WITHDRAWN

PRAISE FOR *MY MOTHER'S SON*

"David Hirshberg has written an engrossing novel that belongs in the canon of great American Jewish literature. Filled with stories of concealed truths, shattering discoveries, and unconditional love, *My Mother's Son* is a twenty-first century exploration of the formative American Jewish experiences of the twentieth century. It transports the reader to that other time even as it speaks to the urgent concerns of today."

—DAN LIBENSON, founder and president of the Institute for the Next Jewish Future and co-host of the Judaism Unbound podcast

"Sometimes it's the lies we grow up with—more than the truths—that define who we are and where we come from. That's the message of David Hirshberg's coming-of-age novel, *My Mother's Son*. Through the eyes of young Joel, we witness essential elements of the mid-twentieth century: the scourge of polio, the magic of baseball, the repercussions of war, and the development of modern Jewish-American culture. But above all, we come to understand why Joel is his mother's son—and how that phrase resonates for us all. A deceptively simple, profoundly memorable novel."

—BARBARA SOLOMON JOSSELSOHN, author of *The Last Dreamer*

"*My Mother's Son* starts out as a story of a family's life in Jewish Boston and grows as big as a century. Fascism lurks. Polio carries off its prey. Only-in-Boston characters pop up. To wit: Murph Feldman, the Jew of Southie. Time rushes in only to roll back as the stories within stories reveal truths not only about one family and one city, but about America in the 1950s and, by extension, today. Hirshberg is a raconteur who feels no need to stop to get a sip of water."

—PAUL GOLDBERG, author of *The Yid* and 2017 Finalist: Sami Rohr Prize for Jewish Literature, and 2016 Finalist: National Jewish Book Award *Goldberg Prize* for Debut Fiction

"Reading *My Mother's Son* is like opening up a time capsule and sifting among the treasures. Nineteen fifty-two Boston comes alive as David Hirshberg weaves the artifacts of that year into the fabric of his poignant narrative. This provocative novel is the colorful description of life as seen through the eyes of thirteen-year-old Joel, and at the same time, a telling and re-telling that allows adult Joel to process and decipher the truths and richness of all that transpires."

—JEANNE MCWILLIAMS BLASBERG, author of *Eden: A Novel*

PRAISE FOR *MY MOTHER'S SON*

"*My Mother's Son* is a richly sprawling and singular Jewish-American saga. It echoes with an unwashed Boston brogue and a heart that beats with a Holocaust past. And it entertains with wit, humor and secrets both dark and luminously incandescent."

—THANE ROSENBAUM, author of *The Golems of Gotham* and *Second Hand Smoke*

"David Hirshberg's engrossing debut not only captures the coming of age of a young boy in the wake of WWII, it also layers hidden identities, family secrets, and larger-than-life characters from Boston's past into a story that will leave readers deeply satisfied."

—CRYSTAL KING, author of *Feast of Sorrow*

"Only occasionally does a novel like this come along—one that sculpts a vivid, irresistible portrait of a life and times. Evocative of the 1950s, with cinematic flashbacks and flash-forwards, it is clever, poignant and funny. Hirshberg allows the reader to eavesdrop on complicated 1950s family intimacies that had been clouded by years of denial, secrecy and self-preservation. What he exposes are the riches left behind, those that reveal the truth of the human condition. This is a book worth reading, probably more than once."

—MITCH MARKOWITZ, screenwriter of *Good Morning, Vietnam*

MY MOTHER'S SON

City of Boston
of Birth
November 7, 1939
Color
Sex Male
Joel
Place of Birth
Boston, Massachusetts

MY MOTHER'S SON

[A NOVEL]

DAVID HIRSHBERG

BEDFORD, NEW YORK

Published in the United States by Fig Tree Books LLC, Bedford, New York

www.FigTreeBooks.net

Jacket design by Christine Van Bree Design
Interior design by E. J. Strongin, Neuwirth & Associates, Inc.

Library of Congress Cataloging-in-Publication Data Available Upon Request

ISBN number 978-1-941493-22-9

Printed in the United States

Distributed by Publishers Group West

First edition

10 9 8 7 6 5 4 3 2 1

CONTENTS

To Ann

PROLOGUE

The yin and yang of my life

When you're a kid, they don't always tell you the truth.

They tell others that they don't want to hurt you or they think you won't understand. But in reality, it's just easier if they tell you what makes *them* feel good, or what gets them out of a jam.

That, as you devotees know, is how I opened each radio show five nights a week for forty-seven years. I write it down now on the anniversary of my last show as I glance at the walls of the studio, where they taped up a photo of me from each year, a mélange of shots that arrested a moment of time, but they appear to be a film strip if you sweep your head from beginning to end, taking in all the pictures, a short reel that exposes customs of dress, grooming habits, and attitudinal stances—the outsides, the two dimensions that others recognized when they saw the me that they thought they knew. I'm all too familiar with these men, some of whom I loved; others, well, let's just say I've taken my leave without rancor but sometimes with embarrassment. No, I don't deny the veracity of the glossies, the snippets that captured me with mustache, clean-shaven, long-haired, crew-cut, with wide lapels (thank God, no Nehru jackets), thin ties, aviator glasses, contacts, tie-dyed T-shirts and cashmere sweaters, often wearing the red-and-blue Braves cap, the *Boston* Braves that is, which meshes nicely now with my speckled beard that still has a wisp of reddish strands, a trick designed to fool me into thinking that I'm younger than I am.

I acknowledge the optimism behind the first one, the 1964 headshot where I'm still in my army uniform, having mustered out only a couple of weeks previously from active duty in West Germany. I'd gone to my first interview wearing it, perhaps to impress the station boss; he was, after all, a high muckety-muck in the reserves, having won ribbons in Korea, but the real reason I wore it is probably more mundane, given that this was still the era in which it was said that girls liked men in uniform.

He listened to tapes of some of my shows from Armed Forces Radio. Then, suppressing a smirk, I presented documents to him to bolster my case, including an article in the *Berliner Morgenpost* about my private meeting with the president after he gave his famous "*Ich bin ein Berliner*" speech the prior June. Prominently displayed on the page was a photo of him smiling broadly at me. I could tell that the station manager was impressed. He asked me if I had any other things that would support my candidacy for the position. I retrieved an article that came from my college newspaper my senior year, 1961, which featured a picture of me with a famous radio humorist sharing a beer at a local hangout, where I interviewed him about his stories that captivated young and old alike, regarding his time growing up in the Midwest during the Depression and afterward in the War years (when it's capitalized and used as a standalone word, it always refers to World War II). And finally, I handed him an amusing piece from my high school paper that reported on a discussion I had in 1957 with my dog, a black Lab, who was lamenting the fact that the Russians sent dogs into space and all we sent were mice. It contained a shot of him with a caption underneath that said, "Depressed that he couldn't be Muttnik."

I got the job.

I can recall the opening of my first show without resorting to any notes: "On May 10, 1952, when our soldiers were bogged down in a war in Korea, our doctors were battling the polio epidemic, and our elected officials were assaulting each other in a political campaign, my brother Steven and I surreptitiously witnessed a shakedown that enmeshed us in the events of the day in a way that affected us for the rest of our lives. I was twelve and a half and my brother was fourteen." I've spent the intervening time between then and now giving tidbits of what happened that year, intermingled with other observations about actions big and small, parochial and ubiquitous, that've occurred since those days.

Most studio visitors take in the pictures on the wall chronologically, examining closely, pointing, noting something in the background, muttering to themselves, stepping sideways a few feet, wash, rinse, repeat, engaging me in small talk about some particular thing that catches their attention, usually relating it to an event in their lives. Once a year my brother would take the occasion to bring a new photo; he'd step back, alternating peering between it and me and it and the other shots, and give the imperceptible head bob, which intimated that he could differentiate the glint from the prior year, the presentation as opposed to the pose, the body language that only he could interpret.

When the last photo was hung a year ago, Steven's intense scrutiny of the sags, the creases, the squint, the distractedness that's unambiguous to a sibling, was a signal as obvious to me as a Morse code SOS. It's time, life was tapping out, dot dot dot, to say good-bye, something that he'd just done, having announced to his partners his intention to wind down his appointments with patients by the end of the year.

I wondered if what my brother noticed was caused or exacerbated by my recent finding of a trove of handwritten papers that'd been nestled within the inside pocket of a valise, stashed in my house for almost thirty years, the keepsake that reminded me of a trip my aunt had made more than seventy years earlier, now exposed as the chintzy vessel that housed the real treasure.

I initially misinterpreted my brother's advice as a call to retire, when in fact he was simply urging me to walk away from a daily grind, a two-hour radio show five nights a week, Sunday through Thursday from eight to ten. From your letters and emails you marveled at my ability to riff for 120 minutes, seemingly off the cuff, a stream of consciousness about my life, starting with when I was a kid, right after the War, with my friends Noodge Mauer, Myandrew, Frankie, my brother, our respective love interests Zippo and Susie, The Guy on the Radio, and my dog—adults making guest appearances, certainly never getting star billing. I take pride in your encomiums, thank you, but it wasn't as if I made it all up extemporaneously. I'd get up early, come into the studio before anyone else—solitude in moderation can be an ally if you get along famously with your conscience—and establish an endpoint from which I'd work backward, a deductively logical reverse process that served me well, a way in which to come up with an outline, the sinew that was all that was necessary to begin construction of the body scaffolding for my soliloquy.

A few months ago, Steven accepted a dollar-a-year position at the university hospital, coordinating efforts to better understand and treat post-polio syndrome, the legacy of the epidemic that we thought we'd conquered, only to be fooled years later in the same way the balloon of our unbridled optimism following the surrender of Germany and Japan in 1945 had been pierced by the Korean War in 1950. Witnessing him make the smooth transition into a new role eased the process for me to do the same, and that shouldn't have surprised me. He'd led the way for me throughout my childhood, and while I was grateful, it wasn't until I was an adult that my admiration for him was further enhanced as I recognized that no older sibling had been there for him, the curse of the firstborn.

Yes, the last picture on the wall was the trigger for Steven to offer that I, too, move on, which I did halfway through 2011. At first, my agent suggested that I go through the station's archives and pull out my favorite shows from each year, have them transcribed and edited, a surefire way to deliver a product to members of my audience, a built-in group numbering about 250,000, the result of national syndication that brought my show far beyond the Boston metro area. While this might've made sense financially, it was something I could've done while still at the station showing up five nights a week and didn't reflect the change that my brother and I both felt was necessary.

After my last broadcast, they were kind enough to allow me to come by the studio to write, at dawn, when it was uncannily quiet, a perfect setting, the only sound being the sporadic whoosh of the air-conditioning kicking in, generating an autonomous shudder, my body anticipating the cool blast that would remind me it was summer, a necessary cue to a person who's in a space with no windows and no other stimuli other than what he conjures up on his own. With each shiver, I'd get up and pace, much as I did when the green light went on and the young woman in the control room provided the nod-smile that indicated the lavaliere mike pinned to my lapel or collar was live, a silent admonition to remind me not to clear my throat, crinkle paper, or talk back to her when she'd occasionally contact me through the earpiece.

Many times, in the middle of a program, I'd glance over to the wall opposite the photos, where I'd hung my Braves baseball cap and a souvenir bat, the former highlighting fond memories of going to the park with my friends, the latter being the proximate cause of a relative's death and another man's murder, these two objects together bringing forth a sobering juxtaposition of the yin and yang of my life.

But there'll be no more control room signals, no more hushed voices in my ear, no more green lights, no more writing the outline for a two-hour show. No, that's all behind me. Now it's about act two, a bit of uncharted territory. I feel like Marco Polo, whose mission was clear but who couldn't tell you much about the outcome until he finished his journey.

So I start by staring into a mirror that I've hung next to the most recent picture on the wall. Reflected in it is a story both personal and universal that I'd skirted around gingerly for all these years, a memoir about betrayal, disease, gambling, death, bribery, persecution, kidnapping, war, politics, escape, loyalty, forgery, unconditional love, depression, marines, theft, girls, and a dog. In it you'll find extraordinary revelations about members of my family and the world we lived in, beginning at a time when I caught a glimpse into adulthood, or, as I think about it now, perhaps this was simply the first peep into the rearview mirror of childhood.

I told my brother that unlike my radio shows, here the adults take stage, front and center, exiting only when they depart, leaving behind their legacies, forever in the penumbra of my imagination and displayed through my actions, behaviors, and wants.

"You are your mother's son," he said definitively and presciently, "so despite the fact that I've been there all along, I don't know what you'll reveal or withhold or how you'll interpret your life."

"My mother's son," I said in a way to hear the phrase in my own voice. "Is that a double entendre?"

He smiled as he cupped his hand around my neck, a wordless gesture that conveyed both affection and recognition that it was the perfect time to take his leave.

1.

A couple of drunks
clinging to
each other for
support

Our aunt and uncle lived nearby in a garden apartment close to the Fens, a fancy word for the swamp that was what remained of the Back Bay. To get there, we'd ride our bikes through the grasses that sprouted next to the remnants of the tidal pools, which were more than twice an adult's height and swayed in the winds that blew off the Charles. We were always careful to hurry out while there was still sunlight, before they'd gang up with the thistles on the flowering bushes, bending down to us, begging us with eerie rustles to stay at night with the ducks, geese, rabbits, raccoons, and bats that countered our reign during the day.

Steven and I'd usually time our arrival to when Uncle Jake got back from the track, our welcome enhanced by the aromas of the German-style bittersweet pastries and strong coffee Auntie Rose would prepare for her husband, a prelude to a much later meal. He'd sit in an overstuffed chair with a large pillow behind his head and his feet on a hassock, eating his snack, drinking his coffee, and going through the mail, tossing the obvious bills onto the side table and using a letter opener to pry the glue from the back of the personal envelopes, almost reverently sliding the insides out, then lowering his glasses to swiftly peruse the contents, reading the German, French, and Yiddish ones aloud, knowing we couldn't understand, and lip-reading the ones in English.

"*Mein Gott im Himmel*," he shouted frequently (we didn't know why he was talking about *his* God in heaven, was his different from ours, this was something that we wondered about later back in our room), then would shake his head, reverence replaced by disdain, rummage through a file cabinet, select a copy of a note he'd written, and deftly staple the letter he received that day to it, then place it back in the folder within the cabinet. The letters he received were typewritten and usually embossed with an emblem or some other mark, while the ones he pulled out of the file were handwritten, in his own script, which we could tell, as we'd received letters from Uncle Jake when we were away in Maine. His intensity when reading the letters would abate only after he'd file them away; we could see the red recede from his face, like the ebb of a tide, which was the sign we could ask our customary question.

"What is it, Uncle Jake?" one or the other of us would inquire, the patterns of our conversations having been established years earlier. It was as if we were in a play, knowing we'd utter these lines day after day, yet despite the repetition, we knew to stick to the script, not to throw anyone else on the stage off-kilter by an extemporaneous remark.

"News but no news," Auntie Rose would reply, and Steven and I'd pivot to look at her and then back to Uncle Jake to see if he'd elaborate or simply take a sip of the coffee or a bite of the cake, leaving us to wonder what she meant. It was always the same: sip and bite.

To whom he wrote we didn't know and agreed that it would be intrusive to ask, and anyway, he wasn't going to reveal anything to us, so we let it go and didn't bring it up to Auntie Rose or anyone else in the family. Instinctively we understood that this ritual was even more important to him than his job because he never complained when there was a snowstorm and he couldn't get to the track, but the fact that the mail couldn't be delivered made him anxious and irritable.

He'd come back to us after he settled down; he'd start up with a comment on the stamp, which he'd delicately peel off and place in a folder on the end table next to his chair.

"Take a look at this," he'd say, holding the light blue four-pence British stamp with the picture of the beautiful young queen. "You know what 'ER' means?" he'd inquire, then explain before we had a chance to respond, "Elizabeth Regina, which means queen, in Latin of all things."

"I was there once," Auntie Rose chimed in, then sought her way back into the kitchen to get some hot chocolate for us, as if to choke off any questions we may have had about a trip to England that surprised us, as Maine was as far away as we thought anyone in the family had gone, with the exception of Papa, our grandfather, who'd go to the furniture factory in North Carolina once a year.

Stamps were a means for Uncle Jake to reconnect to his old world and to establish his identity in the new one, but we never thought of them as a device. On rainy days, we'd strap our albums underneath our yellow slickers and spend hours with Uncle Jake, listening to him tell us stories about the countries from the stamps he'd peeled off letters, while we sat on the floor, combing through approvals that came in the mail for twenty-five cents in clear cellophane packages, using magnifying glasses to make sure we could distinguish between flat-plated prints and rotary press prints, counting perforations, looking for missed cancellation marks, checking single-line watermarks, hoping against hope to find the one-in-a-million mistake, the next upside-down airplane that'd be worth all the money in the world that we'd then give to them, a bribe for Auntie Rose to tell us what she meant when she said "news but no news."

Uncle Jake's passion for reading the letters was matched by his obsessiveness when it came time to get up early in the morning and listen to the shortwave radio. On those school vacation days when we got to stay overnight with them, we'd pretend to be asleep, nestled in between the radiator and the sofa in our fort in the living room, when we'd hear him stir at 6:00 a.m., which would be followed by the sound of his slippers scuffling on the wooden floor; then at precisely 6:10, the announcer would intone somberly in a foreign language. It would go on for ten minutes and stop abruptly at 6:20, when Uncle Jake would turn it off, never uttering any words, usually making grunting or hissing sounds. We secretly turned the radio on twice, once after Uncle Jake went to work on a weekday and the second time on a Saturday, when the station wouldn't come in. Because we didn't know if this was something he kept from Auntie Rose, we asked neither of them about it, just chalked it up to one of his peculiarities, a harmless eccentricity probably having something to do with his not being born in the United States.

When we'd leave, Auntie Rose would make us promise not to tell Mother that we'd gorged on her homemade cakes and cookies, which were always laid out on the kitchen countertop, the scents from the cinnamon, raisins, chocolate, and warm jams as palpable to us as the sweet smoke from Uncle Jake's pipe. We had to be vigilant, though, since she also made special snacks for animals that were arranged side by side with our treats. Occasionally, we'd see her in the Fens, taking nuggets out of a bag that hung around her neck, feeding the ducks and geese that lined up more orderly than we did at Hebrew school. On the block, neighborhood dogs and alley cats would traipse behind her, abandoning their natural animosities for a few moments to receive the succor and gentle words from our aunt. When we were ready to say good-bye, she'd tousle our hair or pinch our cheeks and give us a kiss that became more of a nuzzle as the years went by.

At the end of October, we knew not to visit for a month, Mother having told us simply *it was that time*. So we stopped going until we got permission, which we'd receive in the beginning of December. This was just the way it was. We'd overheard snippets of conversations between Mother and Dad about *that time of year,* and for the longest stretch, we thought that Auntie Rose and Uncle Jake just didn't like the onset of the cold, the overcast skies, and the shorter days.

Steven and I talked about our aunt and uncle's November hibernation.

"It's as if they're humanized bears living like the ones in the storybook," Steven said.

"Yeah, but in this case, they don't have any baby bears," I added.

To head off a conversation Mother didn't want us to initiate, she said, "Uncle Jake and Auntie Rose's reclusive month of November is due to *the troubles*."

At first, Steven and I thought this must be related to the Troubles we'd read about in the *Weekly Reader*, something to do with the Irish fighting the Irish, although that still didn't make any sense to us either. This was one of those times when it looked like we were going to get into a discussion that was clearly uncomfortable for Mother, so she pulled out an ace of spades, her special way of having the last say, her words spilling out with no pause, to emphasize that it was futile to come back with a rejoinder: "Your Aunt And Uncle Need Their Rest."

As I got older, I could tell when Mother was going to give one of her pronouncements. I got the "I'm Telling You This For Your Own Good, So You Could At Least Pretend That You're Listening" speech when she thought I wasn't paying attention. I was the recipient of the "Your Father Worked Day And Night So You Could Have A Nice Life" speech to make sure I didn't take things for granted. And each time I left the house, she'd wrap her arms around me, squeeze me hard, and murmur, "I Miss You Already And You'll Always Be My Baby Boy."

Our friends thought Auntie Rose was entertaining. Once, when Noodge Mauer and Myandrew came with me for after-school snacks, she bolted for her bedroom and paged through the name-your-baby book that she kept by her night table, looked under the Ns and Ms, and came back tsk-tsk-tsking.

"Something's amiss, boys, see here, there's Norman and Mychal but neither Noodge nor Myandrew."

Once, she let the phone ring until it stopped, saying, "No one's home," feeling no necessity to answer despite our urgings and anxieties. "More cake?" she offered us through an additional dozen rings. She was paying attention to us and was not going to be interrupted by someone who'd divert her focus.

Steven and I adored her even when we were invisible to her, which occurred more and more as we approached the beginning of November. Occasionally we'd find her alone in a darkened kitchen, not acknowledging our presence, while we'd scarf down one of her confections, then give her a peck on the cheek and bolt for the door. We were never sure she knew we were there.

Yet her attentiveness (she listened to the rat-a-tat effluvia that erupted from us about sports or bikes or school as if it were the most important thing spewing from the depths of our souls) and kindness ("Here, boys, it's cold, take my scarf"; "Remember to go to the drugstore to call your mother if you're going to be late"; "I'll walk behind you with a flashlight so you'll stay on the path in the Fens") more than offset her oddities, and we were drawn to her as if we were planets kept in an orbit around her by the grip of an invisible force.

She was a bit taller than Mother, and although they looked a lot alike, you could see where a fraction of an inch more between the eyes or less on the slope of the nose could affect an appearance in a disproportionate way. She was, in a word, pretty, and when she was standing next to Uncle Jake, both arms entwined in one of his, he became the envy of every guy they passed on the sidewalk. Little did anyone know that my aunt and uncle's pose was akin to that of a couple of drunks, clinging to each other for support, more noticeable when Uncle Jake's legs got weaker, which caused him to stumble along.

Uncle Jake had darkroom eyes, which drew you into his world, slowly, as it took a while for people to adjust to his personality. Blinking and straining were common until the outline of his nature would begin to emerge, initially in blurry blacks that would add lighter and more vibrant colors only when a mutual acclimation process had taken place.

He had what I can only describe as a War look: someone who hadn't been able to get an umbrella in time to ward off the storm clouds. He would be forever drenched by a deluge of grief and loss, which showed up in a downcast expression and an inability to talk about the future. He could be short with people he didn't know and would answer questions he had asked others before they had the chance to respond. He was an authority on almost any subject, and his vast knowledge generated resentment from those who couldn't possibly understand how he had come to accumulate it.

Yet when he was around us, his gruffness had a playful element to it, and we wouldn't shrink from his offers to take us with him on errands. On car rides with Uncle Jake, he'd sing "Bei Mir Bist Du Schön," "By Me You Are Beautiful," which, by the way, could've meant only that he was daydreaming about Auntie Rose. We'd listen to this Yiddish tune, originally popularized by the Andrews Sisters, good Lutheran girls, which most folks probably thought was a Bavarian folk song sung by kids in lederhosen when they went off to school hopping and skipping, accompanied by their German shepherd or schnauzer.

Every half hour he'd pull over so he could stretch his legs, a necessity for him to avoid cramping; these repeated exercises were helpful to reduce the pain caused by his limp even if only for a short period of time.

I can't tell you how much we loved Uncle Jake. He was the first adult who'd look us squarely in the eyes, not dismissing us merely because of our ages, which is what most grown-ups would do. He'd listen and we knew it wasn't the kind of listening that we could tell was phony, as when someone would mumble an "okay" or "uh-huh," ostensibly acknowledging your comments or presence but, really, we could've been prattling on about our bathroom habits, they had no idea what we were saying. It was clear that Uncle Jake *cared* about us and showed us the deference that, in truth, we hadn't earned, but now it's apparent that it was part of his teaching process, a technique that he hoped we'd absorb and pass down to the kids we'd come in contact with when we got older.

Those of you who've got relatives like this know what it's like to have someone invade your heart who, unlike an unwelcome intruder, stakes out a claim for territory that you're never willing to cede even with princely recompense.

And although I wouldn't have expressed it this way out loud back then, I had the same admiration and affection for my brother, so close in age, so much more knowledgeable and sophisticated, a bit intimidating truthfully and a tough act to follow, but I never felt as if I got the hand-me-downs or the short end of the stick. Sure, I was "dickhead" sometimes but it wasn't uttered in a nasty way, no different from when he called one of the Braves a moron for making an error.

As we got older, the difference between our ages seemed to diminish proportionately to the similarity of our exaggerated height, and oftentimes we'd get stares from people who didn't know us, assuming we were twins. Today, of course, the vernacular would be expressed in terms of cloning but a couple of generations ago it was all about carbon copies, and despite the inferiority of the blue-inked yellow paper compared to the crisp, white, digital printouts we have now, it was a more accurate reflection of how we were presented to the world, as smudges and erasures would more naturally display the fact that we were not exact duplicates. We both had dark hair but Steven's ringlets were curlier than mine and his smile was more vertical compared to my more horizontal orientation. Perhaps what increased the number of double takes were two sets of opaque brown eyes that seemed to dart or alight simultaneously without overt communication emanating from either one of us.

Uncle Jake was born in Germany, or East Prussia, or Austria, or Hungary, or Poland, or that slice of Poland, Galicia, that nobody remembers anymore, or maybe it was in Prague or somewhere in the Pale of Settlement, supposedly a pretty big place though nowhere does it appear on a map and no one at school or the library had ever heard of it. He spoke German, that much I can tell you, because we'd hear him at the pastry shop near Sears, Roebuck on Park Drive, where there were maps on the walls of Germany and pictures of a large guy on a horse wearing a uniform with something that looked like a pointy-topped ice bucket on his head and newspapers with stories from Frankfurt and Hamburg, which cracked us up. He spoke Polish when he talked to the ladies who'd cross and recross themselves a hundred times when he'd run into them at the laundry down the street from Noodge Mauer's parents' store. And he spoke Yiddish with Old Uncle A when he didn't want us to know what he was talking about.

Uncle Jake had a beard as a young man in Europe. He showed us pictures of himself that he'd taken out of a shoe box, yellowed pictures of people we didn't know in front of signs we couldn't read, next to cars we didn't recognize.

"I shaved for the first time when I was twenty-three," he announced proudly, which made us laugh; we couldn't imagine him with a beard.

"It just doesn't look like you, Uncle Jake," Steven said.

"Yeah, more like Jingles," I chimed in, convulsed about how he looked like Andy Devine on *The Adventures of Wild Bill Hickok.*

"Who? What?" he responded, not connecting with my TV reference, then added a "Ha!" when he understood he was the butt of the joke. "Mr. Smarty Pants thinks he knows a lot," he said to Steven, making sure I caught the side of his smile. "We didn't know of such things when I went to school in Berlin," he added, diverting attention back to the shoe box of photos. "My school was a *Gymnasium*," he continued, which faked me out, because I thought that meant he was always playing sports indoors, like basketball or volleyball or wrestling, yet we never saw a picture of him in athletic clothes.

Sensing a continental divide, he quickly added, "*Gymnasium*, boys, with the *g* sound like in *get*, is the German word for school."

So I, Mr. Wise Guy, asked, "Then is *school*, with the *sch* sound like in *shoulder*, the German word for gym?"

"No," he said, "*schul* means synagogue," and with that, he trumped my remark without making me feel embarrassed at my attempt at humor.

Uncle Jake was born in 1900 and came to America in 1938, but how he got here was something that we weren't supposed to know.

"When you're older," he'd say each year on our birthdays, when we'd ask.

"Older than what?" I'd ask, since we knew he wasn't going to tell us.

2.

And that's how I met Rose Mischal

One morning in the spring of 1952, Dad rather solemnly asked us to come out of our room to the kitchen, where he told us that Uncle Jake had gotten polio. "He's not in an iron lung, boys," he reassured us, but we wondered what he'd be like, could we continue to visit him and Auntie Rose (yes, once he got out of the hospital), would he be able to sit in a chair out back and watch us play (again yes), but still, it was going to be different, we just didn't know how, and this uncertainty provoked an anxious discussion once Dad left for work.

Steven: "You think he'll talk funny? I mean, does it affect the way you speak or is it just his legs don't work?"

Me: "What do we say to him, we can't just pretend he's fine, is it okay to look at his legs?"

Steven: "I guess, but don't stare, sneak a peek at them when he's not looking at you."

Me: "Can we catch it? If I give him a hug, can I get polio?"

Steven: "We can say good-bye to car rides with him."

Me: "Someone'll have to push him in a wheelchair, probably us, I hope not in the Fens, it gets too muddy in there."

Dad had told us to be home by three in the afternoon pronto, so we raced home from school and took the stairs up the three flights two at a time, then burst in the door expecting some surprise, only to find everyone including Dr. Richards waiting for us.

"Pull your pants down," Dr. Richards ordered, just like that, no hellos, no nice to see you, no presents, no treats, no let me tell you what's going on, no nothing but "pull your pants down," which we did, "underpants down below the crack, fellas, and bend over the hassocks" that'd been lined up waiting for us.

As soon as our stomachs hit the hassocks, Dr. Richards jabbed a horse needle into our tushes, first Steven's, then mine.

"That's it, boys," he said with satisfaction, and that's how we got one of the first injections of gamma globulin, the drug that was supposed to prevent us from getting polio. My face flushed pink, needles pierced my trunk in a pattern that led up past my neck to my head, and I became a bit wobbly. From the back, Mother caressed one hand around my ear and braced me against her side, gently rocking for a while until I looked up to her and told her I felt fine. Only it was Auntie Rose.

"Thank God you're going to be protected," Mother said, her eyes riveted on us, my eyes asking where was Dr. Richards and his miracle drug before Uncle Jake got sick, so why should God be thanked? In the end, the gamma globulin was all for naught, it had no effect, unless you count a fraudulent peace of mind, for the real polio vaccine wasn't available for two more years.

Papa thanked Dr. Richards and made sure we shook hands with him, an introduction into the adult world of acknowledging care and concern despite whatever temporary pain is associated with that person's actions.

Back in our room I said to Steven, "We have to get to Uncle Jake in the hospital, he'd want to see us, we're like his kids, and besides, we have to hear the story of how he came to America, we'll never be satisfied if we hear it from someone else."

"Zippo can help us," Steven said.

"What are you talking about?"

"She can sneak us into the hospital, she's a candy striper."

And that was that, as Uncle Jake would say.

Juliette Bouchard never knew why they called her Zippo. The guys in Steven's class always said she was as easy to turn on as the lighter. One touch and she got hot.

Zippo was to meet us at Noodge Mauer's parents' store the next morning. I went into the basement storeroom, where I helped my friend open boxes of things that would be brought up and placed on the shelves at later times. Steven was in the store, waiting for Zippo.

After about a half hour or so, I went back upstairs, catching the sight of Zippo's profile as she bounded out the door and onto the sidewalk.

"Do you think she can get us in? To see Uncle Jake? Soon?"

Steven nodded in the affirmative but his head was elsewhere and his eyes were glued to Zippo's retreating figure. I heard him murmur something; it might have been "second base" but I wasn't sure so I didn't pick up on it.

That afternoon, we waited outside the hospital and sat on the lowest of the front steps, Steven looking up the skirts of the candy stripers as they ascended into the building. Suddenly, Steven stared at a candy striper getting out of a car. The overhead sun shimmered off her ponytail, which flopped back and forth as she made her way hurriedly toward the front entrance. The strap of her bag was over her right shoulder, and with the bag on her left hip, that meant the strap accentuated her emerging figure, something she must've figured out as soon as her body began to take shape. We stood up straight, the way we did whenever we'd meet guys we didn't know at Papa's office. She was looking down but when she got near the first step, she looked up and gave us a huge smile.

"Hi Joel," she said. It was Zippo.

"Hi Juliette," I said, quickly remembering not to call her Zippo.

"Hiiiiii, Stee-venn," she said, "hiiiiii" and "Stee-venn" being spread out over about five seconds, in rhythm to her hips, swinging back and forth. I couldn't take my eyes off her strap.

They chatted for a minute or so, seemingly oblivious to my eye rolling, coughing, finger snapping, and humming, all designed to get them to stop so we could go inside to see Uncle Jake.

She finally noticed me, and said in a way that I could interpret only as her thinking I was a nuisance, "You're early, be back in an hour and meet me right here."

"How come?" I asked.

"It's not as if Uncle Jake's going anyplace," Steven replied, as if to ingratiate himself with her.

With me in a huff, we headed west to Longwood Playground, thinking about how we'd kill some time. Out beyond Francis Street, we passed an abandoned house. We looked at the shattered windowpanes that once reflected back the sounds of songs and whistles and teakettles and exploding popcorn and spinning washing machines and crackling wood and the noise from sibling rivalries and arguments over homework and dating and money and politics and in-laws. But all we could see now were the cracked walls and cobwebs and threads of drapes that'd been cut on the shards of glass, fragmented by the rocks and snowballs of bravado, hurled a safe distance in front of the broken fence that somehow still kept everything at bay. Every neighborhood has one of these. We were frightened, yet were drawn to it. We always wanted to sneak up and take a peek at what things could've been, what they might become. We skipped past it several times before we had the courage to walk up the creaking steps and touch the door, which kind of groaned when you made it swing on the hinge, as if to say: "Don't come in! Don't come in! Go away! I don't want you to see me like this!"

When we got back to the hospital, Zippo was waiting, and as she saw Steven, she began her sway, automatically, as if someone had turned the key and you didn't have to hit the ignition button simultaneously, it just started like magic. I was yammering on about the Braves and noticed that they were holding hands. Out in front of the hospital, Zippo told us to wait, she'd be back in a minute, and up the steps she flew, Steven cocking his head low to get another look. She returned quickly with two visitor passes for room 302, and in a matter of minutes we entered Uncle

Jake's room. There were no contraptions, no medicine bottles, nothing, just a bed and a chair. He was sitting in the chair, hat on his head, blanket on his lap, no different from what he looked like at home. He didn't budge when we came into the room.

"Uncle Jake," I whispered, "Uncle Jake, it's us, Joel and Steven, we came to visit you, we know we're not supposed to be here, but we wanted to come anyway, Uncle Jake, can you hear us?"

He was asleep. Steven and Zippo sat on the bed, holding hands. I took out a crumpled-up Scott stamp catalog from my back pocket and went through the American section, looking to see if I had enough money yet for the three-cent General Kosciuszko 1933 150th anniversary, mint, commemorating the time he became a US citizen.

After a half hour or so, Uncle Jake woke up. I was directly in his sight, and he raised his arms up slowly, outstretched, the way Mother did whenever she saw a baby. I let him swallow me up. Steven hugged him, and he tipped his hat when he was introduced to Zippo. Uncle Jake was unconsciously maneuvering a coin between his fingers, then for the first time that day, he spoke.

"East Boston," he said softly.

"What do you mean, Uncle Jake, 'East Boston'?"

He drew the blanket up near his chin, and with his droopy eyes and fedora pulled down low on his forehead but with the brim turned up, he reminded me of the Mexican gunslingers taking a siesta on the Cisco Kid show.

"That's where the ships came in, to East Boston."

"What ships, what are you talking about?"

"The ships that came from Europe, the passenger ships, they docked in East Boston. You know that's where they originally wanted to put the Statue of Liberty," he added slowly and softly.

Steven gave me that look, the look that says *he's nuts*, but he couldn't say that out loud to me.

"Uncle Jake, that's the airport, we can see the airport in East Boston from Papa's office, that's where the planes land, there aren't any ships there," Steven corrected him, respectfully.

"That's where the ships came in, that's where they docked, before the airport, for chrissakes, that's where I landed, that's where I first set foot in America," he said in the kind of rasp you get when you need to clear your throat but you keep talking because you have a point to make and nothing is going to stop you.

"He wasn't born here?" Zippo mouthed silently to Steven.

Clearing his throat of phlegm, he said, "I came by boat in '38."

I was flabbergasted that he'd answered so robustly; just a few moments earlier, he'd been in a stupor. As glad as I was that he had now shifted himself up, was making eye contact, and had expressed some energy, it was also unsettling, not knowing whether he'd stay on this course or tack back to lethargy. Although I was learning a lot about the world of adults, this was my introduction to the vagaries of the tricks the body can play. If it'd been someone other than Uncle Jake, I might've just said he was off his rocker and not given it another thought, but when it's someone close, a member of your family, it's not as easy to be so flip.

"I knew English, we'd studied at the gymnasium and you could still get foreign newspapers at that time, so I'd get up early and put on the jacket with the star and buy a British paper to find out what was happening."

Steven and I realized that now was the time that Uncle Jake was finally going to tell us the story of how he ended up in America, so we shut up and didn't let it bother us that what we'd waited practically our whole lives to hear, Zippo was finding out the first time she met him.

"Come here." He motioned to us. "Get closer, I have to tell you a story. It's not a bedtime story," he went on as Steven, Zippo, and I took positions lined up with our legs dangling over the side of the bed, facing him in the chair, "and there's a lot I can't tell you, maybe some other time, maybe never . . ." He seemed to drift off, eyelids down about three-quarters, before jerking his head back, willing himself to continue, pulling up the memories as if he were an old nag circling a well with his harness tied to a rope hauling a bucket up to the surface. "Back there, then." He hesitated, and I suspected he was having trouble saying *Germany*. "You know something about what went on in Europe, just before the War?" We three nodded, each of us likely having different images in our minds of the Gestapo, the camps, the destruction. "These were uncertain times for the outside world but one thing was certain for us: we were doomed, the Jews, as a people, as a part of the *Volk*. There were all sorts of rumors, we had to wear the stars on our clothing, I couldn't practice medicine with a gentile, we didn't have much to eat, we all thought there was going to be war," he said quietly. He had turned his body to be in a position to stare out the window and for an instant I thought I saw one of his legs move, a twitch really.

"What about the star, Mr. Goldblum, what did you mean by that?" Zippo asked.

He didn't answer her but I was pretty sure it was because he didn't hear her, he was staring intently out the window seeing the people, places, and things of 1938. Eventually, he started up again.

"It took me a long time to decide to leave. I couldn't tell my family, they'd be against it and I didn't know how to take them with me."

Silence.

"A friend, a gentile, someone I'd worked with, agreed to my plan, at great risk to himself and his family. From a fire or a traffic accident or a murder, there would be a body brought to the hospital without identification and my friend, a doctor, God bless his soul, would issue a death certificate for Jacob Goldblum and explain that he hadn't known the man was a Jew or else he wouldn't have treated him and anyway, what did it matter, it was one less Jew to deal with."

Silence.

"I was dead, officially, and wrote this all down in a note to my family, so they wouldn't think I was really dead, although I'm sure they thought I'd be caught and hanged so they probably sat *shiva* for me starting that very night."

Steven put his right index to his lips, a way of telling Zippo not to ask about shiva, that Steven would explain it to her later.

Silence.

"A boy I knew from the gymnasium, an Aryan boy who had married a Jew, was a customs official in Hamburg."

He drifted off again, was silent for quite a while, which we assumed meant that he was asleep. We didn't know how long we should wait it out and debated leaving, disappointed that we hadn't heard the whole story.

Uncle Jake awakened with a start. "I gave him some cash. In return, he stamped my exit card and guided me to the boat. The exchange was uneventful and took less than thirty seconds."

Silence.

This was one of those stories that wasn't long on details but I knew not to interrupt as it could result in him forgetting where he was or, worse yet, going off on a tangent and not reaching the end of it. Every once in a while, I found myself leaning slightly forward to become caught in Steven's peripheral vision, a simple slight nod or facial tic substituting for words, receiving a reciprocal response from my brother, indicating that we were both getting the gist.

"I stayed much of the time in my cabin, which I shared with another man, whom I suspected was also a Jew passing, but we kept to ourselves other than to say 'Good morning' or 'Excuse me' or 'Thank you.'"

Silence.

"Seven days, seven days of storms, seven days of rolling and pitching, seven days of asking myself what had I done, seven days of retching and crying, seven days of thumbing pictures, seven days of reading English, seven days of practicing sentences, of pretending to walk down the gangplank, holding my head up, smiling broadly, scanning the crowds, imagining to look for relatives and friends who'd be waving handkerchiefs and jumping up and down, seven days of wondering where I'd sleep the first night, where could I get dollars, was there a schul near the docks, could I get a license to practice, was my English good enough, would I still be a Yid. Seven days."

Silence.

"We landed at the port. I stood on the dock, amid dozens, hundreds of people, alone. I watched my cabinmate get hugged and jumped on before he disappeared into the crowd. I saw the cranes lowering trunks, valises, duffel bags, furniture, and even cars onto the docks. I stood there with a suitcase, wearing my hat and coat, figuring out what to do, wondering if my passport that said I was Dieter Harald Eberhart would be rejected if the immigration official found out I was circumcised."

Silence.

Then Uncle Jake closed his lids and for a second or two, Steven and I both leaned forward and made the same face—pinched eyes, stretched mouth, and slightly raised brows—as if we could communicate an urging to continue, tinged with disappointment if he stopped, silly, of course, as he couldn't see us. He snapped back and caught us in a hunched position from which we had to straighten up immediately, otherwise we might've cracked our heads together.

He continued without acknowledging our proximity and the accident that was barely avoided. Honestly, at this point in his reverie, I'm not sure he even remembered where he was and to whom he was talking. He'd kept this bottled up for so many years that it seemed to us that he was reading from a book, one that was printed on the inside of his eyelids so it didn't matter to him if his eyes were open or closed.

"A young woman approached me and asked if I spoke English. 'Yes,' I said. 'Are you a Jew?' she asked. I froze. I said nothing. It's over, I thought. They'll send me back. She touched my arm and said the *shehecheyanu*. Tears came to my eyes then rolled down my cheek when I heard the celebration prayer. She took out a handkerchief and dabbed at my face. There were too many tears for the cloth. I cried for a full minute or so without moving, without saying a word. I took the cloth from her and buried my face. I expected that when I opened my eyes she'd be gone."

Silence.

"She was still there. 'I'm from the Hebrew Immigrant Aid Society, HIAS,' she said with a warm smile and handed me a card that said so in many languages. 'I'll be your guide until you're settled in Boston.'"

Steven and I knew all about HIAS, that was where Papa started out at the turn of the century, so I was pretty sure I was going to follow this part better, and anyway, he was now in Boston, Germany was in the past, which for me meant I could relax a bit and even show a small smile of familiarity.

"'You've docked in the port of East Boston, an island close to the city, and we'll board a small boat once we claim all of your belongings and go through customs,' she continued.

"'My suitcase is all I have,' I told her.

"We arrived at what looked like a dilapidated tenement near the docks. It was a rooming house.

"'You'll stay here for a while and take your meals here,' she said, and left me in a room on the fourth floor. There was a bed, a chest, a sofa, a lamp, a chair, a rug, and a bathroom that I'd have to share with the others on the floor.

"I fell asleep on the sofa, soundly, for hours. I woke up in the afternoon and stretched. My hand thrust into the crevice at the back of the sofa and felt something hard. It was a coin. It was from Austria and was minted in 1904. I gave it to the young woman from HIAS when she checked on me at dinner. She gave it back to me and said, 'On your last day you should take a German coin and put it in the sofa. They're left to remind you that others have experienced what you're going through, that you're not alone. There are dozens of coins in each sofa. My father started this tradition when he came to Boston in 1894, when he was ten years old. He's now in the furniture business and supplies the sofas like the one you slept on as well as the beds and rugs and lamps and chests that are in every room of the HIAS building.'"

"Papa?" I mouthed to Steven.

"And that's how I met Rose Mischal," he said exhaustedly, his chin practically resting on his chest. We could see his head slowly rise and fall with his breathing.

"Auntie Rose!" Steven and I exclaimed together.

He finished and lay back against the headrest. His left arm flopped onto the night table where a nurse had placed a glass of water and the day's paper. Then motionless, except for rhythmic breathing. We assumed he had drifted off. We made for the door.

"Did you see his leg move?" I asked when we got to the staircase.

"You never told me your uncle was a doctor," Zippo mentioned.

"He's a vet," Steven corrected her.

"He works at the track at the end of the Blue Line," I added, trying to be helpful.

"Something's fishy," Steven said. "I mean, he could've told this to us years ago. What gives?"

"People say stuff when they think they're dying," Zippo suggested, in a reassuring way until she realized the impact of what she had said, then turned her head to avoid seeing our reaction.

december 6 1919
dear diary

misses bean told me no when I asked her to be a brownie. I hate her. Anyway I will be. she is mean. She made me eat a sawsidge in front of the other kids. They laffed at me. I told mamele. at recess Polly felt the top of my head. I told her to stop. she did it again. Now the boys try also. But not Milty. he is nice to me. his family has diner with us on Fridays.

Your frend Rose

3.

He was the first adult we didn't have to address as Mister

We lived in a row house inside the westernmost border of Boston, poor cousins to the elegant brownstones near Coolidge Corner, a couple of miles west on Beacon Street in Brookline. The ones on our street were sheathed with irregularly shaped red bricks marked with occasional streaks of green copper residue etched by years of water having overflowed cluttered gutters, surrounded by mortar that exuded black mold. Once in a blue moon, one of the houses would get hand-scrubbed by Italian immigrants who'd jack up a platform that hung by ropes strung around a vent on the roof, an anxiety-provoking setup that had neighborhood mothers scurrying to the other side of the street, holding their children's hands tightly, and admonishing them in colloquial dialects never to walk near the buildings when one of the scaffolds was suspended in the air.

Our apartment had three bedrooms, one for our parents, one for our maternal grandfather, and one for my brother and me. We lived in the middle of the block so we had only two sets of windows. The ones in the front had the blinds closed most of the way so the people across the street couldn't see us so easily when we were in the living room. In the back, our parents' bedroom door was usually closed, so the bulbs in the hall ceiling were on all the time, regardless of the time of day. Our room, the one I shared with Steven, was on the left, and directly across from us, Papa had the room that would've been the den. Our bathroom was off-limits to us on Sundays between nine and ten, when Papa was in there reading the funnies and smoking a cigar, which he wasn't allowed to do. It'd been Nana's rule, no smoking in the house. He'd observed it when she was alive, and although Mother didn't like it, she allowed him this one indulgence.

Our room was next to the kitchen, so we knew when to wash up early (potato latkes and brisket) and when to have a stomachache (flanken and farfel). When Old Uncle A would come down from Maine, he would sleep on the sofa in the living room, something that was off limits to us because we'd drool on the needlepoint pillows that Nana had made just after she got married to Papa.

Out back were the garages, which were circled by an extra-wide driveway, big enough for the coal truck and a couple of cars to fit side by side. The guy who drove the coal truck wore a bandana and his shirt was always open so you could see his undershirt, even in the winter. His belly hung over his belt, like in the newsreels when the glaciers jut out over the fjords far enough for the folks in boats to drive under them. We could hear the truck before he made the turn to come into the driveway, what with the coal scraping against the sides as he bounced from crater to crater across the rutted asphalt. It hadn't been repaired any more than the loose banister on the second-floor landing or the large glass window high up on the second floor of the garage that shattered when it was hit by a line drive on July Fourth, causing reverberations we couldn't imagine at the time.

When the coal truck made the turn from the road into the driveway, it would pick up a little steam on the straightaway and you'd hear the gears screech and the engine groan, and the driver would start this howling, bouncing through the ruts, as he raced the engine in neutral.

"I'm gonna scare the bejesus out of youse kids," that's what he said, every time, when he smacked the front bumper into the ash cans that were lined up between the chute and the stairs.

"Jesus, Mary, mother of God," he'd say as he'd raise the back of the truck, swing the chute out from the basement window, and open the gate to the roar of the coal, which made us yell to be heard over the din. This spectacle became the subject of our conversations along the row at precisely six o'clock when all of us had to come inside to eat. That and the stuff he wore around his neck, the medallion and the cross with the figure on it that Dad would say was the size of the Bunker Hill Monument.

His name was Rocky; he was the first adult we didn't have to address as Mister. Rocky Morone, which rhymed with baloney, something we never mentioned to him. "Morone Coal Delivery" was painted in fancy script over the doors on both sides of the cab. When I was about ten, Rocky would bring his kid with him if he was late or if he came on a Saturday. He was four years older than Steven. Rocky's son was the first kid we were allowed to call by his last name.

He'd wear a pink shirt opened halfway, with the ends of the sleeves rolled up almost to the shoulder, tightly holding what we presumed to be a pack of cigarettes against his arm. His pants were so tight around his body that he constantly pulled at his crotch, readjusting himself, Mother noted, admonishing us to keep our hands out of our pockets unless we were retrieving something, a euphemism that we understood to mean that we shouldn't play pocket pool. His pants were draped way below his belly button, tethered to his body by a two-inch-thick garrison belt with a brass buckle in the shape of three large letters—USA. He was planted in engineer boots with fake grommets lined in a vertical pattern on the outside. He carried a comb in his back pocket that was more valuable to him than his wallet. The straight slim handle fluffed the curl that hung down over his forehead to the bridge of his nose, while the teeth separated tiny Wildroot-stuccoed rows that would meet at the back in the duck's ass style prevalent in the North End. This was run through his shiny hair as often as we aimlessly pounded a ball into a mitt.

Had we, for argument's sake, seen him for the first time when we were goofing off outside near Papa's office, I'm sure we would've instinctively shied away from him, probably would've pretended to investigate an anthill or an abandoned tire, anything to avoid a confrontation with a hood, which was how he would've been described by the Irish guys working on Papa's loading dock, who would've been mumbling in sotto voce: dago this and guinea that.

While it's not true that clothes make the man, we do seem to have either inbred or environmentally inspired reactions to people at first glance, depending on their exterior. In this case, to have judged Rocky's son viscerally would've been a serious mistake. Yes, he was as foreign to us as the waiters at Mr. Lee's Chinese restaurant, but while his clothes, diction, and customs were alien, his mannerisms belied his appearance, and Mother, of all people, was one of his biggest fans, not surprising since his politeness and respectfulness elicited an ace of spades pronouncement each time after he left: "I Know You Boys Will Mind Your Ps And Qs When You Are In Mr. And Mrs. Morone's House."

Us? We had wiffles, hair cut short all over the head, which neither allowed for parts nor resulted in mats when we wore a cap. Most of the time we wore dungarees, sometimes lined, plaid shirts, and when it got chilly, a blue jacket on which Mother had sewn a Braves patch over the heart.

Morone would sometimes stay after Rocky delivered the coal and play ball with us. He was great at running bases, three flies up, as well as fungo, and taught us many curse words, some in Italian. He'd use them when he didn't have to. We'd practice his strut and his intonation, accenting words on different syllables and using our new vocabulary out of context. Girls liked Morone and so did we. He talked about them incessantly. You can imagine our amazement when he described his version of third base, for up until then it'd been a garbage lid or a pizza box in our make-believe baseball stadium out back, and now it was something like the Holy Grail, even if we didn't know what that really was. He had a first baseman's glove, the long kind that looks like the end of a vacuum cleaner and has two pockets, one for the thumb and the other for all the fingers. After he'd tag us out he'd stick it up in the air and say, "Fungoo," loudly, which we thought was just his North End pronunciation of fungo. We never corrected him. But we did start to ask some kids if they wanted to play "fungoo," wildly sticking our gloves up in the air. Their parents told them not to play with us anymore.

It was out back on the macadam where Mother, Dad, Papa, Uncle Jake, Auntie Rose, and Old Uncle A would set up their wood-and-canvas folding lawn chairs in the lee of the garages to get out of the sun if they wanted to spend time with us when the weather was good. They'd come in groups, or by themselves, drinking two cents plain, watching us play ball, keeping up a constant stream of chatter to us or to the other adults, seemingly adept at three things simultaneously: talking; watching; and fiddling, with knitting needles (Mother), rolls of paper tape (Dad), ledgers (Papa), photos (Auntie Rose), letters (Uncle Jake), and stamps (Old Uncle A).

Not much consequential went on when they sat sipping and talking, but I do remember when Uncle Jake opened a letter, sank low in his chair like when the air is removed from a rubber tire tube, and fell to the ground, all of us rushing to right him and help him inside. It was not long after that when we were told he had polio.

4.

Mother and Dad were not immune to the hysteria

In 1952, Boston was in the throes of a polio epidemic. The spawning of new cases was measured by all the charity events for grown-ups to raise money for the victims, who had to live for years in iron lungs, those coffin-like contraptions, up to seven feet long, in which people lay on their backs and saw through a mirror fastened to the top corner of the machine. Nowadays, of course, you can exist with a small tube inserted into your throat, attached to a portable ventilator, but back then, well, this was your only option. Polio was the first disease Steven and I knew about, although it was difficult in the beginning to understand, because whenever Mother said the word, she lowered her voice to a pitch barely audible, the same pitch she used later on when she'd talk about cancer.

"You can't play with any friends if there's polio in their family," Mother intoned.

"So what?"

"You want to live in one of those machines, Mr. Know-It-All? Go, go play, play with one of those kids, I should have a cripple for a son."

I left in a huff for Noodge Mauer's house, taking my mitt, but in truth it was as much to see if Susie, his twin sister, were there. I'd had a crush on her since we were first allowed to go outside and play by ourselves. I'd see her skipping rope or playing hopscotch and would always linger to do goofy kid stuff, like slip in to do double dutch with her on the rope or hop like a kangaroo next to her, throwing my own stone in parallel to what she'd chalked out on the sidewalk. I guess I was a bit of a show-off, but she liked the attention. I hardly actually exchanged words other than things like, "Noodge in the house?"

Or, "Careful not to step on the line."

Or, "Watch me pick up the stone between my knuckles."

Whereupon I'd get something back from her such as, "He's got his mitt on, waiting for you."

Or, "I wouldn't if you didn't get so close to me."

Or, "Big deal, I can do it with my toes."

You get the picture.

I made excuses to spot her during recess and to catch up with her when she walked home by herself. I usually took my bike to school and would do figure eights around her before pedaling off with a "See ya," hoping she'd call out for me to come back, overjoyed and suppressing a smile when she made the most innocuous comment: "We're supposed to have a hurricane tomorrow, you know," which had the same gravitational pull back to her that the earth was able to exert on me, preventing my wheels from leaving the ground.

In the spring, she was out of class for a week and I found myself missing her but not wanting to ask Noodge Mauer in front of others, so I waited until we were playing three flies up out back.

"Hey, I haven't seen Susie for a while," I called out casually after I'd caught the third ball and switched places with Noodge Mauer to pick up the bat.

"Oh, I guess I didn't tell you, she's sick," he said.

"Be back in school next week?" I asked hopefully.

"No, not likely, I mean she can't even walk."

"Why, did she break a leg, is she in a cast?"

"No, nothing like that," and I breathed easier. "She got polio," he said, as matter-of-factly as he then added, "Hey, you didn't catch that, you trapped it."

My ears instantly pounded so loudly I thought others would be able to hear the beat of the internal drum, reverberating with my racing heart as I imagined Susie in an iron lung, no longer able to skip rope, play hopscotch, or eventually marry me.

"Is she, you know, in one of those *things*?" I queried, unable to use *iron lung* and *she* in the same sentence, while at the same time noticing a cracked voice that wasn't related to my near coming-of-age status.

"Nope," he replied, "she's lucky," and in a sense, she was. Others were paralyzed and many died.

Because the term *infantile paralysis* generated such disquieting fears, it was rarely used in colloquial conversations but never far removed from anyone's thoughts. We'd had outbreaks in most years after the War but by the spring of 1952, it was an epidemic, dominating newspaper coverage as much as the stalemate in Korea and the "Draft Ike" movements that sought to convince General Eisenhower to leave his post as president of Columbia University to run for president of the United States. When the weather warmed, the dread increased, as it was presumed that stagnant waters where mosquitoes hatched were the breeding grounds for the virus, so the word went out from mother to mother, over backyard clotheslines, telephone party lines, and exchanges with the grocers, bakers, and milkmen, about stories, true and false, concerning so-and-so's kid who got it because she didn't towel off after swimming, but as incorrect as those turned out to be, the anecdotes mushroomed and were transformed into admonitions not to jump through puddles or share a tonic bottle. We became paralyzed as a society.

Mother and Dad were not immune to the hysteria. We were told to stay away from the Fens. Most parents weren't sending their kids to school after Memorial Day, so it wasn't that unusual when they sent us off on a two-week trip at the beginning of June to Palus Island off the coast of Maine, where Old Uncle A had a camp. Dr. Richards said the worst of the season would be past within a few weeks.

Steven and I took the Flying Yankee from North Station to Portland, carrying our duffel bags over our shoulders, imitating the way the sailors at the Charlestown Navy Yard did, for the half-hour walk to the wharf, and made our way to a bench on Commercial Street, waiting for the skiff that'd take us to Palus Island. From a few miles or so off the western edge of the island, we could see Old Uncle A waving on the dock, nonstop, for the fifteen minutes or so it took us to make the crossing. Steven and I marched up the hill and threw our bags onto the back of a horse-drawn wagon. We were the only kids at the camp. Everyone else was old, Papa's age it seemed, and several old ladies looked like they could've even been Old Uncle A's mother. We had breakfast the next morning in a big open building, and all the old folks made such a fuss over us. "Sylvia's," more than one person remarked to another when we got up for seconds.

Old Uncle A told us that the island was ours, go, play, do, be back in time for supper. We hiked down to the water where the rocks were slippery and the seaweed got entangled in our sneakers. It smelled like the fish market on Harvard Street near Coolidge Corner in Brookline, where Papa would take us to get smoked salmon, sturgeon, whitefish, and trouties, which he'd eat whole, lock, stock, and barrel. We skipped stones to the closest lobster traps, and once we climbed back up the hill, threw rocks at the buoys bobbing in the cove. We saw seals sunbathing on rocky crags that jutted up from the ocean and clapped our hands and made seal sounds. They stared at us. We waved to some lobstermen wearing bright yellow slicker pants and to some guys on a small fishing boat who all waved back. We debated whether we would die if we ate what looked like wild blueberries and decided it was worth the risk. They weren't very sweet but we couldn't get them down fast enough. Out by a promontory we found wild strawberries and mushrooms and that became our lunch. We made a bat out of a tree branch and played three flies up with a frayed tennis ball. Late in the day we found a small stream where we took off all our clothes except our underpants and made like beavers, creating dams and bridges with the rocks from the bottom. We dried off in the late afternoon sun, counting birds and finding faces of people we knew in the clouds. We must've dozed off for a while because we got back to the big house when everybody was eating dessert.

In the evening, we sat on the porch and listened to one old person after another say to someone else, tell them about so-and-so, oh no, they wouldn't be interested, yes, they would, tell them, go on. Some of them were a little difficult to understand, they had accents. They didn't seem like Americans. They'd frequently mention names that had no connection to what they'd been saying, but for the most part we could figure it out, except when they'd tell a story for fifteen minutes and then give the punch line in Yiddish, which would cause them all to either laugh or nod with approval. We'd sit there with idiotic expressions on our faces and remind ourselves to ask Old Uncle A later, but we never did. This is how we spent two weeks at Palus Island, away from the mosquitoes and polio.

5.

That bat
would've been involved
in two deaths,
ten years apart

Myandrew and Noodge Mauer were always included when we had other kids around, along with Frankie, when he could sneak away from his old man's ranting and raving. The three of them went with us to the next home game, on Saturday, against the Pirates. They showed up around noon, biking over from Boylston Street having picked up Noodge Mauer from down the block where he lived on the second floor over his parents' shop, which sold comics, tonic, and gum—the stuff we had to have—as well as cigarettes and magazines and something called numbers, which we never saw on the shelves but that the adults used to say they could get there. Steven led us, he knew the way across Beacon Street and Commonwealth Avenue, right to the Charles. We were to meet Morone at the gate near third base, which now had recently been given a new connotation to us such that just saying it, we had to lower our voices. Mother packed our lunch boxes, and on the way, we stopped at Brigham's to load up on jimmies, which we didn't have to pay for since they were there on the counter for the people who sprinkled them on their cones. We locked our bikes together and wrapped the chain around a telephone pole onto which Steven climbed a couple of rungs to make sure he could spot Morone.

Noodge Mauer, Frankie, Steven, and I were wearing dungarees and T-shirts and had our mitts handy in case we were in a position to nab a foul ball. Myandrew was the only one who didn't have a crew cut, his blond hairstyle like the hit singer Gisele MacKenzie's, a high bouffant on top of the forehead with long flaps over the ears; it reminds me now of the fur-lined caps that hunters wear in the winter.

On days in which we had assembly at school, he'd wear his burgundy jacket; underneath there'd be a rosé shirt, red-and-white-checked pants, and white socks. He looked like he'd spilled some Passover wine on a cheap tablecloth and walked away, leaving the napkins for his sister to mop up the mess.

Once, Mother told us, she met his mother at a back-to-school night and all that lady did was blather on about her son's clothes, outfits he'd create from remnants of things she'd put aside for the needy. In one of the only times I can remember Mother using a mocking tone, she imitated my friend's mother, saying repeatedly, "My Andrew this . . . my Andrew that . . . my Andrew blah, blah, blah," each time slurring the "my" and "Andrew" into the elision that forged his identity, a one-word moniker with the emphasis on the *y* so we'd say it and hear it as *my-YANdrew*.

At the ballpark that day, he was wearing his Hood ice cream truck outfit: white shirt, white pants, white shoes, and a thick garrison belt with a giant silver buckle that I swore could actually dispense change.

Frankie gave us some Sen-Sen, which was an indication that his father had washed out his mouth with soap that morning, a pretty regular occurrence given the number of packets he kept in his lunch box and jacket pockets.

Steven spotted Morone from the pole. He was squinting as the sun glistened off his sheer silk jacket, which had birds and symbols we couldn't decipher on the front. When he got to where we were, we gathered around him, as if he were the campfire radiating heat and we were the Cub Scouts running around him in circles. On the back, his jacket said "Korea."

"It's a gift from my cousin Little Alfredo, he sent it to me with a note to join up and ship out, wish you were here."

We took turns wearing it, gingerly, not wanting to have it drop on the ground where your sneakers would always get stuck in the gum-, beer-, tonic-, mustard-, ice-cream-covered cement that ushered you into the stands by the third-base dugout.

After the seventh-inning stretch, we were about to sit back down when the guy on the PA system said, "Ladies and gentlemen and boys and girls, please keep standing while the police honor guard marches out from the stands behind home plate." They were pushing a kid in a wheelchair. He was waving to the crowd, baseball glove on his right hand, legs braced with metal and leather straps.

We all stared intently, nervously, not knowing whether to cheer, so we took our cues from the adults and politely clapped.

The procession stopped on the mound and a guy came onto the field with a megaphone, the kind that cheerleaders used, and we got quiet. He introduced the kid and his parents and although he was shouting, the wind took some of his words so all we could make out was something like, "He's . . . polio . . . generous . . . dig . . . pockets . . . coins . . . cups . . . ushers . . . doctors . . . money . . . cure . . ."

On cue, the ushers came racing back from where they'd been smoking and had cups that said "Timmy Fund" on them, and we dug into our pockets to find some coins to give so that the kid could one day get out of his wheelchair, and we'd invite him to come play ball with us out back near the garages.

Before the start of the top of the eighth inning, Frankie bought a souvenir bat, one signed by the whole team.

"Hey Joel, could I keep it at your place out back in the garage?" he asked.

That way, his father wouldn't find out what he did with his money or have another means at his disposal with which to clobber him. Neither Frankie or I could've conceived how that bat would be involved in two deaths, ten years apart.

6.

These were the things I knew, for sure, in Boston in 1952

After the game, we biked to Papa's store, staying downstairs in the showroom, having noticed upstairs in the office that there was a roomful of men with him who didn't work at the store. At sixty-eight, Papa was the unquestioned head of the family.

His mane was pure white; it was thick and encroached upon his face from both his forehead and temples, and with his weathered creases, he resembled the cabins we'd see in the winter that'd been buried under a blizzard. His gray eyes had the effect of frost that prevented you from peering completely inside, so you had to assess his demeanor from other means: his voice, mannerisms, and various visual cues. It was his voice that gave you the best opportunity by which to judge him: his sounds had a musicality that could dazzle or calm you, up and down scales, major and minor keys, from adagio to presto, from basso to profundo; you never dozed off during one of his performances.

Steven and I got our height from him; he was over six feet tall and we yearned for the day we could look him squarely in the eye, which we did when we were in high school. When we got a little older, he'd tell us that God was playing accordion with the three of us, as he was shrinking while we were expanding.

We pronounced his name with the accent on the second syllable, Pa*pa*, the way Eddie Fisher would later sing in "Oh! My Papa." Papa was a storyteller, an entertainer really, someone who could spin yarns into fabrics that never seemed to fray at the edges. The best were the tales that he'd tell us when Old Uncle A was in from Maine. Papa loved to regale us with stories of people from the Bible. Only you wouldn't hear about any of these in Sunday school, as those Bible characters didn't play dice and prophets weren't scolded by their mothers for holding jousting contests with tree branches while riding donkeys, which were called asses back then. He'd also enthrall us with fables that Aesop never knew, where guys like Odysseus would meet people who were trapped inside animal bodies. They thought like humans, they imagined they could act like us, and they saw themselves as regular folks. We accepted, willingly, stories of men talking to birds and goats and fish. And they always ended when the hero looked into the eyes of a bear or a dove and deep inside saw a little Greek boy who'd been transformed by a testing god and had now gained wisdom beyond his years, having experienced life from a new perspective. At the conclusion of each story, Papa would give us a wink, which initially we didn't know how to construe. Only after a while did we catch on that while, yes, these were entertaining tales and sure, he presented them as if it were a performance, he really didn't mean for us to be passive members of the audience only to applaud with smiles and oodles of laughter when he gave us the tip off that the story was over. He was encouraging *us* to be little Greek boys, right here in the USA, something that I did eventually internalize and was able to demonstrate by the end of 1952.

To get to Papa's furniture store, we used to pick up the trolley just as it went underground and get off before it went under the harbor. In the back of the store, through the door marked Employees Only, you could walk straight to the warehouse where the trucks backed in to unload the furniture or you could go upstairs to the offices and mingle with the visitors; they'd keep their hats on so you'd know they wouldn't be staying long. Some of the visitors were friendly enough, they'd pat us on the back of the head and make a remark to Papa about our size or manners, notwithstanding the fact that we'd more than likely been rambunctious down on the selling floor. Many would give us a coin or two, nothing much, some would show us a card trick, others would have the smell of beer and cigars on their clothes, and one guy would always, and I mean every time, extend his hand to us and ask us, "Howja like to shake the hand of the man who shook the hand of John L. Sullivan, wouldja now?" Not waiting for a response from us, he danced on his tiptoes, threw some lightning-fast phantom punches, left jab, right hook, and we ducked, fearful he was going to connect, then saw Papa's grin and felt the boxer tousle our hair, then offer his huge gnarled hand. We shook it, not having a clue as to whom he was talking about. Nevertheless, we'd spend the entire ride home on the trolley extending our hands to each other, asking each other if we'd like to shake the hand of the man who shook hands with John L. Sullivan, trying to imitate his brogue, and pretending to drink a beer and smoke a cigar. We never knew his name; he became The Boxer to us.

Upon entering the showroom, you'd be overwhelmed with a swoosh of leather and wood polishes, a mixture that Papa said was a means of giving customers the feeling that they'd entered a parlor on Beacon Hill, but to us, it was more of an antidote to the pine-scented cleaners that the fellas who didn't speak English would lather on the floor after closing.

Steven and I loved to play games in the store. You'd be amazed at what you could do with a couple of hassocks and wastebaskets. We played baseball, where the ball was two or three pieces of paper squashed together, held in form by some of the tape we'd pinch from the loading dock out back. The bat was your arm and the hassocks were the bases. "I'm the Braves," I'd always claim first, which meant that Steven had to be the visiting team, usually the New York Giants or the Brooklyn Dodgers.

We played iron lung: "Hey Steven, watch me scrunch up my legs into this large wastebasket, let's put it on top of a coffee table so only my head and shoulders are showing and I'll scratch the inside of the basket in a rhythm, it'll be just like the noise the machine makes when it allows the people to breathe."

We played Korea: "Joel, look what I did. See this rubber band?" He'd wrapped it tightly around his index finger, looped it around the thumb, and hooked it onto the pinky, whereupon he shot me as I scrambled for cover behind a chair tank or a dresser jeep.

And we played election: we marched around the store, chanting, "We need Adlai badly," over and over again until Papa would rap on the window at the back of the store up on the second floor and make the gesture of scraping his thumb against his neck. That was the admonition to calm down and we would, moving a sofa in front of a console with a ten-inch round screen to watch Roller Derby or wrestling.

To a kid, baseball is leather mitts, rubber balls, wooden bats, insignias, pennants, parks, and hot dogs. Polio is doctors, hospitals, shots, paralysis, wheelchairs, and lowered voices. War is salutes and medals, pretend battles, make-believe deaths, days off from school, guns, and parades. Politics is elections, speeches, buttons, flags, handshakes, history, and rallies.

These were the things I knew, for sure, in Boston in 1952. They were truths. They were no less true than the knowledge that my parents wouldn't lie to me, that the mystery of girls would never be revealed to me, that death came only to the old, and that man's best friend was a dog.

By the end of that year, I can tell you that I still believed the thing about the dog.

7.

What if

Lot's wife

hadn't

turned around?

When we arrived at our grandfather's store after the Braves game, I plopped down on a couple of sofas and immediately began to slip my hands between the cushions and the backings in search of coins that had fallen out of the pockets of customers, a habit I asserted was not exactly stealing, it wasn't as if the coins had been purposely placed there the way they were at HIAS. On a good day, I'd get twenty-five to fifty cents, a nice haul that I could use to buy stamps.

Papa rapped on the window and called us upstairs.

We went around the room, shaking hands first with the men we knew, Murph Feldman, Moses O'Neil, Derby Canurbi, and Chief Stinkowski, addressing each as Mister, remembering Papa's warning to unremember everything we'd hear in the office. We shook hands with a few guys we didn't know, answered a few chitchatty questions the guys asked us, then proceeded to go back downstairs. Murph Feldman held the door and walked down the steps to the loading dock behind us.

"Hiya, kiddos. Would yas like to make some extra dough?" he asked. "There's a quarter for each of ya, ya can earn it twice a week, come back tomorra and I'll tell yas about it." A quarter? Twice a week? I imagined all the things that we could treat ourselves to at Noodge Mauer's parents' store and how many Braves games we could go to and how much extra we could give to the Timmy Fund.

Murph Feldman always smoked cigars, wore suspenders, called every man "fella" and every kid "kiddo," and seemed to know everyone. He was a lot shorter than Papa, although he weighed about the same, likely a result of his prodigious consumption of whiskey, which he invariably referred to as "the water of life." He bristled at the notion, suggested by some, that he was a Falstaffian figure, although Papa once wondered, if Shakespeare had invented the character as having come from the Emerald Isle, whether Murph Feldman would've embraced the analogy with élan.

When Papa would have a party for the guys on the loading dock, which we were invited to, Murph Feldman would wear the most raucous Irish costumes, all gussied up in green, shamrocks, tartans, and leprechauns. Afterward, they'd have the real festivities at the pub across the channel on Thomson Place, where we weren't allowed in on account of our ages. Murph Feldman grew up in South Boston where it wouldn't do to go by the name of Meyer, that just wouldn't fit in. So his friends called him Murph and Papa said that even his mother would say Murph outside of the house, it was safer that way, but it was Meyer inside, that was for sure.

"I'm the only Irish Jew in Southie," he'd say, "and I kin make the brogue as good as the guy who shook the hand of John L. Sullivan."

I can still hear Murph Feldman speaking to the guy named McSomething-or-other on the loading dock, "Hey boyo, got langered at the shebeen last night, don't you know?" or, "Gonna search for a good beor to have a craic with, eh?" then looking at me as if I were wearing the befuddled appearance of the dim-witted, that hesitant smile and half-squint look that'd cause him to exclaim, "Well, Janey Mac!" and walk away, slapping the back of whichever Irishman was around, a gesture intended to cement their comradeship and to draw a distinction between us and an authentic *Irish* Jew. Later, Steven explained to me that he was pretty sure it was all about the guys on the loading dock getting drunk and horsing around with girls they'd meet late at night at the bar across the channel on Thomson Place.

We unlocked our bikes and rode west past the warehouses near the wharves and steered around the wooden pallets and garbage cans, creating a new game, the kind of spontaneous unscripted thing that kids did then, on their own out of the sight of their folks. Steven suddenly skidded to a stop around the corner of a building and when I got there he was patting a large black dog with splotches of blue dabbed on its ears, forehead, flews, and front paws, as if someone had practiced painting by numbers on it. It didn't have a collar and had been asleep on the other side of a trash bin stuffed with mostly empty gallon cans and still-wet blue brushes when Steven had nearly run over its tail. Steven called it "boy."

"How do you know?" I inquired.

"It's got a dick, dork head," was his response.

We played with the dog for a few minutes and threw a stick that he fetched and brought back to us, dropping it at our feet, waiting for us to throw it again, which we did for about ten minutes, then played moron in the middle, throwing the stick to each other with the dog not having a chance to get it from either of us. We said good-bye to the dog and rode west, past Faneuil Hall and around the Boston Garden, where the road started to slope downward slightly on the way to Kenmore Square. We stopped at a busy intersection and I swatted at a fly on my right calf, the one exposed to the air because my pants were rolled up so that the grease from the chain wouldn't rub off on them. I swatted again and again and the third time I smacked against something that turned out to be the head of the dog that had been licking my calf. He'd followed us from the warehouse.

"Come on, we don't have time," Steven said authoritatively. "The dog'll eventually turn around, just don't pay any attention to it."

We tied him up in our garage out back, wolfed down our dinner, surreptitiously stuffed pieces of bread and potatoes into our pockets, then went out back, supposedly to have a catch but really to feed and play with the dog, which we were going to take back the next day. When it started to get dark we tied him up again, put an old mat that said "Welcome" next to where he was sitting, and walked backward toward the row house, watching him all the way. He navigated the mat in tighter and tighter circles, tamping it with his paws, going on forever. I went over to him and tried pushing him down but he resisted, still going in circles. I got down on his level and patted the ground. That didn't work, either. Finally, I started talking to him, slowly, as if he were a recent immigrant who knew no English, except that I didn't shout. I used to watch the men at Papa's office when they got no reaction from someone they suspected didn't speak English very well. They repeated themselves, constantly getting louder, then they slid into the pidgin form in exasperation.

"You take this envelope to Sal, Sal, the barber."

(Louder.) "Sal, the barber," gesturing to their heads, making a little scissors with their fingers, doing a snip-snip all over their heads.

(Louder still.) "Sal, over in the North End, North End, the barber, pole, red, white, blue, pole, envelope," pointing north as if the gesture had any more meaning than the direction of the door.

(Shouting.) "You go, Sal, barber, envelope, give, snip-snip, North End, got it?" and off they'd go, where, no one knew, which could mean trouble, big trouble for guys like Sal the barber in the North End, if they never showed up.

We got up early the next day, had a quick bowl of cereal, untied the dog, gave him a bagel, got on our bikes, and headed east for the warehouse district, still a little sore from Dr. Richards' injections. What a sight. The dog was like a PT boat, darting here and there looking for North Korean ships, radar on full 360-degree scan, running what to us was a random pattern but to him must have been an ingenious deception to confuse the enemy. I imagined I was a cruiser, sleek against wave and wind, proudly flying the flag, while Steven was the aircraft carrier, the raison d'être for the convoy, launching his jets of sweat, firing his guns of excitement, searching the horizon for some R&R at a friendly port of call.

We went to Papa's store first to use the mimeograph machine. We ran off twenty-five copies, let them sit out to dry, then put them in an envelope and hopped on the bikes and took off with the dog in tow and came upon the corner of the warehouse where we originally found him. We tacked the "Found Dog" sheets on the front door of the warehouse, on the sides of other buildings, and on telephone poles leading in a spoke pattern in all four directions. Back to Papa's, we bounded up the steps, shushing the dog to be quiet and leaving him a bowl of water near the loading dock. We burst into the office, hoping to find Murph Feldman, eager to earn the quarter a day that hadn't been out of our thoughts since the moment he mentioned it to us. Murph Feldman wasn't there and our hearts sank. Then we heard the clank from the chain in the toilet and out he came, drying his hands on what looked like a couple of dozen paper towels, somehow not igniting them with his lit cigar, his unintentional bathroom deodorizer.

"Hiya, kiddos," he said, "step into my office and let's discuss our transaction," which meant nothing to us.

I whispered to Steven, "Where's the part about us earning two bits a day?"

"Here's the deal, kiddos," he said, laying out a dozen envelopes on a card table and a list of names and addresses. "All ya gotta do is on Tuesday take an envelope to each guy on this list, and on Thursday pick one up from a name on a list I'll give yas. Don't open'm, do ya hear me, make sure ya don't open'm, like I says, and just hand it. Make sure ya give it to the actual guy whose name is here, and the same on Thursday, ya bring it right back here, okeydoke?"

"And we get a quarter each day," I said.

"A quarter."

"Each."

"Each of yas. Ya not deaf, are ya kiddo? I don't need no deaf and dumb kid doing this important job, do I? Ya grandpa didn't tell me ya was deaf and dumb, ya not, are ya?"

"No sir," said Steven.

On Tuesday, Steven grabbed the list that contained a dozen names and I stuffed the envelopes into my basket. Off we went to earn our due. Steven yelled out, "Ya deaf and dumb?" in a mock Murph Feldman brogue as a response to one of my questions that he was pretty sure he'd answered previously. In kind, I turned and asked the dog, who came with us every day that summer, if he was deaf and dumb. He gave me a certain look and I never asked him again.

We went first to see Sal the barber in the North End.

"You Murph's kids,'cause I thought his kids were older?" he asked and we explained who we were. "You Yids all right," he added, "your grandpa and Murph. Here, here's a quarter, for each," he said and our sense of excitement went off the chart. Braves games, comic books, penny candies from Noodge Mauer's parents' store, mail-order air rifles, stamps on approval, slingshots, pink rubber balls, neat's-foot oil for our mitts, all the stuff that we needed, we could see within our grasp. We crossed off Sal the barber's name and Steven rearranged the list so that we wouldn't be zigzagging all over town, we could start in the North End and work our way west so that the last stop was near our house and we could be home by six o'clock.

As long as we were in the North End, we went looking for Morone on the next block, where Morone Coal Delivery and his uncle's company, Alfredo's Hauling, shared a driveway. We went around back. Morone was there with Rocky and Big Alfredo, Little Alfredo's father. They sat in folding chairs around a table with another guy we'd never seen before, playing dominoes. We were introduced amid a whole lot of exclamations of "Hey!" and Rocky pretended to box with us, his hands coming so fast and furiously, his crucifix flying out from under his undershirt nearly hitting me in the face, that I thought he was going to connect, but he made sure to keep this big grin on so I didn't get scared. The new guy was wearing a light brown shirt, had a blue tie on, and had pressed blue pants with a stripe down the outside of each leg.

"Sergeant Wilson," he said to each of us and thrust his hand out first to shake with Steven and then with me. Rocky saluted and Big Alfredo put his glass in the air and said, "Sal-u-tay," which we thought was Italian for *salute* and pretty neat so we put our right hands over our brows and said, "Sal-u-tay," giving a crisp version of the Boy Scout salute, something we'd seen Myandrew do on those nights he'd take off for meetings where he'd practice how to get found after he pretended to be lost.

"I'm off to Parris Island," Morone said. "I'm shipping out before the end of summer then joining my cousin, Little Alfredo. I'm going to Korea."

"Semper fi," shouted Sergeant Wilson, who'd bolted up straight as a rail.

"Semper fi," Rocky and Big Alfredo yelled, in unison, on their feet.

"Semper fi," Steven and I cheered, saluting furiously.

We stayed a few minutes, watching them throw back some drinks that they wouldn't give to us. After they finished, we saluted and excused ourselves because we had other envelopes to deliver. Biking down Snow Hill Street, we were abreast of each other, the dog off to the side, when I yelled out to Steven, "Is Paris an island?"

"What's semper fi? I hope it's not another Italian curse that'll get us in trouble," Steven said, and I added the same for sal-u-tay. We agreed not to say anything to anyone else.

We made the rounds of the other names on the list, then headed home, where we tied the dog near the mat in the garage. On the way up the three flights, into the bathroom and then to the kitchen, we practiced the routine we'd devised. It was time to beg for a dog.

"Please, please, please, oh, oh, oh, can we get one, can we get one, please, please, please, we'll take care of it, we promise, please, please, please."

Ever the accountant, we anticipated Dad would first say no but then would make up a list of the chores we'd have to do, calculating how much everything we were going to need would cost, so we practiced our response that we'd pay for it with the money Murph Feldman was giving us for delivering envelopes.

We went out back to play running bases with Noodge Mauer and we showed him the dog, swearing him to secrecy.

"What if someone calls your house, you know, in response to the notices you put up?" he asked.

"Holy crap, I hadn't thought of that," I panicked, first because we'd lose the dog, and second because they'd kill us for lying and not telling them about the dog that we'd had for a day and a half. Our only solution was to go and tear down the "Found Dog" signs we'd put up, but we were tired from biking all over kingdom come and wouldn't dig into our treasury to take the trolley.

"We'll do it in the morning," I said unconvincingly, then played with the dog.

We never went back to the warehouse to pull down the signs and no one ever called to claim the dog. We never tried to find the dog's owner. And we didn't feel guilty; this was a concept that we could readily define but not actually feel. Like many other emotions that are learned, we can't really comprehend what something like guilt is until we reach a certain age, which we hadn't done by that time.

We pulled off our charade with the dog for a few more days when Dad finally gave in and told us we could go to the pound, but under the condition that the dog would sleep in the basement or out back in the garage and that we'd take care of it so as not to bother Papa or Mother. On Saturday afternoon when Auntie Rose was there, we brought him up the stairs, having come from the pound, so we said. He walked in as if he owned the place, bounded through the rooms, Mother after him telling him not to pee. He made a beeline for Auntie Rose and put his head on her lap. She wet a hanky with her tongue and tried to wipe the dried paint off his face. Everybody referred to him as the blue dog so it's not surprising that he became known as BlueDog, with the accent on *Blue*. He never slept in the garage, not once.

In many ways, BlueDog changed my life. I could say things to him, could practice speaking to others, imagining him to be a person, and when I heard myself, I could gauge how it'd sound to others and if I didn't like the way it came out, I'd have the opportunity to fix it without negative consequences. Some people do this in their dreams, where they really shine, they say all the right things, knock out all of their opponents, have the snappiest rejoinders, and the like. Then they force themselves to wake up and jot down something but it's completely unrecognizable in the morning.

We went on our routes for Murph Feldman twice a week, biking in the waterfront, downtown, the North End, and Southie, going to meet the men whose names were on the envelopes. We took BlueDog with us every time. With the dough we made from Murph Feldman, plus what we snared from the sofas in Papa's showroom and the occasional coins from the men in Papa's office as well as the extra that the guys like Sal the barber in the North End gave us, we went to a Braves game against the New York Giants on July 1.

Who could've predicted what would happen as a result of a serendipitous occurrence that day at the game, the catch of a foul ball in the eighth inning?

What if Lot's wife hadn't turned around?

November 8, 1923
Dear Diary,

I still sometimes wet my bed if I forget to get up and go. So then I take the sheet and my underpants and put them on the radeater to dry out. I don't want my sister to find out.

We went to temple to pray for mamele. Uncle A is teaching us to read Hebrew. I know how to say the shma. My sister acts like she is my mother. Uncle A says when she annoys me I should say oy gevalt. He told me how to spell it. I asked him what it means? He says it is the same as when someone rolls their eyes up into their head. I roll my eyes up and stare into the mirrer. It doesn't work. He says it is not Hebrew. Yiddish. It is what he can speak. He talks to Daddy like this when they don't want us to know what they are talking about. That's how they tell secrets. I have a secret.

Goodnight,
Rose Mischal

8.

Hey, gimme my cut, chief

Murph Feldman sat on the sofa in front of the bulletin board that was crowded with notes, some for the Tuesday envelopes, some for the Thursday envelopes, and a few that he didn't recognize, those with names and instructions for furniture deliveries, pickups, and bills. He knew nothing about the furniture business despite the fact that his business card said "General Manager" and the telephone number was Papa's store's number. He and Papa went way back. They met working at HIAS when they were sixteen or so, around 1900. After Papa told Murph Feldman about the coins in the sofas, it took all of Murph Feldman's restraint to walk down the halls and pass by the easy pickings.

Old Uncle A told us that as a Jew, a poor Jew, an immigrant Jew, Papa wasn't able to get the jobs that others could; you had to be Pilgrim, Brahmin, establishment, or connected. Papa tried and failed to get a job on the trolley, the police and fire were out (you could be Irish but not Jewish), and the banks wouldn't give you credit so you couldn't open a store. He stoked coal on a steamship that took passengers from East

Boston up the coast, to Marblehead and Portsmouth and Old Orchard Beach and Bar Harbor and then on to Halifax and back.

He'd shovel coal during the days but got to spend the evenings on the cool deck waving to the crowds on the beach. On the nights he'd stay on the boat, he'd clean up, have dinner, and then go up on the deck, where he'd play pinochle with the men and entertain the ladies with stories concocted from the escapades of the mates from the steamships that docked at East Boston. Streaming in from the four corners of the world, these sailors would entertain all comers at the bar across the channel on Thomson Place, which served, for all intents and purposes, as the schoolhouse for young immigrant men like Papa. With the stars shimmering between the whitecaps of the waters of the North Atlantic, Papa would tell of his purported adventures with the natives in the South Seas, of whaling near Cape Horn, of logging old growth in the Northwest, or of serving as a mule guide in the red rock desert of the Arizona Territory, none of which, of course, was true. He'd speak of the girls in grass skirts wearing only clam shells on top, of holding on for dear life in the rigging while the harpoon guns were firing over the crests of the breakers and, when they'd hit, of the jolt and the backlash when the whale lurched down, stretching the rope taut. He'd tell them of scaling a sequoia with the spikes of his shoes barely grabbing the foot-thick bark at two hundred feet in the air, and of spending the days in the desert with the burros at temperatures of 110 degrees and the very same evenings huddled with three dogs for warmth around a campfire in the freeze of a July night.

He knew how to control his voice, speaking softly, then wham! he'd explode with his fist pounding into his hand for emphasis, his voice detonating so loudly that the percussion waves would lift the ladies' skirts and set them all aflutter. He was always careful not to step over the line, not to be too forward, not to have the ladies more interested in him than in their husbands. For the fellas, he'd do card tricks, pick a card, any card, he'd pull cards out of their ears, and he'd turn up the very card they'd selected. He was a master with money, having spent hours at HIAS with the coins he'd found in the sofas, rolling them from finger to finger, turning mils into pennies and then dollars into twenties. They called him Frenchie for Michel, which was what they thought Mischal was.

He left the boat one night at Bar Harbor in Frenchman Bay, finding a general store, and spotted some canned goods, nuts, dried fruits, biscuits, and a woman who smiled shyly at him. Papa once told us that he fell in love with Nana at first sight and honestly, we never knew if this was an apocryphal tale, but it didn't matter if it was true, embellished, or fiction. In the frame above his bed in our apartment, Nana's face reminded me of Mother's and Auntie Rose's. You could see the hint of the smile that Papa saw that day on the coast of Maine in the first decade of the 1900s.

As he was piling provisions into his knapsack, the woman who would turn out to be my Nana turned to face Papa and extended her arm.

"I'm Sylvia Feiner," she said, and her bracelet grazed his forearm. He noticed a six-pointed silver star among the charms. As he gently touched the charm, he winked at her. And that's how they met, Nana and Papa, two young Jews on the coast of Maine, one who would embark on a journey that would turn out to be as dramatic as one of his stories, the other to die during the time of the flu pandemic following the Great War. "I thought you were, you know, one of *us* when you walked into the store and secretly hoped that you were looking to find the camp on Palus Island." Papa showed no recognition, so Sylvia continued. "Off the coast, there's an island that the refugees from Europe flee to when they find the city life of Boston so different from their rural life in the shtetls. We have about a hundred people at any one time and they're supposed to stay a year or two before moving back, to Boston or on to another place, but they rarely leave. They've been overwhelmed, by the language, by city life, by the loss of the neighborhood, the loss of family, the loss of community," she said and then invited him to spend the night on the island.

Early the next morning as the sun was struggling with the mist, he pointed to the three-story houses. "It looks like the village where I grew up," he noted. "See? They have the same large sweeping roofs but here they look like they're made with seaweed instead of knitted with thatch."

"Inside they have an area that's open all the way up to the roof, with the second floor being as much a balcony where people sleep," she remarked.

He guessed there were about three-dozen houses. Three additional ones were off in the distance in the promontory.

"With the smoke pouring out of each one of those three, if you aligned yourself just so, you'd think that a huge ship was leaving port from the middle of the island," he said. She smiled coyly at his keen observation.

"It looks like there aren't any children," he noted as they strolled around, "and most of the people are much older than we are." She nodded in agreement.

They were all friendly to him but quickly lowered their voices when he was near and spoke in the language of his youth. Miss Feiner introduced him to Abraham Auerbach, the caretaker, at dinner on that first night. Papa described his life on the boat, and her eyes lit up with his fanciful stories of his make-believe travel and exploits.

"Why surely they know it's just entertainment, that these are stories. I bet they probably think you're paid by the steamship company to amuse them!" she exclaimed.

"I sure could use the money," he responded.

When all were gathered in the great room of the largest building, Papa amused them with the tallest tales, tales so tall that they couldn't stand up without support, which the crowd provided. They became extemporaneous fabulists, lurching into uncharted territory, reaching new levels of absurd occurrences and clever wordplay. That night, the stories seemed to go on forever until there was a loud tympanic crash, as Mr. Auerbach dropped a plate filled with halva on the stones in front of the fireplace. Everyone laughed and it drained them dry, the magic disappeared the way Papa made coins evaporate into thin air.

Later, Papa wanted to know who the island residents were.

"They're the folks who come down the gangplank and don't have anyone to greet them," she replied. "They're the farmers and the smiths and the milkmaids, they're the boys who didn't want to play and the maiden aunts. They're the people who were swept along with the ebb tide but who found out they simply couldn't swim ashore."

Papa stayed for three days, leaving early after there'd been blue sky at night. He knew he had to get back to the boat, where he'd continue his entertainments and pick up his half-pay check in Halifax along with a little pocket change, which would be good because he made plans, right then and there, to return someday to Palus Island, to return to Miss Feiner.

Back in Boston, Papa started to make plans for the future. He worked the docks of East Boston and loaded the belongings of the immigrants onto carriages, sometimes taking them to the HIAS tenement and other times to houses of relatives. Playing pool one night with Murph Feldman in Southie, Papa came up with a new business idea that wouldn't require a bank loan.

"Let's meet the immigrants at the dock in East Boston, we'll take their belongings for free, we'll refuse to take any money, even any coins that they try squeeze into our hands as I imagine they will. They'll hug us, we'll earn their respect, respect that'll translate into loyalty, which we can trade once they get settled for furniture; they'll need beds and lamps and chairs and tables." So with seventy bucks from a summer of hustling with Murph Feldman and playing craps with a young tough named O'Neil and the Irish boys in Southie, Papa had the bankroll to start the business, which he did by buying a wagon that'd serve as his transportation for immigrants and then to deliver the goods.

He'd buy secondhand stuff and take the detritus that the Brahmins would leave out on the curb in Beacon Hill, fix it up and haul it onto the wagon, whereupon he'd parade around the settlements where the immigrants congregated, not so much selling as much as schmoozing and entertaining, eventually getting around to the offer and the bid, if not this time then next. He went to the North End, the Italian part of town, and to Southie, where he always had Moses O'Neil with him, and out to Dorchester, the only place he was asked to come inside, which he did, for a drink and a look at the daughter that was the real reason they wanted to make his acquaintance. The daughters' huge smiles betrayed their shyness and set them apart from the older generation. Papa laughed, drank, ate, sometimes sold some furniture, and all the time thought of Miss Feiner.

He was thinking of her when he went to play pool with Murph Feldman, he was thinking of her when he was carrying a chest strapped to his back up the fourth flight of stairs in the late August heat, he was thinking of her when he saw a young boy dart between a horse and a trolley and get clipped by a Stanley Steamer coming in the opposite direction. Papa ran to where the boy was lying, picked him up, and brought him to his wagon. He was relieved to see no blood and there probably weren't any broken bones because with all the movement, the kid wasn't screaming. Moaning, that was it. Moaning with his eyes closed. The driver of the car came close, first daintily stepping over the trolley tracks and making sure he didn't brush his clothes against the wagon, or Papa, for that matter.

"Why, he ran right in front of me, everyone saw that, what's a person to do with these ruffians all over town," the driver said, pleading his case to the small crowd who'd assembled around the wagon.

"I'll take him to the settlement house," Papa said.

"Well, you're a good man and here's something for your troubles," the man offered, then anxiously withdrew an envelope from inside his coat pocket along with some cash and placed it in Papa's hand and whispered, "It's for the kid, for a doctor, for an undertaker, or for you, here, take it." Then he was gone, back over the tracks, stepping as if he were in a field of cow patties or doing some new dance, like they did in the silent movies when the bad guys shot the ground under the good guys' feet and the words come up on the screen, saying, "Dance, pardner."

As the driver was leaving, a handsome Irishman of medium height with his hair parted just slightly left of center, wearing a waistcoat, a vest, a shirt with a turned-up collar, and a bowtie appeared, leaned over the suddenly quiet boy, and spoke to Papa.

"It's an honor to have you in my city," he pronounced. "Whether Jew or Italian, you'll always have a place in Boston; you can count on me as this young man has counted on you." He bowed graciously to Papa, who awkwardly bowed back, then handed Papa a card that was immediately stuffed unread into his pocket.

As soon as the well-dressed man who gave him the card was out of sight, the kid opened his eyes, extended his hand palm up, and shouted to Papa, "Hey, gimme my cut, chief."

And that's how Papa met Chief Stinkowski. He couldn't have been more than ten or so, yet pulled off a scam in front of dozens of folks who'd believed that he'd really been hit by the fancy car driven by the rich guy. Papa gave the kid half of the cash, kept the other half for himself, more than enough money for Papa to take the Boston and Maine all the way to Bar Harbor and back, and then some. He shoved the envelope into his pocket and told the kid he was going to take the train to Maine the next day and would be back in a week.

"See ya 'round, chief," the kid said, Papa assuming he'd never lay eyes on him again.

On the train to Bar Harbor, Papa reached into his pocket for a handkerchief and found the card the well-dressed Irishman had given him. It read "John Francis Fitzgerald, Mayor, City of Boston."

He arrived at Palus Island just in time for dinner, Mr. Auerbach serving and fussing, Miss Feiner watching Papa do his tricks, helping the oldest to their seats, listening to their woes, consoling them with stories, then assisting Mr. Auerbach by cleaning the tables, taking out the trash, and repairing a chair. She stood back, seeing how he had nestled into their community effortlessly with charm and grace, and imagined the disappointment they would all feel when he'd leave in a few days. Her ache was not simply for them, she realized later that night when she couldn't get to sleep. How was it, she wondered, that this man, barely a man, had intruded without imposition? Was it that he had spent his youth in an American city? That he was the dream for those who lived nightmares? That the faces and sounds and struggles of these people mirrored those of his upbringing? Or was it that he was a Jew following traditions that were imbued within him, unconsciously, out to repair the world?

She imagined life with him, life without him, wondered if this was love. She approached Mr. Auerbach in the dining hall, whom she looked to as if he were a revered *onkl*.

"How do I know?" she asked him.

"Listen to your heart," he replied, "not to what anyone else says."

"When I see him, I get excited, I smile, I can't wait to speak to him, to hear his voice. But I shouldn't leave the colony and he won't stay here, this isn't a life for him."

"Or for you either, Sylvia."

"But who else'll be the mortar that won't crack with the weather of daily life?" she asked, then self-consciously attempted to reassure herself that no one other than Mr. Auerbach had heard. "This is a burden that'd be difficult for me to bear."

"How would you feel seeing Solomon Mischal's back diminish slowly as he drifts toward the mainland alone?"

"Oh," she swooned, then said nothing for a while. Fidgeting with some silverware, she resumed, "I worry about an emptiness that'd settle in the bones of those who reside here on Palus Island if I were to leave, and this I'm not sure I could abide."

"There comes a time when you have to decide what's best for you and you alone, and this decision isn't unlike those made by the folks who chose to come here, having left loved ones over there." He pointed out over the Atlantic.

She hugged him and went back to her house, thinking about Mr. Auerbach and his decision to remain on Palus Island.

After dinner, she asked Solomon Mischal to walk with her out back of the main house, where they could hear the waves crashing. It was an awkward moment; she didn't know how to start the conversation and was also a bit nervous, thinking that perhaps her feelings were unrequited. She began several times and he noted her stops and starts, a sign to him that this walk was about neither sea breezes nor seal sightings.

"May I?" he asked, and with that simple question, to which she responded with an affirmative nod and a smile, he grasped her hand in his, sending a jolt of electricity through her body that Papa told me many years later he thought he could actually feel. Right before they crossed through the light that shone over the door at the back of the dining hall, yet when they were still out far enough in the shadows of the old pines, he asked if he could kiss her, and before she said yes, she knew they'd be leaving Palus Island together.

This was, we found out years later when Old Uncle A made his last trip south to Boston, a first for both of them. Not just first love; first embrace, first kiss. It seems odd to us now that such a tiny spark could detonate the kind of passion that would be sustained for years through calamities great and small. How is it possible that someone simply knows based on such a limited set of data points? we now ask ourselves. Is there really love at first sight, or is it a matter of pheromone interactions? I can tell you this: we never asked Old Uncle A either about any of this or if he'd ever had a first.

Sylvia rose early on her last day on the island and made the rounds of each of the houses, posting lists of the things that she routinely told the residents, designating a person at each house with the responsibility to perform the tasks, to mark down each day that they were done and to leave the list tacked to the wall outside the front door so Mr. Auerbach would know. She straightened out the clothes that were lying about, stacked the books near the night tables, and wrote down the instructions that each person needed to have, knowing that these would find their ways into the crevices of the sofas, under the beds, wedged in between the dressers and the walls, lost as bookmarks, all within a few days of her departure.

She gave each person a kiss and a prolonged hug to Mr. Auerbach, who helped Papa lift her trunk into the skiff for the start of her trip across the bay. She told herself she couldn't look back, she'd cry so, and she didn't want Solomon Mischal to think her tears were for the uncertain future with him. When they got to Boston, he helped her off the train and lugged her trunk to the street, where they spotted a kid sitting on a wagon, peering under his brimmed cap into the crowd. He waved and yelled out when he saw Papa.

"Chief, over here, over here, chief!"

Papa guided Miss Feiner to the wagon and was astounded to see the kid, Chief Stinkowski.

"Pleased, ma'am," the young boy said in an uncharacteristic show of manners, touching his cap, then immediately scampering to load the trunk onto the back of the wagon.

"Aren't you going to introduce me to your young friend?" Miss Feiner asked Papa. "I'm Sylvia," she said, extending her fingers, the first woman's hand Chief Stinkowski had ever held.

October 28, 1927
Dear Diary,

Today I stayed home from school. My head hurts. So does my stomach. I am dizzy a lot. I told my sister I had a cold and pretended to cough and blow my nose.

I listened to the radio. I heard them sing Aint she Sweet. I know the words but fell asleep when I was singing along.

I made hot chocolate so Daddy would have some when he came home. Some of his friends were here for dinner. Daddy made coins disappear. Uncle Murf showed me some card tricks. Mister Magwire laughed and winked at us when Daddy told his stories. We had fun but I threw up when they went home. I will not be going to school tomorrow. Maybe never again. None of the girls like me. The boys do. My sister says I should be careful because they all want one thing. I don't know what they want so if I stay home they will never get it. Ha!

Forever yours,
Rose

9.

Serendipity is an instrument that we can never learn to play

Morone and I went to a game not long before he shipped out to Parris Island; he was accustomed to wearing his marine uniform and I had on my Braves cap. In the inning after the Timmy Fund coins were collected, big Earl Torgeson stepped up to the plate for the Braves and sent a foul our way. I jumped out of my seat, stretched my left hand, the one with the glove, as far as I could, and felt a thump and a hand simultaneously. Standing on my left, Morone had gone for the ball, and his right hand cupped the right side of the ball that was partially in my left hand, the gloved hand. Our hands were pretty much at the same level, and we kept the pose for a few seconds, not sure if we actually had the ball or not.

In our delirium, we didn't notice the guy with the felt hat who snapped a picture of the two of us, intertwined, me in shorts and a T-shirt, Morone in his marine khaki shirt, blue tie, and blue pants with the stripe running down the outside seam. After the game, we bolted down the stands and tried to get the attention of big Earl Torgeson as he was packing his gear in the dugout, so we could get his autograph on the ball we'd caught. Leaning over the rail, I shouted,

"Earl, Earl, Earl," so loudly you'd think he would've made eye contact, just to shut me up. I got a tap on my shoulder, and the grown-up with the camera asked if I would come with him and would I bring the guy in the uniform with me.

Oh cripes, I didn't know that I couldn't lean over the rail.

I didn't mean to yell at Mr. Torgeson.

Mother will kill me.

Do I have to give the ball back?

The guy with the camera told us that he wanted us to meet someone, and proceeded to take us down a flight of steps underneath the stands and along a corridor that led through a door to a couple of grubby offices. The smell of beer and cigars was palpable.

"Wait here, fellas," he said, and the two of us stood around, looking at the photos on the wall, shots from as far back as 1915 when the stadium was built and one of Babe Ruth, who played for the Braves in 1935. After a while, the guy with the camera came back with another man, who was wearing a vest and a pocket watch.

"This here's Mr. Perini, the owner of the Braves, say hello," and we dutifully stuck our hands out to shake.

"Would you like to have the ball you caught autographed?" he said, and as if on cue, big Earl Torgeson entered and stuck this huge paw out that engulfed mine and pumped it like he was fixing a flat. Mr. Perini gave him a pen, and the photographer took pictures of him writing his name and date on the ball, of us with him, of us with the ball, and of us with Mr. Perini and Earl.

Mr. Perini came over to Morone and me and put a hand on one shoulder of each of us. "How would it sound," he wanted to know, "if you guys want to come back tomorrow, for free, to sit in the box with me and meet the Braves?"

How would it sound? It sounded as good as watching *Ramar of the Jungle* or *Mr. Peepers* every night. It sounded as good as a day at Norumbega Park, ten miles west of Braves Field out in Auburndale, where you could canoe, play softball, picnic, and ride on the carousel.

The next morning, I picked up the *Herald Traveler* on the front stoop and took it upstairs for Dad. He liked to read it first thing, he said, to find out how the other half lived, but really, it was his way of getting a feel for the ponies before he called Derby Canurbi, one of Papa's cronies whose nickname we had to unremember.

Steven and I were in our room, lining up toy soldiers for an epic battle, when we heard, "Holy cow!" shouted from the kitchen and then again and a third time.

"Joel, Joel, holy cow, you're in the paper, Joel, holy cow, holy cow!" Dad shouted, and in we scampered to the kitchen. There, taking up most of the back page, was a picture of me, the day before at Braves Field, with Morone by my side, our arms stretched straight up and the ball, the ball that Earl Torgeson fouled off, safely in our combined grasp. The caption read, "Call in the Marines!" and Dad said, "It's a double entendre, it has two meanings, it's the sportswriter's way of saying that the Braves need some assistance or else another seventh- or eighth-place finish is coming." I told Dad about the catch, the photographer, the meeting with Mr. Perini, and our invitation to the game that afternoon.

I was proud of having my picture in the paper and especially since I was side by side with Morone. Even though he was six years older, Catholic, and a working-class kid from the North End, I looked up to him in a kind of hero worship. He was so different, almost exotic, something a bit forbidden, a hint of danger surrounding him. I wondered if Papa and Murph Feldman had any of the same feelings when they first encountered Moses O'Neil.

Morone never talked down to us; we were like little brothers to him, and although he never set out to teach us anything, we learned from him—about girls, of course, but also about how to wend your way in the world when you weren't born with a silver spoon in your mouth. He could adapt to different situations quickly, playing the hood in his part of town when it served a purpose and playing the polite dinner guest at our house when being served by Mother. "Yes, ma'am, more kugel, please, raisins with noodles, I have to tell Ma."

Steven came with us to the park that day and we all sat in Mr. Perini's box. We met all the VIPs who'd stop by the box and greet Mr. Perini, who introduced us to everyone, including Dr. Goodman, whose picture was on the front of the paper all the time at those fancy shindigs for raising money for the kids with polio. His hand never seemed to be separated from the bag next to his leg that said the name of the hospital on it, as if he'd be able to save a kid the minute he suspected him of having the disease by whipping out some magic potion and rushing to his side. Next to him was lanky Mr. Carlson, cigarette dangling from his lips, the sportswriter from the *Herald Traveler*, whose face and trail of smoke we recognized from the back of the paper, where his column appeared every day the Braves played, whether in Boston or in one of the other seven National League cities. *Everyone* knew Mr. Carlson, he was as well-known as the players, a guy who'd "Give it to you Straight!," the slogan he'd made so famous that the mayor and the other hotsy-totsy folks would crib it into their speeches, after paying homage, naturally, to Mr. Carlson, as if by making a reference to him, they would cause some of Mr. Carlson's essence to rub off on them, too.

Right after we sang "The Star-Spangled Banner," Mr. Perini walked out on the field near the mound and, using the megaphone, told everyone that he had a special guest on hand and directed our attention to the Braves dugout. After a few seconds, a boy two or three years older than Steven emerged and the crowd roared.

"Who's that?" I asked no one in particular, then heard folks yelling out, "Timmy!" with more enthusiasm than I ever heard any of them yell with during a game.

It was Timmy, *the* Timmy, the Timmy of the Timmy Fund, who came out onto the field, supported by a couple of Braves, waving his Braves cap at the crowd. Mr. Perini grasped Timmy's hand with both of his own and then gave him a ball. Dr. Goodman had this huge smile on his face and applauded vigorously, whipping his head from side to side as if to make sure that the crowd wouldn't stop its appreciation for this kid who was conquering polio. Then Mr. Perini pivoted his position such that the megaphone was pointed toward us, and he asked the crowd to welcome Morone and me, the kids whose picture was on the back of the *Herald Traveler* catching the foul ball.

Morone put his hand on the rail and was over in a flash. I could imagine him vaulting out of a landing craft as it hit the beach in North Korea. I idled my way over the rail, managing not to catch my shorts on the metal post. Mother would've been pleased. I trailed him to the mound, shook Mr. Perini's hand, and stood next to Timmy, not knowing whether to shake his hand, remembering Mother's stern warning that I can't play anymore with someone who has polio. "You nev-er know," she'd say ve-ry slow-ly, slightly nodding her head up and down for an eternity after she spoke, as if to mean she really did know but just wasn't going to let on how she knew so don't ask.

Mr. Perini had the Braves players support Timmy as he approached the mound, stepped on the rubber, and assumed the pitching position. Just like that, big Earl Torgeson stepped out of the dugout and went into a crouch behind home plate. Timmy wound up, a little dramatically, I might add, but that was okay, he probably hadn't gotten to see too many games, having likely been cooped up in a hospital, and let one fly over big Earl Torgeson's head. The crowd laughed and applauded and Timmy raised both hands over his head in triumph.

Mr. Perini said to Morone, "Have a go, son," and as if taking orders was something that he'd gotten used to, Morone wound up in a great imitation of Lew Burdette and let fly with a fastball right down the middle. Big Earl Torgeson gave him a thumbs-up and flung it back to him. Now, I'll never know if Mr. Perini was going to ask me, too, to throw out a ceremonial first pitch, because before he could say anything, I grabbed the ball from Morone, stepped to the mound, and ripped one into big Earl's mitt. It made the good sound, the one you could hear on the radio, the whumpf thud that came over WBZ at night that probably meant a swing and a miss.

Mr. Perini thanked us and the photographer took pictures of us on the mound and at the plate and we got to meet all the players, who came out on the field. On the way back to the stands, Mr. Perini asked Morone and me, "Would you like to help the ushers in the seventh inning pass the Timmy Fund cups around?"

"Could my brother do it too?" I asked.

Mr. Perini gave me a smile and said, "Why not?" in that special way adults have of asking a question when they're really giving you an answer.

After we collected coins for the Timmy Fund in the seventh inning, Morone left and Steven and I took the cups down to the office where

I'd first met Mr. Perini. Some guy there told us to leave the cups on the desk and to plan on being there the next day to help out again with the collection.

"I'm not sure we can," I mumbled, "we've got to go to our grandfather's store."

"Same time tomorra, kid," the guy said, never looking up and apparently not listening to me, but as we didn't want to let Timmy down, we gave each other a doltish look and said sure, we'd come back the next day. On the other hand, maybe he actually did hear us but simply didn't care about what a couple of kids had to say.

We got to Papa's store late the next day because we had to fix our Soap Box Derby car. Some of the nails had gotten loose so we pounded them in the garage with the bat that Frankie had bought at the Braves game as a souvenir and kept at our house so his father wouldn't find out and use it on him as a cudgel.

We overheard Derby Canurbi shouting and saw him gesticulating on the phone in Papa's office. Steven and I've since talked about what would've happened if we hadn't seen Derby Canurbi that day, or if we'd seen him but hadn't had the curiosity to try to figure out the meaning of the words he said, or if he hadn't spoken them at all. What if we'd never met the kid who'd become the symbol of a city, a region really, fighting a disease that was to us what the flu pandemic of 1918 was to our parents? Would we really be different people if we hadn't known a guy who was going into the marines to fight in a war, whom we might never see again?

These were chance encounters, and we know that serendipity is an instrument that we can never learn to play. We listen to its sounds and take action or ignore it, for better or worse. And honestly, we won't know how the cadence of our lives will be affected at such a time, but in retrospect we can evaluate how we reacted and make our assessments. It's many years later that we well up with emotion and express either happiness or resentment at actions taken or avoided. *If only we could've known in advance* is a common lament, but to me it misses the point. Not knowing is the essence of life, and this uncertainty makes it all worth living.

The door to Papa's office swung open, and before Derby Canurbi slammed it shut, we heard fragments that lingered in the air for days, like the confetti that never seemed to reach the ground when they threw it out of windows and off of roofs for special occasions, at the end of the War and on Thanksgiving for the parade: "Chief . . . Braves . . . bank . . . envelopes . . . Milwaukee."

"What'd he say?" I asked Steven after the door slammed and Derby Canurbi was in Papa's office.

"Something about the Braves," Steven said, "but there was other stuff, too, he mentioned Chief . . ."

"Yeah, Chief and the bank, that's all I heard."

"Something about Milwaukee, too, what could that mean? Oh yeah, and envelopes, he said envelopes," Steven remembered, and we both bolted upstairs to get the envelopes from Murph Feldman. He was paying attention to Derby Canurbi, who was talking on the phone, Murph Feldman nodding and writing notes on the back of one of Papa's invoices. We waited for a kid's hour, ten minutes or so, and left with the list that had the names and addresses inside a large envelope. We took off through India Street on the way to Milk Street and stopped in the shade of a Hood truck where we got a couple of Hoodsies and a cup for BlueDog.

We looked at the list to figure out where we were headed and the fastest way to get there. Allston, straight out on Commonwealth Avenue.

"What's this?" Steven asked, as he pulled a piece of paper from the envelope. "It looks like something Papa needs. It must've been in the envelope by mistake."

"Turn the paper over, what's on the other side?"

The piece of paper was an invoice form, and on the back were the notes that Murph Feldman had taken when Derby Canurbi was on the phone.

"What's it say?"

Steven read it and we tried to decode it at the same time. "It's just words: 'Milwauk $10Gs Perini 2 to 1 office after game Zeidler Balt.'"

"What's it mean?"

"I don't know but something about ten thousand bucks, that's what they mean by 'Gs,' and it has something to do with Mr. Perini."

"'Milwauk' and '2 to 1' and 'Zeidler Balt'? I don't get it," I stated out loud as much to myself to see if it'd trigger something.

"I don't know, maybe it'll come to us at the game this afternoon when we collect the coins for the Timmy Fund," Steven said, and we mounted our bikes, taking off toward Allston on a Murph Feldman assignment.

At the game, we normally would've been obsessed with screaming out "Magpie" at Sal Maglie, the New York Giants' pitcher, and baiting Leo Durocher, the manager, who'd come out of the dugout with arms flailing at the slightest provocation and would scuff the dirt with his spikes all over the umpire's pants. But we both seemed distracted, and at one point, Steven turned to me and said, "When we overheard Derby Canurbi who said something about Milwaukee and the Braves and Chief, I think the 'Milwauk' from Murph Feldman's notes is Milwaukee, but I still don't know who Zeidler Balt is." It was clear that Steven had been obsessing about this the whole time we were on our bikes and handing out envelopes.

After we collected the coins in the seventh inning, we went down the steps and heard voices in the office through the closed door, which was a first. Neither one of us can explain why we did what we did, but we did it without saying a word. Instinctively, we climbed up the ironwork that supported the stands and curved over the office, which was tucked under an arch as an afterthought. On the curved office roof was a grate that covered a fan, and although there was smoke filtering out, from cigars mostly, we leaned on the curve of the roof and peered down through the filter, having placed our coin-filled popcorn cups behind the support on the ground and covered them up with an old broom and mop. We saw Moses O'Neil and Chief Stinkowski along with two other men we didn't know. Chief Stinkowski was so big he blocked much of the view.

People always called Chief Stinkowski *Chief* because of the way he stood with his arms folded and a scowl on his face, and because, with his black hair, he looked just like the Indian mascot of Shawmut Bank. It also didn't hurt that he grunted a lot and his English wasn't great, so you thought of him as a Tonto figure from *The Lone Ranger* and it all fit together. Chief was Polish, but no one, I mean no one, called him a

Polack. Once, I saw him pound a nail into the wall at the loading dock with the heel of his hand in three blows, boom, boom, boom. He was from Malden, five miles north of the city, where nobody met your gaze on the street, as eye contact could start a fight and if you were an outsider, well, you'd lose. He'd left home at ten and, as Moses O'Neil tells it, apprenticed himself to Papa. All anyone knew about him was that he was the youngest of five children and that his parents never learned English and Chief Stinkowski never learned Polish. His brothers and sisters had to interpret for him. Once, Moses O'Neil asked a few questions about Chief Stinkowski's family. "Salt," he replied, and Moses O'Neil passed it promptly and changed the subject.

Chief Stinkowski called everyone he met *chief* as well, the way some folks use *mister* or *fella* or *boss* or *bud*. "Hey chief," he'd call out to Moses O'Neil and they'd up and leave Papa's office or the bar on Thomson Place. "Chief, what's the line?" he'd ask Derby Canurbi as soon as he'd finished making his morning calls. "Okay chief," he'd say to Murph Feldman when handed a note that he'd glance at quickly and then tuck into the pocket watch slit in his trousers. He never called a kid anything, though, no salutation, nothing; sometimes he didn't even acknowledge that you were there.

We were careful not to wriggle or speak to each other on the roof of the office as we imagined someone spotting us, then hearing Chief Stinkowski saying, "Get 'em," the prelude to a stampede out of the office that would end with him wringing our necks.

"So what's it worth to ya?" Moses O'Neil asked a guy wearing a gray fedora.

"You mean to move?" Gray Fedora inquired.

"Nah, to not have anyone know," Moses O'Neil said.

"Well, they're going to find out, sooner or later."

"Finding out sooner's not better," Moses O'Neil said in what could only be taken for a command.

"How much, chief?" Chief Stinkowski asked, rubbing his thumb and middle finger together rapidly in front of Gray Fedora's face.

"We delay the news, it's dough for them, big dough, they'll place bets all over," said Fourth Man to Gray Fedora.

"Big dough as to when, bigger dough as to where," Moses O'Neil added. "Some of that dough to youse guys, it's free, no one knows, just us, so whaddya say?"

"How much, chief?" asked Chief Stinkowski, who'd taken his wallet out the way a gunslinger withdraws his firearm from the holster at the card table, not so much to shoot it but to let the poor hombre know it's time to fold his cards and get outta town.

"We were thinking twenty grand, there are lots of mouths to feed," said Fourth Man.

"Ten," said Chief Stinkowski, who was already laying out the hundred-dollar bills one at a time in a neat pile on the desk where we'd usually place the Timmy Fund coins in the popcorn cups.

"Ten grand, it's nice, we have a deal," said Moses O'Neil, putting his arm around Fourth Man, which was his way of saying take it or leave it. "Not a word," he said as Fourth Man scooped up the money from the desk. "Nothing about when or where, got it?"

Gray Fedora and Fourth Man divided up the bills.

"If Zeidler finds out, my goose is cooked," Gray Fedora said to Fourth Man.

"The mayor'll never know," Fourth Man said, trying to reassure Gray Fedora.

"Dial this number as soon as you know when," Moses O'Neil said and called out a telephone number that Gray Fedora wrote down on one of the bills. Steven and I recognized the number as the phone at Papa's office.

"Back to Milwaukee, boys, it's been a pleasure doing business with ya," Moses O'Neil said, pushing them along, then took an extra-deep puff of his cigar, cocked his head straight up in the air, and exhaled a billow of smoke as thick as a cumulus cloud, which got sucked into the fan and blasted into our faces. How we didn't betray ourselves is something I've never figured out.

"Milwaukee's gain is Baltimore's loss," said Fourth Man, reflecting some confidence spawned by the acquisition of the bills.

"Milwaukee Braves sounds good," said Moses O'Neil, "'cause there wasn't no Injuns in Baltimore anyways."

Gray Fedora, Fourth Man, and Moses O'Neil started to laugh, but Chief Stinkowski didn't join in. As they moved out of the room, Moses O'Neil told Chief Stinkowski that he was going to call Derby Canurbi, *ASAP*, which neither of us understood, so we screwed up our lips and cheeks and silently repeated the word in the hope of grabbing a meaning.

We were still too scared to move or to talk. After a minute or so, Steven broke the ice, softly, conspiratorially, in case someone came back into the room, so they wouldn't hear us.

"Do you know what's happening?" he whispered.

"Is Moses O'Neil going to Milwaukee?"

"No, you dope, the Braves are, they're moving to Milwaukee, the team is going there. Didn't you hear that?"

"What do you mean?"

"What do I mean?" He sat up and crossed his arms like Chief Stinkowski, and in a great imitation that made me laugh, which would have given us away had someone been in the room, he said, "Braves, Milwaukee, move."

The concept of moving a sports team was something I wasn't familiar with. It didn't make any sense to me.

"You mean they'd play there, not here?"

Steven nodded.

"Why? Why would they move to Milwaukee?"

"Money," Steven said. "I guess they can make more money there."

Now, I must confess, this was something that also made no sense to me. It had simply never occurred to me that baseball was a business, like Noodge Mauer's parents' store or Sal the barber's place in the North End.

"The stands are mostly empty here so I guess the Braves think that there'll be lots more fans at the games in Milwaukee."

"Then why did they mention Baltimore?" I asked.

"Probably Mr. Perini could move the team to Baltimore if he wanted, as well as to Milwaukee, I guess."

"But they're going to Milwaukee, not Baltimore, and they're not staying here, right?"

"Right," he agreed.

"So Mr. Perini knows?" I asked.

"Obviously, dick-for-brains, it's his team, they can't go without his permission."

We were silent for a while.

"Then what about the dough, the ten grand? Did you see the stacks of bills? Holy cow. Ten thousand bucks. Jeez."

"Derby Canurbi's involved, you heard Moses O'Neil say he had to talk to Derby Canurbi."

"'ASAP,' he had to speak with him 'ASAP.' Do you know . . ." I started to ask, but Steven cut me off.

"I don't, really, don't know what it means, maybe it's some secret code that Moses O'Neil uses with the others," Steven ventured.

"We'll ask Dad, he'll know." Which was true, Dad had an answer for everything, he'd lay it out on paper or verbally, in terms we could understand, never chastising us for not knowing, praising us for asking for answers or guidance.

"So there's a bet going on," Steven concluded.

"A bet? What kind of a bet? What do you mean, 'bet'?"

"What do you mean, 'what do you mean, "bet"'? A bet. They're going to bet when the Braves will move and where they'll move to."

"You can bet on that? I thought you had to go to the track to bet," I said.

"You can bet on anything, it doesn't have to be horses or dogs. Don't you say 'wanna bet' to me all the time?"

"Yeah, but I just say that. I don't give you money."

"Well, betting for dough is what Derby Canurbi does, and Moses O'Neil is going to tell him that the Braves are moving out of Boston and that they're going to Milwaukee. Derby Canurbi will get on the phone and call guys and ask them if they want to bet on this, and that's what they do for a living."

It had never occurred to me. Really. I guess I'd never thought of Derby Canurbi as having a job. He just talked on the phone to lots of guys all over town about the horses and the dogs. A job I thought was something like what Papa had or what Dad did, adding up numbers on this really neat machine that made a lot of clanking noise on the kitchen table before it came to a rest and Dad would say, "Aha," which led him immediately to write a number down on a piece of paper, that he'd squeeze afterward into a ball and toss across the room into the wastepaper basket. He got upset when it didn't go in and would leave the room with all the balls of paper scattered on the floor, which would cause Mother to say to no one in particular, although it was loud enough to hear even if you were in the bathroom, "I SHOULD LEAVE THIS FOR THE MAID?"

"What does Moses O'Neil do?" I asked Steven. "Does Murph Feldman have a job? Does Chief Stinkowski work?"

Steven paused. "They're all in it together, I guess," is what he answered, and although it actually explained nothing and wasn't a direct response to my questions, it satisfied me somehow.

Steven had the ability to put things together, quickly, like an adult. He'd figured all this about the Braves' move, both of us having been presented with the same information, yet he was able to make something coherent out of disparate words, phrases, and body language, the way a sculptor crafts a block of clay into a recognizable object. What I took away was neither jealousy of my brother nor doubts about *my* ability to become an artisan. No. Taking pride in what he could do actually fueled my confidence that this was something that I'd be able to accomplish as well. Little did I realize how quickly this would all come about.

10.

He looked like Moses did, that's all, so don't never cross him

Derby Canurbi burst into Papa's office having taken a call from Chief Stinkowski and Moses O'Neil, who reported that they had confirmed the move, and that it was to Milwaukee, not to Baltimore.

"Solly, the Braves are moving, it's money in the bank!"

"Get on it now," Papa ordered, "news like this can't be suppressed, word's going to leak out."

Derby Canurbi raced for the phone and proceeded to give the dope to his best clients, none of whom seemed interested in the substance of the call, only in committing an amount and selecting a particular day.

Derby Canurbi was born Archangelo Canurbi, somewhere over there, and although he said he'd fought in the War, no one was quite sure which side he'd been on. His passport said he'd come to America in 1919 but his accent said more like 1949 and anyway, Murph Feldman got it for him, so all bets were off. His family called him Arky but he was Derby to his friends and enemies alike, and he hung out at the crack of dawn at Suffolk Downs. He'd take a little spiral notebook and record all sorts of stuff, what the horses were eating, what the grooms would say, how the track looked, anything to get an edge. It wasn't a good morning unless his pencil was worn down, and that's when he'd up and go to Wonderland, where they raced greyhounds, and repeat the routine, this time with the dogs. By noon, he was back in Papa's office, on the phone, writing down names and numbers, which he'd give to Murph Feldman, who'd put some of this stuff into envelopes, which were placed in the safe until 3:00 p.m.

Arky had made his name by betting heavily on a horse named Hooch, an old-timer, way past his prime, who shouldn't have been able to go the distance, a full two miles, in a race on August 1, 1951, at Suffolk Downs. Early that morning, Arky got a message that Hooch had mounted a female named Sparky and it seemed to make him five years younger. He was a spunky colt again, and Arky put out the word on the phone back at Papa's office that Hooch was good enough to win the Kentucky Derby, that's how fast he was and wouldn't you know it, old Hooch won that afternoon and paid forty-eight to one, set a track record for Pete's sake, and Arky Canurbi became Derby Canurbi, the go-to guy of Boston racing.

Derby Canurbi had started out with horses and dogs at the Boston tracks and then gravitated to numbers, cards, and dice at bars and clubs throughout the city. He had a regular game at the bar across the channel on Thomson Place, where the guys would meet once a week to play craps and determine who'd get the plum jobs at city hall and at the police, fire, and sanitation departments. When the bigwigs played, so would Moses O'Neil, and if you got invited to that game, a guy would call you and say, "Holy Moses and the high rollers," and hang up. That's all he'd say and you felt like a made man so you'd show up in your Sunday finest with wads of cash.

"Gotta be worth a hunnert, easy, he-he," Derby Canurbi chortled when Murph Feldman walked in. "After our cut, you got a lot to give the mayor's grandson," he finished. "Where's he, anyway?"

"With some old ladies in Brookline today," Murph Feldman replied, looking at a piece of paper on the bulletin board.

"Too bad Honey Fitz ain't alive to see this," Derby Canurbi said.

"What do you mean by 'this'? The grandson and the election or *this*?" Murph Feldman said, laughing, as he rubbed his fingers against his thumb, the universal sign for money.

Steven and I'd met Honey Fitz's grandson for the first time earlier that summer. We'd been playing marines down in the showroom when Papa motioned to us from the top of the stairs to come on up. As we entered the office, Papa's pals were all there along with a younger guy with a lot of hair, neatly combed, and a big toothy smile; the pals were slapping his back while they pumped his hand. We lined up in the lee of Chief Stinkowski's bulk and prepared to shake the guy's hand.

"I bet it's John L. Sullivan," I said under my breath to Steven.

The visitor walked in front of me and asked, "Who've we got here?" extending his arm while making eye contact with Papa, as if he'd already figured out who we were.

"I'm Papa's grandson and I deliver envelopes on my bike, with my brother, here"—I nodded to Steven, who was standing next to me—"and we go all over the city and we get a quarter a day from Mr. Feldman, each!" I exclaimed and pointed to Murph Feldman, who winked at me.

"What's in those envelopes, son?" Honey Fitz's grandson inquired.

I kind of raised my shoulders up a couple of inches, turned my palms up, and had the look of a kid who'd been caught red-handed and couldn't think of anything, nothing, that he could say that wouldn't get him in more trouble.

I looked to Steven. He shrugged, too, stuck out his hand, and said to the visitor, "Nice to meet you, Mr. Sullivan," whereupon the pals burst into the kind of laughing that you see in the funnies or, better yet, at the movies on Saturday morning, when they used to show the Three Stooges making fun of the ritzy folks.

After the visitor left, Papa came over, put his arms around both Steven and me, and said, "*This* guy's grandpa was mayor, many years ago; he's a congressman and now he's running for the Senate."

Moses O'Neil announced, "Drinks on me!" and the crowd flew down the back steps in a commotion, out the loading dock, and to the pub across the channel on Thomson Place, where we weren't allowed in on account of our ages.

Moses O'Neil was a Jew the way Murph Feldman was an Irishman. He looked like a fire hydrant, all red with freckles and hair, short and squat, muscled with tattoos that twitched along his arms when he grabbed or lifted something. Even his fingers had muscles.

"Let me tell yas how he got his nickname, kiddos," Murph Feldman told us. "When he was at a bar, see, and someone looked at him kinda funny, he'd bust him up good, and then when the guy was on the ground, he'd hover over him and point at the guy, just the way Moses did, ya see the picture of Moses pointing to God, huh, and he'd get this Old Testament look, just pointin', and the guy on the ground would be scared to death. He looked like Moses did, that's all. So don't never cross him," Murph Feldman warned, and I made sure I never crossed in front of him and told Morone not to make the sign of the cross when Moses O'Neil was around.

The story was so great that Steven never contradicted Murph Feldman that the painting was of God pointing to Adam.

11.

It came out the same way The Guy on the Radio would've said it

We climbed down from the roof over the office and retrieved the popcorn cups with the Timmy Fund coins that we'd stashed out of sight. We took them into the office and put them on the desk and then wended our way home, had a quick dinner, and went to our room.

Sharing a room was never a hardship, notwithstanding its small size, which didn't concern us, in spite of it being stuffed to the gills with books, games, toys, sports equipment, stamp collections, comics, homework (in English, easy, in Hebrew, hard), and an RCA console radio that included a record player, which we called a Victrola back then, a brand name, referenced much like Kleenex, which I still search for when I buy tissues. We got it only because Papa took it as a trade-in for a TV, which was starting to replace the radio at the center of families' home entertainment activities. But for us, hooked on listening to voice and sound effects and imagining facial expressions, costumes, and sets for *The Lone Ranger*, *Bob and Ray* (whose thick New England accents made us feel right at home), and *The Green Hornet*, this magical box brought another world into our lives, so we treated it with reverence, not even allowing ourselves to put our junk on top of it, lest it scratch the highly-polished burl wood. After our homework was done, after we'd cleaned up the room and ourselves, after we'd fought our last toy soldier battle but before we got too tired, we'd slip under the covers, turn out the overhead bulb, and stare at the pulsating yellow light from the RCA radio as if the words we were hearing came from this jaundiced glow, a lipless, headless, eerie thing that captivated us as soon as we heard the sound of the kazoo, heralding the entrance of The Guy on the Radio. The rhythmic da *da* da da da, repeated over and over, would give way to him singing, "The *bear* missed the train, the *bear* missed the train, the *bear* missed the train, and now he's walking," which was his fractured version of "Bei Mir Bist Du Schön."

No one knew what he looked like; these were the days when anonymity was a prized possession that some famous people were able to retain without fear of it being stolen. "You're better off not knowing," was what Papa said, "just like it was good we weren't aware that the president had polio and couldn't walk." To Papa, Roosevelt was the president, no matter who occupied the Oval Office.

Yes, but Uncle Jake had polio, he couldn't walk either, and yet everyone knew all about that.

The Guy on the Radio captivated us by talking about how his old man lost his job during the Depression.

"He pretended to go to work every day but really made the rounds of the fire department, the post office, the police department, and the tavern, meeting other guys just like him wearing brown striped suits, yellow ties, wing-tip shoes, and fedoras, which didn't seem to sit on their heads at a rakish angle anymore. Every Friday, he'd open an envelope and pull out the cash that he'd give to Ma, cash that he'd squirreled away for a rainy day, cash that he knew would last only a few months, then what would he tell her, what could he say about the charade he'd been carrying on, but he couldn't think about that and besides, he was sure that he'd get a new job before the dough ran out. After a couple of months or so, after the novelty of his rounds wore off, after he had nothing new to say to the guys at the fire department, the post office, the police department, and the tavern, after he was scared he'd pop out of, say, the tavern and spot Ma at ten in the morning, after he felt it was too easy to feel sorry for himself, after the angle of the slide seemed to get steeper, after the descent got faster, after all the afters began to run together in a blur worse than any time that he'd tied one on at the tavern, well that's when he decided to take charge of the befores, and that's when he started on the road to recovery, the road that took him back to a job, back to an honest paycheck, and back to self-respect. He went back to his boss, the one who'd let him go because the old man's salary was greater than the premiums that his customers could pay, and told him he'd work for half pay and would make the collections himself, pay for his own gas, and there'd be no expense account. The boss listened, didn't interrupt, let the old man state his case. His unaccustomed silence seemed to deflate the old man, but when he was finished, the boss stood up and shook the old man's hand so hard you would've thought he was pumping the well dry on a Saturday night."

When I woke up, I wasn't sure if that'd been what I'd heard from The Guy on the Radio or if it'd been one of my dreams. Was it *his* story or mine? Or both? It sure was different from what I usually dreamed about, being the hero of the game, that kind of thing. The old man was The Guy on the Radio's father, so the fuzzy picture I'd formed based on the voice over the years morphed in my dream into someone with thinning gray hair who looked to me a lot like an older version of my vision of The Guy on the Radio. The funny thing was that I had a clear picture of the boss, yes indeed. He was tall and skinny, about Dad's age, a cigarette dangling from his lips, smoke pouring out of his nostrils, ash floating onto his clothes before he absentmindedly swiped it away in a dismissive motion as if to question how it got there in the first place.

It hit me. "Steven, wake up, wake up, we've got to go to the boss and tell him how he can keep the Braves in Boston, get up, get dressed, come on."

I shook the bunk beds for emphasis, which elicited a "Cut it out, will ya?" He leaned over the edge and his upside-down face said, "I don't know how to do that, and besides, Mr. Perini won't listen to us, we're just a couple of dopey kids."

"Not Mr. Perini, not that boss; Mr. Carlson."

"Mr. Carlson? The sportswriter for the *Herald Traveler*? The guy who sat in the box at the Braves game with Mr. Perini and Dr. Goodman? He's not the boss, knucklehead."

"I know, he's not the boss of the *Braves*, but he's the guy who can tell everyone in Boston that they can't let the Braves go. We've gotta tell him what's going on. We can't mope around like the old man feeling sorry for himself," I added, hoping that Steven would remember what I thought I'd heard on the radio during the night.

"What do we say, what do we tell him, stuff about Moses O'Neil and Chief Stinkowski meeting the guys from Milwaukee and giving them all that dough to find out where and when the Braves will move? Should we say anything about Derby Canurbi betting on this stuff, huh?"

I gave my brother a look that for the first time showed him that I wasn't a nitwit and that he couldn't automatically lord it over me willy-nilly. If nothing else, it made me feel good.

We were lucky that Murph Feldman's Tuesday list took us south. We biked down along the Fort Point Channel, making it to Herald Street in ten minutes, and tied BlueDog up to the bikes out front of the *Herald Traveler*.

"Follow me," I said and we went around the back of the building to the loading dock. There were lots of papers scattered around, the place was a mess, and trucks were pulling in to collect the afternoon edition to distribute throughout the city. There was a door that led to a small office where the kids would go in and collect the papers for their routes and get paid. I went up to a kid who'd just finished his route and said I'd give him fifty cents if I could borrow his shoulder bag. He whipped it off so fast I had to move my head out of the way or else I would've been clobbered. I borrowed his cap for another fifty cents and I promised to meet him the next day and give them both back. I put the cap on, the kind that you don't see anymore, it looks something like a beret and has a snap on the front that keeps the peak together with the top of the hat. Steven went up to another kid and did the same and within five minutes we looked like we belonged.

We asked the first guy we saw in the lobby where we could find Mr. Carlson, the sportswriter. "Fourth floor, kid." He pointed, and up the stairs we went. From the landing at the top, we could see dozens of desks, guys hunched over typewriters clanging loudly like Dad's adding machine, other guys on the phone, some wearing hats, others green see-through visors, and nearly all of them smoking. The noise lifted the clouds of smoke to all corners of the room.

"We're looking for Mr. Carlson," I said to a guy typing furiously, who cocked his head to the right while neither skipping a beat nor making eye contact with us. Down the corridor between rows of identical slate-gray desks we saw a nameplate tacked onto the bulletin board above a desk piled high with newspapers, slips of paper, ticket stubs, buttons, banners, and a typewriter that made so much noise you would've thought it was Rocky's coal truck bombing down the driveway, gears screeching to scare the bejesus out of us. It said "Arthur Carlson, Esquire."

"Mr. Carlson," I said and I guess because of my voice, he turned around, surprised to see a kid in the newsroom. A cigarette was cemented to his lower lip by saliva. The smoke ran straight up his nose and then out his mouth.

"Yeah, kid, off your route a bit, huh?" he said, stealing a glimpse at our caps and the paper bag. "What, whaddya want, kid, I'm busy, I'm on deadline," he said without looking at us. And with a flourish, he pulled the paper out of the typewriter, jammed in another, and kept on typing, kind of talking the story out, adding an "okay" and a "jeee-sus" and an "I'll fix that, yeah that's it," as the ash kept getting longer and longer.

"Mr. Carlson, we have to tell you something," Steven said. "Something important."

"Tell me, kid, tell me something important, something more important than the latest word on Sam Jethroe's eyes," he said, which was what everybody talked about at Braves Field on account of the fact that Sam wasn't hitting, or fielding well, just two years after he was the rookie of the year. "Come on, c'mon, c'mon, tell me something I don't know, tell me something that doesn't involve comparing Charlie Grimm to Tommy Holmes," he said, referring to the new versus the old manager of the Braves. "Tell me when Ted Williams comes back from Korea, he's killing the Sox by being over there and not here," he said, referring to the star Red Sox outfielder who'd volunteered to be a pilot in Korea instead of playing left field at Fenway Park. "I'm *list*-nin'," he practically sang, "I'm all *eeeears*," he continued, taking his hands off the typewriter and putting them up behind each ear, bending them forward, gazing in our direction, the way we'd move the rabbit ears on the TV in Papa's showroom toward BlueDog, which seemed to get rid of the snow. "Speak, speak, speak for chrissakes, speak already," he practically commanded, his voice rising to compete with the din.

"The Braves are moving to Milwaukee," I yelled out, and just like that, the room got quiet, the fingers stopped hitting keys, guys stopped speaking into the phones, all you could hear was the clackety-clack of an automated typewriter. "They're going to play next year in Milwaukee, they'll be the Milwaukee Braves and they're leaving Boston," I continued shouting, as if my screaming at the top of my lungs would be heard by Mr. Perini, who'd be shamed into reconsidering the move.

Mr. Carlson looked around the room at the other sportswriters, who were all staring at us. "What are you saying, kid, that you know something, that you know the Braves are moving, you know this, how do you know this, who are you, where'd you kids come from, the Braves are moving to Milwaukee, that's what you know, how'd you get here, how do you know this? Wait, I know you, I know you kids, I've seen you kids before, how do I know you, what's your name, is he your brother, sit down kid, here, sit, get another chair, sit down, right here, and tell me what you know and how you know it."

So Steven and I sat and told Mr. Arthur Carlson, sportswriter for the Boston *Herald Traveler*, and everyone else who'd gathered around, what we'd seen and heard from our position perched on the roof of Mr. Perini's office, all in great detail, except we didn't tell Mr. Carlson that we knew the names of two of the men in Mr. Perini's office. It came out of me as fast as the BBs from the guns we'd secretly ordered using Morone's address, having saved up from the work we'd done for Murph Feldman. It came out the same way The Guy on the Radio would've said it, I know, because all the men had their eyes fixed on us and no one interrupted.

When I stopped, no one said anything.

Then Steven asked, "Who's Zeidler?"

"The mayor of Milwaukee," one of the newsmen responded in a tone that seemed to acknowledge we might not be a couple of morons making stuff up.

"Where's Smitty? Smitty here? Anyone see Smitty?" Mr. Carlson asked no one in particular.

"Here, here I am, excuse me, I'm here, coming," said a voice that was making its way through the crowd. It was the photographer, the one who'd snapped the picture of me and Morone catching the ball together at Braves Field, the same guy we'd seen later at Mr. Perini's office and again when we tossed out first pitches at the park the day we met Timmy, which was how Mr. Carlson thought he knew us.

"Smitty, listen up, I want you to take these boys . . . what're your names?"

"Joel."

"Steven."

"Show them downstairs and take a few shots of them, you know, for posterity," he chuckled, referencing a word that was new to me. "Now, I've got work to do." He then swiveled his creaky old chair around and with a conductor's flourish, whipped the piece of paper from the typewriter with his left hand, balled it up, threw it in the wastepaper basket, and with his right hand jammed a new one into the machine, then started to type furiously.

We headed to the stairs with Smitty.

"Be here tomorrow at noon, fellas, you will, won't you, don't forget, noon, tomorrow. And hey, don't tell anyone, I mean no one, not your folks, other kids, no one, you hear, not one living soul about the Braves moving, about your being here in the newsroom, nothing, you got that? Traps shut."

As we traipsed behind Smitty, we were arrested by Mr. Carlson's booming voice before we got to the staircase. "Hey, Joel, Steven." We turned around with the fear that grips kids when an adult raises his voice and a punishment is in the offing for an unknown offense.

He took a huge drag from his cigarette, exhaled a puff that nearly obscured our view of him, and bellowed, "You did good, kids, real good," and I'm pretty sure I perceived a wink through the dissipating white cloud. I floated down the stairs.

Steven said, "Look, if we could keep quiet about the envelopes that we delivered and never trying to find the owners of BlueDog, then we could keep this under our hoods, too."

When we got home no one was there. We played a few games and then fell asleep. We woke up with Mother, Dad, and Papa in our room. I don't know if they stood there while we slept, waiting for us to get up, or if they rustled a little bit to get us up.

"Uncle Jake's back in the hospital," Dad announced. "He's had a setback."

He'd been out for a month or so, and while he wasn't playful anymore, Auntie Rose would still drive around back to where the garages were, take the wheelchair out of the car, and push him to where Mother would be seated, knitting, while he went through his mail and we played ball.

"Dr. Richards says it's not too serious," Mother added, emphasizing the word *serious*, while Steven and I shot glances at each other because we'd fixated on the word *too*.

"When's he coming home?" I inquired hopefully.

"We'll know more tomorrow," Papa answered. "They're doing some tests."

"Dinner'll be ready in a half hour, boys, can you wait?" Mother asked rhetorically.

We asked lots of questions at dinner, beginning with what's the word *ASAP* mean, and quizzed them about Milwaukee, which Papa explained was in Wisconsin, where a lot of Germans lived who drank beer and ate fatty meats. "Not like the kind we get from Mr. Burgas, the kosher butcher," Mother added, then continued, "Whose Son Studied Hard And Became A Doctor," a thinly veiled exhortation that we took as an ace of spades pronouncement.

"Can we go visit Uncle Jake in the hospital?" Steven inquired.

"We'll see," Mother replied, which was her way of saying maybe, which really meant no.

June 17, 1935
Dear Diary,

Today, my sister announced her engagement. He is smart, handsome and successful. An accountant. They are so much in love. He even kisses her in public. How modern. I am sorry that mama did not get a chance to meet him, she would have been proud. He is kind, even asking me both for my blessing and if a December wedding would be alright with me. I am always better by then.

My father says it is a good sign, a mitzvah, Jews can still celebrate despite what is going on over there. The yekkes like Uncle A never say Germany anymore. And they call the leader Horowitz. It doesn't make any sense but nothing seems to anymore so it's not worth asking, I won't get a straight answer anyway.

I made a friend at the circus. Ida. She is the other Jew. Her father was killed in the Great War. I had a dream in which my father married her mother. But not now, back then, just after mama died, so I could grow up with a YOUNGER sister. Ida and I eat lunch together, sitting on the benches of the Public Garden. Except when it rains or snows. Also, except when it's November. Then I eat alone with the animals. They are my friends, too. Sometimes I see Ida watching me as I speak with them. She smiles and waves. So does the ringmaster, I catch him staring at me. He is not Jewish, however. Someday, I will meet a Jewish man who will love me, the way my sister is loved. I know it. Ida says it will happen to her as well.

With hope,
Rose

12.

The bird princess of Africa

Other than the inscrutable references to *the troubles*, Steven and I didn't know why Auntie Rose would've turned out differently from Mother. Auntie Rose was the introvert whereas Mother was the one who strode confidently through life, managing her household and family with aplomb, her ace of spades pronouncements the outward manifestation of her ability to measure the pulse of life without instrumentation. Mother had set her sights on and married a most eligible bachelor; as far as we knew, Auntie Rose didn't have what Dad called 'gentleman callers', despite her good looks. Whereas Mother put up with BlueDog, Auntie Rose loved him, which really didn't surprise us as we'd seen her in the Fens with the ducks and geese. We saw this again when Old Uncle A came down from Palus Island. He took Steven, me, and Auntie Rose to the Franklin Park Zoo. We split up when we arrived. Steven and I went to the building that housed the monkeys and the apes, where we imitated them and they imitated us. It was extremely difficult for us not to feed them as they stretched their hands out in gimme, gimme, gimme form. The lions paced incessantly, so we did too, like Groucho Marx all bent over with our hands behind our backs. The giraffes and zebras had big smiles on their faces like they had fooled the lions, who were living right next door but had to have their meals served to them in bowls. We didn't care much for bugs, birds, and snakes, that's not why you go to a zoo, really.

We went looking for Auntie Rose and Old Uncle A. They were up against a fence in animated conversation. As we got close, the zookeeper looked at me and said, "I get a kick out of seeing your mother talking to the animals."

"My mother?" I questioned. "My mother hasn't been to the zoo since I can't remember."

"Isn't she your mother?" He pointed to her. "You look just like her."

"Oh, her," I said, catching his drift. "That's my aunt. Our aunt."

"Well, your aunt comes here to see the ostriches, mostly. Actually, the big one, the one who weighs over three hundred pounds, his name is Peek. Go on, go over there, you can pet him, he loves people and he's crazy about your aunt."

We approached Old Uncle A and Auntie Rose, who encouraged us to pat the ostrich, who accepted our entreaties without taking his eyes off of her.

When we visited Auntie Rose, she was always patting and brushing BlueDog, and more often than not we'd find him sitting perfectly straight with his eyes fixed on whatever she was preparing for dinner, a position he would've assumed only if he knew that she'd be slipping him things she previously would've scraped directly into the garbage can. Afterward, she'd curl up with BlueDog on the sofa, reading to him from books and regaling him with stories about the time she worked in the circus back in the thirties.

She told him, "Of all the animals, I preferred the baby elephant, who reminded me of Shirley Temple, as she wobbled around a lot, in a kind of dance, and trumpeted these childlike sounds. Shirley would nuzzle up against me when the vet was checking out her mother. Shirley was interested in the trinkets from my charm bracelet. The soft breath from her trunk tickled against my skin. Shirley used her trunk to wrap around my neck, a hug that I reciprocated.

"My job was to make the animals happy. Often, this meant distracting them when they were given medications or separated from their mothers. I also had to clean up after them, feed them, and make sure they were groomed. I could spend an hour brushing TR, an old dwarf bear who'd reconciled himself that the call of the wild was the squeal of delight when a kid at the Garden would pat him gingerly with one hand while being held tensely by his father's grip. I could even get the wallabies lined up to hop in a row, trailing after me, and I could play peekaboo with the ostriches. Pretty soon, word got around to the circus master that the animals' happiness could be attributed to me, even though I hadn't received any formal training."

Steven and I loved to eavesdrop nearby when Auntie Rose was telling these kinds of stories to BlueDog. Usually, we'd be on the other side of the room, seemingly reading the funnies, actually straining to hear every detail. In 1952, when Old Uncle A came down from Palus Island, we were in our own living room, early in the morning before anyone else was up, quietly listening to *him* tell *us* a story about Auntie Rose while *we* patted BlueDog.

He began innocently enough, his version of *once upon a time*: "Come closer, boys, it's time I told you a story, a true story that I can vouch for despite having not been a witness."

"How's that?" I asked.

"It's all firsthand, from Uncle Jake," he responded.

Steven's eyes locked on mine, and my slight head tilt back to him acknowledged that I, too, was thinking that we might now be getting the rest of the story that Uncle Jake had told us in the hospital when we visited him with Zippo.

"Fourteen years ago, your aunt took a trip, a trip that changed her life. It's time you knew about it."

What we didn't know was if this was authorized by Mother, Dad, Papa, or Auntie Rose or if Old Uncle A was exercising rights in loco parentis.

"You know that your aunt worked in the circus," he said, a kind of declarative statement that adults make that leaves enough room for a kid to acknowledge that he didn't know without feeling a sense of embarrassment. We nodded yes.

Satisfied, he started. "In early October of 1938, the circus master informed everyone that they'd been invited to tour in England. Your grandfather was alarmed. Rose had never been away from home and the British Union of Fascists was stirring up anti-Semitic ravings via marches, street brawls, and outdoor speeches. Your Papa sought medical advice from Dr. Richards, engaged in long conversations with Murph Feldman, added up the pros and cons in a ledger with his accountant son-in-law, then shared all of his findings with your mother and ultimately told your mother it was her decision to make. Your mother listened to blow-by-blow descriptions of her father's conversations, nodded up and down in agreement with some, expressed skepticism about others by moving her head slightly on the horizontal, but didn't utter a sound until her father had finished. She responded respectfully, 'What does *my sister* have to say?'

"Your aunt pleaded her case in a straightforward manner: she adored her time with the animals, they would need her comfort on the journey, it was only for a few weeks, it was England she would be going to, not Germany, Italy, or Spain, where the men in brown shirts were in charge, and she'd be with the other people from the circus. With inward trepidations but outward manifestations of enthusiasm, they relented and gave their blessings. They watched her go up the gangplank that her forebears had walked down in East Boston, holding her hat to her head and her lone valise in her hand.

"Rose anticipated dinners at the captain's table, clinking glasses, witty conversations with accomplished and well-heeled passengers, dalliances with handsome British mates, descending staircases opening onto vestibules that led one way to the bar, enlivened by sounds of a full orchestra, the other way to the after-dinner rooms, charged with the hubbub of middle-aged men smoking cigars and discussing business deals. Perhaps that's what your mother, dad, and grandfather thought, too, when they waved good-bye to her that October.

"She sent a wireless message that she was having a grand old time. She kept from them the description of her tiny cabin, more like a cell with a bare bulb for light and a toilet that didn't allow enough room for her whole body when she was bent over, expunging the latest meal that moved up and down her alimentary canal in rhythm with the waves. She never mentioned the chill at night, the inability to secure a chair on the overcrowded deck during the day, or the monotonous horizon. She refrained from telling them that she'd sneak down past steerage into the cargo hold to spend nights calming the ostriches and reassuring the dwarf bear TR and Shirley the baby elephant that the terrifying heeling motion and the incessant sounds of the waves crashing and the nauseating smell of the engine room would be over in a few days. She never mentioned her own anxieties about whether she'd made the right decision to go, inasmuch as she'd waved off her family's entreaties without really listening to their concerns.

"Eight days later, they landed in Liverpool. The circus master purchased additional animals whose harrowing and heartbreaking stories soon became evident to your aunt, like the chimp who hadn't seen his mother in more than two years and the cheetah whose legs had atrophied in the absence of being able to run.

"It was a small circus and she was surrounded by foreigners. There was a Canadian who looked like a Mountie with his jodhpurs and brass-buttoned shirt, a Cuban whose tongue was black from chewing tobacco leaves, a Hungarian who'd become apoplectic the moment someone mispronounced *Budapest* without the *esht* sound, a tinker from the west coast of Ireland who'd offer to trade you stuff that you would've sworn had once been yours, and a peg leg from the Faroe Islands who claimed he was descended from Leif Erikson. He insisted that he owned Greenland and had the deed to prove it.

"Within a week, your aunt felt secure and had pushed the memories of the boat trip into the bottom of the valise that contained her clothes and pictures of her family.

"They played the towns and small cities of the north, setting up each Tuesday and taking down each Sunday, Monday being the travel day. They moved in vans driven by the carnybarkers, the ones who'd honk their horns and yell out to the kids who'd always stop at the side of the road and wave.

"She named the ostriches Peek and Aboo, from the game she played with them in Boston. She took turns riding them, to the point where she could race with them and not fall off. The circus master asked her if she'd like to ride in front of the crowd. She practiced on Peek, the male, a three-hundred-pounder who needed to be mounted from a step stool onto a blanket saddle. She told Peek to take it easy; she knew he was capable of more than forty miles per hour. Peek proposed a deal: he'd ease up on the speed if she'd let him set the course. When the ringmaster made the announcement, 'Ladies and gentlemen and children of all ages, I bring to you Rose, the bird princess of Africa,' she extemporaneously stood up on Peek's back and told him to dig his two toes deep into the earth ring with each step so she'd have better balance. And then off they went, Peek moving his head like a turkey, in acknowledgment of the applause and the cheers, your Auntie Rose extending her arms outward, elbows bent, palms up."

"Like an Egyptian hieroglyphic," Steven interjected.

"Or the waiters at Mr. Lee's Chinese restaurant who bring the dim sum that they place on the lazy Susan in front of all of us when we have dinner on Sunday afternoons," I added.

"Yes, both, boys," Old Uncle A said with a warm smile, indicating no displeasure that we'd interrupted. "Now, back to the story. So Peek went round the circle slowly, Rose gaining her balance and confidence. He stepped up the pace and began a zigzag pattern that eventually took them into the aisles and up the rows where the children all reached out to touch the bird that didn't fly and the woman in flight on his back. Flashbulbs didn't disorient her and the picture of them the next morning in the *Liverpool Echo* showed your beautiful aunt wearing a crown and a cape with long ostrich feathers that resulted, the next night, in a sold-out house. The circus master told her the picture was reprinted in London, Glasgow, Dublin, Copenhagen, and Hamburg for sure, perhaps even in the States. Mother, Dad, and Papa saw it in the *Herald Traveler*, I saw it in the *Portland Press Herald*, and Jacob Goldblum, a veterinarian who lived in Hamburg, Germany, saw it in the *Hamburger Anzeiger*. Dr. Goldblum normally didn't have the time to read the newspaper, but now with the rules against Jews, he had little *but* time and read voraciously, remembering things he wouldn't have had the time to notice previously.

"Rose became the featured attraction. Children would bring their parents early and line up to pat the ostrich and to pose with the African bird princess. Young men followed her around the circus grounds, and old men tipped their caps and bowed. The Canadian Mountie proposed to her, the Cuban played his guitar for her, the Hungarian made goulash for her, the tinker presented her with a bracelet that she thought she lost on the boat, and the Faroe Islander offered her the queenship of Greenland. She declined the proposal, listened to the guitar around a campfire, ate seconds of the goulash, kept an eye on the bracelet, and rejected the queenship, explaining that she would have to relinquish her princess-ship of Africa, something that she was not prepared to do.

"The circus master came to see Auntie Rose on the last Sunday in October when they were breaking down the camp. He told her that the African bird princess and Peek had been invited to make a special appearance in a circus in Hamburg and that he had made an arrangement to let her go for the first ten days of November. While she was flattered and excited, she worried about what to tell your mother, father, and grandfather. She'd made a point of informing them she wouldn't be going to Germany, after all. In the end, the excitement was too much to pass up; this was the first time she'd ever been the center of attention. She was, after all, the African bird princess, not just Rose Mischal. And, too, it was Hamburg, close to Denmark, practically on the North Sea, not Berlin or Munich, and only for a few days. So she wrote several messages, dated a few days apart, and instructed the circus master to send a wireless back here on the dates indicated at the top of each page from whatever English town he was in on that day.

"Their first performance in Hamburg was sold out and the anticipation was so great that newspapers covered the story and sent photographers. One of the newsmen acted as her translator as they worked their way through the crowd of children clamoring to see her, to touch her, and to pat Peek.

"'The children want to know why you are not *schwarz* since you are an African.

"'They want to know why your nose is so long.

"'They are curious to find out if you love *der Führer*.

"'The photographer wants to know if the *Juden* in America will bring war to the *Vaterland*.'"

We knew all about the Führer and remembered when we were little that Uncle Jake would refer to us as *Juden Kinder*, but when he said it, it was as much a blessing, not a curse.

Old Uncle A went on, "Rose gave her most radiant smile and ignored the questions. When it was time to start the show, the lights went out, the tuba took up the oompah-pah sound, the glockenspiel signaled the parade of the animals, and the ringmaster came out with the first beat of the calliope. The crowd applauded enthusiastically. The clowns rushed the audience and threw buckets of paper at the folks in the front rows, sending up squeals of laughter. The lion tamer cracked his whip, the big cats snarled and lunged, the people oohed and aahed. The catch of the young girls by the muscular young men hanging by their knees from the high bars caused explosions of 'Bravo!' and standing ovations. When the crews cleaned up after the elephants, the clowns entertained, wearing animal headdresses. Each clown's exit was accompanied by a deep bow as the children made the relevant sounds in unison: *grrr* for the tiger, *neigh* for the horse, *hoooot* for the owl. As the last clown, disguised as a pig, was about to follow suit and bow, and as the children were on their feet cupping their hands around their mouths, waiting to make the *oink-oink* snort, a deep, full-throated voice rang through the tent from the crowd: '*Mischlinge!*' and the throng erupted in spasms of derisive laughter that billowed the canvas high above like a child's hand wave to a departing parent."

Neither my brother nor I had ever heard that word, but somehow, given that Old Uncle A's eyes were closed and he appeared to be in a trancelike state, we knew not to interrupt.

"After the intermission, Auntie Rose, the bird princess of Africa, came out with Peek, and the crowd became ecstatic. '*Prinzessin, Prinzessin, Prinzessin*,' they chanted. She stood tall on Peek; round and round the circle she went, gathering speed. The noise was deafening, the sea of faces was blurred, the air was electric. The wind picked up her cape and made her figure appear to float above the bird. Mothers held their hands clasped to their chests, fathers took off their hats in homage, the other members of the circus lined the ring, unable to take their eyes off this magical spectacle.

"With all the people in the audience watching, with all the circus members' eyes glued on her and Peek, with the newspapermen and photographers there, no one saw which one of the kinder it was who threw the marble that hit Peek in the head, dropping him instantly a few feet from the edge of the ring. His arrest was so sudden that Auntie Rose was thrown at close to forty miles an hour into a pole that supported the high-wire bars. A concessionaire standing outside the tent later told a newspaperman that he heard a giant sucking sound, like what happens when all the air is let out of a balloon or a tire. He thought that the tent was going to collapse. This was followed by shrieks and pandemonium.

"A group of clowns ran to where Auntie Rose was lying and lifted her up, running with her body across the open ring to the performers' exit where they loaded her onto a van. A group of animal trainers bolted to where Peek was lying, picked him up, and also deposited him in the van, which then sped out from the harbor around the ornate city hall to the hospital across from the museum. The clowns rushed Auntie Rose inside the hospital, screaming for a doctor, and saw two men huddled in a corner. The clowns breathlessly explained what had happened to the woman they were holding, leaving out no details, and motioned to the van where the ostrich was lying, unconscious. A tall blond doctor proceeded to give instructions immediately. The shorter, dark-haired man snatched a white coat from a rack, informed the animal trainers that he was a veterinarian, and ran to the van, then drove the dying ostrich and the clowns a couple of miles; whereupon the vet ran inside a house and came out with a bag of equipment.

"The vet worked furiously, giving instructions to the animal trainers, who complied with each command efficiently. After a few minutes, the vet looked up and said, 'He'll live,' whereupon the men lifted the vet onto their shoulders and threw him in the air gently three times. 'You are a savior,' one of the animal trainers said, and another made the sign of the cross by putting one arm at a ninety-degree angle to the other. They laughed heartily, patted the vet on the back, shook his hand incessantly. One of them actually bowed and kissed the back of his hand. The vet informed them how to care for the ostrich to make sure he would make a complete recovery. They drove him back to the hospital and then he watched them take Peek back to the circus.

"The vet was told that the woman was in surgery and would be out in about two hours. He went outside and sat on a bench. Several hours later, the tall blond doctor came out and sat next to the vet. He told the vet that the woman had broken ribs, a broken hand, a punctured lung, multiple bruises, a concussion, and this, he said, holding out his hand. His fist opened slowly and the vet saw a silver charm bracelet. 'Look closely,' the tall blond doctor said. The vet examined each charm, not knowing what they represented. As he moved the next-to-last charm, he saw the Star of David underneath and knew why the tall blond doctor had clenched the charm bracelet in his fist. 'She will be able to travel in about a week,' the tall blond doctor said.

"'I'll visit her in the morning,' the vet said, getting up to drive home.

"Auntie Rose woke up late the following day, not knowing then that she was in the hospital.

"'Do you remember anything?' the vet asked, sipping from a teacup.

"'Who are you?' she wanted to know.

"'Tell me what you remember,' he inquired again.

"'You speak English,' she said groggily.

"'About last night,' he persisted.

"'I was on his back,' she began, 'Peek's,' she continued, 'the ostrich,' she added. 'Peek,' she strained to yell, 'where is Peek?'

"He told her the ostrich was fine. 'Go on,' he implored gently.

"She stopped to gather her breath and her memory. 'There were clowns, in animal costumes: a tiger, a horse, and an owl. Oh, and a pig. When the last clown animal was about to bow, the one with the headdress of a pig, I heard this word shouted out and the audience roared.'

"'Word?' he asked. 'What word?'

"She moved a bit, grimaced and coughed up a drop of blood. She put her hand out towards him as if to say stop when he moved closer to her to inspect her mouth. 'Someone yelled, really screamed, and the audience cheered.'

"'What was it?' he asked. 'I'll translate.'

"'My pronunciation will not be good,' she said softly. 'It sounded like *mish*-something, *mish-ling*.'

"'*Mischlinge*?' he asked, incredulously.

"'Yes, that's it, that's what was yelled out. What does it mean?' she inquired. 'Why were they laughing, what was so funny?'

"The vet looked down at her and was glad her eyes were closed. For a minute he thought she was sleeping.

"'Tell me,' she implored, 'what does it mean?'

"Cautiously, he told her about the Nuremberg Race Laws of 1935, briefly explaining the Law for the Protection of German Blood and German Honor, the Reich Citizenship Law, and the Law for the Protection of the Genetic Health of the German People."

We hadn't heard of these laws but we knew what the Germans did to the Jews so we absorbed this in context without asking any questions.

"The vet startled himself with his intimate knowledge and the rational demeanor with which he explained absurd regulations designed to reduce Jews to become less than citizens, less than normal, less than *human* to the Aryan populace.

"He told Rose, 'There is a word, *mischlinge*, that can mean cross-breed or half-caste and is customarily used in describing animals derived from different stocks, like the results of breeding a Boxer with a Rottweiler.' He felt embarrassed but continued, 'The word has a new meaning in the common vernacular—it is now being applied to the children of mixed marriages, where one parent is a Jew and the other a gentile.'"

I thought about a kid in my class whose father was Jewish. The Catholic kids referred to him derisively as HB, a nickname that meant nothing to me at the time until I heard someone call him out as half-breed when I was older.

Old Uncle A's eyes were now open, and he stared at us as if to command us to listen intently; what he was about to tell us was going to be more important than one of Mother's ace of spades comments.

"Jacob Goldblum thought about the likely meaning of the word used in the context of the pig's headdress, the idea that Jews were the offspring of the coupling of pigs with humans. Could it be, he asked himself, that there is such a law, that there is such a connotation for a word in German, in Germany of all places, in the twentieth century? 'Do you understand why it was yelled out when the *pig* was in the spotlight?' he asked Rose, hoping she would comprehend. She didn't answer; thinking she hadn't heard, he lowered his head to within a foot of hers and noticed her eyelids fluttering, straining to retain the tears that would eventually escape and expose her vulnerability.

"He gently pulled the bedsheet up to her neck. She seemed not to breathe. Without opening her eyes, she asked him in a barely audible voice what day it was. 'Thursday, November 3,' he replied. She imagined that she could retract her legs, shift over on her side, curl her arms to her collarbone, and remain motionless under the care of this stranger with the soothing voice for the rest of the month. He took the charm bracelet out of his pocket. 'Your doctor found this in your pocket,' he said. She opened her eyes, nodded acknowledgment of the charm, and watched him slip it back into his pocket. 'Your doctor wants you to get some rest, so I am leaving now.'

"'You are my doctor,' she informed him, and fell asleep. By Sunday, November 6, she was able to sit up and her pain was noticeably reduced. He told her the doctor thought she could get out of the hospital in a few days. 'But no going back to the circus,' he admonished.

"'You're so kind,' she said gently, then touched his hand and asked him again about Peek.

"'Peek is fine,' he said and kept his hand enmeshed with hers, watching her eyelids twitch, then rest. With all the tumult, the uncertainty, the inhumanity that he'd endured since 1933, this was the first time he'd allowed himself the luxury of investing something more than time with a woman. He let go of her hand when he sensed she was asleep and slumped in the straight-backed chair near the window. He debated whether his feelings were influenced by the fact that she was vulnerable and he was a physician. He had to make sure that his emotions were not unduly affected by her physical beauty, which still was apparent, despite her injuries.

"On Tuesday, November 8, it was all over the *Hamburger Anzeiger*. On November 7, a Jew, Herschel Grynszpan, had shot Ernst vom Rath, a German diplomat, in Paris."

How difficult it must've been for Old Uncle A to give us this dispassionate rendering of what he'd been told by Uncle Jake, since he himself was a yekke who'd lived in the City of Light when the bulbs dimmed during l'affaire Dreyfus.

"Calls for revenge flooded the radio waves across Germany. In coffee shops, on streetcars, at bus stops, there was talk of nothing else. Party newspapers with sixty-point headlines were eagerly snapped up. Meetings were called for; business was paralyzed. The performance of the circus was cancelled. The veterinarian made his way to the hospital to meet with the tall blond doctor. 'It is time,' he said.

"On Wednesday, November 9, violence erupted throughout the country. Egged on by the men in brown uniforms—tobacco shop owners, ticket collectors, waiters, bakers, clerks, foundry workers, office managers, deckhands, ordinary people—took to the streets, raced through town squares, marched through cities, looking for Jews and Jewish businesses. 'It will pass,' the Jews said to each other in their homes, which they did not leave that day. 'When the people come to their senses, they will be ashamed of themselves,' they added. Gasoline bombs exploded in stores where once gentile had worked for Jew. Synagogues were burned, men were rounded up and stabbed, women were spat upon and kicked, children were beaten with sticks and shoes. The sounds of bricks shattering the storefront windows rang out street by street, city by city, state by state, yet were heard only by the victims. Jacob Goldblum explained all this to Rose. She shuddered with each explosion of glass from brick or fire and with the cries of the wounded as the two of them peered out of her hospital room in Hamburg.

"Rose thought her shaking was worse than when she had gone out one cool fall night to drop snacks for the animals in the Fens dressed only in pajamas and had to be wrapped in a blanket and set down on top of the radiator when she returned home. The veterinarian thought her shaking was worse than when he had cut his first cadaver and pus from an infected wound had shot into his eye.

"'You remember the tall blond doctor,' he reminded her.

"'Yes, he has visited with me,' she said.

"'When you were brought to the hospital a week ago, I was in the corridor, speaking with him; he's a former colleague, a friend. I will tell you what we were discussing,' he whispered, closing the door. 'Listen to me carefully. This man has agreed to my plan, at great risk to himself and his family. From a fire or a traffic accident or a murder, there will be a body brought to the hospital without identification and my friend, God bless his soul, will issue a death certificate for Jacob Goldblum and explain to his colleagues that he hadn't known the man was a Jew or else he wouldn't have treated him and anyway, what will it matter, it is one less Jew to deal with. I am Jacob Goldblum,' he informed her. 'I will officially die tonight. Once the body of the dead person is here, my friend will remove several teeth, take off all of his clothes, make an incision somewhere and stitch it up, do you understand? Phony medical treatment. He will fill out a form that will say that he did all he could but that Jacob Goldblum is dead. In death, I will live. A boy I knew from the gymnasium, an Aryan boy who had married a Jew, is a customs official. I will drive to see him and will give him some cash. In return, he will give me an exit card so that I can get on a boat and leave Germany, perhaps as early as tomorrow. Do you understand?'

"He paused and then added, 'We will go together, the two of us,' a bold assertion that he hoped would be accepted.

"'Three,' she said, 'the three of us. We will get Peek.'

"And with that simple statement, instantaneously submitted, he had his first confirmation that Rose Mischal acknowledged that Jacob Goldblum was more than a doctor who'd assisted in her treatment.

"Shortly after dawn, the tall blond doctor informed the veterinarian that Jacob Goldblum had died early in the morning and he gave Rose instructions: 'Try not to bend over, walk slowly, hold on to rails when you use stairs, spend as much time as possible lying down, take your medications, carry nothing, rest is the best thing for you.'

"Jacob Goldblum and your Auntie Rose drove to the circus and found the animal trainers, who helped load the sedated ostrich onto the back seat and covered him with a blanket. After a half hour of careful driving, they approached the harbor and he pulled over at the side of the road. Sweat seeped from Jacob Goldblum's brow and under his arms. He suddenly had the urge to pee. He'd been contracting his pelvic muscle for a few seconds, then releasing it, for the entire trip in an attempt to avoid urinating in his pants. He was surprised, as he'd gone to the men's room just before leaving the hospital. He knew, of course, about dysautonomia but had never experienced his autonomic nervous system coming to the fore and taking over control of his body."

I sat transfixed, neither knowing the meaning of dysautonomia nor having the urge to ask Old Uncle A to explain it.

"Rose was asleep, so he recalled a soliloquy from a long-ago drama class to determine if his voice was affected and to his dismay, it was; a croak had lodged in his throat and saliva was filling his mouth. He opened the car door a speck and spit on the ground. Immediately, his mouth refilled. Gastric juices gurgled throughout his alimentary canal, so loud he was sure anyone else could hear. He looked in the rearview mirror to check his pupils. They were slightly constricted, he wasn't surprised, he was anxious and dehydrated, but to a third party, he presumed, it wouldn't be noticeable; nevertheless he put on his hat, brim down on his forehead, and made a mental note not to look anyone directly in the eye.

"Although his papers were phony they looked in order, certainly to a lowly customs official whom he'd known slightly years earlier and who had married a Jew, for heaven's sake, what was he worried about? And it was not a case where this was charity. 'See here,' he said to the face in the rearview mirror, 'he's getting 5,000 Reichsmarks, a not inconsiderable sum, enough perhaps to buy a small house. He might even be happy to see me, we never got into any scuffles, as kids often do, those many years ago, he's getting due consideration, and he's probably not a Nazi, he couldn't be, he married a Jew, at least I think she was Jewish, maybe only half but if it was her mother, she's a Jew; anyway, it's likely that he's just one of those who's going along, I'm sure of it. And to top it off, if I've misjudged the situation and he's an anti-Semite, well, he's probably thrilled that by my leaving the vaterland, it'll be purer than it is today with me in it. Yes, of course,' his breathing slowing to a rate above but near normal, his rational mind trying to regain dominion over his body. He exhaled slowly. 'All is well,' he told himself, 'calm down.'

"He lowered the driver's window to let the cool north wind skimming the Elbe refresh his face and lower his pulse. Within a minute he shivered, the self-induced heat having evaporated; he rubbed his sides by crossing his arms in front of him. 'Good,' he said aloud, 'it'll give me something to say to the customs official, the weather, today, here in Hamburg, and some chitchat about what it'll be like when we get out to the North Sea.' He practiced several lines of small talk, starting and stopping, attempting to be natural, trying to regain the normal timbre of his voice, much as a singer will do prior to a performance, walking up and down a musical scale, searching for the perfect tone.

"He checked on his passengers, still asleep. He started the car and slowly drove down to the entrance of the harbor. He came to a checkpoint. When a soldier asked what he was doing there, he confidently told him that he and his fiancée were visiting an old friend, a customs official. He cunningly gave him her passport first and was rewarded with the soldier's curiosity about the red American document that contained the picture of the beautiful passenger. The officer ducked his head and took in all of Rose Mischal, from long, slender legs up to thin waist, before settling on her perfect facial features, a frequent occurrence with which Jacob Goldblum would become familiar in the years ahead. The soldier winked and he smiled back, a silent, common unspoken exchange between men acknowledging primal feelings of lust and pride. The soldier barely looked at the forms for Dieter Harald Eberhart and waved him on with a hearty '*Auf Wiedersehen und viel Glück!*' Good-bye and good luck! 'Yes, *auf Wiedersehen und das Unglück*,' he said softly as he pulled away, which seemed to wake Rose, who asked what did he say and where were they? 'Past a checkpoint,' he noted. 'We're on the way to the customs official,' but ignored her first question, preferring to keep his wishing of bad luck to the soldier to himself.

"He was halfway home. The customs official exited the door of the small building when he saw the car approaching. 'It's all going well,' Jacob Goldblum quietly observed, recognizing both the punctuality and the visage of the person he remembered from the gymnasium. His heart rate was back to normal and he was not perspiring. 'We will be on the boat in a few minutes,' he said out loud excitedly, glimpsing the gangplank as well as the stevedores bustling to load last-minute cargo onto pallets secured to cranes that looked like giant versions of the Meccano construction kits he played with as a boy. And was that a smile he detected on the face of the customs official?

"'I was expecting you earlier, Jakob, or do I now have to call you Herr Doktor?'

"'Gunter, it's me, just Jakob, your friend Jakob from the *Wandervogel*, I'm the same me.'

"'*Ach*, but those days are over and friends we never were. Acquaintances, I knew your name, and it's just as good, as a Jew cannot be a friend of the volk.'

"'How can that be? I hear you are married to a Jew. Is she also not a friend?'

"'It's a lie, Herr Doktor, do not insult me by suggesting I've married a Jew; only a kike would make such a remark intended to slip underneath my skin, like an insidious virus that spreads the disease of the Jewish science.'

"'I assure you, Gunter . . .'

"'Do not be so familiar with me, Jakob the Jew. Herr Schuttmann, do you understand?'

"'Yes, Herr Schuttmann, everything, precisely.'

"'Show me your papers, Jakob the Jew.'

"'Dieter Harald Eberhart.'

"'Yes, yes, I see it here. Is this your pound of flesh? Stolen from an Aryan? A thief is what I have here, a fugitive, a murderer.'

"'I assure you, Herr Schuttmann, I am neither a murderer nor a thief . . .'

"'You have taken Herr Eberhart's name, this is a crime, I should report you.'

"'Reporting me will not benefit you.'

"'On the contrary, Jakob the Jew. I will get a commendation, my picture will be in the paper, I will be celebrated, you will see.'

"'Yes, I do see , and if that is satisfactory to you, you will indeed report me. But that will not put bread on your table, clothes on your back, or a roof over your head.'

"Ignoring him, the customs official barked into the car, 'Fräulein!' Startled, your Auntie Rose said nothing, while her passport was handed over. He peered at it and at the young woman again and again and seemed satisfied. At that point, Peek awoke from a medicated slumber, puffed up his throat, and made the sound that can be mistaken for a bow scraping over the deep E string of a bass.

"'*Was ist das*' the customs official exclaimed loudly, and Jacob Goldblum instantly began to experience the panic symptoms that had gripped him before he entered the port. Before he could say anything, Rose indignantly responded, 'It's Peek, my pet, he's not feeling well, we must get him on board to take him home.'

"The customs official looked down at his clipboard, scanned the page, switched to English, and said in a rather contemptuous manner, 'I have no forms for an animal, there is nothing here.' He pointed to his papers. 'So you cannot take him. Leave him here.'

"'I WILL DO NO SUCH THING!' she exclaimed defiantly, as if she were drawing from the well of her sister's aces of spades, and was about to continue when Jacob Goldblum cut her off, exited the car, and stood directly between the customs official and Rose.

"'He has to come with us,' Jacob Goldblum said, in a soft tone deliberately designed to lower the inflammation, having realized that she was not acculturated and that her American-style pushback would be met with increased resistance by a lowly government official. 'I am his doctor, he is under my care, he was injured seriously in a circus accident a few days ago, he is recovering, he needs my constant attention.' He was able to get this out without tripping on his words, simultaneously trying to figure out how he could convince Rose to come with him if Peek would not be allowed to go. He lightly touched the customs official's sleeve, felt the man flinch, and knew that his old connection was worthless and that the only reason the man had agreed to the transaction was that there was a bribe involved.

"'*Your* papers are in order,' the customs official said condescendingly, 'and so are the ones for the Jewess. But the dog stays here.'

"'It's not a dog,' came the voice from the car. 'It is an ostrich.'

"'Get it out of the car, whatever it is, it stays here,' the customs official barked and handed the clipboard to Jacob Goldblum, which included an envelope, the place for the money to be transferred.

"Jacob Goldblum was faced with a *Schicksalsfrage*: he could leave by himself, that much was established by the appearance of the envelope, or he could be defiant, make a stand based on principle, decide to remain with Rose and Peek. But he immediately discarded this alternative. A Jew could not stay in Germany, and he would not allow another Jew to remain. He was fifty meters from the boat, and once he was on board he was no longer in Germany, an outcome he could not afford to pass up. He was going and would forcibly drag Rose with him if need be. Yes, she would resent him and the spark that had ignited their relationship would be snuffed out. But it would be a mitzvah and the only offset would be the loss of the ostrich. So be it.

"Jacob Goldblum needed to defuse the situation, so he took out the 5,000 Reichsmarks and stuffed them into the envelope, offering the clipboard back to the customs official.

"'Give me your wallet, Shylock. Empty your pockets, drop your pants, take off your shoes, open your mouth—I will check for hidden valuables—and hand over the keys to your car.'

"'The deal was five thousand, we had an arrangement, only cash,' he pleaded, stung not so much by the heavy-handed attempt at a last-minute shakedown but rather by the realization that the egregiously uncivil orders that came from Herr Schuttmann now reflected the commonly accepted way. The customs official said nothing and tapped his pen against the clipboard. Jacob Goldblum understood that there was now a new arrangement, more money plus the car, which was supposed to have been picked up by the tall blond doctor; it was now added to the deal as well. He handed over his wallet, which contained all of his money, an additional 3,000 Reichsmarks, slipped the keys into the custom official's hands, opened the rear door and enticed Peek to emerge slowly, called softly to the young woman, who got out and walked with him and the ostrich to the gangplank. Neither one of them turned around, they did not exchange any more words or body language with the customs official, they held their heads high and disappeared into the boat.

"Once on board, your Auntie Rose hissed, 'It's inconceivable.' Then Jacob Goldblum vomited over the rail; the retching could be heard above the sounds of the cranes. The contractions came regularly, similar to what he'd witnessed when delivering babies, every few seconds, but here they were from deep within his stomach and beyond; it was as if his insides were commanding his bowels to exorcise their contents as well. Up, up it came, in swell after swell, in light browns and dark reds, in liquids and paste-like solids. He could sense the fumes of bile, a stench that conveyed echoes of his past—slights, harassments, exclusions, intimidations, curses, rejections, humiliations, sneers, and ignominious incidents too frequent to distinguish, they were all jumbled up in a cloud that he rained down onto the dock.

"'*Hineini*,' he shouted with satisfaction when the last of it was purged, recalling what Moses said in front of the burning bush, 'Here I am.' Then he rocked slowly forward and backward in the motion of his fathers and made eye contact with the customs official, who had witnessed this obscene Juden farewell to the vaterland."

Old Uncle A leaned back into the pillows on the sofa; his sly smile expressed satisfaction that he'd let us in on a family secret, a recognition that we'd reached the age that we could be trusted. With his eyes fluttering, he whispered that on his next trip, he'd tell us the second part of the story, how Uncle Jake and Auntie Rose came to America.

He fell silent and within a minute, it was apparent that he was asleep. We'd listened to him for an hour, his English near perfect, unaccented just like Uncle Jake's, a nineteenth-century immigrant recounting a tale of a twentieth-century refugee to a native-born kid who'd turn out to retire as a twenty-first-century raconteur.

"It wasn't in German," I whispered to my brother.

"What? What are you talking about?" he responded in kind.

"What he said, Uncle Jake, when he got on the boat. He didn't say 'Here I am' in German, he used Hebrew."

"So? We say *Shabbat shalom* on Friday nights at services and *kol tuv* all the time and *boker tov* in the morning, and that's Hebrew, too."

"Yeah, but don't you get it? *Have a good Sabbath* and *all good things* and *good morning* are when there are other Jews around. This was directed at the customs official and any other Germans within earshot; they couldn't know what Uncle Jake was saying."

"Okay, then that was the point, I guess," Steven said. "It allowed him to shout at the rooftops without anyone else knowing what he was saying. This was the first time in a long time that he could express his Jewishness in public, without fear of retribution. You know what that means, don't you?"

I did and I understood. I tried to imagine what it would've been like if I'd had to wear a yellow Star of David and couldn't ride my bike all over town and couldn't go to a Braves game or just horse around with my friends without fearing that goose-stepping men were everywhere, ready to beat me to a pulp.

"We're safe here," I said, in the way kids do, making a declarative statement that literally begs the other party to offer a confirmation.

"You mean right here, at home?" Steven asked.

"Not just our place, you know, Boston and the rest of it, the US, America."

"It's where everybody comes to feel safe. I mean the immigrants, this is the place they want to be. They keep coming, no one's going to stop them, and their kids are just as American as you and me."

"That's what Dad would call the bottom line," I concluded, my first double entendre.

Old Uncle A hadn't awakened during our talk. So I had the opportunity to take him in without him feeling self-conscious or me being intrusive. He was spindly yet with a paunch, made more noticeable by his goatee, which seemed to act as a semaphore, bringing it to everyone's attention, all the more obvious when he was in a sitting position. He kept his bearing, enhanced by his smoking jacket, the kind Basil Rathbone wore in those old movies when everyone dressed elegantly and said *rather* when they meant *somewhat*. He still had his hair and his wits, and while the former had thinned, the latter were as thick as they had been when Papa met him on Palus Island fifty years earlier.

We went back to our room.

We were about as prepared to receive all this new information about Uncle Jake and Auntie Rose as Timmy or Susie were primed to get polio. I'd waited so long for Uncle Jake to tell us how he came to America that when he told us the story that day in the hospital when Zippo was there, I felt a pang in my gut as I imagined this lonely man walking down the gangplank in East Boston scared and apprehensive. Now I'd found out that he'd made it up. Old Uncle A had told us a completely different set of events, and I was angry with Uncle Jake for deceiving us and for leaving out so much that we should've known. At that moment, I glossed over his tribulations and ignored his heartache at giving up his profession, being persecuted, leaving his family, and emigrating to a new country. My hurt feelings were what preoccupied me. I felt my pulse in my ears and instinctively put my fingers in them to smother the sounds of rage cascading against the drums, lest Steven hear them and chide me for my selfishness.

"I don't believe a thing about the ostrich," I said. "I mean, really."

Steven was also thinking about parts of the story Old Uncle A had told us.

"How come when we went to see Uncle Jake in the hospital, he said he met Auntie Rose when he got off the boat in Boston, when he really met her in Germany and they came here together?" he asked me.

I didn't have an answer. We were silent for a while.

I could see the wheels turning and Steven finally said, "Maybe because it was too painful for him to speak about what really happened, you know, Nazis, killing Jews in the streets, Mischlinge, and all those bad memories getting past the customs official."

Two things immediately came to mind that I didn't say out loud: that there are things we just can't talk about, like death, for instance—we know they're there but we can suppress them as if they're not; and, well, I was embarrassed that I'd resented the change from the Uncle Jake narrative just a couple of minutes earlier, and now felt shame for my egoism.

What I did manage to say was, "And by the way, in the hospital, did you see Uncle Jake's leg move?"

October 10, 1938
Dear Diary,

Yesterday, the Ringmaster told us that we were going to England. I've never been away from home and November is so close. Also, Ida will not be going. I am scared but do not want to let anyone know it. Ida says it will do me good and anyways, the animals need me.

Dad once took us to the dock where the ships come in to East Boston. We took a tour. It was like a floating hotel. All the mates in their uniforms with shiny brass buttons!

I know my sister doesn't want me to go. She pretends it is the distance but I know she is worried about next month. Dad asks what if I get sick. My brother-in-law takes notes from both of them and writes it all down neatly in two columns. He asked me if I declined, would I still have a job when they got back? I know what they're really thinking. Why is it that they don't come right out and say it?

Tonight, at dinner, my sister asked me what I wanted to do. I repeated what I'd heard from each of them. I told them I understood their concerns. I told them I loved them. I told them I was going. Don't they know what it's like to be me? After dinner, I threw up in the bathroom but ran the water so no one knew.

My sister gave me her favorite valise and showed me the pockets and the places within the pockets that I could use to hide valuables, like my passport and charm bracelet.

I may not be able to sleep tonight,
Rose

13.

What Do I Tell You A Thousand Times?

Mr. Carlson had asked us to come back the next day. When we got near the *Herald Traveler* building, there was a mob scene. Lots of photographers and guys with microphones were being told they couldn't get in and were clamoring for attention. We snuck under their elbows and made our way to the front, with a lot of the guys jabbing us and yelling at us to get out of the way, to go around back where the other paperboys were. Finally, Smitty saw us and opened the door, which had the effect of raising the level of commotion to a point where you would've thought the Braves had just won the pennant.

Mr. Carlson greeted us with a "Hiya, fellas," and handed each of us a piece of paper that he instructed us to put in our pockets and to read later. He asked Smitty what time it was and when told 11:59, he said to us, "Okay, kids, here's what's gonna happen. In a minute, Smitty here will start snapping pictures of us and the guys outside. There'll be a microphone on a podium and I'll go right to it and make a few remarks. Then, when I'm finished, I'll ask the boys in the crowd if they want to ask questions and there'll be a lot of jostling and lightbulbs flashing. So here's the deal. Remember yesterday, when I told you not to say anything to anybody? Remember?"

We nodded.

"Well it's the same today. Nothing. Don't say anything. Just stand behind me and say nothing. Got it?"

We nodded.

"Let's go, Smitty."

We went out the door. The noise was deafening; the guys with microphones and cameras were so close to me I grabbed Steven's arm. Mr. Carlson went to the podium and made a speech about the Braves moving to Milwaukee. The guys with pencils were writing furiously in notebooks with spirals at the top instead of on the side. We didn't say anything, of course, standing there frozen as if still on command from Mr. Carlson, but later, we melted at home, spilling our guts to our parents at the dinner table, despite Mr. Carlson's warning not to tell a soul, alternating with each other, filling in with actual details and embellishing others, making sure our claims weren't so outlandish as to render our story suspect.

To say that Mother and Dad were astounded would be an understatement. Mother was so nonplussed she couldn't come up with an ace of spades, which was a first. Dad commented that it was nice of Mr. Carlson to allow the two of us to be at the press conference but was concerned that the guys with the notebooks would start poking around at the *Herald Traveler* to find out who we were and why we were there. Steven said that they'd assume that we were just a couple of dopey newsboys and that he was sure that no one would recognize or remember us. And that's precisely what happened; or in this case, didn't. It's a pattern of behavior that I've seen repeated over and over again, where members of the herd take their cue from the leader, following one directed path, and are oblivious to the side trails that could ultimately steer them to a better destination.

A few minutes after the lights in our room were turned off, Dad came in quietly and told us not to mention anything to Papa or his pals about what we'd seen and heard. He assured us our secret was safe with him. As he took his leave and was closing the door, he bent his neck around and whispered, "It's all for the good, boys, trust me," and we did, expunging all negative thoughts about the bribery, shakedown, and gambling scheme we'd witnessed because of our father's reassurance.

We fell asleep exhausted from the excitement, only to awake the next morning to the look that meant we were in trouble.

Mother came into our room and asked loud enough to wake us, "WHAT DO I TELL YOU A THOUSAND TIMES?" There were probably a thousand things that she asked us to do or not to do a thousand times, so it was futile to try to respond; as Steven would remind me, we'd only end up admitting to something that she wasn't even thinking about, and boy, would we ever be in trouble then.

I tried to pretend I was still asleep.

She approached the bunk beds with two pairs of wet dungarees, dripping on the Braves rug, raining down on BlueDog, who was still curled up and ignoring her. I wondered why she hadn't taken them from the washbasin directly to the clothesline out back.

"What do we have here?" she asked, pulling out an ink-stained piece of paper first from one back pocket and then from another. I assumed it was my Scott stamp catalog but what was from Steven's pants?

"What if they were invitations to dinner from the queen of England? Wouldn't you have taken them out before you put your dungarees in the hamper?"

Steven jumped over BlueDog and grabbed one of the pieces of paper and furiously tried to read it.

As she left the room, we could hear her down the hall. "You were lucky your underpants didn't come out blue. Is that what you want, blue underpants, do you?"

"It's from Mr. Carlson," he said to me, "the pieces of paper he gave to us before he went outside in front of the cameras. I can't read it, it's all blurry, I can't make it out."

"They're probably identical so put them under the lamp, they'll dry out, then put them side by side and we'll be able to piece together enough from each one to make it out as a whole," I suggested.

We placed them under the lampshade printed with the names of all the cities in North Carolina, a souvenir that Papa had bought for us on a visit to the furniture factory outside of Warrenton, North Carolina, in March of 1945, our first trip outside of Boston. On the way back from North Carolina, we'd stopped in Washington, DC, and gone to a spring training game, which was where we'd picked up the Braves rug.

We held the pieces of paper up close to the light, so close we could start to smell the paper burning. We also blew on them and waved them in the air. In a few minutes, we could see some of the words, although most of them looked like the letters in the horror comic books, all elongated and with blurry edges.

"What's it say?"

Steven was looking from one to the other, filling in the missing or blurred letters as best he could.

"He wants, I think this is it, he wants us, both of us, to meet with him and all the other paperboys out back of the *Herald Traveler* at 3:00 p.m. today, if we want the Braves to stay in Boston. That's it. Here, read it yourself."

Sure enough, when we got to the back of the newspaper building, there must've been a hundred paperboys, but we found the kids who'd lent us the hats and bags and returned them. Mr. Carlson and Smitty, the photographer, came out the door and stood up on a pallet on the loading dock to speak to us. We got quiet.

"Boys," Mr. Carlson opened, sounding like the newsreels when President Roosevelt would speak with a cigarette holder in his mouth. "Boys, I want to thank you, the newsboys of the *Herald Traveler*, the boys who bring the world to thousands of people in Boston, thank you for coming here today so you can be a part of keeping the Braves in Boston. Do you want to keep the Braves in Boston?" he asked and received a thunderous chorus of yeahs and yeses and keep the Braves. "And you think it's a bad idea to have them play in Milwaukee?" he continued, getting back instant nos and lots of boos. "Will you help me? Will you help me keep the Braves in Boston? Do you want to make sure the Braves stay here for 1953 and forever?" We made more noise than before; even the kids who were Red Sox fans were jumping and yelling, so loud, in fact, that all the guys in the newsroom on the third floor and the sportswriters on the fourth floor were leaning out their windows, smiling at us, waving at us, pointing to us while speaking to their colleagues about us in that peculiar way that grown-ups do, as if kids can't see them or know what they're saying.

"Let's keep the Braves in Boston," he said, and as if on cue, the drivers of the news trucks came out of the loading dock, some of them carrying huge stacks of papers, bound up with twine, others with boxes that had tops so we couldn't see what was inside, and a third group with boxes that made the same kind of noise as BlueDog's collar, all clanking around.

Mr. Carlson kept on repeating: "Keep the Braves in Boston," until something clicked and we all started the chant: "Keep the Braves in Boston. Keep the Braves in Boston." The drivers who carried the stacks of papers cut the twine and held up the paper for all of us to see. "Keep the Braves in Boston. Keep the Braves in Boston," a hundred kids screamed out in unison, over and over again. The part of the paper the drivers held up for us to see was the front page, hot off the presses, and it had in the biggest letters I'd ever seen on a headline, "America: Land of the Free." Below it, in the middle, was a picture of Braves Field. At the bottom of the page, in letters as big as the headline, it said, "Boston: Home of the Braves." Kids were cheering, kids were screaming, some kids continued the chant, "Keep the Braves in Boston," some kids were making farting sounds by blowing into their armpits or into their hands between the thumb and index finger, other kids were whistling, putting their first and fourth fingers into their mouths, like Steven, but since when I did it I got spittle all over my shirt, I stuck to hollering and chanting and fake farting.

Mr. Carlson looked like a conductor with his hands open palms down, telling us to be quiet, he had more to tell us.

"Boys, I know how much you want to keep the Braves in Boston and now I'm going to give you the chance to do it. Yes, *you*." He pointed to a kid on his left, and as his arm made the arc of the sweep of the crowd, pointing out different kids, he kept saying "you" and "you" and "you." Each time he said it, we all hoped his eyes would make contact with us and his finger would point to us, the way they said Moses O'Neil's finger would point to a guy, except in that case you really didn't want to be pointed out. All the kids were shouting out me, me, me, pick me, I want the Braves to stay in Boston, me, me, me.

Steven and I were on the fringe of the crowd and when the finger came our way, he stopped, and a second finger, the middle finger, came out to form a V and one side of the V pointed directly to me and the other to Steven.

"Boys," he said, when we all calmed down, "boys, I want you to listen to me." He lowered his voice and instinctively we got quiet, we didn't want to miss a word. "Boys, there are thousands of people, tens of thousands of folks who want the Braves to stay in Boston. Now you know Mr. Perini, who owns the Braves, he wants to move them to Milwaukee." Boo Milwaukee. "My guess is that Mr. Perini doesn't know how much we, the people of Boston, want the Braves to stay here. So you've got to tell them. You and you and you and you and you," he said, sweeping his audience again. "And you know what? You have to tell other people, yes, other kids, but also their parents, that's right, their parents, you've got to tell their parents to shout, just like you've been doing, to shout from their rooftops, to yell so hard that Mr. Perini changes his mind and keeps the Braves in Boston. Kids, do you like to shout?" he asked with a huge smile that was met with an enormous roar that took about thirty seconds to die down, despite the maestro's attempts to bring down the level of noise in the pit.

"You do, you do like to shout. But your parents and other grown-ups, they shout in a different way. That's right. They shout by making their voices heard on paper, did you know that? It's true. Words can shout. Words can scream. Words can be louder than all the noise that you've made today. That's right."

Mr. Carlson turned to face the second set of drivers, the ones with the closed boxes. The drivers opened the boxes and held up what appeared to be postcards.

"Boys, the drivers are going to give each of you a box of postcards. Every box contains a hundred cards. If you want the Braves to stay in Boston, when you go to make your weekly collections, I want you to give a postcard to all the people and ask them to write down their names and addresses and phone numbers, even if it's a party line. Now you'll notice that there's no stamp on the postcard. That's right, no stamp.

Why should they have to pay two cents? No siree. After they fill in their names, addresses, and phone numbers, you take the card back from them, that's right, and bring all the cards back here. That's it. Here's what *we'll* do. We'll deliver them to Mr. Perini. Can you imagine the noise from all these postcards, all these good folks, these sports fans, Braves fans, people from every part of Boston, shouting to keep the Braves here? We'll take these postcards, there should be ten thousand of them, and dump them on Mr. Perini's desk, and Smitty here"—he pointed to the photographer—"Smitty will take a picture of these ten thousand cards and we'll put the picture on the cover of our paper and the noise will be so loud they'll hear us in Milwaukee!"

We all started cheering again.

"Boys, you'll be an important part of keeping the Braves in Boston, yes, that's for sure. And to let you know *how* important, how special you are, we're gonna give you something to be proud of, something to wear so that the people you don't collect from, the people who're not on your routes, those folks will know that you're part of the team that's going to keep the Braves in Boston."

At that moment, the last group of drivers stepped forward and opened their boxes and held up buttons for us to wear, buttons that said "I'm a Brave Bostonian," with a picture of an Indian in the background. We surged forward and it was a good thing that the drivers were up on the loading dock or else they might've been crushed.

Some of the kids put the buttons on their hats, some on their shirts, others on their collars. We stuck the pin through our belt loops. Some of the kids clamored for two.

After Steven put his pin on, he leaned to me and said, "We don't have a paper route. So what're we gonna do?"

"I didn't think of that."

The other kids were lining up for the postcards when Smitty came over to us. "Hey Joel, Steven, let me take a picture of you guys wearing your pins. Here, Joel, grab some of these postcards, and Steven, you take some of the papers and hold the front page up next to your face." He snapped a few more and said, "Go back up to the fourth floor to see Mr. Carlson when all the commotion dies down here at the loading dock."

We waited near Mr. Carlson's desk for a few minutes, leafing through the monthly pictures of the girls on the calendar that was tacked to the bulletin board on the wall at the side of his desk. I had never seen naked breasts before. When I saw Mr. Carlson coming, I pretended to be interested in the schedules of the Braves and Red Sox games, next to the calendar.

He greeted us with a warm, "Well boys, pretty exciting, don't you think?" He showed a wide grin, the kind that can't be suppressed, that makes people wonder if the person is demented or just can't contain himself, almost as if the person's got something to reveal and, if it's not done quickly, will erupt like a volcano. It turned out that Mr. Carlson simply had a surprise for us and wasn't very good at hiding it.

"Here, kids," he said, thrusting two identical eight-by-ten glossy photos into our hands. It was a picture of a postcard and an ice cream scoop, like the ones they had at Brigham's, superimposed on what looked like the front page of the *Herald Traveler*. I had no clue what would have made Mr. Carlson give this to us or why he was guffawing so awkwardly that it made me squirm.

Then Steven burst out with, "It's a double entendre!" and I noted that Mr. Carlson put two thumbs up to show all the other guys in the newsroom who'd gathered around us; they started to applaud.

"The big scoop," Steven said to me, "it's newspaper talk for the story, they got it before anyone else did, the story about the Braves leaving Boston."

Up until that very moment, I'd been a little intimidated by Mr. Carlson, not surprisingly, given our interactions in the last couple of days. But now, he sounded like new fathers do in the movies when they approach folks in the hospital and give them a cigar to celebrate the birth of a baby.

"Happy days, boys!" he said and clapped us on our backs, slightly nudging us toward a table that'd been set up off to the side with ice cream tubs, cups, and scoops, which we dug into as quickly as we scarfed down dinner when we wanted to go out back to play ball, prompting Mother to say, "WHAT? THE RUSSIANS JUST LANDED ON CAPE COD?"

Then Mr. Carlson directed us to some boxes of postcards on another table. "You can put a box on the basket of your bikes and hand out postcards to people you meet while you're wearing the buttons that say 'I'm a Brave Bostonian.'"

We were so excited we didn't know what to say. Really. All I could think of was something goofy, like, "Gee whiz, Mr. Carlson, that sounds swell." I was really excited, no doubt about it, but I kept thinking about the girls in the calendar the whole time I was there.

"Well boys, you can start tomorrow and all I can say now is that you've been for the Braves what Timmy is for polio." He pumped our hands, then gave us a pat on the back accompanied by an open arm sweeping motion in the direction of the door. Smitty walked us out and Steven shook his hand, telling him that he'd shaken the hand of the man who shook the hand of the man who shook the hand of John L. Sullivan.

We put the stacks of postcards in the baskets, rolled our right pant legs up, and rode out to Beacon Street, where we raced the trolley. We were home before we knew it, so we rode over to Noodge Mauer's, where he was having a catch out back of the store with Myandrew and Frankie. We filled them in on all the details, showed them the postcards, let them finger the buttons. They wanted to know if they could come with us on our routes to collect signatures on the postcards, though Myandrew said he'd become a Red Sox fan if the Braves left for Milwaukee, he liked their uniforms better anyway. Susie rapped on her window, wished us good luck, and hollered for me to come up before we left. Steven started to tease me, which made the heat rise despite the sun going down. We played for about fifteen minutes before I excused myself, pretending to need a drink of water, wanting to go see Susie before we had to go home for dinner.

That night, I reverently put the eight-by-ten glossy photo into my scrapbook; later that year, I added pages of the *Herald Traveler* that had pictures of me with Morone and me with Steven, the "I'm a Brave Bostonian" button, and things I couldn't have possibly envisioned at that time.

14.

Did ya know, Solly,
that they spend
more on tea
than a workin' man
spends on rent?

Papa settled Sylvia at the HIAS building and took the wagon directly to city hall. Up the imposing steps, Papa presented the card the mayor had given him on the street a few days before to a succession of guards, who examined it and passed him on to others, whose exterior expressions more resembled the warmth of the August day as he got closer to the mayor's office.

"Your Honor," Papa said when presented to the mayor, "I am the man you met in the street the other day; there was an accident, a young boy and an automobile, you gave me this card."

"And the boy?" the mayor asked. "He is well?"

"Yes, Mr. Mayor, he is here with me, outside, with the wagon."

"What do you do, Mr. . . ."

"Mischal, Solomon Mischal, Mr. Mayor, Your Honor. I'm a furniture man, sir, I greet the immigrants from the dock, I take their loads for free, then I sell them the stuff I haul from the curbs in front of the houses on Beacon Hill. Yes sir, I go all over town, in the North End to the Italians, in the south where I travel with an Irish Jew, to Dorchester and Roxbury where we Hebrews live freely, and all the way out to Malden, where the Polish settled."

Before he knew it, Papa was introduced to a Mr. Maguire, who spoke with such a brogue that Papa had trouble at first, learning later that it was a design, that Mr. Maguire used this technique to induce people to pay closer attention.

"Come back tomorra," he told Papa, and when he did, he started the ritual that would characterize Papa's life and the lives around him for so many years. Papa was given a list and envelopes, a list of names with amounts, amounts to be delivered and to be collected, on Tuesdays and Thursdays, throughout the city as he went on his way taking immigrants from the docks all over town and then selling furniture to them in the ensuing days.

Solomon Mischal and Sylvia Feiner were married later that year. Papa's furniture trade prospered and he bought a second, then a third wagon, hired men to help him, used Chief Stinkowski to deliver the envelopes and to collect from the customers. Within ten years, he had a small store, down by the docks, as well as two children, first Mother and then Auntie Rose. Each week, the men from the mayor's office, Mr. Maguire included, would come to the store, smoke cigars, drink whiskey in the back, open the envelopes, mark the books, put some of the cash in the safe, pocket the rest, play some pinochle, listen to Papa tell some stories, slap each other on the back, and leave for the bar across the channel on Thomson Place when Papa turned off the lights and locked the doors to go home to Sylvia and the two young girls.

The Great War brought few immigrants and many sacrifices as well as a new mayor, but the routine never stopped, even during the influenza pandemic. Most everybody they knew got sick and not a few died, frequently those in the crowded tenements. When Papa got sick, Chief Stinkowski, by then a strapping young man in his early twenties, took on the burden and Papa pulled through with little loss to the business. Sylvia went about as best she could, hacking cough, dry throat, light head, high temperature, tending to those at HIAS, making sure her children were safe and sound.

One day in the early fall of 1922, Mr. Maguire took Papa aside when no one else was in the back office.

"Let's go see a man about a horse," he whispered, in case anyone was snooping whom he couldn't see. Off in the far corner of the room, he leaned in. "Honey Fitz is gonna run for guvana," he said, his brogue as thick as ever. "So's I need a favor, I do. He wants to know if youse and the boys"—here he meant Chief Stinkowski, Moses O'Neil, and Murph Feldman—"would help him, ha ha, off the books, coola boola? He asked me special to ask ya, the mayor did, he sends his regards, personal."

Papa readily agreed; after all, wasn't it the mayor himself who'd helped Papa out when he was starting his furniture business? And this was something special inasmuch as Mr. Maguire mentioned the mayor by name.

"Ya see, Solly, the thing of it is, this conversation never took place, are ya with me, boy?"

Papa didn't have to respond; he'd been around this Boston politician long enough to know where the conversation was going and he well understood the process of getting votes.

"Well, we won't have to worry about us micks, don't ya know, we're as good as gold, darn near to a hunnert percent, I'll drink to that, my friend. And the dagos, especially in the North End, well, the mayor, he grew up there, practically a wop himself, if ya know what I mean. The Polacks, too, good Catholics, ya see where I'm headin' lad?"

Papa saw.

"Now the Yankees," Mr. Maguire started up again, "their investments buy a pol's pound of flesh, no offense, mind ya, and outside of town," by which he meant Boston, "they have the numbers, they do. Have ya ever seen a pope's man in Lexington? In Provincetown? In Amherst? Count 'em up, Solly, count 'em up on one hand, I tell ya. The numbers are against us and the cash is too, by jaykers. Ya can't fight 'em with the nickels the firemen and the transit workers give us, not with the real money the customers' men have and the dough they raise with the wives at tea. Did ya know, Solly, that they spend more on tea than a workin' man spends on rent? That's a fact for sure, so it is.

"They laugh at us, Solly, they think we're eejits, they roll *prátas* on our stoops at Christmas and throw lumps of coal at the kids on All Hallows' and don't be fooled, Solly, they wished ya'd never come here, would've sent the boats back lickety-split, one two three, be done with ya, kicked over the meltin' pot and spilled it into the harbor, they would. Then they'd send a bowsie Paul Revere all over the place, he'd ride through every town and village, 'The Yids are gone, the Yids are gone,' and all the folks would come out, clappin' and hollerin' and whoopin' it up, yes sir. Yahoo!" he sung, loudly, then quickly stifled it and put his arm around Papa.

"And now they're saying that ya're Bolsheviks, communists, and pretty soon ya gonna be blamed for the flu, and don't ya think they'll find another Leo Frank to hang, to *hang*, for chrissakes. Ya can't let them do this, Solly, will ya stand with the mayor, will ya stand for the workin' man, will ya stand for the immigrant, the sons of immigrants? Ya've got kids, Solly, think of them, think of the girls and stand with me, will ya do this?"

Papa stood up straight and nodded.

Mr. Maguire squeezed Papa's shoulder and drew a flask out of his pocket. "Let's drink a *sláinte* to better days, Solly." He took a swig, then recapped the bottle and had it back in his pocket before you could say *gee willikers*. And then he was gone.

Papa took the list of all the immigrants he'd sold furniture to and mapped where they lived.

"Get the locations of all the polling locations in and around Boston," he hollered to Murph Feldman. "Put pins on the map where the working families live and color the street where there's a polling station. Spin the wheel, Murph"—by that he meant get cash from the safe—"enough for five dollars for each name on the list."

"Fellas, that'll do the trick," Murph Feldman said. "It's a week's pay."

"Give some to the kids, too," Papa said.

"We're going shopping, Solly," Murph Feldman exclaimed, excited about the prospect of buying votes.

Moses O'Neil took out the Tuesday list that was from Mr. Maguire. These folks played the horses and the numbers. Then he opened the Thursday list. Included were the names of politicians, executives, city workers, lawyers, union chiefs, prosecutors, a deacon or two—a who's who of who was important in keeping the lights on in the city. The list had started out simply enough, back in 1911, when Mr. Maguire asked Moses O'Neil and Chief Stinkowski to keep an eye on a few cops and department heads whose loyalties were suspect. Moses O'Neil tracked them for days and found out about their girlfriends, their drunken brawling, their gambling, their taking money from defense lawyers, their passing it on to prosecutors and judges. He told Chief Stinkowski they'd hit a goldmine.

"We'll shake 'em down," he said, "and get cut in on the deal."

"Tell Mr. Maguire," Chief Stinkowski said, and of course they did, offering him a piece of the action, which he politely declined with a wave of the hand.

"That's ya business, boys, sure jeez," he said. "My business is keepin' the gurriers in line for Honey Fitz."

Over the years, the list grew to where it had close to five hundred names, some with lines drawn through them, taken off by the Great War, the influenza pandemic, old age, accidents, and the like, always supplemented with new names.

"They'll never learn, thanks be Jaysus," Mr. Maguire would say.

They used the list in the mayor's reelection campaign and in his successful election to the House in 1918, although the Congress threw him out the same year once the extent of the shenanigans became public. Through it all, Mr. Maguire was loyal to the mayor and was back again for the reprise, the run for governor in 1922.

Papa and Murph Feldman used the immigrant lists to go vote buying. They made the rounds all over the city and surrounding towns, regaling listeners with old stories, inspecting the homes, meeting the relatives, taking down a name to see if there was a job with the city, occasionally even interesting some in buying new furniture, as Papa took old furniture in partial payment and resold it to newer immigrants or placed it in the HIAS tenement. He disbursed the five-dollar payments by folding up the bills in the palm of his right hand, pumping the hand of each person in the house who was twenty-one, telling them that they shouldn't turn their backs on a friend, that they were their friends, and that Honey Fitz was their friend, too. When they especially liked a family or found one in desperate straits, they gave the kids five bucks too, Papa making the money suddenly appear out of a kid's ear or pocket.

While Papa and Murph Feldman were buying votes for the mayor from immigrants, Moses O'Neil and Chief Stinkowski were stalking their compromised prey, waiting for them to come out of buildings after the workday was done or greeting them at night when they stumbled out of a bar or a flophouse where they'd taken a woman for an hour. Their proposition was always the same.

"We can be your best friends," Moses O'Neil would say, using his thumb and first two fingers to pull his empty pants pocket out, waiting to be stuffed with some dollars, "or your worst enemy," turning his cocked head to look at Chief Stinkowski. The transgressors always paid up the first time, many with good humor, especially if they were drunk, but few realized that this was an annuity they had signed up for, an insurance policy whose premium would be paid each month.

The money rolled in as Moses O'Neil and Chief Stinkowski upped the ante during the weeks leading up to the election, squeezing the marks, ignoring their squealing and begging, reminding them of the consequences to their families and to themselves if they didn't pay. The amounts they collected, minus their cut and minus the hundreds of five-dollar payouts that Papa and Murph Feldman were doling out, amounted to tens of thousands, a tribute to the efficiency of the collection mechanism and a testament to the vastness of the extracurricular activities of the connected and powerful. The higher the connection, the closer to the sources of power, the greater the willingness of the shamed to pay.

For the most part, collections were easy. Occasionally, Chief Stinkowski would make a menacing move, a gesture toward the victim that would usually elicit a grimace; then they'd watch the prey's hand slide down his pants. Ever wary of a gun or a knife, Moses O'Neil would take a piece from inside his jacket pocket, cock it, and aim, then out would come the wallet, which would be snatched by Chief Stinkowski, who'd pull out what he said was owed as well as a penalty, penance, he'd bark out, before slamming the wallet down on the ground and waiting for the dupe to pick it up. With the mark in this vulnerable position, Chief Stinkowski would look to Moses O'Neil for the sign whether to knee the guy in the abdomen or to pretend to do so, to come up short, which would usually have the same effect: the guy would gasp and fall over, clutching his stomach, which was still full of the wine and food he'd just imbibed with his girl at a posh restaurant downtown.

Right before the gubernatorial election in 1922, they went after a guy from the North End, Leo Tubbs, Tubby to his enemies, never to his friends, who was the assistant commissioner of permits—meaning you had to go through him to get something, whether it was permission to build, a license to serve liquor, the authority to haul garbage, the right to put up a sign. Tubby lived up to his name: he lived large in gait and appetite and he threw his weight around the local haunts so most folks just gave him wide passage. Tubby was on both the Tuesday list (he played the ponies and the numbers) and the Thursday list (by virtue of his job and the various compromising positions he'd found himself in over the years). He'd walk into a speakeasy with a top hat and cane, a cigarette holder in his mouth, and a babe on his arm, and it would be Mr. Tubbs this, Mr. Tubbs that, a far cry from when he'd taken the civil service exam twenty years before, one of the first kids from the North End to get an important job in city hall. Tubby and his entourage carried airs, you could say, airs that began to stifle other people in the room, people who were looking for the opportunity to take him down a notch, all in confidence, of course. Those people asked Mr. Maguire to handle it, which of course he did, and that set in motion a train of events that would culminate in a wreck that no one could have presumed.

Mr. Maguire went directly to Moses O'Neil at the bar across the channel on Thomson Place.

"It's a pure, simple proposition, yeah?" he said. "There's five Gs for ya to get that sleeveen Tubby back to his office, out of his haunts," and Moses O'Neil noted his understanding by reaching across the bar with an outstretched hand that soon found a grand placed into it. Moses O'Neil enlisted Chief Stinkowski to help and told Mr. Maguire that they'd contribute half of the fee, $2,500, plus half of anything they could get on their own out of Tubby to the mayor's reelection campaign.

They stalked Tubby for a few days and caught up with him in the bathroom of the Roxy on Tremont Street a little after midnight. Moses O'Neil walked in behind him and washed his hands, the signal for Chief Stinkowski to come out of a stall and lock the door.

Moses O'Neil gave Tubby a choice: "Listen up, fella, hand over ya wallet and leave nice and quiet out the door; or listen up, fella, hand over ya wallet and leave via the window where yas might not be discovered for a while and when ya is, well, ya might not be recognized."

Chief Stinkowski held Tubby's hands together behind his back using only his right fist. There was pushing against the door, guys raising their voices, hey open up, open the damn door, open this thing, we gotta pee. Chief Stinkowski opened the door an inch with his free hand and snarled, "Beat it," which had the effect of setting the guys at the door running for their lives.

"Back to yer desk, Tubby," Moses O'Neil threatened, "for six months, ya hear, or else next time there won't be a next time."

He emptied Tubby's wallet, removed his gold chain, stuck his hands down Tubby's pants and removed a silk bag with more cash in it, and then landed a roundhouse right into his gut, doubling him over, whereupon Chief Stinkowski released Tubby's hands and shoved him with his foot, sending him headfirst into a toilet. In all, they got about a grand from Tubby's wallet and the silk bag. Mr. Maguire gave them the four Gs they were owed upon completion of the job. They gave two and a half to Murph Feldman for the campaign as they'd agreed beforehand and split the remainder between them.

"Pretty good walkin'-around money for a night's work," Moses O'Neil said, salivating.

Tubby lay low, nursing both his wounds and his ego. He sat at his desk, stayed away from the clubs, and kept his ear to the ground, listening for clues as to who'd done this to him and on whose behalf.

Papa and the boys gathered at the Copley Plaza Hotel on election night, joined by Mr. Maguire at a table not far from the front, watching the guys on a makeshift stage chalk in the numbers as votes came in from the cities and towns all over the state. The mayor looked good early on in the evening, with the results from Boston and the surrounding areas. The immigrant districts voted nine to one for Honey Fitz for governor and the mood was festive, the champagne flowing, the crowd in a self-congratulatory mood, folks thinking about how they'd enjoy the spoils. Around ten o'clock, the lead lessened as towns down on the

Cape and up north near New Hampshire started to report. By eleven, with Springfield and the western areas in the Berkshires coming in, the race was neck and neck and the mood soured. Those in the know knew then that it was all over because even if Honey Fitz led by a little, the absentee votes would break overwhelmingly against them. By eleven thirty, it was all over. The mayor came out and made a speech in which he acknowledged his defeat, congratulated his opponent, and thanked those who'd worked so hard for him, pointing his finger at the faces in the crowd when he mentioned their names. Mr. Maguire took a lame, fast half bow and gestured to the boys at his table, a public recognition that made Papa feel a little better, but he went home feeling glum.

When they dropped him off in front of his place past midnight, he was hoping he'd find his Sylvia asleep, something she'd desperately needed but hadn't been able to get, inhibiting her recovery from the flu, which had kept her under the weather for over a year. He opened the door slowly and stepped gingerly, avoided turning on any lights, not wanting to make any disturbance that would wake the girls. With his first step, he stumbled and nearly fell over, righting himself against the wall in the entryway and managing to turn on the hall light. Sylvia was lying motionless within the folds of her nightgown and robe as if she'd nodded off in a soft, fluffy pile. Papa speculated that she must've been dizzy from the aftereffects of the flu, and the ambulance driver noted her bruised neck, which he thought was the result of her falling violently against the side of the marble table in the hall, then careening to the floor.

Near the end of his life when we were paying our respects at Sylvia's grave, Papa told us that he was in shock that night and couldn't remember either riding in the back of the ambulance or listening to the doctor who told him that Sylvia was dead. He said this as if he were transported back in time and that the ride to the hospital had taken place recently. To the outside world, he'd resumed what could be called a normal life, but we in the family knew he was never the same, despite his business successes and political intrigues.

Less than six months later, Tubby died. Seemed as if the beating from Moses O'Neil had caused internal bleeding that they'd thought they could control by removing his spleen but it never got better, one thing led to another, and he died after a related operation on his broken ribs. Moses O'Neil and Chief Stinkowski held their own private wake at the bar across the channel on Thomson Place while the funeral was going on, and it was that very night that Moses O'Neil got his nickname, as he threatened a guy who told him he wasn't tough enough to knock somebody off.

Mother was twelve, my age in 1952, and Auntie Rose was nine when Nana died that election night in November 1922. Papa told us that although Mother was beside herself with grief, she also sensed a responsibility to her father and sister and became immersed in the activities that she heretofore had taken for granted: she went to the market each day and prepared all of the meals for the family; she scrubbed the clothes in the washbasin, hung them out to dry on the lines out back, and ironed her father's shirts and trousers; she dusted the furniture, mopped the floors, and cleaned the silver; she took her younger sister in the summer on the trolley to Norumbega Park to visit with the animals and in the winter to skate on the Muddy River, which snaked through the Fens. Her hustling and bustling, her coming and going, her chores and obligations were a substitute for the traditional pursuits of an adolescent. Perhaps the challenges of playing the role of a sister-mother and a daughter-wife suffocated her instincts to be only a sister and a daughter. So while she rose to the occasion reprising Sylvia's role (receiving plaudits for her efforts), she also plunged into adulthood prematurely and never learned to cope with the ordinary burdens of the maturation process. Steven and I could, therefore, forgive Mother her peccadilloes—her ace of spades pronouncements, her overprotectiveness, and her penchant for avoiding thorny problems—as we could no more imagine how we would've turned out had we lost a parent.

We speculated, although we couldn't know for sure since Mother wouldn't engage us on this topic, that *the troubles* of Auntie Rose might've stemmed from her being brought up by her sister. She was, after all, just a little girl when her mother died. I was also aware that people reacted differently to the same kinds of problems. Susie, for one, accepted her fate when her parents told her it was part of God's plan; polio was something that happened to her and she'd make do. Uncle Jake, on the other hand, appeared to want to fade away.

15.

The kisses
were more akin to
a detonator rigged
to my childhood

Running up the back steps at Noodge Mauer's house two at a time to see Susie, I gave enough leeway to slip by the figurine hanging on the cross without disturbing him and knocked on Susie's door, a first for me. I told BlueDog he could come in but that Susie had polio so he couldn't jump on the bed, pull the covers off, eat crayons and tissues. In other words, "Be On Your Best Behavior," that's what Mother would have said. BlueDog jumped on the bed and began licking her face, stepping all over her body. She threw her arms around him and kissed him on the top of the head and the cheeks, rubbing his ears. He gave me that dog look that makes humans feel shame. She'd had her bed moved closer to the window so she had a clear vantage point to watch us play ball out back, which she did, even when her brother wasn't playing with us. She'd even seen Steven with Zippo intertwined on the other side of the garage.

She told me how she woke up one day and couldn't move her legs. She'd had them fall asleep before, usually one at a time, so she wasn't scared, but when she couldn't make the sensation go away by shaking a leg with her hands, she called out for her mother and father but they were downstairs in the store and couldn't hear her. She slipped out of bed, hands first, and crossed the room by dragging her body and then proceeded down the steps, feet first, she said, so if she lost her grip her head wouldn't be bashed in. When she got to the store on the ground level, her mother's first reaction was to yell at her, "You've made a filthy mess of your pajamas." "Don't come down here without your clothes on," her father added.

She spent a few days at the hospital, the same one that Timmy was at, the doctors telling her that she was one of the lucky ones, which she couldn't figure out because here she was with no use of her legs and why was she lucky now that she couldn't go to school, dance, play field hockey, or ride her bike?

I never checked with Mother about whether I could be near her and was careful not to mention her name until the colder weather arrived in the fall, which was the time that Dr. Richards indicated was the end of the mosquito breeding season.

We got downstairs with me sitting on the step below her and her clinging to my back as we bumped one stair at a time.

"We must look like a centipede," I said.

"An accordion, especially with the noise of our rears hitting the steps," she noted and we both laughed at that, our voices sounding like we were gargling with each one-step thump.

I helped her into her wheelchair and pushed it out the back door. No one was playing ball there now. She directed me to a spot across the macadam near the garage. At the back, there was a huge old wooden rocking chair, more like a rocking sofa.

"Before we lived above the store, we had a house in Mattapan, and the rocking chair was on the front porch. I had trouble getting into it when I was little because I was afraid that when I put weight on the front it would tip over on me and I'd get hurt. Hey Joel, help me out of the wheelchair and onto the rocker, okay?"

There was room for three and I sat next to her. I pumped for both of us. BlueDog timed his jump perfectly with the rocking motion and sat on Susie's other side. He gave me the *I can do anything you can do* look and licked Susie's ear. The three of us rocked for a while, not saying much of anything. I thought BlueDog was asleep, but he spotted a cat walking by the front of the garage out of one droopy corner of his eye and flew out to chase it. His push off sent us rocking back hard, and Susie's head fell on my shoulder. She kept it there.

"I should get home for dinner," I said and pushed her back to the store.

"My folks are working, leave me in the wheelchair, my father'll carry me up later."

I turned to go and felt a tug at the back of my polo shirt.

"Come here," she said, "I have to tell you something." I turned around. "Closer," she said, "I have to whisper." I bent down to put the side of my head near her face and she kissed me, hard, on the cheek. I turned to face her, not knowing what to do or say. Then she kissed me on the lips. I stayed motionless until she pulled her head back. I felt the heat from my blush.

"Did you like that?" she asked.

I nodded, sounds not coming to my throat.

"Next time, we'll open our mouths, that's what your brother and Zippo do when they go on the other side of the garage."

Steven had told me how sweet Zippo's kisses were, but there was no flavor that I could now identify from Susie. In fact, taste wasn't one of the senses that'd been aroused. There was however a scent, a whiff of possibilities that no longer seemed as out of reach as the White Mountains of New Hampshire, which we had to squint to see when we were on top of the John Hancock Building. I sensed then that the kisses were more akin to a detonator rigged to my childhood, just like the plunger wired into the box with the fuse that the bigwigs pressed at city hall that blew up the docks in East Boston to make room for the airport. There was an explosion that reverberated throughout my body, and its repercussions had an impact on how I saw the world and how I thought that the world saw me.

Later, I'd find out that girls could generate this effect without kissing or even speaking. All that was necessary was a blink or a sway or a smile.

BlueDog and I made our way home.

The next Tuesday we had to deliver Murph Feldman's envelopes and get signatures on the postcards to bring back to the *Herald Traveler*.

Steven and I wore our "I'm a Brave Bostonian" buttons and headed down to Papa's store just before noon to get the list of names. We spent the day mostly in the North End, delivered all the envelopes, got more than a hundred signatures, many more than just the names on the list, as people recognized us from our picture in the newspaper. "Hey, you're the kids in the paper, 'Home of the Braves,' gimme a postcard, I'll sign it for ya, kid." We arranged it so we'd end up near Morone's house.

He was there and so was his uncle, Big Alfredo, who'd just gotten a letter that day from his son, Little Alfredo, stationed in Korea.

"Home before Christmas," Big Alfredo exclaimed enthusiastically, and Rocky and Morone clicked their beer bottles together. "Have a 'gansett," they piped up in unison.

"I'm set to ship out to Parris Island in a week," Morone said, and I imagined seeing him walk up the gangplank onto a huge battleship like the one they showed in the movies when the Japanese signed the treaty ending the War.

In his room, Morone had pictures of his cousin on the wall, a big one of him wearing the white hat and the blue uniform with red piping, staring directly into the camera. He was nineteen but he still didn't look like he had to shave.

Morone told us what Little Alfredo had mentioned to him about boot camp, which first sounded strange, a camp about boots.

He described what it would be like, getting up at dawn, taking an early morning run, having breakfast with the guys, marching, getting a gun, going to the rifle range, doing calisthenics, cleaning up the bunk, studying manuals, passing inspections, telling dirty jokes, reading magazines, smoking, dropping and giving them ten.

He instantly fell to the floor, hands on the carpet, back perfectly straight, toes ninety degrees to the floor, and started to do push-ups so fast you could hardly count to keep up. He finished in a flash. I was scared out of my mind that he'd tell me to do ten; I didn't think I could do one.

"Why do they call it *boot camp*?" I asked Steven, when we left.

"I dunno, maybe they'll boot you out if you screw up or get killed," he answered, and that made perfect sense to me.

Our last stop of the day was with Isaac Burgas, the kosher butcher in Kenmore Square. Mother told us he was an anomaly, a purveyor of meats who didn't eat them, a fact that accounted for the absence of girth, something you wouldn't have expected, just as you wouldn't have thought of our soldiers fighting in Korea as peacekeepers, another anomaly we brought up to Dad.

The butcher told us that the Tuesday envelopes contained money won or lost on the bets that the guys would make through Derby Canurbi back at Papa's office, bets on the numbers, on the horses—they were sometimes called ponies, which was another thing we couldn't figure out—and the dogs at the tracks north of the city, but we were never told about the Thursday envelopes.

"Com'ere, kids," Isaac Burgas said and motioned us toward the back of the counter. "See this calendar?" He pointed to a calendar on the wall that had a line drawn kitty-cornered from top left to bottom right on each Tuesday, and a handwritten number marked on each day in descending order.

"On Tuesdays I get an envelope from Murph Feldman. This envelope." He pointed to the one we'd given him. "When it's a good day, a day my numbers have come in or my ponies or dogs had a good day at the track, I get some dough from Murph Feldman. I place my bets here, on the phone, to Derby Canurbi. Every day. He calls me when he gets back from the track and I tell him to bet on a horse or a dog or I just play the numbers. Sometimes I win, sometimes I lose."

"What happens if you lose, I mean how do you pay Murph Feldman?" Steven asked.

"When you lose, they just take it out of what you bank with him, that's all," he said.

"Murph Feldman's a *banker*?" Steven asked incredulously.

"It's just an expression, boys. We all start by giving him some greenbacks that he keeps in the safe," Isaac Burgas said.

"What if you don't win?" Steven persisted.

"Well, if that happens a lot, you gotta make another deposit."

"Yeah, but what if you lose and the money runs out at the bank and you don't have anymore?"

"Well, that's when you get a visit from Moses O'Neil," Isaac Burgas said ominously, "so you make sure you keep some money all the time with Murph Feldman, 'cause you don't ever want to get a visit from Moses O'Neil," he warned. "And you don't ever want to get on a Thursday list," he whispered conspiratorially, then, sensing that he'd let the cat out of the bag, turned and looked again at the calendar.

"Why, what's special about the Thursday lists?"

He completely ignored Steven's question. "Now the handwritten numbers on the calendar, my young friends, are how I count the days until my son comes home; he's in Korea."

I had the image of a guy who looked like Morone only his uniform was a chicken-blood-stained apron.

"He's a doctor," Isaac Burgas said proudly. "He fixes up the boys who've been shot."

It was easier for us to handle the Thursday lists as opposed to the ones on Tuesdays because most of the time on Thursdays we were in the buildings around city hall. We'd knock on a door, a lady would let us in, and we'd tell her we needed to speak with Mr. So-and-So and that Mr. Feldman sent us. The women were nice to us, called us *honey* and *sweetie*, sometimes touching us on our cheeks or rubbing our heads as they passed by, usually offering to get us water or something to read. Most of the time, they were old, Mother's and Auntie Rose's age, but every once in a while there'd be a girl who didn't look much older than Zippo or Susie and we'd pay so much attention to her that someone else would almost always come by and say, "It isn't nice to stare." Actually, we thought the opposite was true, that they liked the attention, even from jerky kids like us.

The men always came out quickly, most pretending that this was a welcome affair, though their receptionists either couldn't have cared less or knew all along what was going on but still didn't care. They'd emerge from their offices with a nervous saunter and an exaggerated smile, many wearing their wide-lapelled, double-breasted, striped suits unbuttoned, their ties either tucked into their pants or fastened to their shirts with fancy pins, skating on wide, thick-soled wing-tip shoes that scraped with a grating sound, as opposed to the high-heeled snare-drum beats that we heard when the women got up to open the door or go to the ladies' room.

Steven put it all together going up in the elevator to make the first connection of the day. "These Thursday guys, they're not the ones who place bets with Derby Canurbi, that's not it. Mr. Burgas wouldn't talk about it, it's got to be something else. There has to be money in these envelopes they give us. My guess is that the dough's a payoff, you know, so that someone like Murph Feldman won't say anything about what they've done but it must've been pretty bad."

Up until that time, I'd simply pictured these guys outside of their offices as husbands, fathers, uncles, brothers, neighbors, and friends, but now I would see them as marks, plain and simple, guys ensnared by Murph Feldman, transgressor weasels whose squeals had been exchanged for cash, delivered most humiliatingly to a couple of young Jews. How'd they explain to wives or girlfriends the relentless drip, drip of cash going out the door? Had their trysts been worth this quid pro quo? What personal sacrifices were they bound to in the form of steadily more implausible excuses? These debts were never going to be repaid in full, and any thought that there'd come a time when they'd have a clean slate was as naïve as a belief in the war to end all wars.

When they handed us their envelopes, we invariably held them up to the light, something that annoyed these guys no end. Usually, the transaction took a few seconds and the guy disappeared, but every once in a while we had to engage the guy in some idiotic chatter, so we'd pretend to walk and talk like Jughead in the Archie comic books. The routine got these guys so flustered that they'd hightail it back to their offices while the ladies in the front of the office would laugh so hard their curls would come loose. The second time we'd come back to these places, the guys would just give us the envelopes and turn around without saying anything. Then we'd leave the office and, out in the hall, mock the way they walked, by sticking out our stomachs, angling our toes outward, hunching over, flailing our arms, and jumping from the ball of one foot to the other. We got all of the receptionists to sign the postcards even if they didn't know who the Braves were. We never asked the Thursday men to sign them.

16.

Can we count on you fellars?

We brought the postcards we'd collected from the folks we met all over town to the paperboy door at the back of the *Herald Traveler* building and dumped them in a canvas bag marked "Home of the Braves," then left for Papa's store. We gave the envelopes to Murph Feldman, who gave us our weekly pay and said, "Hey kiddos, would yas like to make five bucks each?" Well, would I like to eat ice cream every meal, play baseball every day, get to kiss a girl once a week? I thought. Our faces lit up like Roman candles. Murph Feldman didn't wait for an answer.

"Okay, here's what yas gonna do. Get out to the Badgers Club in Roxbury tonight, we're havin' a meetin' and we need yas kiddos to set up the tables and chairs, put on the tablecloths, empty the trash baskets when they fill up, show the guys where the restrooms are, and help clean up afterwards. Can yas do that?"

For five bucks each we can run around Kenmore Square naked, I was thinking.

"And yas gonna not bother anyone, ya got that?"

Got it, Mr. Feldman, 'cause we's not deaf and dumb, we didn't add.

We were told to get there at seven thirty, and we were there a few minutes early. The door was open. We parked our bikes and walked into a huge room with a giant banner that said "Help Stamp Out Polio!" with the word *Stamp* made out to look like the three-cent American doctors commemorative of 1947. Across the room there were hundreds of chairs stacked on top of each other, jammed against what looked like thirty or more tables. We spotted a man near the entrance to an office and called out to him, "Hey mister, should we start to set the tables up?" When he turned around, we saw that it was Sal the barber.

He had a diagram of the room and places marked out where each table should go. We set the tables up, put on the cloths, each one with a badger symbol embroidered on it. They looked like the lettering on the bedspreads that Mother made for us with our names on them. We placed ten chairs at each table and made countless trips to the pantry, where we got plates, knives, forks, glasses, napkins, salt and pepper shakers, and ashtrays for each table. Sal the barber set up a table exactly as he wanted it, and we'd constantly go back to it to make sure we got it right. It took about forty-five minutes, and just when we thought we were done, a guy walked in wearing what looked like a canoe hat with a ribbon trickling down at the end like a dangling rudder and said, "What about the coffee cups?"

Cups? Coffee Cups? We raced around like lunatics because Canoe-hatman said everyone would be there in fifteen minutes, which they were; they showed up like the incoming tide, a wave of mostly middle-aged and older men hitting the beaches at precisely eight thirty.

Steven and I stood in the back of the room and watched as the tide took a ninety-degree left turn as it entered the room, heading toward the bar set up along the whole wall underneath a sign that said "Cash—Tipping Appreciated." They looked like how Derby Canurbi told us they bet at the track, with guys pushing and jostling, waving bills, to get the attention of the three guys making drinks, calling out names of places, like Manhattan, and guys' names, like Tom Collins. Then I heard a guy yell out for a 'gansett; it was Sergeant Wilson from the marines. A few minutes later, Isaac Burgas, the kosher butcher, came in, talking with Mr. Lee, the owner of the Chinese restaurant. We also noticed The

Boxer, the guy with the brogue and the handshake, in front of Chief Stinkowski and Moses O'Neil. The bartender from the bar across the channel on Thomson Place was served without him having to ask for a drink. Papa and Murph Feldman walked into the room, and we heard a buzz, some applause, and a couple of whistles, and a part opened up all the way to the bar, where they were greeted with back slaps by the very guys who'd been ahead of them waiting to get their drinks and gotten pushed out of the way.

Derby Canurbi came in next, by himself, scratching down notes into his little spiral pad, not looking up while he was walking but not bumping into people either. We stood straight, like how Morone said marines stood tall and proud, and then guess what, Morone came in with his dad, Rocky, and his uncle, Big Alfredo. We scanned the crowd, and Steven pointed out more guys we'd met on Tuesdays and even some of the men from Thursdays, though we were reluctant to make eye contact with those guys in case they'd seen us make fun of them. The place was really starting to fill up and the smoke was thick, so we opened the windows wide and made a doorstop out of napkins to get a cross breeze going. While we were bending down to fix the door to stay open, we heard a familiar voice. It was Dad talking to Dr. Richards. They didn't notice us. We looked at each other the way Clem Kadiddlehopper would make an exaggerated glance on *The Red Skelton Show*. A couple of minutes later, Mr. Carlson and Smitty from the *Herald Traveler* came in and were greeted by practically all the folks in the room.

We heard the clinking of silver against glasses, which meant for everyone to quiet down. Papa was standing in front of the wall at a right angle to the bar, where they'd set up a small podium and a microphone. It squealed as Papa started to speak, and everyone laughed. Papa motioned to a man in the opposite far corner who fiddled with some knobs on the equipment. Papa thanked the Badgers for allowing them to have their meeting there and saluted in the direction of Canoehatman, who reciprocated.

"Thank you for coming tonight," he began. "I think it's fair to say I know each and every one of you, a few for forty or more years; others, it's been my pleasure to make your acquaintances since the War. On the subject of wars, let's raise our glasses and salute our boys in Korea." Applause, cheers, whistles, and hear, hear! He pointed his glass to Isaac Burgas and mentioned his son, the army doctor, and then to Big Alfredo, whose son would be home in time for Christmas. Big applause. He saved his last tribute for Morone, who stood ramrod straight as Papa saluted him; Morone saluted back, and the crowd turned to Morone with sustained applause. We got goose bumps.

I saw Smitty, the photographer from the paper, taking pictures all over the place. He'd position himself in a certain way, raise the camera, more often than not decide against taking the shot, move to another location, set up again, and then presto, the flash would erupt and the plumes would mix with the cigar and cigarette smoke. Once, he must've taken a shot of Steven and me because suddenly I saw blue spots and breathed in the electric smell.

"Friends," Papa continued, "I will stand here tonight and speak to you from my heart." The room fell silent. "Thirty years ago, we had a chance to change the world. Thirty years ago, the man whom we think of today when we say the word *mayor*, thirty years ago, the man who might have been the first immigrant's son to be governor of Massachusetts, thirty years ago, John Francis Fitzgerald, Honey Fitz, lost the election for governor. When Honey Fitz lost, we all lost. Honey Fitz was the champion of the immigrants, whether they be Irish, Italian, Jew, Polish, Chinese. He stood up for people like us, he was one of us. Look around the room," he commanded them. "Look at your neighbors. Look at the person standing next to your neighbor. And the next. And the next. What do you see? Do you see all redheads? Do you see all Roman noses? Do you see all dark eyes and olive skins? No. That's not what you see. You see redhead next to raven head. You see crosses next to Stars of David. You hear Gaelic and Sicilian and Mandarin and Yiddish. You see freckles and blue eyes and pale white skin. You see straight black hair and slit eyes and yellow skin. You see brown men with flat noses and tightly curled hair. You see butcher and barber and furniture salesman and bartender. You see coal deliverer and hauler, you see newspaperman and photographer, you see doctor and accountant, you see men from every walk of life in city government, policemen and firemen and garbagemen, toll collectors, trolley trainmen, taxi drivers. You see insurance brokers and clerks of the court and contractors and men of the trades. Tonight we eat corned beef and cabbage, we drink grappa, we finish with rugelach for dessert. Tomorrow morning we'll have bagels with smoked fish and tomorrow night we will use chopsticks to eat strips of beef and noodles smothered with hot mustard sauce. Tonight, my friends, we come together as the sons and grandsons of the immigrants to honor the legacy of Honey Fitz. Is there a man in this room who does *not* want to honor this legacy?" Each person craned his neck, searching in vain. "Is there a man in this room who doesn't think it's time, time for one of us to represent us, time for one of us to show to all of them who denied us, who prevented us, who put stones in our paths, to heave those stones to the side of the road so that our descendants, our children and grandchildren, won't have those stones in their paths? Is there a man in this room who doesn't think it's time?" There was silence. "It's time, yes sir, it's time." And with that, The Boxer broke out in a rendition of "Sweet Adeline" and the whole crowd sang, just as they sang two years before, Papa told me later, at Honey Fitz's funeral.

As if on cue, a dozen or so young men entered the room, and I remembered the candidate from the day we went to Papa's office. He waved to the crowd as he plunged in; it was like seeing gravity at work, everybody was drawn into his sphere. They swarmed around him so it was hard for him to make progress, but his friends kept wedging him on. I noticed one guy who hung so closely it looked like he was draped on the candidate's back; he was whispering, constantly, into the candidate's ear with each new person who came up to shake his hand or to pat him on the back. Two other guys from the candidate's entourage worked their ways to opposite ends of the hall, one to Murph Feldman and the other to where The Boxer was still singing "Sweet Adeline." Murph Feldman handed a series of envelopes to the guy who must've been the brother of the candidate; he looked as much like the candidate as I looked like Steven. The Boxer stopped singing, but the level of commotion in the room hardly died down as people took up with rhythmic clapping, chanting, and whooping it up. When I stood up on one of the extra chairs, it looked like a giant vacuum cleaner was sucking the guys into the candidate's space and blowing them out to the bar after their greeting. Chief Stinkowski and Moses O'Neil wended through the crowd, gently but firmly grabbing guys who were a little tipsy or rowdy, which had the effect of sobering them up right away. I saw Dad give some sheets of paper to Papa, and they both moved to where we were standing, scrutinizing the papers as they moved toward us.

"How many people you think are here, boys?" Dad asked, and when we said about 250, he said 314, or 316 counting the two of you, meaning us. "At ten bucks a pop, plus what the kids have collected, we've got, let's see, over $6,500, and that's not counting the bar, which I figure could be worth another $500 or so," Dad said to Papa.

"Is it all for Honey Fitz's grandson, the candidate?" Steven asked, and Papa nodded.

"It's for the election, the congressman doesn't get it for himself," Papa replied.

They stood near us not saying anything, watching what we watched for a couple of minutes. "I wanted you kids to see this tonight," Papa continued. "I wanted you to see what the money you collect is for. I wanted you to see what your Nana never got to see."

He moved to a position standing slightly in back of us, and we each felt a hand on a shoulder, first resting, then squeezing a bit.

"Your Nana never saw her daughters grow up and marry good men, she never had the chance to see what an immigrant's son and grandson could be, she never got to see what her legacy was, alav ha shalom."

"May she rest in peace," Steven and I reflexively added simultaneously.

We'd say this when Papa took us, with Mother, Dad, Uncle Jake, Auntie Rose, and Old Uncle A, to the cemetery in West Roxbury, to place a small rock on her gravestone, to say the Kaddish, which we learned by the time we were ten or so. I once asked Dad about these practices.

"Kaddish is a prayer we recite at a funeral, but it doesn't mention death," he said. "It's a praise to God, for life, it's meant for us, actually, the living. It's a way for us to deal with the death, together, to start the healing process."

I understood the words but not the meaning.

"And the stones?" I inquired.

"It's a sign to others that people have been there, mourners, that we haven't forgotten, that the person who died hasn't been out of our thoughts, our memory, hasn't been neglected." I nodded my head, taking this all in.

"It's a ritual," Dad explained. "It's what we do. It's part of why we're a people, why we're still here."

It was usually cold and rainy and we didn't talk much, all jammed together into our egg-shaped '48 Plymouth, Papa driving with his daughters in the front, Steven and me on the little jump seats, and Dad, Uncle Jake, and Old Uncle A on the back seat. At the cemetery, Papa and Old Uncle A would walk first, followed by his daughters, then the sons-in-law and grandsons she never knew. We would stand awkwardly for about five minutes, staring at the marker, with the picture in our heads of Nana as a young woman just before her wedding in the photo that Papa had in his wallet.

The picture had been taken by Old Uncle A, the oldest man we knew, whose white hair, pot belly, and hearty laugh would cause Noodge Mauer to remark that Santa came early to our house. We never told him that Santa didn't come to our house at all or to his either, for that matter. Old Uncle A wasn't sure of his exact age because he was born over there, but he would admit to eighty-four, which Papa said was about right, although how he came to this conclusion we never knew.

Old Uncle A always stored an envelope with some stamps in his breast pocket, and would give us one of the stamps each time he visited. He'd started a collection after he landed at East Boston, it was a way of perfecting his English and history too, he said. He'd show us a stamp and tell us a story about it, some of which was probably true, but since he always had an answer no matter the question, we weren't sure, so as we got older we'd ask more and more until we could figure out if it was a yarn or not.

The stories would start innocently enough, always with a stamp, like the story that the 1898 ten-cent stamp called "Hardships of Emigration" was Nana's idea. She wrote to her newly elected congressman, John

Francis Fitzgerald, in 1895, and Honey Fitz took up her suggestion, but by the time the Brahmins got done with it, it contained a picture of a Conestoga wagon and people from Scandinavia heading out west from Saint Louis. "Would it be so terrible if they showed a group of refugees coming down the gangplank at East Boston kissing the dock and leaving famine and pogroms behind?" queried Old Uncle A, who then made a sound that can't properly be written, it's not exactly *phooey* and it's not *yech* and it has a bit of extra saliva from the back of the throat in it so you know if you've heard it before and you know what it means even if it isn't in the dictionary and no one can spell it.

But the best story was the one he told us about how Papa got the family through the Depression in okay fashion: he never had to lay anyone off at the store and no one went hungry, thanks to the transaction that he entered into in 1932 to sell a set of the first stamps to be perforated, from 1857, all in mint condition. Papa said he'd acquired the stamps in 1904 from some rich guy he did a favor for after a car accident in which Chief Stinkowski, as a kid, may or may not have been hit. Murph Feldman found a buyer, a guy who owed Moses O'Neil a favor, and after all the cuts there was still plenty to ride out the brown storm of the thirties.

The ride back from the cemetery was always better than the ride out; we'd all talk a blue streak and then go have a middle-of-the-afternoon Sunday dinner at the Chinese restaurant, where seeing Mr. Lee cheered up Papa and getting all the food on a lazy Susan was a special treat for Steven and me. Nana never got to see this, but I told her about it at night after we went to bed; I gave her a pretty complete picture, all the details. I told Steven I'd do this, and while he thought it was idiotic, I kept it up, perhaps in the hope that one day someone would tell me all the important stuff that I'd been unlucky enough to miss.

"May she rest in peace," Dad repeated to no one in particular at the Badgers Club.

The guy who'd been standing behind the congressman came over to Papa and whispered in his ear. Papa headed for the microphone and got their attention with a single, "May I have your attention, please." A few guys who were a bit rowdy at the bar got a cuff on the head from Moses

O'Neil and Chief Stinkowski and turned around, belligerently, especially after their drinks went flying all over their clothes, but straightened out as soon as they realized who they were up against.

Papa said simply that he was proud to introduce our congressman, the grandson of Honey Fitz, a man who traced his ancestors to the potato fields of Ireland, the reason they were all there, the next senator from Massachusetts and, he hoped, the first Catholic who would get to be president of the United States. The crowd roared, Smitty's flashbulbs went off constantly, and the wedge cleared the way up to the podium for the young war hero, dressed in a crisply pressed suit, starched white shirt, and silk tie.

He smiled a huge grin, kept his head tilted down and his left hand in his jacket pocket, took the neck of the microphone with his right, and said, "Fellow Irishmen," an opening that got a big laugh from the crowd, which was at most one-quarter Irish. He thanked Papa, not just for the introduction and the event but for forty years of assistance to his grandfather. "May I have the wisdom of Solomon," he said, causing me to turn to Steven and proudly acknowledge that this was a double entendre, "and the luck of the Irish on November 4," which got another big laugh and applause. He didn't talk much about Korea but said we had to support the police action, which I didn't understand as the cops in Boston didn't have tanks and mortars, but he was the congressman so it had to be something that I just didn't know about. He hardly said anything at all about China except to say that President Truman didn't lose it. I wondered how anyone could think someone could lose a whole country, especially one the size of China. Perhaps Monaco, maybe, it was less than a square mile, although with their beautiful stamps it would've been hard to believe that even that place could be lost either. He mentioned the Russians and the bomb and things like they were stirring up trouble. He used the word *resolute* a lot. He said that price controls were a necessity but that they could probably be relieved shortly. This was one of the things I supposed I'd learn about when I was older, the way Dad said I didn't have to know anything about taxes yet.

Then the congressman paused. He pointed to a tall guy with hair thicker than his own, one of the men that'd entered with him, and said,

"You all know Tip." The guy named Tip twirled around and waved as the crowd applauded.

"I'm proud that Tip's going to take my place in Congress, and he'll find out something very important when he moves to Washington: that senators always get beaten up." They really gave a good laugh to that one. Steven mouthed "double entendre" to me, which I honestly didn't get when the congressman said it but figured out later, realizing he was also referring to the Washington Senators, who were as bad in the American League as the Braves were in the National.

"Tip says all politics is local," he continued, and the crowd murmured. Really. It was the first time I'd witnessed a murmur, a word I knew and could define without having heard one before. It sounded like those English movies about prime ministers when the guys in Parliament sitting on the benches make sounds that you can't actually translate as words.

"I'll continue to make speeches about price controls, China, Russia, Korea, and the like, but the only way I'll get a chance to act on any of my ideas is to get elected, and to get elected, I need your help. I need you to do whatever it takes, whatever effort is necessary, whatever you can do to get people to the polls to vote for me. Is someone sick? Get in your car, pick them up, and drive them to the polls. If someone owes you a few bucks, tell them to forget it if they vote for me. If someone isn't sure who they're going to vote for, let these guys know," he said pointing to Moses O'Neil and Chief Stinkowski, which caused howls of laughter. He continued, "Each of you should tell ten friends about our campaign and tell these ten to get ten of their own. We'll turn tens into hundreds and hundreds into thousands and thousands into ten thousands. If you live in an apartment, tell your upstairs and downstairs neighbors to vote. If you know someone is going to be away, go to the post office and get them an absentee ballot. When you write a letter, add a PS about our campaign. When you send a postcard, let the world know about us."

He finished by giving a thumbs-up to Tip, who responded in kind. The audience applauded, hooted, and whistled. The congressman jumped down from the podium and started to shake all the hands that were thrust out to him. Within a few minutes, he materialized in front of Papa, whispered into his ear, grabbed Dad's arm, and pirouetted around when someone called out his name. At that instant, Steven and I ducked under arms on either side of him and were just starting to straighten up when the room turned bright blue and I smelled the smoke right in front of me. In a second, when it cleared, I made a goofy face at Smitty, who promptly snapped another picture. The congressman put his hand out to shake Steven's and said, "Mr. Sullivan," which made Steven blush as he remembered this was what he'd said when we were first introduced to the congressman back at Papa's office. Moses O'Neil, Derby Canurbi, Murph Feldman, and Chief Stinkowski laughed uproariously. They'd rushed over to complete the circle around the candidate. Steven and I found ourselves in the middle with the conversation taking place at a higher altitude. The candidate's men and brothers joined the huddle. No one asked us to leave.

Whenever we'd play football, we'd give signals that a stranger couldn't follow. Down and out. Over the middle. Statue of Liberty. But all the guys on our side knew what they meant and we'd snap the ball, each person carrying out the plan, the intent being not to let the other side know what we were doing.

I heard the words they used above me when I was down in that huddle that night, lists and names, amounts and towns, cards and bags, papers and boys, got its and yes sirs and count on its and no problems, and then they broke the huddle and started to move to different parts of the field. The Boxer turned to Steven and me and said in his singsong brogue, "Can we count on you fellars?" I felt as if I were being tested on a subject after missing the homework assignment. I had no idea what the teacher was talking about. Papa winked at us.

"Honey Fitz would be proud," The Boxer said.

"So would Sylvia," Papa added.

We ate corned beef and cabbage, had our first taste of grappa that night, and jammed so much rugelach down our throats we might've been competing with the guy who wins the hot dog eating contest at Norumbega Park each July Fourth.

January 1, 1939
Dear Diary,

It is bitter cold. We were up half the night in front of the fire wrapped in layers of woolens with Uncle A and perhaps as many as two dozen others. There was no celebrating. A halfhearted raised glass of schnapps sometime near midnight. Acknowledgment came with slight nods. No one smiled. A few quiet sobs.

Everyone wanted to know about Kristallnacht, how we escaped, what is life like for Jews. I told them about the circus, but I couldn't recall the accident. I remember waking up in the hospital and seeing Jacob for the first time. I wasn't afraid since I had no memory. I was in intense pain. I still can't raise my arm above my shoulder and I get winded if I do too much walking. I kid him that even though I'm not an animal, Jacob takes care of me.

I cry a lot. For ima, for the Jews in Germany, for the Jews here on the island, everywhere. My stomach churns. It's hard for me to keep food down.

For the first month, I hardly got up. Jacob is my doctor, my nurse, my friend, my protector. I am in love with him. Hopelessly. He says he loves me. I miss my father, my sister, my brother-in-law, their baby Steven, my family. My ima.

I am the bird princess of Africa, I tell them. They smile, humor me, but do not believe the story of Peek. Moses O'Neil took him to Boston. He will take a Kodak and mail it to Uncle A. Then they will believe me.

Jacob tells them about leaving. There is not a sound in the room. When the fire snaps, they jump. It is as if they don't know how the story ends. He leaves out no detail. When he says, Hineini, they gasp. More than one then begin to cry. It makes me cry as well. I am still afraid.

They ask me about my mother. I tell them what little I remember. They tell me about her. What little they remember. They say I look like her. More than one has addressed me as Sylvia.

They speak to Jacob in many languages. He knows them all. They ask him about their aches and pains. He does the kind of doctoring he did in Germany when he wasn't allowed to practice medicine, only minister to the Jews. They love him.

My headache does not go away. I wonder if November will be year round.

In the spring, Jacob and I will go to Boston. I will know then if he really loves me.

With a heavy heart,
Rose

17.

Dad cooked
the books for Papa
and his pals

We woke up with stomachaches the next morning and stayed in our room until noon. We skipped lunch and went outside to play ball, remembering that Morone had said he'd come over to play with us. We had to be sharp because we wanted to impress him. We were still a bit tired so we hit fungoes to BlueDog, who'd return the ball with drool. We'd snatch it up with our gloved hand, flip it in the air, drop the glove, regrab the bat, and whack it as far as we could. After fifteen minutes or so, Steven knocked one so far it bounced from the garage roof to the third-floor fire escape on the building next door. So we retrieved an old disgusting ball that BlueDog chewed on and used that until we heard the sound of Morone's jalopy as it entered the driveway sputtering and emitting blue fumes. When I showed the ball to Morone, he made a face and said he wouldn't touch it, it would get cooties on his hands and then how could he run his comb through his hair?

"Hey, don't worry about the ball," he said, looking at Steven and me, "you guys got bigger things to worry about."

"Like what?" Steven asked.

"Like helping the man you call The Boxer steal the postcards, that's what," Morone answered. "You're supposed to meet him at the loading dock like he said at noon tomorrow. Got it?" He gave us a thumbs-up, got in his car, and drove off, burning rubber, trailing an acrid smell that was as foreign to us as the nauseous aftereffects of the flamethrowers were to the Korean villagers we'd see running away from their homes during the short newsreels that preceded the cartoons at the movies on Saturday mornings.

"What's he talking about?" I asked. "What does he mean, stealing postcards? And *who* said? What's going on?"

After dinner, Steven told Dad he needed to ask him a question. Shoot, Dad said. Steven told him about the conversation out back with Morone, the one that indicated we had bigger things to worry about, and repeated the bit about stealing the postcards.

"We don't understand what he meant. Why would we want to steal the postcards?"

"If we did," I interjected, "then Mr. Carlson wouldn't be able to take a picture of them being dumped onto Mr. Perini's desk and there'd be no chance for the Braves to stay in Boston."

Dad asked, "Do you remember when the congressman came over to speak with us at the Badgers Club?"

"Sure," we said in unison.

"Do you remember the circle of guys who hovered over you?"

"Sure," we said in unison.

"Do you remember the man you call The Boxer asking you if he could count on you?"

"Sure," we said in unison.

"Do you know what he was counting on you to do?" he asked.

"Do?" Steven asked. "What do you mean, do?"

"Were you boys listening?" Dad inquired.

Uh oh, I thought. The huddle. I'd heard some of the words but wasn't really paying attention. Steven had the same look.

"Look, boys, they decided they need the list of names of the folks who want the Braves to stay in Boston. It's a goldmine of information," Dad informed us. "They're going to visit the folks whose names are on the postcards and tell them about how the congressman is for the Braves staying. They'll do this a few days before the election. They're gonna say they're the congressman's right-hand man and they want them to know the congressman cares about what they care about, you know, all politics is local, you heard that, didn't you? Anyway, that's the deal. You want the congressman to win, don't you?"

"Sure," we said in unison.

"You want to be part of it, don't you?"

"Sure," we said in unison.

"Well then, the only way to get the postcards with the names on them is for you guys to steal them, so that's what Morone meant."

We were taking it all in when Dad stood up, tousled our heads, and said, "They'll be proud of you."

I had never felt happier than I did in that moment, even though Dad hadn't said who the *they* were; I just assumed it was Papa and his pals. To think that my grandfather would want my assistance, would need me to help him, would *rely* on me to do something important for him—well, that was better than the Braves winning the pennant, that was certain. I knew there was something else too: that by including us in the theft, in this critical part of the election plan, he was giving us a sign that we weren't just some kids anymore; we were special, like Papa's pals.

This was a key element of the initiation process into the adult world; if I did well, I'd earn their trust, and that was something that I was going to put in the bank and never withdraw. I knew that Dad would be proud of us as well. Without direct participation in the mischief of Papa's pals, in the absence of the kind of color that characterized Old Uncle A, too young to be the patriarch of the family, and often defined by his mien simply as an accountant, Dad was the kind of adult who'd often be overlooked, recognized for his sturdy hand only after an event, such as a funeral. But we knew when we were young not to misinterpret his quiet demeanor for passivity or timidity. Dad would assert his views conscientiously, quietly, and in a deductively logical manner, which made it hard to try to circumvent his decisions.

And then it hit me. Wham. Over the head. Uncle Jake was the vet at the track. He knew which horse was healthy, which one wasn't. Derby Canurbi took the action on the horses (as well as anything else that people wanted to gamble on) with customers throughout the Boston area. Moses O'Neil and Chief Stinkowski shook people down and made sure they paid up when they lost. Murph Feldman had us take envelopes with cash to guys all over town and bring others loaded with cash back to the office. And who had to know all about this? Who handled the books? Dad. He was Papa's accountant. Dad cooked the books for Papa and his pals. Phony invoices, faked book entries, jiggered bank account statements, false insurance claims, you name it, Dad took care of it. Five-dollar payments to voters? Disguised as day laborer fees to Italian immigrants to deliver furniture. Payments for Papa's pals? Contrived employment contracts. Gains from shakedowns? Rebates from suppliers. Track and gambling winnings? Interest income from pay-as-you-go sales. Campaign contributions? Donations to needy arrivals. Dad's fingerprints, figuratively and literally, were all over these transactions, and no one from the tax authorities would ever have questioned this upstanding CPA.

Dad was in on everything, you just wouldn't know it to look at him.

Listening to him filling us in on what we were supposed to do, we knew he was giving his stamp of approval to the scheme. I could see the liquid building in Dad's eyes, a prelude to a tear that he wouldn't show us, pretending to casually rub his eye and simultaneously give a fake yawn.

I went to bed feeling important.

The idea that I'd be involved in a scheme, a theft, didn't bother me. I wanted the Braves to stay in Boston. I wanted the congressman to win. I wanted Papa to be proud of me. My excitement level was so high I couldn't fall asleep right away. Long after midnight, I was still wide awake. At first, I thought I was anxious about getting caught during the robbery. But since I didn't know the details, I couldn't walk through the steps and see how it could all fall apart. And besides, with Papa's pals somehow involved, they'd be sure to think of everything. I knew, of course, that stealing was illegal, but I figured that the congressman was going to win anyway and really, how many votes do you think we could get for him by swiping some names and addresses? I ran through all the possible reasons for my pulse beating so rapidly. I pictured the congressman getting sworn in on a stack of Bibles with a guy from the FBI following my every move, waiting for me to crack, to spill the beans on the scam. I imagined Susie finding out that I was a criminal and telling her brother that she never wanted to see me again. I envisaged Rocky and Big Alfredo expressing shock that while Little Alfredo was fighting for truth, justice, and the American way in Korea, I was defrauding the very system that he was fighting to preserve.

My heart didn't stop pounding until I conjured up an image of Mr. Carlson as seen through Smitty's lens. He was at his desk but his hands weren't working his typewriter. There was no noise in the newsroom at all. Each person was doing his job, silently. Mr. Carlson was staring at the front page of a newspaper propped against his telephone. The headline was in fifty-six-point type: "Postcards Stolen!" Underneath was a shot of Mr. Perini's desk. There was nothing on it. How would the guy who wrote the column "Give It to You Straight!" explain what happened without making himself look to be the sap? The man who broke the news of the Braves' move, the sports figure whom everyone wanted at the big affairs, the fellow who commanded the respect of the ballplayers, the managers, the executives of the team, would be seen as the victim of a simple hoax. Worse yet, if it was ever revealed that he'd been duped at the time of his greatest triumph by a couple of kids pretending to be paperboys, the humiliation might be enough to make him a permanent fixture at the pub across the channel on Thomson Place.

I jerked my body up to a sitting position so quickly that it startled BlueDog. I realized that by filching the postcards I'd be helping the congressman and making my grandfather proud of me, but that simultaneously I'd be crushing Mr. Carlson's dream of being a key player in keeping the Braves in Boston and preventing him from getting a front-page story, usually out of reach for a sportswriter. I'd solved my racing-pulse puzzle but had done so at the expense of conflicting my conscience. After musing on this for a while, I opted for the theft and Papa's respect. I knew I'd made the right choice and that this was an adult choice as opposed to a kid's choice, which was usually limited to options such as determining whom to play with or which bike route to follow. But that didn't mean that I'd ever forget what my actions would portend for Mr. Carlson.

18.

I sure
could use some
dental floss and
some extra
bullets

The next morning, I heard soft rapping out front, which meant Auntie Rose was at the door. "He's gone," she said to me when I opened it to let her in.

I assumed she was referring to BlueDog. "No," I said authoritatively, "he's here, with us, back in the room, under the bed."

She walked past me, zombie-like, no peck on the cheek, as if I weren't there.

"He's gone," she repeated.

I burst out into tears, now realizing that she was referring to Uncle Jake. I suspected he must've succumbed to the effects of polio in the hospital. Waterworks. Sobbing uncontrollably, I ran back to the bedroom and woke Steven up. The two of us sat on the bottom bunk and cried hysterically. Through my tears, I mustered enough energy to rummage in drawers and closets and came up with things we'd collected on trips with Uncle Jake, like a postcard of the Old Man of the Mountain in New Hampshire, the insignia from Old Ironsides, a window sticker of the Bunker Hill Monument, and the paper coaster from when he allowed Steven and me to have a sip of beer for the first time, all bringing up wonderful memories that generated nervous laughter, seemingly pouring out of us in equal measure to our tears. Doing all of this, I remembered other things we did with Uncle Jake where there was nothing we saved, like once when he came with us trick-or-treating dressed up as Frankenstein's monster and really scared kids, not just because of the costume but also because of his limp, which got more pronounced as the night wore on, making him lurch from side to side. I also couldn't forget the time we got lost on the way back from a farm in Vermont where Uncle Jake had had to go to attend to some prized dairy cows, mysteriously ill. "There was something wrong with their teats," he said, which suddenly made the long car drive worthwhile.

Mother came in and asked what was wrong. I told her that Auntie Rose said Uncle Jake was gone.

"Auntie Rose told you that?" I couldn't speak but nodded my head. "Boys," she said, putting her hands on her hips, "listen to me. Look at me. Look up at me this instant." We angled our heads up but couldn't see much through our tears. "Are you listening?" We nodded. "I was on the phone when you started to cry so loud I couldn't hear anything Uncle Jake was saying, you know he speaks softly now. Do you hear me? Do you understand? Make your beds, wash up, and get ready for breakfast." Then she turned and walked out, heading down the hall to the living room where Auntie Rose was staring out the window.

We could tell Mother's mood based on how she communicated to us. If she needed to make us stand up and take notice, she would use one of her ace of spades pronouncements, delivered like Marta Hansen, the mother on *Mama*, except without the Norwegian American accent. But if she was exasperated, she'd address us as if she were one of Morone's drill sergeants, dismissing us with a command and then exiting from our presence.

"The letter he got, not good news but what would he expect?" she finished, trailing off to find her sister, making it hard for us to catch it all, which was expressly her purpose; the necessity for us to strain kept us quiet and focused on her every word.

We'd been dismissed.

"What's she talking about?" Steven shot at me.

"I guess, you know, out back, when we were playing baseball, he read a letter, remember? He practically tumbled out of his chair, all the other letters spilled to the ground."

"I thought he fell asleep."

"Do you think he maybe fainted?" I asked, wishing Dr. Richards were with us so we could get an answer without guessing.

"From a *letter*?" Steven asked. "Really?"

"Mother said it was bad news."

"No she didn't," he replied. "She said *news*." He left out the part of it not being *good* news.

If it was true, it was befuddling; I couldn't imagine fainting from a letter. "Maybe he hit his head on the macadam," which I didn't see, "and that's why he ended up in the hospital," I said.

"So he's not there because of polio, is that what you're saying?"

"Maybe," I answered hopefully, assuming fainting wasn't going to be fatal like what faced many of the polio patients.

We decided we *had* to go see Uncle Jake without telling anyone else in the family, to find out for ourselves what was going on, as we inferred that he was getting worse. We knew they wouldn't approve. Something just didn't feel right for either of us. We couldn't articulate it at the time, and if you'd asked us then and there to write down what we thought was going on, we wouldn't have figured it out. Chalk it up to kids' intuition, which isn't as insightful as that of an adult, it comes from a different perspective and hasn't got the layers of context that code our perceptions when we're older, but there's no mistaking its legitimacy.

Zippo got us in.

Uncle Jake didn't make eye contact with us. We weren't sure he knew who we were. We asked him about letters. No response. We asked him about the time he fell out of his chair onto the macadam out back near the garages. No response. We switched topics. We blabbered on about having met the congressman at the Badgers Club and wearing the "I'm a Brave Bostonian" buttons and collecting the postcards. Occasionally, I'd jerk my head to point out to Steven whenever I thought I'd seen a twitch in one of Uncle Jake's legs. Uncle Jake moved his lips and out came some stuff we couldn't figure out; we asked him to repeat, we bent so close we could feel his lips, but we still couldn't understand. He'd move his hands all around and then fall asleep. When we got up to say good-bye, Uncle Jake hardly seemed to notice. He was staring out the window, wearing his hat low over his brow.

We left disappointed, getting no information, feeling unfulfilled.

On the way out, my head started to swirl, thinking about all that was going on with collecting for the Timmy Fund at Braves games, making the rounds for Murph Feldman on Tuesday and Thursday afternoons, collecting the postcards for keeping the Braves in Boston, planning to steal the postcards to give to The Boxer for the congressman, worrying about Uncle Jake, anxiously thinking about Auntie Rose, daydreaming about Susie Mauer, and wondering what Noodge Mauer would say if he found out that I was sticking my tongue down his sister's throat.

French kissing was not what Morone was getting. "Hey, I'm going to be celibate at boot camp," he said with a grin, accepting congratulations and envelopes, like he was getting married, at an Italian restaurant in the North End for his going-away party. Steven and I saluted Sergeant Wilson when we entered, "Semper fi," we said and he reciprocated in kind, clicking his heels and saluting back. Rocky was wearing a jacket and tie, although the shirt was unbuttoned and the tie looked more like an elephant's trunk sniffing the brush for food upon command of his growling belly. "Have a 'gansett," he said to us, shoving cups of beer into our hands. "Sal-u-tay to my son." "Sal-u-tay," we said, raising our cups, looking around the room to see if there was any reason not to take a sip. Big Alfredo read a postcard he'd gotten from Little Alfredo after he'd found out his cousin Morone had signed up: "See you all soon, be home for Christmas, semper fi."

We ate things we'd never had before, fried squid, ham and melon served together, veal smothered with melted cheese topped with tomato sauce, pasta that we couldn't pronounce though it sounded like *nookie*, what Steven was trying to get from Zippo. They brought dessert trays around for more than an hour, little cakes with rum and cream-filled pastries that tasted good even with a 'gansett. At the end of the evening, Morone came over to Steven and me and gave us the thumbs-up. We shook hands. He told Steven he expected him to hit a triple with Zippo, hey, you know what I mean. He wished me luck with the Braves and gave me a postcard with his name and address on it and told me to give it to Moses O'Neil and his old man would give him five bucks for the congressman. "You bet," I said, watching him move to the bar where he clicked glasses and semper fied with his father, his uncle, and Sergeant Wilson. I didn't know, was this the last time I'd see him? Sometimes they don't come back, Papa had said, his introduction to us into the adult world of worry, pain, and uncertainty.

A few weeks later, Morone sent us a postcard from boot camp, located on Parris Island off the South Carolina coast. It didn't seem anything like Old Uncle A's camp on Palus Island in Maine, where we'd been sent to escape the polio epidemic raging in Boston in the spring.

I've often thought that it was odd that we were sent to a camp to be out of harm's way while Morone was sent to a camp to prepare for it.

Yet Morone's postcard from camp in South Carolina was surprisingly all gung ho. He had to crawl under wires, up cable ladders, down rope swings, through tire tunnels, keeping his head down while guys shot over him. He got to charge into straw dummies with his bayonet while screaming, "Aaiiiiieee." He said the chow was fine and his boots were lickety-split clean. He was concerned that they'd taken off so much of his hair that he'd have a rough time when they got to go to town, get my drift? He promised to write and ended with "I'm a Brave Bostonian" followed by his signature.

Little Alfredo's letter to his cousin arrived six weeks after the postcard that his father had read at the Italian restaurant on the occasion of Morone's going-away party, the one where he'd written, "be home for Christmas, semper fi." The letter was in pencil and some of the words had been blurred out by water and erasure. Rocky gave it to Steven when he delivered coal, and Steven read it that night when we were about to go to sleep. BlueDog was on my bed. Mother, Dad, Auntie Rose, and Papa were visiting Uncle Jake at the hospital.

> It's really cold. Colder than the day we found the old skates and went onto the Charles. Remember when it started to snow and we couldn't figure out which direction was which? We ended up in Cambridge and

had to walk back three miles over the bridge into the wind. I shake my hands and pound them together. My feet are frozen at night. I cry they hurt so much. Everybody does. I have blisters and they rub against the leather but I can't feel the cuts. We're supposed to dig foxholes but the ground is frozen solid. I have a sleeping bag that I pull over my whole body. It's not long enough and my back hurts from the stuff I carry all day and the hunched over position I sleep in. We get these cans that you twist and heat comes through. They don't help that much, not on your feet, anyway. Some of the local people bring us food. I heard that some of them are PROK and they want to trap you by pretending to be friendly when they really want to kill you. A guy in my squad shot at one last week so they don't come by much anymore. We're on a hill. I can't tell you which one. It doesn't matter anyway.

We can see the CCF on the next ridge a hundred yards away. Sometimes they yell to us. We give them the finger. Every once in a while, we'll hear the roar of the howitzers and the mortars a couple of miles back. Then we wait for the explosion and the shock waves. They make gigantic holes. We stand up and cheer and then drop right back down. Snipers got someone in our unit. He didn't get back down fast enough. Yesterday, we saw a dogfight. This MiG came in screaming over the hill and strafed our position. Out of nowhere came a Sabre. Our guy got behind the MiG and rat-a-tat boom it scored direct hits. Smoke came out of the MiG, then it headed straight down. The pilot didn't eject. The Sabre came back and tipped its wings to us before heading back over our positions. You can't imagine how loud it was. One guy broke his eardrum. We all turned to watch and saluted.

In the valley behind us there are miles of people on carts heading back away from the fighting. When we marched past them there were dead bodies in the carts. Lots of people were covered in blood. Nobody made any sound. It was weird. You just heard the big wagon wheels on the snow. Also the snap and crack as they went over the frozen tracks the tanks made the day before. Those guys are lucky. They get the heat from the engine.

I'm with a great bunch of marines. They're from all over. My lance corporal is from Louisiana. He calls me wop. I call him frog but not when the sergeant's around. We hear all kinds of things. That there's an agreement to stop but the Russians don't want to. Or that someone'll use the bomb. Or that there'll be an invasion up north and we'll circle them. There's a guy who came back to our unit after being stitched up who said we'd all be home by Christmas, that's what he heard from a full bird. But so what, the guy was a doctor.

I have a little calendar. From the bank. I check it off every day. I keep it in my underwear so it won't get wet. I got your package. I gave the gum to the boys. One guy used it to make a plug for his canteen, the top had been blown off. He sends a big THANK YOU. I sure could use some dental floss and some extra bullets. Ha ha, just kidding. Well, there's the whistle, got to go. Semper fi.

"Do you know what PROK and CCF mean?" I asked Steven.

"We'll have to find out from Dad in the morning."

"And full bird?"

"That too," he said as he shot me the finger.

"Very funny, hardy har har. What about wop and frog?"

"Wop's what they call Italians. It's like Yid," he replied, "so don't use it."

"And frog?"

"Beats me," he answered.

I skipped a beat and then said, "Good night, Yid," whereupon Steven reciprocated with a barrage of slurs that'd been tossed at him over the years, including kike, Shylock, Hebe, Jewboy, Christ killer, kinky, and Hymie, which I thought were funny, except the one about Christ, because I had nothing to do with his death, although I did knock him off the wall once going up the stairs to see Susie.

19.

I was feeling
the same kind of oats
that old Hooch
must've felt

We met The Boxer at Papa's loading dock to work on the plan to steal the postcards. We'd rounded up Noodge Mauer, Myandrew, and Frankie, barely getting there on time. Myandrew was wearing a sailor's hat and a kerchief tied around his neck. Noodge Mauer was asking me a thousand questions about what we were going to do and would we get home in time for dinner. Frankie was patting BlueDog, who reciprocated with nonstop nuzzling.

I was a bit leery, mind you. The Boxer was a ramrod-straight six foot four, weighing in at two hundred pounds, and sculpted in his T-shirts with a Popeye-like chest and arms that stretched the fabric to the breaking point. But it wasn't just his physical presence. Sergeant Wilson's brass buttons and ribbons could barely contain his torso yet he didn't intimidate us, perhaps because the marine uniform's symbolism gave off a comforting blanket of protection, much like that of the traffic cops on Kenmore Square, who'd make sure you didn't get swiped by a car when you pedaled across Commonwealth Avenue past Beacon Street and onto Brookline Avenue, where you had a straight shot through the

Fens to our home. His potato-thick brogue was decipherable and his idiomatic English was inflected with singsong refrains typical of other Irish immigrants, so that wasn't the cause for us to be wary. No, I rather thought that it was the cloud of Catholicism that swirled around his presence, that combination of incense, holy water, flowers, oils, and candles, blended together in an aroma that attracts other believers with a sense of familiarity by creating an invisible shroud, and to this day I'm not sure if it represents the boundaries to protect a community or a barrier for those others who don't share their faith. We were told that he attended Mass every morning, and we wondered if he made confessions on account of his manhandling foes both in the ring and on the streets. We never knew of Moses O'Neil, Chief Stinkowski, Derby Canurbi, or Morone ever attending church. They certainly never smelled as if they did. And truth be told, we never wondered if anyone thought we Jews had a particular odor, especially since we had Havdalah services on Saturdays when we lit candles, sipped wine, ate challah, and sniffed the spices that permeated our clothes and hair, a scent that marked our outsider status.

The Boxer greeted us, glanced at my friends, and asked me, "Who's these guys and are they in it or what, Joelboy?"

I introduced him to Noodge Mauer, Myandrew, and Frankie.

"I can trust 'em, I can?" he asked me.

"Trust us, you can trust us," they replied together.

"Do they know what's gonna happen, lad?" he wanted to know from me.

I shook my head no.

He looked down at them and said menacingly, "Then do exactly what I'm going to say, ya not going to tell no one in particular, I mean nobody, not a living soul, so I says. If youse fellars can keep the traps shut, if it can be done, then ya can be in on it. But if there's a risk I'm gonna be banjaxed, well, let's just say then the bunch of ya be fitted for some delph, yeah?"

Despite none of us having any idea what either *banjaxed* or *delph* meant, we knew that they were things that wouldn't be good for us, that was for sure.

Three more scared faces I'd never seen. "But I'm tellin' ya boyos," he added for emphasis, looking at each one in the eye, "if youse say anything, any little thing, to anyone, ya hear . . ." and he never finished the sentence, just looked at them back and forth a couple of times, nodding his head slightly as he took out a cigarette, lit it, and blew smoke in their faces. Then he stood up, a towering figure made taller by his pomaded pompadour, and assumed a pose we'd seen on newsreels, a slightly backward tilt with both arms bent at the elbows, one ahead of the other, fists clenched upward, poised for a match or a camera. Affected for only a moment, it had its intended impact: none of us uttered a word.

He scanned our faces, detected assent all around, then continued. "Laddie"—he nodded to Steven—"when the time comes, youse stand apart, be here on the loadin' dock when the postcards come back, hear me now, they'll need to be sorted and quick, there's work to be done, says me." Steven straightened up, and a slight groundhog smile emerged for a second, but he was careful not to have it erupt again, betraying his pride in this new assignment.

"Youse fellars," The Boxer said to me and my friends, "youse gotta be paperboys otherwise they won't give ya the bags with the postcards," he warned. "When ya get in where they stash the cards, haul 'em over to the truck and be done with it, so I'm sayin'." We all nodded. He lit up another cigarette before the first was finished, drew a long inhale, and pointed in the direction of the loading dock, where we'd stashed our bikes. "Now be goin'," he growled and we raced down the stairs to mount up.

That settled, our job was to find out how many postcards the newsboys had collected and how many more they were expected to get. We biked over to the *Herald Traveler* building to get the forms to be a paperboy from the guy who sat in the paperboy office out back. The guy told us that the only openings were for routes in Brookline and Newton. I quickly said that was okay, we'd take them, before one of my friends had the chance to say something that might've made the guy suspicious. He gave us bags and lists and told us to make trial runs beforehand, how to make collections, where to put the money, and what to say or write when someone wouldn't pay. I sensed that Noodge Mauer was going to ask a question so I shot him a look and gave him a noogie on his shoulder, which distracted him enough to prevent him from continuing.

"Follow me," I commanded quickly and guided them into the building and up to the fourth floor. When Smitty saw me, he gave me a big smile and pretended to take a picture. Myandrew stopped and posed.

"Hiya, kid," Smitty said, "you're in luck, Mr. Carlson's at his desk." I knew my friends wouldn't bother, interrupt, or embarrass me since they'd be completely absorbed by the pictures of the topless girls on the calendars. Maybe they were the inspiration for Steven to get to second base.

"Hello, Joel," Mr. Carlson said, rising from his chair, the first time anyone had done that for me, extending his hand, which I know impressed my friends. "What can I do for you?" he inquired, sitting back down and continuing to type away.

"I was kind of wondering how many postcards you think we've got? I was out back and there seemed to be piles of them."

"How many postcards? Well last I checked, it was more than the number we were going after, ten thousand if I remember. Ten thousand cards dumped on Mr. Perini's desk, how's that going to make him feel, huh? Smitty, how many postcards the boys brought in?" Smitty came over and handed him a tally sheet.

"Let me see, with today's haul, here it is, twelve thousand, almost. Won't that make a pretty sight, Smitty. Can you get them all into a good shot?"

"Are you going to stop now that there are twelve thousand?" I inquired.

"What do you fellows think?" he asked of everyone and no one. There were a few looks goods offset by a couple of get some mores that floated by from the desks near Mr. Carlson. "I guess we'll stop soon, let's say Saturday afternoon so Smitty here can take a picture that we'll put on the front page of the Sunday edition."

I reported this all back later to The Boxer. "For sure, boy, we gotta move'm out on Saturday, noon, don't ya know."

Saturday would be the day I'd be involved in a heist to help the candidate. When I think about it now, I probably would've refrained from doing it if I'd been, say, two years younger or two years older. At almost eleven, I would've been too scared, and at almost fifteen, been concerned with peer ostracism. But at almost thirteen, I was feeling the same kind of oats that old Hooch must've felt the day he got up and won the race, setting the track record at Suffolk Downs in 1951.

20.

He said it the
exact same way
that Mother said
"we'll see,"
which meant no

"There are three ways ya can rob someone," The Boxer told me. "First, ya can use force, so it is. Like a gun or a knife or your fists." With the mention of each of the three means of force, he first mimicked a gun with his right hand, then made a slash with his arm, and ended with his fists clenched, which caused his biceps to bulge. "Or maybe ya just threaten the gomey," he continued. "But ya gotta be able to back it up, 'cause a threat with nothing behind it is where the sissies get hurt. Okay now, ya can also pull an inside job. That takes time, ya gotta get to know someone who works where ya wanna steal, ya gotta make sure they don't rat ya out, ya gotta believe they can do what ya want them to do, and ya gotta pay 'em and pay 'em enough so's they don't come back and do the blackmail thing."

"What's the third way?" I asked.

"The third way is ya get someone else to do it so ya can say to the cops, 'Hey, I was with my oul fellaman,' or 'I didn't know that's what they'd be doin', they just showed up with the stuff at my house, there's no crime in being home, no way.'"

I was the third way. The Boxer told us that at noon on Saturday, Mr. Carlson would be out of the *Herald Traveler* office visiting with Mr. Perini at Braves Field, a meeting he'd written about in his column. Smitty, the photographer, would be on the fourth floor, probably in the darkroom. The guy who sat in the paperboy office out back would be there eating lunch. Noodge Mauer, Myandrew, Frankie, and I would show up a little before noon, wearing caps, with paper carriers slung over our shoulders. And that's how it started, just like he said.

When we walked into the paperboy office, the guy recognized me although he didn't say anything; his mouth was full and he had a rind of bologna stuck to his mustache. I took advantage of his mouthful and told him that Mr. Carlson asked me to haul the postcards outside so Smitty could take a picture of them.

"You can call Smitty," I said, nodding to the phone, knowing he wouldn't. "I brought my friends to help, the new kids with routes," I said. We walked past him before he answered, The Boxer having told us that demonstrating confidence was an essential element in the commission of a crime. We opened the rear door and saw the postcards dumped into big canvas carts, the kind Steven and I'd seen the cleaning ladies push all over the floor in the office buildings downtown when we got there in the late afternoons on the Thursday rounds. There were thousands of postcards, perhaps even more than what Mr. Carlson had thought. We pushed the carts out to the back lot. A *Herald Traveler* truck appeared, engine running and back door open. The driver had a Braves cap pulled down low over his forehead, wore sunglasses, and had a bushy mustache. He came out from the other side of the truck and helped us lift the carts onto the back, turn them over, and dump them in a pile.

When we were finished, I went to the fourth floor to get Smitty. One of the guys on the floor told me Smitty was in the darkroom, so I talked through a screen that had cloth on both sides to keep the light out.

"The guy in the paperboy office out back needs you to take some pictures of the postcards that we've loaded onto the back of the truck and are going to be delivered to Mr. Perini's office this afternoon," I lied to Smitty. "It's all for the story." I handed him a typed note I'd received from The Boxer, who told me it really came from Murph Feldman, that said for

Smitty to meet Mr. Carlson at the ballpark so he could also take pictures of Mr. Carlson with the postcards and of Mr. Perini as the cards were being dumped onto his desk in the office.

"Mr. Carlson gave the note to the guy in the paperboy office who's asked me to find you, as he isn't supposed to leave the paperboy office unattended with all the dough the paperboys collected."

Smitty took lots of pictures of the postcards and posed us in various positions in the truck, on the pile, in the pile, under the pile. We were all wearing our "I'm a Brave Bostonian" buttons, even the truck driver. At one o'clock, when we were finished, I gave an envelope to the guy in the paperboy office. It had a note that said "thank you" wrapped around a twenty-dollar bill.

"Who's it from?" he asked, his gums still working the sandwich so it came out more as "zits from," which I found especially funny. It looked like Murph Feldman's handwriting. The Boxer had told me to shake the hand of the guy in the paperboy office and to tell him he was shaking the hand of the boy who shook the hand of the man who shook the hand of John L. Sullivan.

"Really, wow, holy cow!" he said, or at least I supposed that's what it was, having trouble concentrating when his mouth was working his food like a washing machine.

"No kidding." I nodded assent. I told Smitty that we were leaving, whereupon the driver closed the rear door, got in, and started to drive away. As he passed Smitty, he pulled down his window and said, "See you over at the ballpark."

We'd been told to bike back to the loading dock at Papa's store. When we got there, Steven was directing a group of young immigrants unloading the postcards from the back of the truck and showing them how to identify them by address and then place them in piles on top of the names of towns that'd been marked on the floor in chalk in his writing. I couldn't figure out how they'd stolen this newspaper truck and how they were going to get it back. Then I watched as The Boxer slid a penknife very gingerly under the "*Herald Traveler*" sign that we thought had been painted onto the side. The paint seemed to lift off in one piece. It was a thin sliver of rubber. He gently pulled the rubber down and as the newspaper's logo curled under its weight, you could see letters that actually had been painted on the side of the truck appear. After a few seconds, I was able to make out Alfredo's Hauling on the side. It was Big Alfredo's, Morone's uncle's truck! He peeled the other "Herald Traveler" signs off and we went upstairs. From the top step, we could see into the front seat of the truck, and I noticed a Braves cap, a pair of sunglasses, and what could've been a mustache. The driver had been The Boxer in disguise, and even we'd been faked out. Murph Feldman emerged from the office and greeted us with a "Hiya, kiddos" and handed each of us a crisp, new ten-dollar bill. He patted me on the head and with a big grin told me it was good to know that I wasn't deaf and dumb.

During the next few weeks, the piles of postcards for each town were delivered to a person who'd go through them and pick out the names of the folks he knew personally. In the North End, Sal the barber was the contact; in Kenmore Square it was Isaac Burgas the kosher butcher; in Southie, it was the bartender across the channel on Thomson Place. Each area had a captain, and the captain would appoint lieutenants who would assist him. When the army was finally assembled, they deployed more than a hundred guys throughout Boston and eastern Massachusetts, culled from the lists of friends and those who owed them favors. They vowed to make a personal contact with each and every name on the list, to let them know that the congressman shared their views on the importance of keeping the Braves in Boston, that the congressman cared enough about them to send someone to their house to speak with them, and that this was the kind of senator that they needed in Washington. The captains paid the lieutenants from the kitty that Papa and the boys had collected, including the proceeds from the big dinner a couple of weeks back at the Badgers Club.

That night, Steven, Noodge Mauer, Myandrew, Frankie and I went to the Braves game. Mr. Carlson spotted me and told me that the postcards never showed up. He was agitated, jittery, fumbling for words, smiling in an exaggerated way to elicit sympathy from me, behavior that was intended to result in me giving up the goods, not that he suspected me, but maybe I knew something that could put him on the right track. Smitty had seen the truck take a right turn out of the lot, he said, and I confirmed that it did, by nodding, but I couldn't tell him that instead of heading toward Commonwealth Avenue, it swung around a warehouse and headed back to the dock where Papa's store was located. He went on to say that Smitty was distraught that he couldn't take a picture of the postcards dumped all over Mr. Perini's desk, which was going to be on the cover. His switching of the hurt from himself to Smitty was my first exposure to a trick that adults do when they want to get your sympathy: I'm not concerned about me, no, it's this guy here, the poor shlub, who's going to get knocked down, we've got to find a way to help him out. I didn't say anything at all, just some head bobs and tics, not wanting to reveal something that would lead Mr. Carlson to suspect I'd had a hand in the theft. And in truth, I'm not sure I was capable of speaking at that point, having a guilt-induced cramp so bad I had to excuse myself to go to the men's room, something that Papa told us never to do in a place as grimy as the ballpark. Taking a leak and reminding myself not to touch anything, I decided I was going to ask Murph Feldman if after they finished using the postcards could they have someone dump them off in bags at the *Herald Traveler* at night, no one would know.

"That's nice, kiddo," he said the next Tuesday when I got to him, "I'm gonna think about it." Though he said it the exact way that Mother said "we'll see," which meant no.

Biking back home, I wondered what would happen if Mr. Carlson found out I'd been in on the theft of the postcards. I wondered what would happen to me if any of my friends spilled the beans on the post-card theft. And as long as I was wondering, my mind raced to Uncle Jake, and I wondered if I'd ever see him again.

21.

Remember when Papa said something about the Holy Grail?

Noodge Mauer went to religious instruction on Wednesday afternoons. That meant I could visit Susie. She'd greet me by telling me what she'd seen during the day from her window, usually things like Steven and Zippo on the other side of the garage after school, or this guy who called himself Herbert Hoover, who'd walk around the neighborhood playing "Hail to the Chief" on a Jew's harp. Occasionally, she'd tell me of strangers she'd seen on fire escapes, couples shouting at each other, a kid throwing rocks at a cat, or a lady spending fifteen minutes in the milk truck on Wednesday mornings.

I told her that my uncle Jake's legs would move, well, twitch sometimes, and she got excited and asked me questions about it. I wanted to know if she felt anything in her legs. She told me to go ahead, pinch them, and I did. She said I could squeeze them as hard as I wanted and it'd be okay. I didn't squeeze hard but I told her I did. I kept my hands on her legs, they were long and shapely, beautiful in their stillness. They were smooth and I felt enough sensation for both of us as I moved my hands practically up to her hips.

She told me that we each had to tell the other a secret. This way, we'd be friends forever. She told me to go first. There was no way I was going to tell her about stealing the postcards. No way would I ever reveal that Steven and I were the ones who'd climbed up on the roof of Mr. Perini's office underneath the stands to listen in when Papa's pals paid the guys off to find out about the Braves' move to Milwaukee. So I told her about the letter that I'd gotten that day from Morone.

> I got into a bit of trouble today being called wop by this one guy. I told him to shut up and he kept it up so I busted his lip. It's all swollen and he looks like Jersey Joe Walcott all puffy in the face after the second round. I had to drop and do fifty with all the guys yelling, standing around me in a circle. Anyway, that shut him up but another guy started in with dago this and dago that and I couldn't coldcock him cause he's my drill sergeant but if I could I would.
>
> I look like a total jerk with no hair and the slop they call food you wouldn't feed to BlueDog. What I wouldn't give for some gnocchi and a tartufo.
>
> We had a ceremony for some guys who got killed. They brought these coffins onto the parade grounds and fired guns before they loaded them onto trucks that went to the train station. The flags on the coffins will be folded and given to their parents. If my father gets a folded flag instead of a silk jacket with the birds on the back, he'll kill me a second time. It's supposed to be like an icebox in Korea and this guy who just came back had a finger frozen off or something. Okay, there's the bugle, see you.

"What's a wop?" Susie asked.

"It's what people call Italians when they don't like them," I said authoritatively.

"Like kike, for you," she said matter-of-factly.

"Yeah," I responded, understanding that Susie was making a word association, nothing more. Yet it stung in an unusual way as I imagined Morone, in South Carolina, with no other Italians around, no family, no friends, no familiar food or weather, being called wop by someone who meant it as an insult, likely an invitation to a fight in which he'd probably have no one come to his defense. I wanted to be there for him, not as an almost-thirteen-year-old but as his peer, someone who'd stand up and say to the other guy, "I'm a wop too, and you'll have to go through me before you can take him on." That was what he'd do for me, I was sure, if the roles were reversed.

"You're not going to show that to his father," she said.

"Of course not," I replied, "he'd be frightened that his son was going to be discharged for fighting," which, once I said it, sounded ridiculous; I mean, that was what they were training for, wasn't it?

"Anyway, here's *my* secret," she began conspiratorially, her lips so close to my face that I wasn't prepared for what came next, as she crossed her hands to grab opposite sides of her sweater and pulled it up over her shoulders. I had two instantaneous thoughts of anticipation: the obvious one and the other, the delight I'd experience in telling Steven I'd finally slid safely into second base.

Back home, I told my brother about Susie Mauer but swore him to secrecy. He told me that he'd been with Zippo that very afternoon. She'd found a room at the hospital that no one used anymore and they turned off the lights. He'd gotten to third base. "How could you tell, I mean in the dark?" I queried. He gave me a look: slightly rolled eyes and a glance to an invisible audience, his exasperation a sure sign that he thought I was a complete dope.

I picked up Morone's letter and read it again. Something was bothering me. I showed it to Steven.

"Did you notice," I said, "no more gung ho stuff, no more cowboys and Indians, no more semper fis?"

"You think he hates boot camp, he misses being home?"

"It kinda sounds to me like he doesn't want to be a marine, he doesn't care about joining his cousin fighting, and he certainly doesn't want to go to Korea and come back dead."

I imagined Morone dead, lying face up in a casket. I winced and shook my head to free myself of this thought, the way BlueDog would shake his whole body to get rid of the water after going for a romp in the Fens.

Steven thought for a bit and then came out with, "Hey, Morone may have a problem, you know, if he wants to get out of the marines, but you've got just as big a problem, you better believe."

"What are you talking about?"

Steven continued, "Look, Mr. Carlson was going to have Smitty take a picture of all of those postcards dumped on Mr. Perini's desk, right? He was going to put that picture on the cover of the paper and he'd write a big article, a follow-up to the press conference he had when he broke the story of the Braves' move to Milwaukee. He's probably written the article and is just itching to get the picture on the front page. Front page! A sportswriter with a front-page article. Well, if there are no postcards, there's no picture, and with no picture, there's no article, and no article means you've got one angry Mr. Carlson. You know what I would do if I were Mr. Carlson? I'll tell you. I'd launch an investigation into how the postcards were stolen. And guess what? They don't know who the driver is, he never gave them his name and he wasn't a regular driver. And they can't track down the truck because it wasn't even a real newspaper truck. They don't know Noodge Mauer, Myandrew, or Frankie's names, either, because you made them sign up for paper routes with phony names. You see where I'm going?"

I did, I wanted him to stop, I was getting clammy and my head was pounding.

"They know you and will figure out lickety-split that somehow you're involved. Even if the guy at the paperboy office out back couldn't remember you after he's seen you lots of times, you went up to the fourth floor and got Smitty, who came down and took pictures of you and the rest of them with the cards in the back of the truck. First thing Smitty's going to do is finger you. What are you going to do when they get you in a room and turn the desk lamp around and shine it into your eyes and say, 'Okay, kid, level with us, who's in on it with you?' Sure, you won't want to rat on your friends but do you want to do time in a reform school while everyone else is out having fun and some other guy on the outside is feeling up Susie's legs and putting his tongue down her throat? Are you prepared to spend your days in woodshop with junior Stinkowskis and O'Neils who'll put your fingers in the vise or on the table saw and the only way they'll not crush them or cut them off is if you say you love Jesus? Huh? And even if you say it, they'll crush them and cut them off anyway. Do you think any girl will want herself felt up by a guy with a crushed hand missing a couple of fingers?"

I was in a tizzy. Did I become a turncoat and get retaliated against? Did I keep my trap shut and hope for the best? A real schicksalsfrage, as Uncle Jake would grumble in German.

I threw up. I used it as an excuse in the morning not to go to school.

After dinner that night, Steven and I told Dad and Papa what Steven had said—that Mr. Carlson was going to figure out that I was in on the theft of the postcards.

"Instead of a story on the front page about the Braves moving with all the postcards on Mr. Perini's desk, there'll be a picture of me and the story of how I stole the postcards," I interjected. Papa sat motionless for a minute, then said he could take care of it.

"Don't worry," he said to me earnestly, "I'll make sure that doesn't happen."

"What're you going to do?" I queried.

"I'm going to speak with Murph Feldman," Papa answered, and Dad added that we should go back to our rooms, he needed some time alone.

"To cook something up," Steven whispered to me before we turned on the radio.

Papa called Murph Feldman and told him that it was likely that I would get caught in the postcard theft and that this could blow up big. If Mr. Carlson found out that I was behind the theft of the postcards and how they were using them, it could mean trouble for the congressman, Papa told him. Murph Feldman said he'd take care of it.

On Sunday morning, Papa told us a story that we could never repeat. I agreed and said I'd cross my heart and hope to die.

Papa admonished, "Don't ever say that. Don't ever say cross your heart and hope to die. Don't say keep your fingers crossed and don't knock wood three times or even say knock wood. Jews don't say these things, they're for gentiles. Only."

We nodded in agreement.

Papa started up again and said, "We fixed the Mr. Carlson problem, boys."

Nothing had ever happened with Mr. Carlson. No phone call, no invitation to his office, no one sitting me down in a chair telling me to confess, no hot lights, no noogies applied to the side of my head, nothing.

"How'd you do it?" I asked Papa excitedly. "What gives? What'd Murph Feldman do to make this all go away?"

"We all knew that Mr. Carlson was more furious that he didn't have a story for the Sunday paper than he was about the actual theft of the postcards. Don't get me wrong," Papa insisted, "he was certainly embarrassed about the theft, which took place at his paper of all places. But for a sportswriter to get a story on the front page of the paper is like, well, I can't think of any other way to say it, like the Holy Grail, but don't ever say that yourselves," he admonished, and hurried back to his narrative.

"Let me tell you what Murph Feldman did," Papa continued. "Remember when you two snuck up on the roof of Mr. Perini's office the day the guys from Milwaukee came to meet with Moses O'Neil and Chief Stinkowski?"

"Sure," we said in unison.

"Well," Papa continued, "Murph Feldman went to Mr. Carlson and told him that you boys not only heard about the Braves moving when you were on the roof of the office but that you knew that bribes were paid so that people could place bets on where and when the move would take place. That would be a major scoop, a sportswriter uncovering a big-time scandal. Front-page stuff for sure. And to top it off, Murph Feldman handed Mr. Carlson an envelope with $5,000 in it and Mr. Carlson promised that he and Smitty would swear they got an anonymous tip about the whole thing, which meant that Moses O'Neil and Chief Stinkowski were off the hook."

"And me, too," I exclaimed.

"You bribed him!" Steven shouted unabashedly.

"There was a catch," Papa added. "He can't publish anything on this until after November 4."

"Why's that?" Steven asked.

"Because we want to make sure it'll take place only after election day."

And, as Uncle Jake would say, that was that.

Later, I asked Steven, "What's with crossing your heart and hoping to die, crossing your fingers, and knocking wood? Why can't we say that stuff?" I wanted to know.

"I think the crossing stuff has to do with, you know, the cross, Jesus."

"Knock wood three times, do you know about that?"

"I asked Zippo and she said that the cross was made out of wood and knocking three times is supposed to bring good luck from something called the Holy Trinity, whatever that is."

"Remember when Papa said something about the Holy Grail and that was something we couldn't say? Why is that?"

"Well," Steven answered with conviction, "I kind of think it's something beyond third base because Zippo says that I'm close to finding it."

September 5, 1939
Dear Diary,

I have hardly slept in 4 days. Everyone goes to bed with the radio on to hear the latest news. Edward R. Murrow from London. No one says Germans. Nazis this and Nazis that. I told Jacob not to tell anyone that he is from Germany. He has no accent but works on th's, which still come out with an s sound. I'm sure anyone will think it's just a slight lisp. I'm worried about his papers. My father and Murph Feldman say I shouldn't be concerned but I am anyway. He is angry and yells at the radio. I let him. What if this had happened when we were there? I try not to think about it but I do anyway.

I am getting big. Bigger than my sister before she had Steven. I'm tired all the time. Jacob comes home early from the track to be with me.

Ida says hardly anyone comes to the circus. They will have to close. I won't go back. I take walks in the Fens and drop bread crumbs for the ducks and geese. They follow me around. Jacob and I went to the Franklin Park Zoo and they let us in to see Peek after he told them he was a vet and had treated Peek but he didn't say where.

Jacob and I talk about what we are going to do. First we say this and I get scared and nervous and then we say that and it scares me as well. My sister is a wonderful mother. Privately, Jacob whispers wunderbar with an emphasis on the v sound and we both laugh. It's the first time we've laughed in days. I try to imagine what it'll be like. Both ways. I settle on one and then the other. I shake sometimes. I love to hold Steven but am relieved when they go home. Jacob tells me I won't be able to make up my mind until I imagine it is the future and I have no regret about what I did. Either way. I love him so.

Sadly,
Rose

June 29, 1942
Dear Diary,

For several days, I have not been in any physical pain from the circus accident. I can raise my arm above my shoulder a little. I am hopeful.

Joel cannot pronounce the second syllable of Jacob. Jake! Jake! Jake! he cries out like the newsboys who yell Extra! My husband is forever named, much to his delight. Privately, I call him Jacob, something I can hold on to from the past.

Out strolling, Joel runs ahead of us, trips and falls, but gets up right away as if this is the way it is. I wish I could accept life that way. Steven dotes on him, teaches him games, he is so patient. It is rare that either of them cries. I bend down to hug them. They are too heavy for me to lift.

Jacob and I are at peace with this. Our tears are for joy.

Jacob wants to volunteer but knows he can't. Mr. Maguire has arranged a meeting with Honey Fitz to find out if he is able to speak to someone in Washington about having Jacob provide assistance. Translating or something to do with maps, that kind of thing. Dad and Murph Feldman say that's OK.

My sister spends her days at HIAS, which has been turned into a convalescent home for Jewish soldiers after they've been discharged from the hospital. She gets home by three. My brother-in-law helps out at the army recruiting station on the corner of Columbus and Clarendon. I have Ida by my side at the Badgers Club, preparing packages for the boys overseas. Every once in a while, we get a thank you note. These brighten our days.

There are so few men around. No one goes to the track or buys furniture. Dad sold some more stamps this week to a man on Beacon Hill. They still have money, he says, lots of it.

Today it was beautiful and hard to imagine that there was a war. Then we go home and listen to the radio.

Your Rose

22.

I wouldn't be the one to tell any of this to Papa

Ever since we'd started delivering envelopes for Murph Feldman on Tuesdays and Thursdays, we went to Sal the barber to get our hair cut. With a wiffle, all he had to do was run the shears over our heads as if we were sheep, keeping the top part flat and a little longer at the front, which we'd brush straight up with the help of some stickum. The whole procedure should've taken about a minute, although Sal the barber would stretch it to about ten so we'd think we were getting our money's worth. However, we didn't travel to the North End, rain or shine, for better barbering. We went there and happened to get our hair cut in between looking at the pictures in the girlie magazines, listening to the guys placing bets at Suffolk Downs, watching Sal the barber's kids taking cash from guys and stuffing it into envelopes and marking down numbers on pieces of paper, and waiting for Sal the barber's wife to bring in espresso and biscotti, smells that swept the cigar and cigarette smoke out back along with the hair on the floor, collected by the new immigrant relatives from Calabria who knew little more than "Hey!" and "Yo!"

While we were waiting, we'd read comic books and listen to the ball game on the radio. We heard the gray-haired guys talk about the good old days, but here they'd give their punch lines in Italian, which was really no different from what we were used to when Old Uncle A or Isaac Burgas finished up a story in Yiddish. At Sal the barber's, the old fellows would lean back in the chair as Sal the barber applied a hot towel to their faces to loosen up their pores, then applied shaving cream. He would strop a single-edge blade in a rhythmic motion for a minute or two and then start to scrape just below the sideburn in a swift and effortless motion, swiping the blade on a towel that hung over his belt before making another gentle scrape on the guy's cheek or chin. We couldn't wait until we were old enough. For Halloween one year, we mixed sour cream with water in a little bowl, whipped it into a rich lather, applied it to our faces as a beard, then colored it with ground black pepper so we could go as the men at Sal the barber's. But we sneezed so much the sour cream sprayed all over the kitchen, and what started out as a fantasy turned into a nightmare as we had to make the place spic-and-span before Mother got home.

We timed our visits to the days when one of Papa's pals would need a trim and a shave. That was when there was the most excitement, generated from the moment one of these guys walked in as if he owned the place. We especially liked it when Murph Feldman was there. Sal the barber would labor over his head, making sure every hair was in place. Murph Feldman would take the handheld mirror himself and pass it behind his head, instructing Sal the barber on individual hairs so he said, but really spying on who else was in the barbershop, we suspected. He also got a shave each time and a special treatment, which seemed to us to be a nap under some hot, steaming towels.

We went to Sal the barber's next after Papa told us that Murph Feldman was going to be there. Derby Canurbi came with him. When Murph Feldman spotted us, he waved and said, "Hi ya, kiddos," making us celebrities in the eyes of the other kids waiting to get clipped. Sal the barber must've known he was coming at a prearranged time because he had a chair ready. He hung his jacket, threw a sheet over his body, leaned him back, brushed the shaving cream on, stropped his blade, nodded to one of the immigrants who came running over with a shoe-cleaning kit, made eye contact with another who brought a cup of espresso in one hand and a chair in the other for Derby Canurbi, placing it close to where Murph Feldman was sitting so he wouldn't have to sit near the goofy kids like us or the immigrant relatives who couldn't speakity American while he was waiting to be next.

Suffolk Downs was closed for the season, so Derby Canurbi wore open-necked, colorful silk shirts with palm trees and sunbursts, never mind that he was freezing his rear end off, this was his way of connecting with the boys in the sun working the stables at Hialeah Park in Miami. Sitting next to Murph Feldman, he had the phone brought across the room, where he'd carry on two conversations at once: on the phone with the guys at the track and with Sal the barber and Murph Feldman, never skipping a beat with either party.

I tried to mimic this, burying my head in a magazine, angling my ears to receive maximum input from their conversation, but it didn't work too well. I loved to listen to these guys, whether at Papa's office or down at the loading dock, and this was a golden opportunity to soak in their language and pick up on all the latest goings-on about town. So I moved up closer to where I could follow most of what Derby Canurbi and Sal the barber were saying and the same for when the towel came off Murph Feldman. There was the usual stuff, about horses and bets, and they mentioned some of the names from the envelopes we delivered. At one point, when the towel came off, I was pretty sure that Murph Feldman said he'd get Sal the barber the papers he needed for a liquor license for the café that his wife had opened in the neighborhood. What I didn't know was whether this would be a real license or simply a piece of paper that would fool any cop or city inspector who'd go over it with a fine-tooth comb.

They reminisced about Uncle Jake and the horse that won the big race in 1951 and gave everybody a big payday. They carried on like Steven and I would, laughing and snorting and interrupting each other with a "Do you remember this," then sucking in some air, fuel for the next burst of rapid-fire recollections. Murph Feldman was laughing so hard he wiped the tears from his eyes with a dirty towel, leaving splotches of shaving cream and hair all over his head. This set Sal the barber off making exaggerated gestures of humor to Murph Feldman, all the while hissing in Italian for the immigrant kids to bring clean towels to him, *capisce*?

They laughed and slapped each other on the back and the thighs, then began recalling the list of things that folks had done with the money they'd won betting on Hooch. Murph Feldman had made the down payment on a house for his daughter in Brookline, Sal the barber had renovated the storefront nearby and opened a café for his wife, and Derby Canurbi had sunk his winnings into a share of the Club Bingo on Highway 91 in Las Vegas, Nevada. Later, we found out, he almost sold his stake because the club was just breaking even, but he put it off, an investment strategy that worked in this case, as the property had just reopened in 1952 as the Sahara Hotel and Casino.

Old Uncle A had told us that Dad had put his winnings from Hooch into savings bonds to pay for Steven's and my college education, that Papa had donated all his newfound gains to HIAS, that Uncle Jake had contributed to the building of a new veterinary clinic at the track, and that he himself had bought plate blocks of the entire 1902–03 stamp series, which included likenesses of Martha Washington, Daniel Webster, Henry Clay, David Farragut, and John Marshall, figures that he'd read up on at the library in Copley Square.

After their hilarity had run its course, Sal the barber said, "Listen up, fellas," to Murph Feldman and Derby Canurbi, "I got something important to tell you and it concerns Leo Tubbs and Moses O'Neil." It was as if all the yukking up had been the appetizer and now Sal the barber was going to serve the main course.

"Leo Tubbs?" Murph Feldman said. "I haven't heard that name in thirty years."

I knew the story about how Moses O'Neil and Chief Stinkowski had cornered Tubby in a bathroom of the Roxy in 1922 and how he'd died six months later from the beating. I pretended to be engrossed in my comic book as I maneuvered my chair imperceptibly closer to where the three of them were talking, enabling me to absorb the conversation before it evaporated. They didn't notice my move or that of BlueDog, who now was curled up with his head resting peacefully on his hind legs, asleep not a foot from the barber chair.

Sal the barber filled them in. A few days earlier, one of the old men having a shave seemed to drift off in the barber chair and mumbled something about having killed a mick, a Yid mick, no less, a revenge thing, and he tried to spit over his shoulder but ended up drooling on the smock.

"I didn't pay much attention at first, an old guinea on his last legs would rather come here and make a confession to me under the influence of the hot towel, such a *criminale* hadn't seen the confession booth since his altar boy days. Anyway, a Yid mick sounded like it might involve you," Sal the barber said, locking eyes with Murph Feldman, "excepting the fact that you're here alive and well and you've never lost anyone, no one's been cut in your family, so maybe he was talking about Moses O'Neil, a mick for sure and a Yid it might seem to an *il vecchio* from the North End. But then again, Moses O'Neil's got no family and he's something like a spring chicken for his age, so this old *sicario* couldn't've been talking about him."

Murph Feldman sat up in the barber chair, Derby Canurbi put down the form he was writing on and hung up the phone, and I lost all subtlety and pretense and stared at the three of them.

"It was clear to me that this man in the very chair you're sitting in"—he nodded to Murph Feldman—"had been an *assassino* way back when and had something to get off his chest."

Murph Feldman started to rise and speak but Sal the barber motioned for him to sit, he had more.

"Here's what I got: the old man said that he'd been with Tubby, Leo Tubbs, the night that Tubby had gone into the bathroom at the Roxy and had come out beaten and bruised. I coaxed out of him that Tubby found out later that the guys who'd attacked him were the mick mayor's men, here he was talking about Honey Fitz, and that he'd asked this guy to track them down and kill them. The old man said that Tubby told him back in '22 that killing the two guys who beat him up was too good, that he should find a way to kill them every day, to make them wake up and regret that they were alive each and every day. I thought that was it, the guy was breathing so hard I prayed to the Holy Virgin that he wouldn't die in my chair. I raised the back, took off his smock, and started to give him a hand getting out of the chair. He looked directly at me and choked out softly, 'On election night, *finito*,' then dragged his thumb across his throat as if he were slicing someone's head off."

I was spellbound. You could've told me the Braves were moving back to Boston or Auntie Rose had never been on an ostrich in a circus and I wouldn't have processed it, not twitched a muscle, I was so focused on what was going on with the three of them.

Sal the barber continued, "I had to try to figure out exactly what it was I'd heard from the old man. So's here's what I did: I went to visit Mr. Carlson at the *Herald Traveler* and made up a story that I wanted to see the newspaper headlines of the day I got married, so I said, November 8, 1922, which was the day after election night. Mr. Carlson put me in touch with the guys who were in charge of the archives and I went scouring through the paper to see if there had been a death on the seventh, a murder that would've been reported on the eighth. I saw a notice that Sylvia Mischal, Solly's wife, had been discovered dead a little after eleven that night, when he'd come home from the Copley Plaza Hotel where he'd attended the gathering that had been hoping to celebrate the comeback of Honey Fitz, you remember, in the race for governor. Boys, there was no other death article reported that day that in any way related to a Yid mick. I pored over the papers for the following two days, hoping to find other deaths that might point me away from the conclusion I didn't want to reach."

"The Yid mick could only be one thing," Murph Feldman announced, "Moses O'Neil."

I knew that Moses O'Neil wasn't Jewish but the name Moses was Jewish and O'Neil was certainly a mick name.

"And, well, here's the thing," Sal the barber said to Derby Canurbi and Murph Feldman, the original Yid mick. "I went over to the old sicario's place, he lives above the pastry shop over there." He pointed out the window, but Murph Feldman and Derby Canurbi didn't crane their necks, kept their eyes glued to Sal the barber. "I told him he needed to come clean, he could do it with me, it'd ease his conscience, and after a bit, I coaxed him into telling me what happened that night thirty years ago. Who knows, maybe he even confused me with a priest, what's it matter," and from that, I guessed that Sal the barber had likely impersonated one to receive the confession.

"It was hard to hear, I had to put my ear practically on top of his lips, he smelled like death and with every second or third word there'd come spittle, it was all I could do to keep close to him, but I had to know, he was fading.

"So's he tells me, and I'm pretty sure I got this right, some words I couldn't figure out, anyway, he says that Tubby found out that Moses O'Neil was the guy and ordered the assassino to get him for the beating, to make him die a little death each and every day, by killing his wife. Tubby sent this guy because he was too ill to do it himself. The effects of the beating Moses O'Neil and Chief Stinkowski had given Tubby were taking their toll and he was mostly bedridden by October of 1922. Tubby told the guy to make the move on election night, as he figured that Moses O'Neil would be at the Copley Plaza and his wife would be home. He drove to the neighborhood, took along an accomplice, and parked the car a block away. They dressed as Western Union messengers with a stack of yellow envelopes. They also had penknives and coat hangers under their coats, which they needed to pry open the outside door. Once inside, they walked quietly up the stairs and knocked softly on the door of the apartment. They heard a woman approach the door and listened for the sound of her sliding the metal cap off to the side of the peephole.

"'Western Union,' one of the men said.

"'Election results,' the accomplice added.

"The woman saw the men in uniform and thinking that someone had sent a telegram announcing the mayor's victory in the gubernatorial race, excitedly opened the door, only to have one of the men grab her head from the side and, in a lightning-fast motion, twist it while the other held her body taut. He said she died instantly and slumped to the floor. Then the two of them left immediately."

I was confused: I knew that Moses O'Neil wasn't married and my Nana died that night, but from the aftereffects of the flu.

Then I froze like I imagined Little Alfredo's bones did, shivering at night in Korea. My heart started to race; it was beating so loudly I thought others could hear. I felt as if I'd been whacked on the back of the head by one of Sal the barber's leather straps. My Nana's death—it was just another story, although *story* sounded more like *lie* to me at that point. But why did they want to kill Nana? Papa had nothing to do with Tubby's death. It was Moses O'Neil and Chief Stinkowski.

No one spoke for a while. Then Derby Canurbi said, "I bet it was Sylvia," and I didn't know if he was just so used to saying the word *bet* that it came out that way, but it didn't matter, he wasn't getting up to go to a phone.

Murph Feldman asked Sal the barber, "You sure about this?"

Sal the barber nodded yes.

"It had to've been a mix-up," Murph Feldman said.

"A simple mistake," Sal the barber agreed. "So here's the last part: this guy tells me that he and his accomplice reported back to Tubby that all had been done as requested, but when Tubby inquired the next day with some friends on the force, the only death reported from the night before was Sylvia Mischal, the wife of a furniture store owner, who'd been found by her husband slumped near the front door, waiting for him to come home; she died from the aftereffects of the flu. The two assassinos had tailed Moses O'Neil the previous day and saw him entering the apartment where Solly lived, then left, not realizing it was just a visit, that he didn't live there. The funeral took place the next day at a temple in Brookline."

"Kol Israel," Murph Feldman interjected, as if he were remembering the day.

"Tubby sent a colleague who spoke good English to the synagogue to report on who attended the service, and it was only then that they realized that they'd killed the wrong person," Sal the barber finished.

The three guys sat there not making a sound, not moving a muscle, surrounded by the chaos of the barbershop; it was like watching a snapshot inside a movie.

Did Papa know? Did he have any idea as to how his wife had died? Was there an inkling, a lingering suspicion, did he fear that his daughters had witnessed a crime unfathomable to a child? Did Mother know anything? Had Mother put any of the pieces together?

I did wonder whether Papa's pals would eventually say something to him. Especially if they were going to tell Moses O'Neil. That's what they began chatting about. Derby Canurbi said they had to and was holding the phone, but Murph Feldman was pretty adamant that telling him would lead to Moses O'Neil apologizing to Papa and then the cat would be out of the bag and what good would it do?

I did get my hair cut, by Sal the barber no less, after Papa's pals left, and when he asked me, "What's up, daddy-o?" I said, "Nothing much," and glanced at my Scott stamp catalog while he pretended to need ten minutes to do what he knew he could do in one.

I decided right then and there that I wouldn't be the one to tell any of this to Papa. Steven might've caught a little of the conversation but he was otherwise engaged with a girlie magazine, and I didn't bring it up to him until thirty years later.

23.

Kristallnacht, they said, they all knew about Kristallnacht

Old Uncle A had given us the straight scoop on how Uncle Jake and Auntie Rose made it out of Germany onto the boat in the harbor at Hamburg but hadn't gotten around to telling us how they got to Boston from Hamburg. Our anticipation was so great that within minutes from the time he walked through the front door on his next visit, we cornered him in our room, shut the door, plopped down on the rug with BlueDog, and enticed him with a cup of his favorite tea to settle into the leather chair, along with our promise to give him our undivided attention.

He was flattered, but I suspect we didn't need to do anything more than ask. He nodded his head a bit, as if to recall where he'd left off, and then, with a smile, started his engine, slowly and noticeably softer than what we were used to hearing and with a few throat clearings sprinkled here and there.

"Your aunt and uncle found a place on the boat for Peek with a seal bound for a zoo. It was a freighter that had room for about thirty passengers. They were assigned one room. Neither of them said anything, as they didn't want to jinx their escape. On the first night, Uncle Jake slept on the small divan in the room, untroubled by either its lack of comfort or the rocking against the waves once they cleared the Elbe River and reached the North Sea.

"The captain told them that they would stop in Antwerp, Glasgow, Reykjavík, and Halifax on the way to Montreal. Your aunt asked the captain if they would pass near the Faroe Islands.

"'And after Montreal,' your uncle, the newly named Dieter Harald Eberhart, asked the captain, 'how do we get to the United States?'

"'Herr Eberhart, Montreal is our final destination,' the captain replied.

"Jake stiffened as rigidly as when he saw the men with the swastika armbands confront an old Jew on the street. He wasn't given to outward manifestations of panic, but his mind raced with the speed of electricity searching for an outcome from the maze of negative possibilities. How could he get to the United States? he wondered. He had no visa.

"Your Aunt Rose reacted to the hot flashes of light emanating from his eyes. 'You will come to Boston with me,' she declared authoritatively, holding his arm, exchanging their roles as caregiver and patient. 'I will send a wireless.'

"With the stops for loading and unloading cargo, it took twelve days to get to Montreal. It was bitter cold. Going up on deck for a few minutes a day was the limit. The crew was constantly scanning the horizon for icebergs. They checked on Peek each day, and the veterinarian found him to be in good spirits. The African bird princess told him that the seal enjoyed having Peek as company.

"They spent most of their time in the small community space near their cramped room. She asked him how he became a vet. He told her that he wasn't officially a vet, that he had gone to medical school in Berlin and graduated in 1932. By the following year, the SA was orchestrating boycotts of Jewish businesses and intimidating Aryans to stop them from using Jewish doctors and lawyers and accountants.

"'First, I was told I could work only in a hospital and couldn't set up a private practice. Then, I could see patients only in the emergency room. Finally, I could treat only Jewish patients in an emergency. That didn't matter much as most Jews started to stay away from hospitals. We developed an underground railroad like what you had before your War between the States. Jewish doctors would go to the homes of Jewish patients. We couldn't carry our bags with instruments and medications. They'd be stolen. We strapped them against our bodies, jammed them into our socks and coat pockets. Once, I saw an older Jewish doctor put his stethoscope on top of his head covered by his hat. I found out later that a group of youths came up from behind him and knocked the hat off his head, found the stethoscope, and strangled him with it.

"'I'd treated many gentiles in my neighborhood so most looked the other way when I went out on my Jewish patient rounds. Soon, however, I started to run out of medications. I could set fractures, deliver babies, bring down fevers, lance boils, apply compresses, reduce pain, clean bedsores, even pull teeth. But my diabetic patients couldn't get enough insulin. My former colleague, the tall blond doctor, would sneak out as much medication for me as he could without arousing suspicions. This was as much a problem as a blessing, you see, because then I would have to choose which patients I would give it to. This is what we call a schicksalsfrage. I would have to play God. How would I decide? Is the small child with his whole life ahead of him more deserving than the young father who is suffering to feed his family? Giving life to one would more than likely mean taking the life of another.

"'Here I was, ministering to the sick, becoming paralyzed with indecision, my stomach churning, unable to eat, having difficulty sleeping, wracked by pain, with no one to offer me counsel or succor, keeping my pretenses up, being strong for my patients, offering hope to their families. Think of the anticipation of it! They would see me walking down the block, not knowing if this would be the day I would inject new life into their loved one or infect them with the insidious disease of despair. I had trouble concentrating, and even reading was impossible. I'd lie at night sweating and thrashing.

"'Two years ago, in the summer of 1936, my supply of medication from the tall blond doctor was stopped. The pharmacist became suspicious. My ability to practice was compromised. I no longer thought of myself as a doctor. I would still be invited to houses, but it would be for dinner, where the unwritten rule seemed to be not to talk about the patient in the other room. Then, one night, walking home, I noticed a man was following me. I'd stop and turn around and he'd freeze, pretending to look at his wristwatch or observe the stars in Orion's belt. He trailed me for several blocks and then disappeared. Suddenly, I was startled to see him pop out of a bush directly in front of me. I thought this was it. My last moment would be at the hands of a man from the SA at ten o'clock at night, less than a mile from my home.

""""Dr. Goldblum," the man called out in a hoarse whisper, "I am sorry I surprised you, Dr. Goldblum, please, do not be scared. It is I who should be scared, talking to a Jew late at night. Do you remember me, do you know who I am?" He was vaguely familiar and in desperate need of my acknowledgment so I said yes. "I need you to come to my house," he explained. "You are the only person who can help my little girl, so please, come with me to my house, we will go through the park and around the back entrance." I informed him I could not treat his daughter, it was forbidden and dangerous for me, dangerous for him as well. "It is urgent," he ordered, in a tone that had changed from pleading to commanding. I felt I had no choice but to follow him.

"'We walked briskly through the park and on to his house. He motioned for me to go to the back door, and in a minute, it opened slightly, enough to slip through sideways, although it was difficult, there wasn't a light on in the house. "Follow directly behind me," he counseled, "so you won't bump into any furniture." I didn't trust him. I couldn't remember who he was, couldn't identify any markings in the house, and was expecting the worst. He opened a door and told me it led downstairs to the basement and that when the door closed behind me he would turn on a flashlight. "There are no windows in the basement," he informed me. At the bottom of the stairs stood a little girl. She was about six years old. I noticed a scar near her left ear when she turned her head and her hair swirled off her face. I remembered who she was. She'd been walking with her dog and had been sideswiped by a car. Her head had knocked into a metal basket by the side of the road, and she was unconscious when she was brought into the hospital. I could still treat gentiles at that point. I had cleaned the wound, stitched her up, checked to see that there was no other damage, and told her father that she'd be fine.

"'I asked why I was now here in a basement, the little girl looked perfectly healthy to me. "Please, come here," he said, and I saw a body under an old blanket.

"'"I can't take care of your other child," I said, "I'm not allowed to practice medicine anymore. You should take him to the hospital."

"'"It is not a child," he said.

"'I bent down and saw that what I'd thought was a blanket was the fur of a German shepherd. "I'm not a veterinarian," I said. "You should take him to the animal hospital tomorrow morning."

"'"But you said you would take care of me if anything went wrong," the little girl begged. She looked at her father. I looked at her father. She tugged at my sleeve. "But you said you would, you said."

"'Whenever I said good-bye to a child who was discharged, I'd want to make the child feel good about the hospital and about doctors. Invariably, I'd say something like, "Next time you need me, I'll take care of you, but I hope there is no next time!" Evidently, my offhand remark was a commitment to her, and there I was.

"'I examined the dog. He was listless, yet his tail flopped when I was examining him. His gums were discolored and his eyes were glassy. I didn't want to treat him. What if he died? They'd accuse me of murdering their pet. Don't think that this is out of the question. There are those who think that Jews suck the blood of Christian children at Passover.

"'"I suspect that your dog has been poisoned," I told him, "perhaps by eating some medicine, perhaps something else. I cannot treat him, I don't have any equipment, he needs to go to the animal hospital."

"'"You will treat him," the man snapped.

"'I paused to gather my wits. "Only if you have what I need," I countered. I requested some charcoal, a knife, some sugar, and carbonated water. I ground up the charcoal into fine bits and made a slurry with the carbonated water. I added a bit of sugar. I worked the slurry until it became a sweet mud. Then I got on the floor, instructed the father and little girl to comfort the dog, opened his mouth, and massaged the mud slurry into the back of his tongue. Fortunately, for him and for me, he was receptive. For fifteen minutes or so, I fed him the charcoal pie. The three of us stroked his fur for two hours. He slept. It was midnight. The little girl was asleep, her head on her father's lap. We did not speak. Suddenly, the dog started to run in place. A few minutes later, he belched, then threw up. When I patted his face, he picked his head up. Just before dawn, he stretched and we helped him to his feet. "You must leave, quickly," the man said. He left the little girl asleep next to the dog and led me up the stairs and to the back door. He extended his hand. As I extended mine, he put twenty Reichsmarks into it and told me to hurry.

"'Within days, I was receiving calls at night. So-and-so will be in a car outside your home at nine. Take a trolley to this-and-such address and be there by ten. Once, my doorbell rang at midnight and a man walked in holding a cat. I treated them all. Most did well and if others didn't, I wasn't told. I was paid, in cash, an amount that they thought was appropriate. They never said thank you and I never said you're welcome. That's how I became a vet.'"

"You understand, it wasn't official," Old Uncle A said to us. We nodded and he continued.

"While Jacob Goldblum was waiting for Peek to be unloaded in Montreal, the African bird princess made a telephone call. In half an hour, a small truck approached the dock, and a man waved to Auntie Rose. They put Peek in the back with the two small suitcases and drove off. Auntie Rose introduced the veterinarian to the driver, a man named Moses O'Neil. They drove due east all day and at nightfall approached a border crossing to the United States. The veterinarian was scared as his papers indicated he was a German named Dieter Harald Eberhart and he did not have a visa for the United States, only for Montreal, Canada, the port of disembarkation. He showed his papers to Auntie Rose, dread in his eyes. 'Here,' Moses O'Neil said, handing him a document. 'Here's ya passport.' It was a United States passport for Jacob Goldblum, born in Boston, Massachusetts, on the very date that Uncle Jake was actually born, in Germany, or East Prussia, or Austria, or Hungary, or Poland, or that slice of Poland, Galicia, that nobody remembers anymore, or maybe it was in Prague or somewhere in the Pale of Settlement.

"They crossed the border without incident. They stayed in Jackman, Maine, overnight and proceeded to the coast in the morning. Throughout the trip, the veterinarian told them what life had been like in Hamburg before 1933: about sailing on the Binnenalster or the Außenalster, where you could dream of flowing to the North Sea and beyond, about strolling through the Planten un Blomen, a park where you weren't allowed to pick any of the flowers, about wandering around in the new wing of the Hamburger Kunsthalle to see the postimpressionists and Picasso, about doing business in the Rathaus, an official building so big and ornate you thought a king had to live there, about taking visitors to the old buildings of the Krameramtsstuben, seventeenth-century reminders of the Hanseatic League, about being a Germanic Jew, so different from what it was now like as a Jew in Germany.

"When they got to Bar Harbor, Auntie Rose told Uncle Jake that they would stay for a while on an island off the coast of Maine before they went on to Boston. Old Uncle A put them up in the main house. They helped him with the chores, but mostly they talked with the immigrants, whose number had declined by more than half in the thirty-odd years since Sylvia had left. Jacob Goldblum could speak to each one in his or her native language. He told them about what was going on in Germany and what he thought was going to happen. He described the horrors of the lives that the Jews lived, not only in third-person reportage but also in first-person witness. Auntie Rose told them about the African bird princess, Peek, and the accident. Not one of them believed her, she being the daughter of the fabulist Solomon Mischal, yet they all peppered her with questions nonetheless and told her to repeat parts that they especially liked. Jacob Goldblum told them about practicing medicine and becoming a vet and the Night of Broken Glass. Kristallnacht, they said, they all knew about Kristallnacht. They didn't believe a word about Peek, but then again, who could make up such a story?

"Moses O'Neil drove straight through to Boston and delivered Peek to the zoo. Murph Feldman had rooms prepared at HIAS for when Rose Mischal and Jacob Goldblum arrived in Boston. Moses O'Neil and Chief Stinkowski paid a visit to a man they knew at Suffolk Downs and got him to agree that it would be a good idea to hire another vet for the track.

"'We got just the guy, he's Europe's most famous vet, he even knows how to fix ostriches, so horses are child's play to him,' said Moses O'Neil.

"'Here's something for ya troubles,' Chief Stinkowski muttered, stuffing an envelope into the guy's inside coat pocket with one hand and putting his other around the back of the guy's neck.

"Papa thanked Murph Feldman for arranging the passport and the veterinary school diploma; Murph Feldman passed on the appreciation to Mr. Maguire. 'There'll come a time,' he said, 'when I'll call on ya fellars, and ya won't want to disappoint me or Honey Fitz, will ya now?'

"In May of 1939, Auntie Rose and Jacob Goldman took the train from Bar Harbor to Boston. She was three months pregnant, due in November, when they arrived at North Station. She brought with her a marriage certificate that Moses O'Neil had handed to her in Montreal, dated Sunday, November 27, 1938, stamped by the clerk of Suffolk County, city of Boston.

"Auntie Rose could navigate to the accounting office where her brother-in-law worked, could visit her father a few blocks away, and made it to the zoo, where Peek was recuperating from his journeys. She would sit near a big enclosed area with other birds and docile giraffes and zebras. They would talk for hours, oblivious to the stares of the parents who'd instinctively grab a child by the polo shirt or overall straps and pull him or her back, making wide berth around the lady sitting on the ground, talking to the animals.

"Jacob Goldblum took the trolley to Suffolk Downs and inspected the horses. He'd never treated one before, so he'd gone to the public library and those at the medical schools, spending hours learning about the physiology of the horse. To make up for his lack of knowledge, he decided to trade on his foreignness, knowing Americans' predisposition to defer to Old World sensibilities. Because he knew so little, he was quiet and asked his colleagues for their opinions. In this way, he gained their confidence, agreeing, yes, yes, you are exactly correct, while applying his prodigious intellect at night learning about the very issue he had pretended to opine on during the day. Within a year, he was appointed head veterinarian.

"Before the baby was born, the veterinarian brought Auntie Rose to the track to assist him with a particularly difficult problem concerning a three-year-old horse that appeared to be fine physically but would often not eat and frequently had to be scratched. The owner was even thinking about the glue factory in order to get some return on his investment. Auntie Rose told her husband that the horse simply didn't like his stablemate. 'It's a personality conflict,' she said. 'He's depressed with his living arrangements, so if you want him to race, change his stable.' Jacob Goldblum told this to Papa and the boys one night when they were playing pinochle back at the office above the furniture store. Murph Feldman asked the veterinarian when the horse was scheduled to race again. 'I'd like to come up and see a depressed horse,' he said. They all laughed. Jacob Goldblum switched the horse to another stall and invited the gang to the track on the day of the race. The horse came in first.

"A week later, Derby Canurbi visited the doctor turned vet at HIAS. He gave him an envelope, an engagement present, he said. It was enough for Jacob Goldblum and Auntie Rose to start looking for an apartment that would be big enough for them as well as the baby. Mother was a great help to Auntie Rose and took pride in showing off her little sister with the big belly when they took their walks in the park. Auntie Rose would lock arms with Mother, who'd be pushing her stroller with Steven around the neighborhood.

"In September, war broke out in Europe. They all feared the worst. Jacob Goldblum and Auntie Rose took some comfort in their having made it out the year before. They pretended that as long as they didn't read anything specifically bad, there was hope.

"On Tuesday morning, November 7, Auntie Rose's water broke and Mother, Dad, and Jacob Goldblum took her to the hospital. It was a beautiful day, Indian summer, and they were all glowing in the abnormally warm morning sun. The nurses took Auntie Rose in a wheelchair and told the three of them to sit in the waiting room. In a couple of hours, the nurse reappeared and told them that the labor was proceeding normally, Auntie Rose was not in too much pain, and that the baby would be out in an hour or so, not to worry. About an hour later, the doctor came out. 'Rose is fine,' he said, and they were relieved. He paused. They were all silent. His demeanor suddenly changed. He put his hand on the veterinarian's shoulder and said softly, 'I regret to tell you that the baby has died. It was stillborn. A boy. We did all we could do. Rose is unconscious. She doesn't know.' 'I'll go in and wait until she wakes up,' Jacob Goldblum told the others."

We thanked Old Uncle A for telling us this final part of the story of how Uncle Jake came to Boston and retreated to our room.

"I wonder how Auntie Rose must've felt when she woke up after giving birth, only to be told that her baby had died, that she'd never get to hold her son, the way Mother could with you and me," I said, then added, "Maybe that's how *the troubles* started."

"I don't think so," he said. "Dad said he knew all about her oddities when he met her here in Boston, and she was sixteen at the time."

We were silent for a minute or so.

"Well," I started up again, "if Mother and Auntie Rose were out strolling together in September and October, then *both* of them would've been pregnant. Mother would've been out to here." I placed both hands more than a foot from my stomach. "With me," I said. "I was born on November 7."

"I guess it was Old Uncle A's forgetfulness," Steven said, unconvincingly.

"As long as we're asking about stuff, can you please tell me how Old Uncle A is our uncle?"

August 5, 1944
Dear Diary,

Mrs. Napolitano came back to the tailor shop today. It's been 3 months since her son was killed. They still have the black bunting up. They won't take it down until the war is over. She hands us our clothes and we lightly touch her arm. We don't talk. No one does. That's just the way it is.

Mr. and Mrs. Mauer won't speak German anymore in their store. English only. It's an acknowledgment, Jacob says. It's patriotic, my sister says. They're both right.

Jacob spends most afternoons downtown in a tiny office on Devonshire Street translating English into colloquial dialects of German for our troops as they advance from France and Belgium into the western part of Germany. He has a whole section devoted to curses. He reads them to me and acts out how he would say them if he were a GI interrogating a Nazi. This brings him his only happiness outside of the family.

He hears things that don't get into the papers about how the Jews are being gassed. He types notes to his supervisor urging him to bring them to the army air force generals in Washington about bombing the rail lines leading to the camps but never gets a return. He is not sure the notes are ever delivered.

I have trouble eating and ask him not to tell me the things that he hears and especially not to tell Uncle A when he comes down this fall.

I don't ask about his family. He has never spoken about them. I used to wonder if he left a wife behind. Or a child. Especially in November when I'm out of sorts. He loves me and that's enough.

I cannot write any more tonight,
Rose

May 8, 1945
Dear Diary,

The war is over in Europe. Everyone was out celebrating in the streets. It is like New Year's Eve in the twenties. But we haven't left the house. Jacob sits by the radio, switching frantically from CBS to NBC to ABC to Mutual. When I am out of the room, I hear him talking in German to the console. He tells me he will go to his office tomorrow and start writing letters.

They told my sister at HIAS yesterday that she will be needed more than ever. They said to expect thousands of refugees in the next few months. Jacob says they will be let out of the camps only to be killed by the people who live nearby. I dreamt that they arrived in boats at a dock in Palestine, which looked a lot like East Boston.

There is still a war in the Pacific. We hear rumors about an invasion of Japan. There are wreaths on many doors, Gold Star flags in many windows. I shudder when I see them. Ida's brother is at the Chelsea Naval Hospital. He is a marine and was shot on the beach at Iwo Jima. He will be fine although she tells me he may limp. He has never seen his sister's baby. He can't wait! I'm so lucky. I see Steven and Joel every day.

I thought I lost my ration books this morning and got upset. Jacob had moved them when he got up this morning to listen to the radio and my sister had placed a copy of Life on top of them near the radiator. I am angry that I can't control myself. I have all year to plan for the next November yet I can't seem to prevent it. When will this ever end?

My father is still in mourning for the president. He says that when the war is over and there is no more rationing, he will drive to Hyde Park to pay his respects.

Yours,
Rose

May 14, 1948
Dear Diary,

We listened to the ceremony of Israel's independence on the radio, which we stared at as if it were the person speaking. Not one of us moved a muscle for the entire 15 minutes. When it was over, we joined those in Tel Aviv in saying the shehecheyanu. We cried and laughed, sang the Kiddush and drank a sip of wine. I had never had a drink in the morning before. I wish Ima could have been with us today. Every day.

We know that the Arabs will invade. More Jews will die. Why does it have to be this way? At Kol Israel earlier tonight I said a silent prayer for Ida's brother who made aliyah last year. If he weren't married, I think that Jacob would have gone with him.

It is almost 10 years since Kristallnacht. Our escape. It's hard to believe what's happened in so short a period of time. I hope 10 years from now I will be better, Jacob will find his family, Ida's brother will be safe and sound.

The boys looked so handsome. They know many of the prayers. There are times like this that I wish I could say something.

Kol tuv,
Rose

June 26, 1948
Dear Diary,

The Germans are now our friends. We have to save those who live in Berlin or else they will starve. We do this for the German gentiles, Jacob says and adds what did we do for the German Jews? He is going mad with anger and frustration. No word from the Red Cross, the Swiss, or the U.S. government. He writes new letters every day, few reply and those that come do not bring any news. He doesn't say who he is searching for. Them, my people, he tells anyone who asks. Is he hiding a secret I want to know?

I know how secrets live within and eat you inside out. Now I have nightmares. They won't go away. I must carry this burden alone. It hurts so I cry, softly, not stirring my husband, I do not want to waken his ghosts, too. We are perfect for each other.

With hope,
Rose

June 25, 1950
Dear Diary,

Oh God, another war. More death. No news. No more to say.

24.

Everyone was saying that the fix was in

When the paper came each morning, it got divvied up according to a well-established pattern. Steven and I would read the sports section, and we had to make sure we put it back together just as it came, because Dad needed to see the racing results, which were right next to the pages that included the box scores for the baseball games and articles on what happened the day before to all the teams. Mother and Papa read every word of the front page and followed stories when they said to turn to page this-and-such. They also read the editorials, sometimes aloud to each other, even though the other person had already read them.

It seemed as if each October morning was no different from any other with the Braves having finished in seventh place, thirty-two games behind the Brooklyn Dodgers. There was an article about the team; it said that Mr. Perini was negotiating with the mayor of Milwaukee to play in a new stadium, and there was another article about how upset the folks were down in Baltimore because they thought Mr. Perini had promised to move the team there. There was a guy who'd made a scarecrow, dressed it in a suit, stuck a picture of Mr. Perini on its face, and hung the thing from a lamppost in effigy, which I guessed at the time was a part of Baltimore like the North End was a part of Boston. It also said that Mr. Perini needed to have cops guard his house all night long, but it didn't say why. Dad pored through the racing results, circling some in colored pencil, making Xs through others, while Papa buried his head in the main articles on the front page, mostly about the war and the upcoming election.

There was a story about the Seventh Infantry Division of the army, which was dug in along the main line of resistance and was up against the Forty-Fifth Chinese Division on either side of Hill 598, also known as Triangle Hill. There was a speech made by John Foster Dulles, when he received an award from the Theodore Roosevelt Memorial Association in New York City, telling the audience that what the communists feared most was that General Eisenhower would be elected president. An article about Adlai Stevenson quoted him as saying, "I have been thinking that I would make a proposition to my Republican friends . . . that if they will stop telling lies about the Democrats, we will stop telling the truth about them." There was coverage of the daily activities of the congressman and his opponent and the news that the congressman would be speaking that night at Faneuil Hall downtown. There was a picture of some kids getting prepared for Halloween in ghost and goblin costumes.

Papa invited us to go with him to Faneuil Hall that night to hear the congressman. As we approached the building, there were lots of pretty girls handing out buttons that had three initials on them in red, white, and blue and the words "for Senator" outlined in blue. We were still wearing our "I'm a Brave Bostonian" buttons, clinging to them as if this would somehow keep the team in town. We put the new buttons on. Everyone was buzzing about this old tycoon named James Wolf who'd bought a rival to the *Herald Traveler*, the *Chronicle*. It had just endorsed the congressman in his race for the Senate. Everyone was saying that the fix was in. I looked at Steven, not knowing what was broken, but all he did was shrug his shoulders, letting me know that he hadn't a clue, either, as to what this meant. I pretended I had to go to the bathroom but really went off to speak with The Boxer. I told him I knew about the fix, you know, the thing with Mr. Wolf of the *Chronicle*. The Boxer winked and said the old man came through, didn't he. I kind of made an agreeing face even though I didn't know who the old man was. Later that night, Old Uncle A explained that certain folks had some dirt on Mr. Wolf and used it to blackmail Mr. Wolf into making the paper come out for the congressman. But he never told us who the old man was.

"Who do you think it is?" I asked Steven later.

"It can't be Papa," he pronounced definitively. "Maybe the congressman's father is all I can think of."

"What did he mean by dirt?" I asked.

"Girls and stuff, crimes, drinking, cheating, things like that," Steven said. "The old man, whoever he was, must've known about something that Mr. Wolf did, that's called dirt, and he probably threatened to tell the world unless Mr. Wolf got the paper to endorse the congressman."

I wasn't quite sure what dirt was but it sounded real good if you had it on someone else and it seemed to be a real scary thing if someone had it on you. Nevertheless, it sounded a lot like what Murph Feldman did for a living.

Inside Faneuil Hall, the band was playing, old guys were getting up and hugging each other, and all the girls and younger women were at the front, eager to get a close-up look at the handsome congressman. The Boxer got to the microphone, held up his hands, said a couple of good evenings, welcome, glad you could be here. He acknowledged some folks from the audience, who stood up and got applause. Each time, Papa told us who the person was and a little anecdote about him, usually with some reference to Papa knowing him or meeting him or one of the pals doing a favor for the guy. The Boxer introduced Tip, the guy running for the congressman's seat. He made a pretty good speech, but the crowd was antsy, you could tell.

Finally, the congressman was introduced and everybody stood up and cheered. He waved, which caused his jacket, still buttoned, to ride up on his shoulders, making him look like a kid waving to the camera at a bigwigs' party. He talked about the same kinds of things he had at the Badgers Club. He was funny. He smiled a lot. And when one of the girls in the front squealed, he broke into this huge grin and all the other girls swooned. He jabbed his finger into the air a lot, kept moving one hand into his jacket pocket, then removed it, grabbed the lectern with both hands, and then repeated the sequence of gestures. He made a very tender statement about his grandfather, Honey Fitz, the former mayor.

"Growing up, I've been blessed with brothers and sisters who are my best friends, a mother who's strict but whose rules were meant to keep me focused on the worthiest goals, a father who supports and encourages me." He paused, then resumed, "In the two years since my grandfather's death, I've been able to better understand what this man meant to me, by replaying the films of him in my memory, by listening to others who'd been touched by him, and by reading the history of what he did, why he did it, and how he did it.

"My opponent has said that I'm but the shadow of another man," he said, the hall so quiet you could almost hear the waves lapping against the docks two blocks away. "However," he continued, his voice strengthening, "if that shadow is the one cast by the deeds of my grandfather, if that shadow covers the whole mosaic of the American people, then it represents the shadow of light, a light that I hope will shine so brightly that it will cause the denizens of darkness, of the past, of those who hold on to the status quo, to scurry away, where they can't find sustenance, as you will no longer allow them to feed at the public trough."

The speech wasn't supposed to end there and he tried to finish but it was hopeless, the place was in an uproar. Steven and I were jumping up and down, and lots of folks picked up the metal folding chairs and were slamming them together. They belted out his initials in a cadence that reminded me of our cheers at Braves games. He waved, then stepped back and put his arms around Tip and The Boxer. Papa looked at us and said Honey Fitz would've been proud of him.

The papers were reporting election polls; they had replaced the polio counts as the warm weather receded.

Papa said, "The endorsement by the *Chronicle* is helping, and the postcards are also having an important effect. Hundreds of people in the postcard army have made thousands of trips to people's homes."

It was true. Myandrew had told us that a nice man in a double-breasted suit had come to his house to talk with his mother and father. The man adroitly changed the subject from the congressman's support for keeping the Braves in Boston to the importance of having a senator who cared enough that he'd send people like him into houses like theirs to talk about what was on their minds. Myandrew's parents decided to vote for the congressman then and there, despite the fact that the guy spilled coffee on their sofa. His mother said it was all right, you see, we were going to redo it anyway. Myandrew decided to make a double-breasted suit out of the slipcover once his mother had the new one installed.

Noodge Mauer pestered the daylights out of his parents until they relented and agreed to let a member of the postcard army make a visit. Frankie never brought it up, lest his father think that some guy was going to come into his house and tell him what to do, or worse, lest the guy show up when his father wasn't home, which would spell doom for his mother.

Every day, the polls reported a slight increase for the congressman, and as the election drew near, we woke up with anticipation and excitement and raced down the three flights onto the stoop to see the scorecard in the *Herald Traveler* from the day before. We took great pride in seeing the positive effects of the postcards that we'd stolen.

25.

No one here's going to tell us, that's for sure

A few days after the rally for the congressman at Faneuil Hall, we saw Dad writing on a yellow pad early in the morning; the unopened newspaper was on a kitchen chair. Most of the time we saw him adding up numbers and jotting short scribblings, so it was kind of weird to see a couple of pages of handwriting.

When we approached him, he pretended to reach for a cup of coffee or make some other move that would result in him covering up the page so we couldn't see what it was he was doing.

That afternoon, after school, no one was home. There was a note on the yellow pad. It said that they had all gone to the hospital. There were instructions for what to do about dinner and a reminder that children weren't allowed to visit; those were the hospital rules. I took the yellow pad and held the back up to the light. I could make out where there'd been impressions from the earlier writing that Dad had been doing in the kitchen. It was tough to interpret these marks, but eventually I could make out the letters *a-b-i-t*. We played with the letters, wondering if we were missing one, say an *h* that would make *abit* into *habit*, or interpreting the handwriting incorrectly, changing the *i* into a *u*, but nothing seemed to work until Steven glanced at the paper, which was opened to the obituary page.

"The *a* is an *o*, and *obit* is short for *obituaries*," he declared authoritatively. At that very instant, it hit us. Uncle Jake was dying or maybe had already died, and Dad was starting to write an obituary. Steven called Zippo and explained that we needed her to get us in to see Uncle Jake again, this time it was urgent, ASAP.

Zippo met us in the hospital lobby, whispering to follow her and to look like we belonged. She was all set to go into her act with the volunteer who gave out visitors' passes when there was a bit of a commotion in the lobby and the volunteer got up quickly from behind the reception desk to see what was going on. As she passed us, Zippo motioned us to a door that led to the stairs and told us to go, go, go! The three of us took them two at a time.

There was no one outside Uncle Jake's room. We opened the door quickly. There was no one in his bed. I knocked on the door of the bathroom. No answer. I opened it slightly, not wanting to get it slammed into my face. No one was there.

"Maybe it's the wrong room," I said.

Zippo rolled her eyes to the tag on the bed. It read: "Dr. Jacob Goldblum, no restraints needed."

"Is he already dead?" Steven wondered.

"Maybe they're in the cafeteria or something," I said hopefully.

"Something's strange," Zippo said. "His slippers are here. Why would he leave his room without his slippers? It doesn't make sense."

We raced down to the ground floor. Now there were many more people in the lobby, everyone was running around, there was a cop talking to a doctor. Zippo went up to the volunteer lady, who was back at the desk. She told Zippo that there'd been a problem, an accident really, well, perhaps not an accident, she wasn't sure, it was awful.

We sidled over to the other side of the lobby and jostled through the crowd. We saw a group of doctors tending to a man on a stretcher. A good place to get sick, I thought. The cop told all of us to give the doctors more room. When the crowd drew back, I saw Auntie Rose and then noticed that the man on the stretcher had no shoes on. I bolted toward her and did a hook slide around the cop as he started to make a move toward me. I caught the outside of my left sneaker on the floor and the momentum pushed me into a standing position right in front of her, in time for her arms to close around me in a move that if we'd practiced all week we could never have pulled off again. She held me so tightly that I couldn't turn my head to see Uncle Jake, which was just as well, because Steven told me later there was a lot of blood and Zippo added that he was banged up. The cop backed off when he saw I must be a family member; then I spotted Mother, Dad, and Papa. They never said a thing about our being at the hospital. We never got Mother's "You Don't Listen To Me, I Don't Know What To Do With You" speech.

It was hard for me to believe. Uncle Jake was dead. I had glanced at him for a few seconds only. Dad told me later that it was best. "You want to remember what he looked like when he was taking you for rides or out back when he was watching you play ball or at his house when he was reading his mail." He was right.

What hurt, ached actually, was the knowledge that I wasn't going to see him anymore. What troubled me then was *my* loss; what troubled me as I got older was my selfishness at not recognizing Auntie Rose's loss.

Right before the funeral, we got little black ribbons that were cut almost in two and had them pinned to our lapels on our hand-me-down jackets, mine from Steven and Steven's from Dad. We sat in the front row. Dad went up to the bima and took out a sheet of yellow lined paper, unfolded it, and read. He told us about how Uncle Jake arrived in America, and I must tell you, I was a little bit expecting a new twist on things, having heard one story from Old Uncle A and another from Uncle Jake himself. Dad pretty much stuck to the script that Uncle Jake had told us in the hospital. There was no mention of Peek the ostrich, the circus accident, how he became a veterinarian, looking out the window of the hospital with Auntie Rose during Kristallnacht, the boat trip to Montreal, getting across the border with help from Moses O'Neil, spending time on Palus Island, coming to Boston for the first time with a marriage certificate that said he'd been married in Boston, comforting Auntie Rose when she gave birth to the stillborn.

"Jake mastered English like Shakespeare," Dad said, "and he was the best damn vet at the racetrack. He took special pleasure driving the boys on his trips to minister to sick animals, singing 'Bei Mir Bist Du Schön,' whereupon Dad belted out the first few lines as if he were one of the Andrews Sisters, which gave rise to a release that I later understood was a critical and necessary result of a good funeral speech, for it gave a legitimacy to a cry that could be masked behind a full-throated laugh.

Auntie Rose had her head on the sleeve of Mother's dress for most of the funeral, where it left a tearstain so deep we could still see it at the end of the shiva. Occasionally, Auntie Rose would make quick, successive nods, probably in response to Mother's questions, are you okay, do you need anything, that kind of thing. After the service, she walked steadily behind her husband's casket, frequently appearing to shiver despite the unseasonably warm temperature. Dad helped her with the shovel at the cemetery, but she didn't need any assistance when she picked up a rock and put it on the family headstone. On the way home, in the Cadillac Murph Feldman arranged for us, Mother took the lead, telling anecdotes about Uncle Jake that got us to reflexively build on them and laugh. As composed as Auntie Rose was in the car, her grief was profound. I could sense that by the way she wrapped her hands around her elbows; she was unconsciously trying to emulate the hugs that Uncle Jake would give her each night when he came home from the animal clinic at the track. She added a bit to Mother's stories, as if to ease *our* pain and to make her presence less intrusive. I noted that her verbs were all present tense.

"Didn't you think it was funny that Dad didn't mention anything about polio?" I mentioned to Steven later.

"Or how he died," Steven agreed.

We told each other that we'd ask Mother or Dad later, but just as we hadn't searched for BlueDog's owners, we never brought it up. Part of it was that we were so grief-stricken that he'd died and so frightened from having seen him dead at the hospital that we simply didn't want to talk about it.

"Let sleeping dogs lie," I whispered to BlueDog when we were alone later that night out back, after the shiva.

Isaac Burgas brought over platters of cold cuts, Mr. Lee's son delivered noodles galore, there was smoked salmon, sturgeon, whitefish, and trouties from the fish market on Harvard Street near Coolidge Corner in Brookline, and Rocky and Big Alfredo made sure there were lots of cannoli, tartufo, and biscotti, which everyone was dunking into the gallons of coffee that Mother was pouring in the kitchen.

When the doorbell rang, I went down and retrieved the yellow envelopes, then raced upstairs and read telegraphed condolences from the old people who lived on Palus Island who were too frail to make the trip, and from the congressman, who sent his best to a family that had lost an immigrant who'd had the misfortune to have lived through the worst and then had the fortune to have died with the best. I couldn't figure out what was fortunate about dying but what did I know?

Zippo was there, which made Steven glad, and Noodge Mauer arrived pushing Susie in a wheelchair. Myandrew was in a black suit, black belt, black shirt, black tie, and black shoes. Sal the barber wanted to know who the little goombah was. Frankie could only stay for a while, as his father had told him that he'd heard of gentile kids never having been seen after they went to a Jew ritual, so he was waiting outside in the car and would come in with a tire iron if Frankie wasn't out in fifteen minutes. Papa's pals stayed for the entire afternoon and night. Derby Canurbi could be heard in the bathroom with the cord from the phone in the hall preventing the door from being closed completely, allowing us to hear him talking about spreads and over-under and vigorish and push and laying off, things that might've been double entendres for all we knew. Anyway, it was something we needed to talk to Dad about, probably at breakfast the next day. Chief Stinkowski planted himself next to Auntie Rose. Initially, Mother was anxious about this, but as the evening wore on, she said it was a relief, as his presence made folks avoid lingering and making small talk, which might have upset Auntie Rose. It seemed as if everyone we knew was there.

Murph Feldman came into our room, where we had gathered with our friends. He'd navigated through a couple of glasses of wine and needed to explore a different ocean for a while. Everyone knew he was the guy that Steven and I had worked for delivering envelopes all over town. He told us that he knew Uncle Jake from the very minute he came to Boston in 1939, saw him frequently at the track, and thought of him as a son. He told us a funny story about Uncle Jake at Suffolk Downs officiating at the marriage of a couple of the horses. He'd put up a canvas tent as a *chuppah*. Murph Feldman let each of us taste the wine and swear we wouldn't tell. He wanted to know a little about all the kids, and with the lubrication brought on by the wine, they all opened up, especially Noodge Mauer, who proceeded to pester him with questions about the furniture business, the track, Uncle Jake, and Chief Stinkowski and, after he got the answers, ask again a little bit differently. Murph Feldman asked Zippo about being a candy striper, and he wanted to know about Frankie, who left after exactly fifteen minutes. He asked Susie about her polio and she talked for ten minutes straight. After she finished, we were all quiet, and I wondered if this would be the opportunity for Murph Feldman to get up, stretch, say some nice things to us, tousle my hair, speak a little Irish, and rejoin the adults in the living room. Instead, he said to Susie, "Kiddo, despite the epidemic hereabout, ya the first person I've ever really talked to who had polio."

I gave a look to Steven that transmitted the message we'd hear from Mother when she'd see some guys stagger out of a bar and say, "THEY'RE FOUR SHEETS TO THE WIND, BOYS, AND THAT'S NOT A SAILING TERM."

"You mean except for Dr. Goldblum," Zippo said.

"Jake had polio?" he asked. "Poor guy, with all his demons, polio too, oy gevalt."

"What do you mean, Mr. Feldman," she pushed ahead, "'with all his demons'?"

"Uncle Jake had polio," I stated. "You saw him, in the wheelchair."

"And at the hospital," Steven added.

"The hospital?" Murph Feldman questioned. "The hospital, did ya say, kiddo? Did ya ever visit him at the hospital, I'm sure ya did, you're his nephew and a good boy, of course ya did. Tell me, was there an iron lung in that hospital room? Was there?" He looked around the room at both of us. "No, of course not. Did ya ever hear of him getting fitted for braces so he could learn to walk?" He turned to Susie. "Lassie, do ya know what I'm talking about?"

"Yes, sir." She practically saluted.

"Well if he didn't have polio, Mr. Feldman, what did he have?" Zippo asked.

"And what did he die of?" Susie wanted to know.

Murph Feldman looked hard at Steven and me, realizing for the first time that we didn't really know, that we'd been told he had polio and never thought otherwise. He said nothing for a few seconds and then pointed his right finger toward his right ear in a circular motion, something I knew was a symbol for tetched, loco, crazy, a motion I'd done behind Noodge Mauer's back many times.

Noodge Mauer wanted to know what he meant by crazy, how did he know Dr. Goldblum was crazy, what did crazy people do, and on and on, he was driving us all nuts. Myandrew wanted to know if crazy was a disease. Susie said she had physical therapy a couple of times a week and was told she might be able to walk with a cane soon. Zippo kept saying he was right, there was never any stuff in the room that polio patients had. How could you die of being crazy? we all wanted to know.

I noted to Steven, "Remember I told you I saw his leg move."

"I saw it too," Steven said softly, trying to piece all of this together.

"Susie, show us how you can move your leg," I said.

While we were yakety-yakking, Murph Feldman saw this as the perfect time to exit. "I said too much to yas," he said and was gone.

When everyone left and the whole family had gone to their rooms, we went out to the living room, where Dad had fallen asleep on the sofa. He was snoring. We woke him up. He was a little disoriented. He called me Jake and then corrected himself.

"What's up, boys, besides me?" he said wearily.

"Tell us about Uncle Jake," Steven pleaded.

"Old Uncle A did, boys, don't you remember?"

"Tell us the truth," I pressed.

"The truth, boys, is what he told you, with an allowance here and there. What he told you, about Germany, and coming to America, that, boys, was the truth."

"He didn't have polio," Steven blurted out, too loudly.

"Murph Feldman said he was crazy, nuts, and he didn't have polio," I said, backing up my brother.

"Even if he is, was, loco, how do you die of that?" Steven inquired.

We asked him to tell us what he had, what he died of, why they told us he had polio, and why they kept all this from us.

"We're not leaving until you tell us," I said defiantly.

We plopped down on the rug, a sign that we weren't going anywhere. BlueDog had followed us and had his head in my lap.

I wondered if Dad had ever prepared for this moment. He started slowly, building momentum like a train pulling out of the station, reaching full throttle within a few sentences, as if pulling the burden of truth wasn't as heavy a load as a made-up story. "It's all true, all true about Uncle Jake in Germany during the 1930s. I'm not so sure exactly where Jake had been born, the countries kept changing boundaries and it doesn't matter to the story. He'd been an outstanding student in medical school and a very promising physician. He was well-liked by gentile and Jew alike. The part you were told about being forced out of medicine and learning to be a veterinarian? All true. The part about what it was like to be a Jew in Germany in the thirties? All true. The part about being in the hospital the night that Auntie Rose was brought in, having been injured from her fall off of Peek's back? True. The part about being in the hospital during Kristallnacht and watching the fires burning and the Nazis marauding through the streets and listening to the sounds of the sticks cracking on the heads of Jews and the shop glass windows bursting from the stones and the pressure of the fires? Yes, yes, yes, true. And the trip to Canada on the boat, being met by Moses O'Neil, getting across the border, again all true. Perhaps an exaggeration here and there, maybe a bit of hyperbole, yes.

"Boys," he continued, alternately locking eyes with each of us, "you can only imagine what it was like. You can hear me tell you, you can read it in books, you can listen to the survivors; they even have recordings of the SS and the SA telling people that they were only following orders, *we didn't know*. You can gather all this in but unless you lived it, lived through it, you really can't understand it. That's true as well.

"Some people," he went on, "some folks have put it out of their minds, just like they did when they went to the hospital, right here in Boston, and had the tattoos, the numbers they'd been given to identify them in the camps, removed from their forearms, blotted out, so you can't see them anymore. Others changed their names, they wanted a new start in life, so Cohen became Cronin, Weiskopf became Whitehead, Schwartz became Black, Kohn became Kent. Others said God had abandoned them, there is no God, and became atheists or agnostics or Ethical Culturists. And some, some of them came through it without any physical scars. Like your Uncle Jake. No tattoos, no scars from being struck on the head, that's true, no time in the camps, none.

"'You're lucky,' people would say to Uncle Jake and others like him. 'You got out, you came to America, you became a vet, you married, you have much to be thankful for,' they said, especially at Thanksgiving. Saying 'you have much to be thankful for' had as much meaning to Uncle Jake as someone saying 'have a nice day.'

"Do you boys know what depression, anxiety, and insomnia mean?"

We nodded because we'd heard the words, yet they would take on real meaning only as we got older.

Dad went on, "Do you know what it means to feel tired when you haven't exercised, worried when you can't control an outcome, awake when your body craves rest? Do you know about weights that're so heavy they crush you yet no one else can even see them? Can you imagine what it must be like to be nervous about something as routine as driving a car, when bam, you hear a honk in your ear or, worse, a backfire from a truck that has you jump out of your seat, sweat oozing from every pore, wondering if you can control the car at all? Have you ever heard that being tired and being unable to sleep are two different things and that more often than not, you're awake all night, that's when the tigers come, and you finally get some shut-eye at dawn, just when you've got to get up and are anxious that you'll be driving soon and fearful that the weight can fall on you again?

"No, Uncle Jake didn't have polio," he confirmed. "It was just easier to tell you boys that he did. You saw that your uncle's leg bothered him. It ached, you saw how he shuffled along, and it got noticeably worse when you were in Maine in the spring. He was the doctor so we didn't bombard him with too many questions. It was likely a knee or a hamstring, you know, that steel-like rod that you can feel on the backside of your thigh." Instinctively, Steven and I both felt our hamstrings. "When he'd grimace, we'd inquire and he'd shrug it off, mumbling something about getting older, trying his best to minimize it. He fumbled with a cane, but it didn't help much, he couldn't get his balance. It was his idea to get a wheelchair and, well, once in it, he decided that it'd be best if we were to tell you that he had polio, you know, with it going around, it wasn't that unusual. And no one who knew Jake was surprised by seeing him in it, after years of observing a progressive decline in his walking."

It was the perfect alibi.

"Okay, I understand, but Dad, what did he die of?" Steven asked.

Dad hesitated, took in a breath as if to give himself an extra boost, and said, "Boys, this may be hard for you to comprehend: he died from despair, his inability to come to terms with what had happened to six million others, his helplessness to rid himself of the guilt of surviving."

He stopped to assess the impact of what he'd just told us. We neither said anything nor moved a muscle so he continued after a few beats.

"Oh, there were times when he experienced happiness, don't get me wrong. His love and affection for Auntie Rose was genuine. Being a vet at the track allowed him to practice medicine without the necessity of interacting with difficult patients. He got a kick out of the hushed calls to Derby Canurbi, giving the inside scoop, and it also gave him the satisfaction of paying something back to Papa and the family. And, of course, you two"—he looked straight at Steven and me—"you boys were his pride and joy, make no mistake about it.

"No, he didn't die from polio. He died from Kristallnacht."

"What?" Steven blurted out.

"Yeah, but he wasn't harmed, and he got out too," I interjected quickly, not really understanding how someone could die of something when he wasn't even injured by it. Dad was silent but we could tell this was a prelude to more explanation, so we waited until he was ready to go on.

"When you read the sports section after knowing that the Braves won," he continued, "you make a beeline for the box score, don't you? You want to know how it happened, what went on, even though you know the end result."

We nodded in agreement.

"It's the same with death, boys, the very same thing. You read an obituary, the first thing you look for is how the person died. What does it matter? The truth is, it doesn't, but you do it anyway. You may read that the guy suffered a heart attack but you need to know more so you keep reading, and lo and behold you find out that he had cancer, had it for years so the heart finally gave out and they wrote that down on the death certificate, but you know he died from the cancer, from years of his body running down. Do you see what I mean?" he asked hopefully.

"I think so," Steven said. "It all *started* with Kristallnacht."

Dad nodded affirmatively. "Fourteen years, all that time smoldering, burning up inside, until the fire—the War, the deaths, the loss of his family—it finally consumed him."

We sat there for a full minute or so, no one talking, letting it all sink in. We thanked him, kissed him good night, and went back to our room. We didn't say very much for a long while. I thought Steven was asleep. Then he leaned over his rail and said to me, "Hey Joel, I get it about him being sad and all . . . so then what'd he really die of? Dad actually didn't tell us. How do you die of despair? And he wasn't in his room, he was there on the floor of the hospital with no shoes on."

"No one here's going to tell us, that's for sure," I answered back.

We fell asleep.

You could see from the minute we awoke the next morning that things had changed.

Auntie Rose was on a mission not to talk about her husband too much or she'd cry her eyes out, so she spent time in her kitchen baking desserts for us. Mother was on a mission to be as normal as possible: "It's Not That We Want To Forget Him But We Have To Keep On Going." Dad was on a mission to avoid Steven and me, lest he be cornered again and not know how to get out of answering more questions.

As we raced out the door that morning to get the school bus, we couldn't help but notice that the newspaper was opened to the obituary page and that there was an announcement about Uncle Jake; it contained some of what we knew of his life story but it didn't say how he died.

26.

Grown men
danced together
doing reels
and jigs

On election day, we biked to Papa's office where there was a flurry of activity: guys were coming in from all over, both phones were being used all the time, and we were put to work on the mimeograph machine. Murph Feldman told us to run off a couple of hundred copies of a flyer about the congressman that we would tack up on phone poles when we were coming and going. In addition to his bets on the horses and the dogs and the date of the Braves moving, we overheard Derby Canurbi taking bets on the election, so that he was in a position to win no matter who won. We saw the guy named Mr. Maguire, Papa's pal who'd worked for Honey Fitz; they squeezed each other's forearms, some kind of secret handshake, Steven and I thought, which we practiced and then waited for a time to use. They mentioned Mr. Wolf, the guy who owned the *Chronicle*, whereupon Moses O'Neil interjected something about a fox in a chicken coop and they all laughed.

At the election night party at the Copley Plaza, we got to sit at the table with Papa and his pals. Papa said it was time for someone whose family was not anointed to get elected. Steven and I had gotten a whiff of what Papa meant when The Boxer closed the evening at the Badgers Club by leading the group in the famous ditty:

I come from good old Boston,
The home of the bean and the cod;
Where the Cabots speak only to Lowells,
And the Lowells speak only to God!

It wasn't lost on us that the congressman's opponent was a Cabot, someone Papa thought was no different from presidents he didn't like, including Taft, Harding, Coolidge, and Hoover. Papa could wax on about Wilson, Roosevelt, and Truman, the only president I was really aware of. "Give 'em hell, Harry," was another thing Steven and I would say to each other after we'd met someone named Harry, when we were alone, just the way we'd shake hands when we were imitating The Boxer.

There were boards of names and numbers all over a temporary stage. Murph Feldman was sneaking dollops of champagne into our glasses. As the early returns came in, it was clear that Tip was going to win the congressman's seat and that General Eisenhower was winning in a landslide. It was nip and tuck for the congressman in his race to become only the third Democrat in Massachusetts history to be elected to the Senate. Around eleven o'clock, the radio carried the news that his opponent had conceded, and the place went into pandemonium. Paper horns like the ones you blow into on New Year's Eve appeared and everyone tried his hand at being Louis Armstrong. Grown men danced together doing reels and jigs. The Boxer sang "Sweet Adeline," and a lot of the older guys joined in, some with tears in their eyes. One after another, people went to the microphone and thanked everyone for helping with the victories. Mr. Maguire made everyone at our table stand up for a bow, and Murph Feldman motioned for Steven and me to get up as well.

A little before midnight, the congressman showed up. Everyone stood and applauded for five minutes, nonstop. The young women from the campaign were screaming and squealing, inching closer to him as he idled up to the podium. Right before he started his speech, Papa said it was time to go home. We waved good-bye to the pals and made our way to the car. Papa was silent. We were babbling away. When we got home, we bolted through the landing to tell Old Uncle A about the congressman and the victory celebration. We were so excited we didn't notice that Papa wasn't with us. We went back looking for him. He'd stayed down at the street and was staring at the front door. He was silent and wouldn't respond to our entreaties to come upstairs. In the apartment, we asked Dad if he knew what was wrong.

"Isn't Papa happy the congressman won and Tip did too?" I asked.

"Was he so upset that Adlai lost badly?" Steven wanted to know.

Dad listened to us and said, "Boys, your grandfather is very happy for the congressman and for Tip, and I'm sure he's feeling bad on account of General Eisenhower's win. But that's not why he's sad. You see, tonight is the thirtieth anniversary of your Nana's death. She died on election night, 1922."

27.

He was a hero, a real hero, and undoubtedly saved all of our lives

When you're a kid, you have no reason not to believe everything they tell you or, for that matter, everything you see or hear. Cynicism is an acquired taste, no different from broccoli rabe or chenille or op art. I had no reason not to believe at first that Uncle Jake came to Boston by himself, since that news originated with my beloved uncle personally. And why would I question the accounts of Papa at the turn of the century, especially since I had witnessed some unusual goings-on fifty years later? Stories of Auntie Rose in the circus were believable, after all, I'd seen her at the zoo with an ostrich. You have to admit, too, that almost anything was possible from the likes of Derby Canurbi, Chief Stinkowski, Moses O'Neil, and Murph Feldman, having had firsthand knowledge of shenanigans that would be grist for any mill that subsisted on the public's right to know. There does come a time, however, when it becomes too much for a kid to swallow everything whole, and you find yourself on the part of the curve where you're more comfortable looking to the frightening uncertainty of the future than you are to refighting the wars of the past in such a way as to try to position yourself to win.

It's the moment you realize that you're becoming an adult, for better or worse. Although I wouldn't have used the phrase back then, I knew this was an inflection point for me.

In the days after the election, the preternaturally warm temperature that enabled us to wear T-shirts was abruptly replaced by a dank atmosphere that hid the upper floors of the John Hancock Building as well as the tops of our heads, now covered by woolen caps knitted by Mother. Frost calcified the pumpkins that normally started to rot, and black ice made our Tuesday and Thursday routes increasingly hazardous. In addition, with the shortening of the days, Mother insisted that we come home when there was still some light, which exacerbated our problems because we now had to pedal on a slippery surface and God knows Mother would've had a conniption if I ended up at Hebrew school with my arm in a sling and unable to hold the Torah. Somehow, she would've felt that I'd been diminished, but I wondered if that'd be in her eyes or God's. After suffering for a few days under these conditions, we told Murph Feldman that we couldn't help him anymore. He understood. He insisted that we come back in the spring and that he'd give us a raise.

Steven had extra time for Zippo, and I spent more time with Susie. Noodge Mauer had to know, we figured, but he never pestered me with questions, and his parents were so busy at the store that most of the time they never knew I was upstairs. I brought my stamp collection over and told her all about plate blocks, first day covers, sheets, and strips, and she taught me how to play hearts, which was fun, and then canasta, which I thought was for old ladies, and then bridge, which was only for kids who couldn't play sports, so I made her promise that she wouldn't tell anyone.

Steven and Zippo would rendezvous at the hospital, where she'd find a storage room or a seldom-used staircase. He no longer kept a scorecard, but I had a pretty good idea of the outcome of the game.

We got a postcard from Morone that ended with "See ya," so we wrote him back, "See ya soon." Rocky delivered coal and told us that he and Big Alfredo were getting everything ready for a big Christmas homecoming for Little Alfredo. His promise to invite us to the party had us dreaming of Italian pastries. We figured that Morone was going to get a pass and be able to make the Christmas party too.

A week after the election, on Armistice Day, Papa got a phone call from Isaac Burgas, the butcher. He told him it was very important, could he come right over to our house. Usually, Isaac Burgas was ebullient, but when he walked through the door, his facial creases seemed more pronounced, as if the valleys had been eroded by a storm surge of tears. With the faint smell of the slaughterhouse, BlueDog materialized and sniffed at his feet and legs, settling in front of him. Isaac Burgas absentmindedly patted him as he spoke. He'd received a call from his son, Daniel, the doctor, who was in Korea, that afternoon at four. It was six in the morning where Daniel was calling from, in Seoul. He told his father that he had just come back from treating soldiers at the front and that he had some news about a young marine from Boston, Alfredo Morone, who died a hero. Daniel had remembered that his father had told him the story of this marine and his cousin, and he wanted him to know that he had died. The doctor said that he wanted to tell him right away and that he'd write everything he knew down in a letter he'd compose that night.

At the very moment that Isaac Burgas was in our living room, Sergeant Wilson and another marine were marching up the front walk of Big Alfredo's house in the North End. They were both wearing their dress blue class A uniforms, and the other marine was carrying a US flag, folded up. When Big Alfredo opened the door, he knew instantly why they were there.

Steven and I had never been inside a church before. It had a lot of stained glass and statues of Jesus and members of his family, I guessed, figurines all over the place. Up front, there was a marine honor guard, and the family sat in the first row, Morone included, having received a forty-eight-hour pass. The priest said Little Alfredo was in a better place now, which caused me to give Steven a *who's he kidding* look, what with Little Alfredo in a casket up front and soon to be buried in a cemetery. We went back to Big Alfredo's house, which was so crowded that not everyone could fit inside. There was a flow from the front yard through the house out the back and around to the front again, people paying their respects to the family, chatting softly with friends, and eating plates of food from the neighbors and the local restaurants.

Isaac Burgas brought the letter he'd received the day before from his son, and he waited until the crowd thinned out so he could give it to Big Alfredo in a quiet moment. Rocky and Morone invited Papa, Murph Feldman, and Isaac Burgas to come next door to his house, where his brother could read in peace, and Papa nodded in assent when our eyes asked if we could tag along. We sat in Rocky's living room. Isaac Burgas handed the letter to Big Alfredo, who fumbled getting it out of the envelope and then couldn't read it out loud. My bet was with his heavy tears, he couldn't distinguish one letter of the alphabet from another. Rocky took it from his brother, gave it to the butcher, and asked him to read it.

Here in the hospital in Seoul, shock and infections are our worst worries, we lose the most men from that. We're on for twenty-four hours or more at a time, the wounded come in at all hours of the day and while you're supposed to triage, how do you make a decision to stop working on some guy with a bullet that hit a major vein in favor of a guy coughing up blood from shrapnel that punctured his lung?

I can tell you that nothing has prepared us for what we're up against here. You rotate through a six-week period in the trauma unit in the States and you think you've seen it all. Let me tell you, that's kindergarten, Dad. You pray for those nights when it's the equivalent of a car accident or a knife stabbing or someone having difficulty breathing or a kid with a hundred and three. By the end of a couple of hours out here, my smock looks like yours, all bloodstained, coupled with pus and vomit. And instead of dealing with a chicken or lamb, I'm working over some guy who could be a neighbor or friend or relative and is usually nineteen or twenty or occasionally some NCO who's still only thirty or so. They're filthy, having been without a shower or a change of clothes for a week or more, and they're skinny, what with the C rations they've been eating. They shake from the cold, from the wounds, from the fear. And, if you can believe this, these guys are the lucky ones. They've made it from the front to a hospital and they're still alive.

In the hospital, I could only imagine what it was like in the field, vulnerable to enemy fire, especially at night, in the cold, without proper conditions, without all the equipment, with the sounds of the fight, the wheels of the trucks, the whoosh of the canons, and the cracks of the sonic booms, combining to sound like a war opera—where you know the overture but have no idea when the fat lady is going to sing.

Despite the fact that Isaac Burgas hadn't read a word yet about Little Alfredo, no one said a thing and no one motioned for him to hurry and get to the part about how Morone's cousin had died.

A month ago, I was rotated out to a field unit. We headed west into the hills. Within twenty-four hours, I could tell why the guys came in cold, dirty, and hungry. It's hard to imagine being trapped in proximity of savagery and fear when life goes on relatively normally in a city thirty miles away.

The locals have learned the insignias of the medics and the doctors and sought us out at all hours of the day and night. This presented us with an acute moral dilemma. To treat a refugee with the medication that would run out when we needed it for a GI was a predicament none of us wanted to face, yet how could we deprive such needy people of our capabilities?

Steven silently mouthed the word *schicksalsfrage* to me and I nodded.

We could have used double or triple the supplies, not to mention the number of medical personnel, and we still wouldn't have made that much of a difference.

The conditions we work under are appalling. How do you get things sterile in the field? Imagine opening someone up in a tent where the flaps are blowing, smoke is coming in from outside, diesel fumes are everywhere, and we're wearing yesterday's bloodied clothes. And who isn't sneezing and coughing, who isn't bringing up phlegm from his toes? And how are we supposed to hold our instruments steady when our bodies are shaking from the cold, our hands have no feeling, snot is dripping from our noses onto our patients, and our intestines are wracked with pain from the combination of C rations, impure water, and the proliferation of pathogenic bacteria?

One day last week, it was my turn to go for a stroll—that's what they say when a doc is called on to accompany a patrol up on the main line of resistance. The theory is simple: most of the wounded on late-night patrols have been hurt by light arms fire, snipers usually, and the blowback from when somebody kicks a trip wire, detonating a land mine. If we can patch these guys up faster, they can resume their places, and fewer reinforcements will be needed. The patrols are made up of six to eight soldiers or marines. None carries more than a rifle, a handgun, and some grenades. Their job is to probe the enemy lines, to find out where the land mines are, to determine if the line is vulnerable, to silence the snipers, and to intercept the PROK and CCF forces that are doing the exact same things to our lines. We all envisage the same thing, going up to the crest of a ridge and coming face-to-face with an enemy patrol coming up the other side. Or worse, going up and opening fire on a patrol coming up the crest from the opposite direction only to find out it's one of ours. We aren't allowed to use our radios as this would tip off the enemy, but it also prevents close coordination with our allies.

I was with a group of marines, there were seven of them. We were to probe up a ridge from which the snipers had been picking off our guys, and to do it quietly. I wrapped all of the equipment that could cause noise, such as splints, syringes, and IV lines in bandages and blankets, and the others made sure that canteens and shovels and other things that could bang metal were left at camp. There was little moonlight, which made it difficult for us to see as we reached upwards to steady ourselves by grabbing onto a crag in the rocks or a branch that would jut out into the path. At each ledge, we'd gather together and try to figure out where we were in relation to a map that we'd look at with a small flashlight, standing around it to make sure the light wasn't visible to anyone else. We argued a bit, quietly, differing as to where we were. I was more consumed with trying to figure out how we'd get back. I wanted to make some trail markers but knew this would be rejected as providing a route for the other side to find us.

What with the bitter cold and being in an unfamiliar place and having to concentrate on getting one foot in front of the other and not falling off the ridge, there was no time to even think about the enemy. No one was thinking about getting shot or shooting, for that matter. So when it all started, it was as if it were a surprise. A trip wire set off a flare, and for the instant that it went up before it unfolded, it was just a hiss and a poof. As the light descended on us, the bullets screamed so loudly that we couldn't tell if someone had been hit. We dropped to the ground and rolled over the edge of the cliff. There was enough for us to hold on to, crouched below the sightline. We were under cover so no one was firing, waiting to see where they were coming from and not wanting to waste bullets or lives. Whether it was a sniper, a patrol, or the first wave of an attack, I couldn't tell. Suddenly, there were a couple of loud explosions above the ridge, and the machine-gun fire from the spot in the front stopped immediately. One of our guys had lobbed a couple of grenades and scored a direct hit.

The noncom motioned us to follow him as he made his way down the slope. We were all right until the angle of descent approached forty degrees, and we were faced with a direct drop to the bottom, perhaps seventy or eighty feet straight down. It was at this point that I saw the transformation of an ordinary guy into someone with remarkable insight, stamina, and leadership. Without saying a word, one grunt leaped from the ridge to a branch of a tree and caught it squarely, where missing it would have meant a major trauma or even death. He moved along the branch like he was at basic, one hand over the other, until he reached the trunk. Without hesitating, he climbed the tree nimbly and quietly, apelike, to a place about fifteen or twenty feet above the ridge where he could have a vantage point over both the enemy and our position. He splayed his fingers wide and flashed them twice, indicating that there were ten of them, and he indicated the direction that they were crawling on the ridge. He motioned the marines to circle back and they did, making their way to a position near the ridge behind the enemy. We could see the marine in the tree following the movement of the enemy. He held his left hand out so we could see it, and it had three fingers, then two, then one, then none, and with the none, he opened up and caught them completely off guard, as they had approached the ridge anticipating that any fire would come from below and in front. Simultaneously, the marines lobbed grenades and then began firing from the ledge behind them. The firefight lasted a few minutes, maybe twice as long as was necessary, but you can't stop the adrenaline and you can't take a chance by not continuing to fire, so you keep on doing it until you realize that the shaking that you're feeling is from your buddy's hand wracking your shoulder while screaming in your ear, which you didn't hear.

After they stopped, there was silence for a couple of minutes and the noncom motioned all clear. At that point, I heard the moaning and turned to see one of our marines with blood coming out of his uniform near his shoulder. His rifle had been shattered and the bullet must've ricocheted off and hit him in the soft tissue of his arm. I found the bullet easily, pressed against the wound with one hand, and checked the rest of his body, not finding anything else of concern. The marine was conscious and told me he was okay. They held the flashlight and I passed a small 4x magnifying mirror that I'd picked up from a dentist in Seoul over the wound to make a closer inspection in order to see any residual particles of lead, then finished cleaning the wound as best I could. I shot him up with penicillin. We hoisted him onto the shoulders of two of the guys and told the wounded marine to keep the pressure on the bandage with his other hand.

We started back, the noncom leading, then the two marines holding the wounded man and two other marines in the rear, practically walking backward. There were six marines, one was missing. The kid in the tree. I went back to the ridge to give the kid an assist but didn't see him. There was no noise, no sound of boots digging in, no huffing and puffing coming up the hill. The others had fallen in behind me. Then it seemed as if we all looked into the tree at the same time and saw him slumped over a branch, lifeless. It took a major effort for two of us to climb the tree and to lower his body down and then to carry him back up to the top of the ridge to start the trip back.

We got to the base without incident. The kid with the shoulder wound lost a considerable amount of blood but was transfused and will make it. I had paperwork to fill out and checked the dead marine's dog tag. It said Alfredo Morone. They told me he was from Boston. I put two and two together and called you as soon as I got back to Seoul. You can tell them that he was a hero, a real hero, and undoubtedly saved all of our lives.

At this point Isaac Burgas stopped reading, leaving one more paragraph unread, something he'd get to later, then stood up and hugged Big Alfredo, softly whispering "Hero" into his ear. One by one we hugged Big Alfredo, Rocky, and Morone. As we walked through the door to go back to Big Alfredo's house, I could hear Murph Feldman whispering to Papa. Something about Morone. Papa responded by saying something like, "Just take care of it."

We approached Morone in his cousin's living room and asked lots of questions about boot camp. It was a struggle, first because we knew so little to ask and second because Morone seemed not to care so much to answer. Steven said it was like losing your brother, he and Little Alfredo were like that, they lived next door to each other, had the same last name, were only a year and a half apart in age. They even had a string between their windows up on the second floor, a waxed string that was stretched taut to an empty orange juice can on each end, so they could talk to each other privately.

That night, Steven and I played war with a deck of cards, played battleship with pieces of paper, and shot marbles on the rug. But since we had just come from Little Alfredo's funeral, it wasn't the same. The games were listless; we went to our bunks. I couldn't help but think of Little Alfredo, lying there all alone in his coffin.

I started rattling off questions to my brother:

"Do you think Little Alfredo could hear us, I mean at the funeral parlor?

"Does your soul leave your body and go up to heaven and can you really look down on us and see what we're doing?

"Do they try to tell us stuff, you know, to get our attention to do or not do something?

"I heard that the last thing you saw is what's on the inside of your eyelid and it's there forever. Do you think that's true?

"Even if they can't talk to us, do you think dead people can talk to each other?

"Is that why relatives are buried near each other?

"What happens if you're burned up or you disintegrate in a plane crash, does that make a difference between you and someone else if they're buried?

"Do you believe all the stuff about hell that Noodge Mauer says?

"Do you think old people know stuff about God but won't tell us?

"When you pray, do you think someone is listening? And I don't mean if you pray out loud.

"When people say they've prayed and prayed and nothing happens, do you think it's the wrong prayer or that God doesn't care? Steven?"

He was either asleep or faking it, and I wasn't going to take any chances, he might kill me.

I tossed and turned, which caused a little bit of growling and digging in for position. After a few minutes of this, I sat up and said the following out loud so only BlueDog could hear. "Here's what I think I should do: write an obituary for Little Alfredo. Do it like it appears in the newspaper. Then, I'll get a picture of him from Morone and use the mimeo machine at Papa's and print this up. I can give it to Big Alfredo and Rocky and Morone."

And like that, I fell asleep, BlueDog nestled into my back. Neither of us moved a muscle until the alarm went off the next morning.

I started on the obituary for Little Alfredo the very next day. I had to find out so much information about him: what he liked to do, what he collected, who his friends were, where he went to school, as well as special stuff that related to him and his cousin. I had to be crafty, no letting on that I was doing this. In a short period of time, I knew that he liked shop, smoked Camels, drank 'gansett, had a girlfriend named Gina, worked on cars, and played junior varsity football. I also found out that he always talked about going back to Nauset Beach on the Cape, where he'd made a sandcastle Nativity scene when he was eight, that he spent every Sunday morning when he was little at his grandmother's after early church services, that he once ate an entire pie for breakfast when he got up one morning and his mother then made him eat a full meal afterward, which he threw up on the sofa, you can thank Jesus for the plastic cover, she said. I retrieved multiple Brownie snapshots of him, many with his cousin, others with his girlfriend and in his uniform.

Within a week, I had enough to get hold of the typewriter and mimeo machine at Papa's office and played around with the layout until I got it to look like the obituaries that appeared each morning in the *Herald Traveler*. I brought the obituary for Little Alfredo over to Big Alfredo's house and gave it to him when Rocky was there too.

Over the years I subsequently visited with them, it was always on display on a table near the phone. Who knows, maybe they put it out when they knew I was coming over, but even if that were true, it wouldn't diminish the memory I have of watching them page through it for the first time, lightly touching each picture and tracing the words with a fingertip, then gently grabbing my cheek.

When I showed the obituary to Mother, she playfully suggested I make another one for the Braves; after all, the Boston Braves were as good as dead, they were going to show up next year as the Milwaukee Braves. When it was completed, I showed it to Papa's pals at the store, and they insisted I make a mimeograph for them, which they put on the bulletin board. The next time I went, I noticed that everybody had scribbled dates on the Braves' obituary, and Steven told me that Derby Canurbi and his friends had made bets as to the specific date that it would be announced officially that the Braves would pull up stakes and move. Most everybody was guessing around the start of the New Year, but just to be a contrarian, I wrote March 13, 1953, and put my initials next to it. Derby Canurbi told me that he'd give me a hundred to one if I gave him a buck and Steven said do it, you can only lose a dollar, so I did.

A week or so later, I was greeted at Papa's store by Murph Feldman who handed me a hundred bucks. "Hey, kiddo, ya won the bet for the date when the Braves would make the announcement of the move to Milwaukee." I gave fifty dollars to Dad to put into a savings account, gave twenty-five dollars back to Derby Canurbi to bet for me, and kept twenty-five dollars, spending the first ten on the "Hardships of Emigration" stamp that Nana had thought was her idea. I added the remaining fifteen to my stash of coins and bills that'd accumulated from the work I'd done for Murph Feldman.

It was years later when I was reading Mr. Carlson's book on the story of the Braves' move to Milwaukee that I was struck by the date on which the official announcement of the move was made: March 13, 1953. That did turn out to be the precise date I picked when I placed my bet with Derby Canurbi, but the thing is, Murph Feldman gave me my winnings four months prior to that day.

28.

Mother started referring to me as "young man"

On the last school day before Christmas vacation, Papa told us at dinner that he'd be going down south for a few days. Steven and I became ecstatic, thinking we'd go on another trip like the one we went on in 1945 with him. Unfortunately, he said, we couldn't go this time, he needed to take Murph Feldman and Moses O'Neil. We were disappointed, of course, but then again, we figured we'd be good for some presents when he returned, perhaps because he'd feel guilty that he couldn't take us with him. On the other hand, we wondered if he felt that being cooped up with us jabbering nonstop for hours on end was a lot to put up with, even for a grandfather.

Our disappointment was short-lived. We decided to go to the movies and asked Zippo and Susie to come with us. Mr. and Mrs. Mauer had some reservations because we'd have to take Susie in the wheelchair, but they agreed once they saw how excited she was. There was a small theater about a mile from where we lived. We left with plenty of time to spare and it wasn't particularly cold, although Mrs. Mauer had insisted that Susie take a blanket. I must admit it took a lot to move the wheelchair, and I could just imagine the effort it took her to do it by herself. In all the time she'd been in it, I'd never heard her complain. It was difficult getting her up the steps, and we had to sit in the back because otherwise the wheelchair would block the aisles. We loaded up on buttered popcorn and Good & Plenty. When I reached for the popcorn, Susie grabbed my hand, and at first I thought she was letting me know the popcorn was off-limits, but then when she held on to it I knew she just wanted the contact. It was like when BlueDog would manage to have one paw touching my leg or arm, no matter what position he assumed or how much I squirmed around. It felt good. Steven and Zippo were in the balcony.

The main feature was *Ivanhoe*. When he was jousting and stuck another guy square in the face, we both gasped and turned our heads at the same time. We spilled what was left of the popcorn on the floor, and as I leaned over her to get the bag, she instinctively grabbed the bars of the wheelchair and moved her legs a couple of inches to make it easier for me. For an instant, neither of us realized what she'd done. Then it hit us. She squealed, which caused lots of other kids to turn and look at us because a squeal didn't go with what was going on in the picture. I whispered, "Can you do it again?" and she could, not much, and not without effort, but there was movement. Then I remembered Dr. Richards saying that not all paralysis was permanent and that many people got partial or even full use of their legs back after a while. I wasn't sure I believed it because Mother had said, "THEY SAY THAT TO GIVE THEM SOME HOPE." I kept my hand under her blanket, officially to feel if there was movement, but that was just a ruse that both of us understood. On the way home, Zippo came up with the idea of having Susie meet the kids at the hospital, the kids with polio, who could see that there was a reason to keep doing the exercises, this would give them something to strive for, she said. Right before Christmas, when Susie could almost cross her legs, Zippo had her appear at the Christmas party, and she was the hit of the show, even more than Santa.

I put the ticket stub for the movies into my scrapbook and even pasted in a couple of the popcorn balls that we'd spilled on the floor, but they got crushed and all that was left was the dried paste, which I colored yellow, though it never looked the same. I reviewed the scrapbook with BlueDog as my audience, starting with the obituary for Little Alfredo, throwing in commentary, extra stuff that I hadn't thought about at the time or that I just ad-libbed because the thought came to me and it was funny, or I added something or answered a question that came to mind. I pretended that I was The Guy on the Radio. It took me about an hour to get through the whole thing, and when I finished, I looked at BlueDog and realized that I should've included him a little bit more and not just for comic relief. After all, I could point out the various times since he'd been part of our household that he'd been present at important events as well as the times here in the room and out back when I spoke to him as if he could really understand.

With the gelt I got for Hanukkah, I bought a secondhand typewriter, supposedly for homework, which pleased Mother no end, as she envisioned this as my first step toward making the honor roll. I had enough left over for a bigger scrapbook as well as scissors, paste and glue, pencils, crayons, string, cloudlike cutouts for short inscriptions, and typewriter paper for when I had a lot to say. I put in duplicates of cancelled stamps and the stories about them that Uncle Jake and Old Uncle A had told us, which made the stamps something more than used postage. I started with the Constitution ratification stamp of 1937, which was issued on its 150th anniversary. It was Uncle Jake's favorite; he'd told us that every time he used one, it made him proud to be an American, which I'm not sure he officially ever was, even if he had papers to prove it nonetheless, courtesy of Murph Feldman.

For Christmas, Noodge Mauer got a toboggan, which we used at Parsons Field with Myandrew, Frankie, and BlueDog from morning to dusk, taking hot chocolate in thermos bottles and getting sandwiches from Mrs. Mauer that I surreptitiously scraped the butter off with the plastic knife I sequestered in my pocket for precisely this purpose. Myandrew got a real fancy bike with gears from his father and also knee socks from his mother, so the grease from the chain that didn't have a guard wouldn't get onto his new gabardine pants. Frankie's mantelpiece stocking got stuffed with saltwater taffy, his father's favorite. Susie got a pair of ballerina slippers and something even better, word that she could go back to school if her legs continued to make progress and she could get around on crutches.

Despite the deaths of Uncle Jake and Little Alfredo, notwithstanding my participation in a crime, and regardless of the impending loss of my baseball team, I could look back on the year and focus on the good things: I got a dog whose presence enabled me to gain confidence in speaking to adults, I was consistently getting to second base with Susie, I'd earned the respect of people like Murph Feldman and the rest of Papa's pals, and I'd improved my Hebrew to the point where it wasn't hard anymore, a tribute of sorts to Uncle Jake, who'd have been proud to hear my voice in another language. Mother started referring to me as "young man," especially in front of adults, so I presumed I was growing up.

I could feel it, sense it, both physically and emotionally. The obvious manifestation of the transformation was in my voice. Sometimes squeaky, it could go up and down an octave in one sentence, embarrassing to me but accepted by others as part of the natural way of things. From the start of the year, my interest in girls had skyrocketed; I'd gone from indifference to excitement, fueled partially by hormonal changes but also, I suspect, by my observations of Steven with Zippo and my interactions with Susie. There was more. I felt at times like the animals that can sense a thunderstorm long before we can, or others that are able to pick up trembles on the ground before seeing a charging buffalo herd. Something was coming that would suppress my jerky and goofy tendencies and sit me at the grown-up table of life. I was on the cusp of adulthood and desperately wanted to make sure I didn't tumble backward.

In the time between Christmas and New Year's, I was looking forward to the return of my grandfather from his trip down south. What I didn't know then was that upon his return, I'd find out three things that would alter my life as profoundly as the events I'd just experienced in 1952.

29.

This was supposed to have been settled by the "war to end all wars"

On his way back from the South, Papa called to say that he was in Hartford, Connecticut, and would be home in about four hours. He asked Mother if she could set the table for three visitors, Murph Feldman, Moses O'Neil, and a guest, which would require Mother to have nine place settings, necessitating us to find the board that fit in the middle of the table as well as to lug our desk chairs from our room. We were all wound up. We wanted to hear about the trip, were curious to find out about the visitor, and, naturally, were interested to know if we would get anything out of it. Around 5:00 p.m., we saw the army-green, egg-shaped Plymouth turn down the driveway out back and head for the garage. Papa honked and we waved back, hopping over the ice patches and careening into the side of the car. Murph Feldman got out first. "Hiya, kiddos," he said and clapped us on the back. We gave hugs to Papa and shook Moses O'Neil's hand, peering into the back seat where the guest was sitting. Papa opened the door and a young man in a strange getup emerged. He was wearing a black hat, not really a fedora because the brim was wide all the way around and there wasn't a snazzy crease or a silk ribbon running around it, like the one worn by Boston Blackie. The mystery man had a full beard and mustache, and extra curls like tufts hung down past his ears. He was wearing glasses too, so while there was a lot of him, well over six feet from foot to top of brim, you couldn't really say you could describe him. You sure could draw a picture of his outfit, though, which consisted of a long black coat over a black jacket and black pants with a white shirt but no tie. You could see little pieces of yarn emerging from where his shirt tucked into his pants; it looked like he must've stuffed the end of a Persian area rug into his drawers and it was peeking out to get a glimpse of the New World.

Papa introduced us to Mordecai, who nodded and let out a barely audible hello. He seemed to evade eye contact and was inclined to wait for direction from Papa to take even a step from where he was standing. Murph Feldman hung back with us as Papa marched Mordecai up the stairs, then told us that Mordecai was nineteen, had lived in South Carolina, was an Orthodox Jew, would be staying with us for only a day, and then would be moving on. Steven said that he thought he was a rabbi or something, and I said I couldn't believe that someone only nineteen could have that much of a bushy beard. Murph Feldman informed us that if we didn't shave, not even once, we would look like this when we were nineteen.

At supper, Papa said the trip had started out, strangely enough, in the North End. Moses O'Neil pointed out that before they could get on the road, they had to have a set of dress blues, the marine corps outfit that was worn on special occasions, so he borrowed the one Sergeant Wilson had had on when he informed Big Alfredo that Little Alfredo had been killed, telling him that he needed to give it to someone who was going to be in a school play.

Mother told her father that there surely must be a story here. "Why don't you tell us what happened on your trip?"

You could tell that Papa was eager to get into his storytelling mode.

"Murph Feldman had everything he needed in his briefcase," Papa said, but he didn't say what it was that Murph Feldman had. "I had the car serviced and off we went, headed for South Carolina, a trip we could make in about four days. It was almost precisely a thousand miles, with overnights in Philadelphia, Richmond, Virginia, and Raleigh, North Carolina. We were careful not to exceed the speed limit, ate at diners, stayed at inexpensive motels where truckers pulled up, and didn't speak to anyone other than a waitress to order food or an attendant to pump gas. We got to Beaufort, South Carolina, in the middle of the fourth day, and he"—Papa pointed to Moses O'Neil—"went directly to the local Catholic church to give confession."

"Was everything all right?" Mother wanted to know.

"Yeah, nothin' coulda been better," Moses O'Neil replied without seeming to get her drift. "I had someone get me the priest, and I stepped inta the confession booth. I told the father that my son, my only son, was gonna be shipped out to Korea the next day and I was all in favor of that, I'd been a marine in World War II, served in the Pacific, and make no mistake about it, the commies have to be stopped."

I was confused. In all the time I knew Moses O'Neil, I didn't think he'd ever been married, let alone had a son. Steven and I exchanged looks.

"See, the thing is," he continued, "I said to the priest, my son was never baptized and if somethin' were gonna happen to him over there and he dint come back, well, I couldn't live with myself, seein' him burn in hell forever, all because my wife, God rest her soul, my wife and I never had a proper baptism for him, on account of her being a Unitarian, practically not even a Christian woman, but anyway, she's gone now, may she rest in peace, and I decided I had to do this for my son, that's what a father's gotta do. Help me father, for I've sinned by not doin' this for my son.

"So's I showed the priest the orders for my son to ship out as well as a letter from my son askin' for a proper Christian send-off prior to getting on the troop transport, scheduled for the next day. The priest offered to baptize my son and I told him I'd be mighty grateful but I'm in a pickle because the ceremony would have to be today and my son is at Parris Island at the Marine Corps Recruit Depot down the road, and the only way I could get him a special pass at this late date is to have a priest come with me to make a special request.

"The priest told me I looked spiffy in my dress blues that still fit so well, and the two of us got in the car and drove to Parris Island, arriving around five o'clock."

Moses O'Neil abruptly got up from our dining room table, announced that he had to see a man about a horse, and walked off to the bathroom. I was staring at Mordecai, who had taken off his hat to reveal a skullcap, which I'd only seen in a synagogue. I wondered if when he took off the yarmulke there was another, smaller hat underneath. Maybe he had a teeny-tiny hat for each hair. Nobody asked the obvious question: Who was this guy and why was he here? It was possible that we'd know by the end of the story of the trip to South Carolina, but it was just as possible that we wouldn't.

Moses O'Neil returned and started right up.

"We told the guard at the entrance why we were there and he made a phone call pronto, relaying our request up the line. While we waited, the guard asked me about my service and I told him I'd been a member of the Fifth Regiment, Second Battalion, First Marine Division in August of '42 when we landed at Guadalcanal on the British Solomon Islands. He asked what it was like. 'Ya gotta imagine the shellin' from the big guns, the guns so powerful that the ship moves sideways thirty or forty feet when the guns blaze in unison. Then there's the landin' in PT boats, runnin' up the beach, diggin' foxholes in the soft sand up to your necks, and fightin' the mosquitoes with the same fury as we showed to the Japs. I was part of a thirty-seven-millimeter gun crew, and by the end of the first day I blew out an eardrum, which still gives me problems today, so's you prob'ly noticed.'

"I spoke with the guard at the entrance for about twenty minutes nonstop, until word got back that they were gettin' my son and would grant him a two-hour pass, that he'd be in the custody of the fathers, me and the Catholic priest, and that he should be back by twenty hundred sharp.

"In a few minutes, my son showed up, and the three of us drove straight to the church, where the priest excused himself, said he'd be back in a few minutes, he had to get everything organized for the baptism, and to stay right here."

At that point, I remembered how Papa had whispered to Murph Feldman at Little Alfredo's funeral, when I caught the end of a few words, "Just take care of it." And now here was the use of a marine uniform, Murph Feldman with his briefcase full of papers that would be useful in many different situations, a trip to South Carolina, to Parris Island where the marines had boot camp, and having confession with a priest about a son that Moses O'Neil never had. God knows Moses O'Neil wasn't in the marines, and anyway, he was too old for World War II, although his description of Guadalcanal was good, I was mighty impressed. With all these people surrounding me, listening to Moses O'Neil and Papa tell the story with occasional enhancements from Murph Feldman, I had an urge so great it spilled out from inside of me. My skin bristled and I absentmindedly scratched it, my temples pounded like a bass, my eyes darted from person to person and alighted on BlueDog. Then, without an excuse me, in the absence of a warning, with no discernable movement from me that would've communicated a timeout to Moses O'Neil, I inserted myself into the narrative in an elision that was seamless, even though when I started, it brought the *now is not the time* look from Mother.

"As soon as the priest was out of sight," I interrupted Moses O'Neil, "you and your son hightailed it out of there, making sure to tell a couple of elderly parishioners to inform the priest that you'd just gone to your car to retrieve a cloth to wipe your shoes, you were embarrassed that there was mud on them, and that you'd be back in a flash. Instead, you headed straight for the motel, where the two of you"—I pointed to Papa and Murph Feldman—"were waiting. The marine shed his uniform, and you"—I nodded toward Moses O'Neil—"cut both yours and the marine's into small pieces, which you took to the Dumpster out back, dressed the marine in new clothes, and headed north, but not before you put South Carolina plates on the car and informed the motel operator that you were headed south for Key West. You made sure you kept under the speed limit and stayed at different motels and ate at different diners on your trip back north. The two of you"—I again pointed to Papa and Murph Feldman—"spent hours instructing the marine on what to say, what not to say, what to do, what not to do, and what was going to happen. You made a couple of phone calls to Boston that night and then went silent until you called here this afternoon to tell Mother that you were coming and to set an extra place for dinner, bringing an Orthodox

Jew named Mordecai with no explanation as to who he is, why he's with you, what he's doing here, or where he's headed.

"My guess is," I continued, sounding like Sergeant Joe Friday on *Dragnet*, "that there's an APB out for the missing marine, we'll probably hear about it on the news as a kidnapping, and the poor priest will likely be in a lot of hot water for aiding and abetting an AWOL marine from Parris Island who nobody in their right mind would believe is sitting right here in our living room in Boston dressed up as an Orthodox Jew." Then I stood up and gave a loud "Yo!" which Mordecai/Morone reciprocated with another "Yo!" and a "Hey!" so loud that I thought Mother was going to have a heart attack.

Morone took off his beard, broke out into a huge grin, hugged Mother, Dad, and Auntie Rose, pumped Steven's hand, and slapped his thighs, the motion and sound for BlueDog to stand on his hand legs, nibble at the *tzitzis*, the fringe from the buried rug, and get his head rubbed.

In all the excitement, I could tell that Mother saw herself as the physician who had set John Wilkes Booth's leg not knowing that he'd killed President Lincoln but was imprisoned for the crime nevertheless. I could hear her pleading with the judge, "My crime was only serving kugel to a guest, Your Honor, it's part of our tradition," something he wouldn't be able to comprehend.

Papa settled everyone down, admonished us to say nothing to anyone, told us that Rocky and Big Alfredo knew what was up but, of course, couldn't acknowledge anything, nor could they speak with Morone until he could arrange for them to get calls when they were at Sal the barber's or at Dad's accounting office. I gave Murph Feldman the *I know how to keep a secret* look. He winked at me. Later, when no one else was near, he leaned over to me, put his hand on my shoulder, and said, "Hey, kiddo, the details of ya reconstruction was off but the gist was a hunnert percent accurate."

Around ten o'clock, Murph Feldman and Moses O'Neil left and Mordecai/Morone came with us while Mother made up the sofa in the living room for him, the same way she did it for Old Uncle A when he stayed with us. Mordecai/Morone let us examine his clothes and we took turns wearing the broad black-brimmed hat and tzitzis, which he said he'd worn even when he was sleeping in the motels. He showed me how to stick the beard on, which I did, then pretended to be Gabby Hayes, saying things like "podner," "bottom land," "draw mister," and droppin' *g*'s like crumbs all throughout the house.

We asked him how this whole thing got started and he said it was his uncle, Big Alfredo, who was so distressed about Little Alfredo's death that he couldn't bear the thought of losing his nephew. At first, he said, Rocky was against it—it was unpatriotic. They debated it for several days, Rocky imploring his brother to give him one single reason that he couldn't perceive as selfish, rejecting every one of Big Alfredo's approaches. What finally convinced Rocky to go along was the last paragraph of Dr. Daniel Burgas's letter, those sentences that Isaac Burgas hadn't read when we'd all gathered together at Little Alfredo's wake. Mordecai/Morone pulled the letter out of his pocket and read the end of it to us:

> The sad thing of it is that sometimes I think it's like a board game, where we take a hill, defend it, lose it, and vice versa. Who's to say who's winning and losing? You sure can't tell from the perspective of us here out on the front lines. We aim, we shoot, and some young Korean or Chinese kid who's loved as much by his family as ours gets killed, just like our marine kids, while they argue for a year in Paris about where to draw a line across the Korean peninsula. And in the end, who will care, what will it mean, no one in Boston or London, or Peking or Moscow for that matter, will do anything differently. In the States, we'll still go to baseball games, college, and restaurants, take walks, meet girls, get married. Well, not all of us will, and that's the part that kills. I thought this was supposed to have been settled by the "war to end all wars," but I guess that was just a 1917 slogan to sell Liberty bonds at 3 percent. I hate to say it but I'll take even money with Derby Canurbi that one day a kid of mine will be writing the same kind of letter home to me, and if that's so, well, tell me, what is really the rate of return on this investment?

Early the next morning, Murph Feldman came over with Moses O'Neil and handed papers to Morone, indicating he was Mordecai Auerbach, born in Maine, parents deceased, only known relative Abraham Auerbach, grandfather. We saw his Mount Desert Regional High School records, his birth certificate, and his Maine driver's license. He packed them into a little satchel that also included a book on reading Hebrew and a mimeographed sheet that was folded up. He put on his beard, gave us a couple of yos! and heys!, then climbed into the car with Moses O'Neil. Around the same time, Rocky and Big Alfredo sat in chairs at Dad's office, waiting for the phone to ring. When Moses O'Neil pulled up to Sal the barber's, Mordecai/Morone got out and went to the back of the shop, where there was a private line. He called the office and got to speak with his father and uncle. They didn't know when they would see each other again, so the call took longer than Moses O'Neil anticipated and this got him agitated.

Finally, Moses O'Neil and Mordecai/Morone headed north out on Route 1, over the newly opened Tobin Bridge that spanned the Mystic River, breezing past Marblehead, Lynn, Lawrence, making Portsmouth, New Hampshire, in under three hours. They stopped at a roadside fish place, where Moses O'Neil quickly told the waiter that the oysters on the half shell that his young traveling companion had ordered were really for him.

"They're *treif*, not kosher, read the mimeographed page for chrissakes," Moses O'Neil commanded. "Ya gotta be careful," he warned, ripping a giant prawn from a shell and dangling it in cocktail sauce to the annoyance of Mordecai/Morone, who was wondering when he'd have the pleasure again of some clams oreganata or be able to have a milkshake and a hot dog at a game. In the car, Mordecai/Morone studied the dos and don'ts of being an Orthodox Jew, and he questioned why he couldn't have been a regular Jew like Steven and me, who didn't seem to follow any of the dos and don'ts yet never seemed to get in trouble.

They reached Bar Harbor, Maine, in two days and found the back roads to Seal Harbor rather easily. Moses O'Neil told Mordecai/Morone the story of picking up Rose Mischal and Jacob Goldblum in Montreal and driving them down to the same dock to make the same boat ride out to Palus Island in 1938. Moses O'Neil had one foot on the gunwale and the other on the island's dock when he heard a hello that was long and drawn out from above the road.

"That's Mr. Auerbach," he said, "ya know, the guy that Joel and Steven call Old Uncle A. I suspect he's been there on that widow's peak of a ridge for the whole day, waitin' to greet us."

Mr. Auerbach began speaking in a barely audible voice without an introduction and told Mordecai/Morone it was okay to remove the beard and take off the broad-brimmed hat and yarmulke. At once, Mordecai/Morone began to scratch his head vigorously, then he quickly retrieved a comb from his back pocket and stroked his head in a two-step motion with the left hand following up the right, which held the comb. It was almost as if he were back in the North End. He was told that the stay would last about a year, enough time for Morone to be forgotten, presumed dead, case closed. Finally, he was told to remember three things: one, that he must wear his Orthodox clothes if he took the boat to go ashore; two, that he was to think of himself not as an Italian, not as a marine, but as a Jew, a scholar of the Bible; and three, that he was Mr. Auerbach's grandson.

Once a week for the next year, Mordecai/Morone would go to the mainland and put in a call to Sal the barber or Dad's accounting office or Papa's store and speak with his father and his uncle. Mordecai/Morone would tell them about his routine, which included acting as the handyman, fixing everything from leaky shingles to backed-up toilets to doors that needed to be rehung to sills that needed to be realigned. The more he took on, the more he liked it, he became indispensable and enjoyed working while the *altekakers* chatted on nonstop, informing him of things they never taught him in school, that was for sure. He went on and on, explaining to his father and uncle about the swath of destruction ravaged on the Jewish communities by the Crusaders across Europe, the banishment and forced conversions of 1492 Spain, the pig's head on the water pump in the Florence town square, the kidnapping of Edgardo Mortara by the pope in 1858, and the underground Nazi railroad that went from Germany through Rome to Buenos Aires at the end of World War II.

"Who was the first Jew in America?" Mordecai/Morone quizzed us one day when we were in Dad's office for the call. Steven and I debated whether it was in Jamestown or Plymouth or Saint Augustine or perhaps some conquistador from Spain who was searching for gold with Cortés or for the fountain of youth with Ponce de León.

"We give up, tell us," I said, and he told us it was Joachim Gaunse in 1585 in the Roanoke colony, and that was news to us and would've been to Uncle Jake too, because he sure hadn't known that when he took us to visit the first synagogue in America in Newport, Rhode Island.

He told us he once asked our Old Uncle A how he was related to us.

"You can become an uncle by blood, by marriage, or by chance," Abraham Auerbach told him, but never indicated which one was relevant for him.

May 3, 1952
Dear Diary,

Jacob doesn't want to take the boys on rides. They still visit, he stays on the sofa, they bring their stamp collections. I give them cookies and I take them for walks in the Fens. Jacob declines, his leg hurts and he's tired all the time. He goes to bed early but lies awake. He's exhausted when he gets up. He went to work only once in the last two weeks. It is difficult physically and emotionally for him to get up and go.

All anyone talks about is polio. Who they know who got it, who died, who is paralyzed, the lucky few who get better. What with the war, no news from Europe, the epidemic, and his leg, he is despondent. I worry that he is giving up.

My sister called and told me to come over quick. I think something is wrong, bad news, but she assures me otherwise. Jacob is not up to it. I dash over and she tells me to sit, wait. I am anxious. Then, the boys burst in with a large black dog with blue paint spots all over it. He is beautiful. He runs all over and makes a beeline for me. Although I am sitting, I am almost knocked to the ground. Everyone is clapping, talking excitedly, patting him, hugging him. We love him instantly. The boys make a leash out of rope and we walk back to our place. The dog nearly pulls Joel over. We open the door, the boys are shouting, "Uncle Jake, Uncle Jake, we have a dog" and let go of the rope. He leaps onto Jacob's legs. My husband has a grin from ear to ear. Would that it could always be so.

Rose

May 10, 1952
Dear Diary,

A terrible day. We were out back at my sister's watching the boys play ball. Jacob got the letter he never wanted to receive. He fell out of his chair. He was bruised but nothing else. We knew what it must have said.

We went home immediately. I knew he wouldn't be able to cry. All his tears were used up, he said.

He is giving up. He sits at the table but doesn't eat. There is silence. He goes to bed but doesn't sleep. For the first time, he tells me that the boys will have to cope without him. I do not tell him that I won't be able to.

I feel if I write my name it is as if I am signing a death certificate.

30.

A foul ball on July Fourth off of Frankie's bat

The kidnapping of Morone and his change into Mordecai living on Palus Island was the first of the three things I became aware of after Papa's trip down south that had a significant effect on me. The second took place shortly thereafter. The whole family went to Mr. Lee's for what we used to call dinner, really a midafternoon meal that took place on Sunday. We sat at a round table in the corner, Mother, Dad, Auntie Rose, Papa, Steven, and me.

While we were waiting for the main courses, Steven piped up, itching to find out how Uncle Jake had actually died.

He knew that if he asked at the table, in a restaurant, he couldn't be ignored. Mother couldn't walk away with a trailing "THERE'S TIME FOR THAT LATER." Each of the four adults gave anxious looks to the others; it was apparent that they wished another to start the conversation. After a moment, Dad began, in true accounting fashion, with a factual representation of what happened in the order in which it took place.

"When I visited with Jake it was clear to both the doctors and me that he wasn't going to hold on for much longer. When I got home, that's when I took out the yellow pad and started to write the obituary."

"Yeah, but how did the doctors know, was he unconscious or hardly breathing?" Steven persisted.

I piped up before anyone could answer. "When we got to his room, he wasn't there. Zippo, I mean Juliette, noticed that something was wrong, his slippers were still in the room. How come?" I inquired.

Mother took up the conversation without addressing our questions. "Uncle Jake had been going steadily downhill throughout the summer. You two are now aware that he didn't have polio." She said this without glancing at the others, which I interpreted as Dad had told Mother, Papa, and Auntie Rose about our conversation. "There was something in Dr. Richards' tone when he called earlier that day, after having spent a few minutes with Uncle Jake in the morning at the hospital."

We could see furtive eye movements among the adults at the table at Mr. Lee's restaurant.

"They called from the hospital in the afternoon, they were really concerned. So we rushed over, missing you by only a few minutes," she said, "but by the time we got there, he was already gone."

She paused, and that's when I realized that her *gone* was not a place but a device that adults use in order to avoid using the word *dead* in front of children.

But then I thought about when Auntie Rose said he was gone when he wasn't. She knew he wasn't dead when she said it, so was there another definition of *gone* that I didn't know about? I almost brought this up. I could sense the words zipping from my brain to my mouth and tongue, yet they were stopped dead in their tracks, perhaps by the same impulse that took control of Uncle Jake's body when he was approaching the port at Hamburg. It was as if a future me were sending a warning to the kid me, signalling that it wasn't always appropriate to say whatever was on my mind. A subconscious flag was being waved in my direction, and the fact that it was perceived and properly translated was another indication that I was on my way to becoming an adult.

Years later, I asked Steven if he thought that when Auntie Rose said he was gone, it was just her way of preparing herself for the inevitable. "It's likely," he said. "It's really no different when we comment that someone's 'a goner' who's been grievously wounded or that 'it's only a matter of time' when a person's in an irreversible coma."

At the table, I put it all together: "He went out the window, didn't he?" and they all nodded. "From his room," and they continued nodding. "And the hospital people brought him inside so there'd be less of a crowd," and the nodding went on.

Suicide was one of those words that we could define for others but whose meaning we couldn't comprehend when it affected us personally. Uncle Jake, the guy who'd spend hours with us, driving, walking, talking, reading to us, the man who knew everything about everything, didn't want to be with us, didn't want to be part of our family, didn't want to laugh and make us laugh anymore. I was hurt. It must've showed because Dad started to talk about how hard Uncle Jake's life was. I understood he was trying not to defend suicide but to put it into context.

"You can hear the words but not really comprehend what it must've been like to have been in Germany as a Jew in the 1930s. We read about it here and your mother and I heard it on the radio, but even *we* never could break through the wall he put up that had no doors or windows for us to walk through or open; we weren't able to discuss any of this with him," Dad stated calmly.

For the first time in my life, I could detect sadness in a voice, a tonal quality that we can both generate and decode only as our brains wire up for adulthood. I thought back to the story of how Uncle Jake left Germany and wondered if the impulsive decision he made on Kristallnacht to leave was predicated upon not having to go through the ordeal of saying good-bye to a family. I couldn't imagine not seeing Papa or Mother or Dad or Auntie Rose or Steven. I still saw Uncle Jake in my dreams, night and day, and spoke to him constantly.

"Even Auntie Rose," Mother continued, turning her head to include her sister into the frame, "who was there during Kristallnacht, couldn't speak of it with him." At that point, Auntie Rose, seated next to me, put her hand on my head, gently drawing it toward her, and kissed me on the cheek, just like Mother would do when I was sick.

I could sense that Auntie Rose wanted to join the conversation as she edged forward in her seat and made eye contact with the other adults, seeking a visual cue that it would be okay to take over. She started slowly, hesitating the way new kids do when they enter a classroom to be introduced by the teacher. "You know about the yellow stars they had to wear on their clothing. That was just the start. You know about Kristallnacht. Jews were harassed, they lost their jobs, they were deprived of papers like passports and licenses to drive and to hold certain jobs. Some people thought it couldn't get worse. Then, after the War began, the Jews were rounded up, first in Germany and eventually throughout Europe. Many millions were brought by railroad cars to camps. Special camps, built in Germany and Poland. That's where people got their tattoos, like prison uniform numbers, burned into their forearms."

I rubbed my left arm from my elbow to my wrist. I knew about the death camps from the *Weekly Reader*, where there were stories about death camp commandants captured in Argentina; Uncle Jake had told us that they were spirited away from Bavaria through Rome.

"There's an *institution*," he'd hissed, "a *network*, and when you're older, I'll tell you all about it."

It was years before I found out how all of these Germans could've escaped detection. We did remember his word for the Final Solution, *Endlösung*, which he'd pronounce with such onomatopoetic energy that we'd have nightmares about men in brown uniforms goose-stepping on slicked streets at night, breaking down doors, shouting and cursing, spitting out orders, and dragging us away to a camp that we pictured as a coal mine: damp, cold, stale, unlit, and claustrophobic, from which there was no escape.

I was fighting to hold back a deluge of tears. Our silence was broken by the appearance of the waiters and the clanging of the silver serving dishes as the tops were lifted up in triumph, with Mr. Lee beaming down upon the labors of his chefs. Since no one even seemed to notice, Mr. Lee put his hands on the backs of two chairs, bent down to a level just above our heads, and started to inquire if everything was all right;

but scanning our eyes, he retreated, recognizing that we were preoccupied and that our lack of excitement about the food being served had nothing to do with any restaurant-related disappointment.

Papa picked up when Mr. Lee receded. "Uncle Jake had experienced the prelude to war and mass exterminations, witnessed the frenzy of the initial violence firsthand, then waited out the seven years until 1945 in limbo. His pent-up energy exploded in a rash of activity that began on May 8 of that year, with the headlines proclaiming V-E Day. On the way to the clinic at the track that day, he went to your father's office, sat down in a small room, closed the door, took out one of his elegant fountain pens, and began the search for his family. While the full extent of the horror wasn't known in terms of the numbers of the dead, Uncle Jake sensed that it was unlikely many had survived. He told me it wasn't that he knew for sure as much as an acknowledgment of a continuum of an historical precedent, Jews having been murdered in the Crusades and in pogroms. I shared his view; we all did. Yet he couldn't be stopped. He never lost hope. There was always a chance, he would say and was especially buoyed when he read about the occasional reunion of refugees with relatives or friends. Each time he showed up at the office, he had the name of a group that was in a particular country or city whose mission was to find survivors, locate graves, and make the appropriate notifications."

I could just envision Uncle Jake concentrating on his letters, making sure whatever language they were written in was perfect, then hustling down to the post office and putting them through the slots with a defiant shove. One thing I knew for sure, he wouldn't have used any fancy commemorative stamp; just the regular purple three-cent profile of Thomas Jefferson.

Auntie Rose, now more confident, added, "Early this past summer, Uncle Jake received a letter—a special letter."

"The one when he fainted and fell out of his lawn chair when he was out back with us near the garages?" I said as a statement that was housed inside a question.

"Yes, that was a letter from HIAS," she picked up. "It was a response to dozens of letters Uncle Jake had sent since the end of the War. Letters to the United Nations, to the governments of Germany, Poland, and the

Soviet Union, to the Red Cross, to the US Army, to the refugee organizations, to the Jewish relief agencies in Palestine, then Israel, to anyone who might be able to assist him in locating his family. Each time a letter arrived, he trembled with anticipation, at first with hope, then later, after they all said the same thing, that there was no record of his family, he dreaded opening the letters. And when he did, he would go through a cycle of emotions: anger, resentment, despair."

I remembered numerous times at his house, seeing him read and then toss a letter away, saying, "*Mein Gott im Himmel*," which now I understood was his way of expressing sorrow coupled with frustration at the absence of any news about members of his family.

"But there was always another organization or government to write to and always another glimmer of hope when he'd read about members of a family presumed to be dead but actually living in Panama or Southern Rhodesia who were united with relatives in Israel or England or here in the States," Auntie Rose continued.

"This letter," I concluded, "the one from HIAS, it said that his family was dead, didn't it?"

"Yes, it did. They'd found a record, names on a list, in an archive somewhere in Germany."

I understood everything that Auntie Rose had said, and I realized that the receipt of the letter was akin to a wind that had extinguished the small glint of the hope fire. But he got the letter in June yet didn't die until October.

"I still don't understand," I said plaintively. "He didn't commit suicide right when he got the letter. How come?"

Having just gone through such a difficult conversation, I expected the *there's a time for everything and this is not it* look from Mother, but instead she took an almost imperceptibly small breath and said, "Kristallnacht."

"Yeah, but that was 1938."

"Kristallnacht is the sound of breaking glass. Shattering explosions of glass, shards showering all over, shouting and screaming," Mother replied.

I don't know how I put it together, honestly I don't. How what flashed next into my mind came to be there is something I think about constantly because I've made other associations over the years by seeming to pluck unrelated images or designs or words or letters out of thin air and then making them fit as if they have no visible means of bonding.

"It must've been when we were playing ball out back on July Fourth," I said anxiously. "Firecracker baseball, when you have to wear your holster and shoot caps off wildly when you get a hit or score a run."

"There were a lot of explosions," Steven added.

"I was up, using the bat we kept hidden in the garage so that Frankie's father wouldn't find out he'd bought it at the Braves game. I whacked a long drive, it went high in the air, the ball hooked foul and made a beeline for the garage, where it smashed into the large glass window high up on the second floor."

"It shattered," Steven added.

"The window exploded so loudly that I hit the deck," I continued.

"Because of the flying glass," Steven said helpfully.

"But also out of fear; the noise was so loud, I just felt that if I made myself smaller, it would cause the bogeyman to pass over me in search of other, larger objects."

I paused. I waited for someone to say something. I didn't want to go on. I was sweating, rubbing my arms vigorously, tapping my feet nonstop. The quiet was killing me. I couldn't take it anymore.

"So what you're saying is that the explosion from the shattering of the large glass window is what set him off? It reminded him of Kristallnacht?"

"He was going anyway, Joel," Dad said in anticipation of my claiming responsibility for my uncle's death.

"It was the letter from HIAS," Papa confirmed. "If it hadn't been the sound of the broken glass, it would've been something else," he said, his way of assuring us that we bore no blame.

I don't remember seeing anyone else at the restaurant at that time, but I'm sure that's just a trick the mind plays on you, the same way Dr. Burgas told us later that when a soldier got his arm or leg amputated he could still feel pain in his lost fingers or toes.

Steven and I burst out crying almost exactly at the same moment. Not little drops eking out of the corners of our eyes. The tears flowed without stop, more like the thousand clowns who get out of the Volkswagen at the circus, you just can't believe that there's another one in there. Yes, we were crying because we were reminded of our uncle whom we'd never see again, and yes, we were crying because the future without Uncle Jake wouldn't be the same. But mostly, we were crying because it seemed to us that we were the ones who'd sent him on his final, downward spiral, which came at him as relentlessly as a black hole sucking in light, leaving no possible outlet for relief.

Anyway, you can imagine that Papa, Mother, Dad, and Auntie Rose soon surrounded us and ignored the stares of the other patrons—the ones I couldn't see, by the way, on account of my tears—to console us, the kids who'd loved our uncle to death.

We heard Auntie Rose's words: "Nothing you did caused Uncle Jake's death. At some point, he probably would've heard a mirror break or a car windshield get cracked or a car backfire or something similar. There was going to be an event, perhaps it didn't even have to be the sound of breaking glass, but something was going to happen that would have had an impact on him the way the sound of the shattered glass from the broken garage window did."

Of course we knew that she was right, but that didn't have any effect on us because if we hadn't smashed the window in the garage *that* day, Uncle Jake would be alive, unless, of course, something else had actually happened to set him off, just like Auntie Rose said.

We went to sleep as soon as we got home. We didn't feel like speaking to each other or to anyone else; I curled up on the bottom bunk and moved BlueDog off the pillow.

Up until that year I knew, of course, that I wanted to be a baseball player, a veterinarian, an accountant, a furniture dealer, or a doctor. That's what I thought about, that's what I'd do when I grew up and finished school and moved away from my parents' home. The reality was I had no clue what I was going to do or to be until I did it; it would be so easy for me today to concoct a trail of events that logically led me to where I now am, but if I did that, it would be grandiose and posturing. In retrospect, I can, however, see the path that started at the beginning of the summer with Murph Feldman offering us jobs, then proceeded to the stealing of the postcards to aid the election of the congressman and to the creation of the scrapbook for Little Alfredo, and continued through the winter with the pretend kidnapping of my hero, when I'd provided the storyline that no one corrected, I'm proud to say. And now this, the connection between the shattered glass and Uncle Jake. I was able to tie together the strands of events and a cast of characters as rich as the family and friends of The Guy on the Radio into a braid that would've made him proud. So it's not surprising that I did in fact become a guy on the radio and a writer, or maybe it's a writer who speaks his craft over the air. Ah, you say now, of course, but if I'd told you I became a veterinarian or a doctor or even a politician, you would've thought ah, well *that* was obvious.

After Morone's kidnapping and evolution into Mordecai, the second of the three things that was uncovered after Papa returned from his trip down south was, of course, the revelation that Steven and I, however unwittingly, had contributed to the premature death of our beloved uncle. Yes, yes, I know it would've happened anyway and we didn't set the fuse, it'd been smoldering out of sight for fourteen years. But what was the third thing?

July 4, 1952
Dear Diary,

Jacob has been sweating, rolling from side to side on the sofa. I put two hassocks next to it to give him more room, so he wouldn't fall off. Despite the heat, he was shaking so I covered him with a blanket. I asked him if he needed to go to the hospital. He didn't answer. Later he spoke. He was not making sense. Maybe he was but I don't understand when he mixes in German. He shuddered and thrashed, then fell back asleep.

My sister was here. We are very worried. My brother-in-law swept up the glass and had the boys bring BlueDog inside so his paws would not be cut. Tomorrow they will go out and sweep again.

I am sitting in his chair, sipping tea, listening to the sound of breaking glass over and over. I will stay up all night.

Wilted Rose

November 3, 1952
Dear Diary,

I know what everyone wants to ask me. Did I know he was going to do it? They don't. They are here day and night, especially my sister. When I mentioned after the funeral that I had something to tell her, she assumed it was about Jacob. But at the last moment, I couldn't let it out. I thought that revealing it would offset some of the loss but that only works in my brother-in-law's books.

They tell me I will get through it. Through to where?

Ida comforts me. She brings Jeffrey with her after school and I watch the boys with him. They build forts for him, they kick a ball with him and the dog and then sit and listen to the radio. I am so proud of them. When we are alone, she tells me she is thinking of leaving Irwin. She says she is bolstered by seeing how I am coping alone. I do not tell her that I am not coping. I do not tell her that divorce does not separate people. I tell her how wonderful Jeffrey is. I say wunderbar, like Jacob would have said it with a v sound. We both laugh.

I will have to face November without him.
Only Rose

December 28, 1952
Dear Diary,

Today we consoled Joel who feels responsible for Jacob's death. My sister asks to no one in particular can you imagine the burden he is carrying? I don't tell her that I can. I am.

Rose

31.

The understanding that I could put things together on my own

I got up in the middle of the night. My head was spinning. I looked at BlueDog and started to speak to him as if he were Mother, Auntie Rose, Dad, or Papa, listening to me attentively at the Chinese restaurant.

"I showed my mettle when I interrupted Moses O'Neil and Murph Feldman with the ending to the Morone/Mordecai story, but I have to be able to do it when no one else is around, when I have no one to feed off, no one to provide the spark," I said softly, in order not to disturb Steven.

I had challenged myself and wasn't going to quit now.

"I remember when Old Uncle A told us about Uncle Jake, the story about his coming to America with Auntie Rose and then her being pregnant. Well, if Mother and Auntie Rose were out strolling just before Halloween in 1939, then *both* of them would've been pregnant. Mother with me and Auntie Rose with the baby that died, the stillborn. But Old Uncle A said that only Auntie Rose was pregnant, and I chalked it up to forgetfulness."

I sat still for a moment, then resumed, "But maybe it wasn't that he forgot. What if Mother wasn't pregnant? What if Old Uncle A didn't slip up? But if Mother wasn't pregnant . . ." I then trailed off.

I sat straight up like they made us do in school when we had a guest visit the classroom.

"Wait a minute, what am I talking about, I've seen my birth certificate, it's in the safe at Dad's office, along with Steven's and a lot of important papers."

Then it hit me with the violence of the bat I'd swung on July Fourth when it hit the ball that shattered the glass window high up on the garage.

I saw Morone's fake letter to his fake father, Moses O'Neil, asking to be baptized, Morone's pretend orders shipping him out two days after Christmas, Mordecai's forged Maine birth certificate/high school records/driver's license, Uncle Jake's false US passport delivered to him by Moses O'Neil at the Canadian border, Auntie Rose and Uncle Jake's made-up marriage certificate that said they were married in Boston before Uncle Jake ever set foot in the States, Derby Canurbi's counterfeit passport, the sham college and veterinary degrees that Murph Feldman gave Uncle Jake so he could work at Suffolk Downs as a vet, and who knows what else, maybe even the letter that Dr. Burgas wrote to Big Alfredo from Korea, you never know.

Was it possible that my birth certificate in Dad's office safe was a phony? That Mother wasn't pregnant with me in the fall of 1939 because Mother had only one child?

If all that was true . . . I hesitated, then asked almost loudly enough for Steven to hear, "Was I adopted?" I sensed I would wake my brother and lowered my voice so it was barely perceptible, knowing BlueDog could hear at any range.

"But how could that be? I look a lot like Steven, so that'd be a strange coincidence, wouldn't it?" Then I stopped short.

"Holy cow, wait a minute, hold the horses, is Auntie Rose my *mother*? *My* mother? Is that why I look so much like Steven? Auntie Rose looks just like Mother. Auntie Rose! Holy cow! She's not my aunt, she's my *mother*. Is that possible? That's why so many people remark that I look like Uncle Jake. And that means Mother and Dad's names as parents on my birth certificate are fakes, courtesy of Murph Feldman. Maybe Auntie Rose named me, was Joel her name, not Mother's? Then the stillborn story had to've been just that, a story. A story to prevent them from having to answer any questions, at least for a while. So when were they going to tell me? I'm sure Steven doesn't know, he couldn't have kept this a secret, no way."

Now, I'm sure you're wondering why I didn't march into Mother and Dad's room right then and there or confront Auntie Rose, but first, remember that it was the middle of the night, and second, I couldn't actually say I was right as I hadn't heard it from someone else, and even if you were to say, so what, this is so momentous, you have to refrain from judging my behavior then against what a kid might do today. Besides, the more I thought about all of this for the next few hours until dawn, it was pretty clear to me that everyone had made the right choice. Nevertheless, I had many questions and was shocked at figuring this all out and wondered if they'd ever planned to tell me. I wasn't sure if anything was going to change, but thanks to Murph Feldman, nobody would ever find out unless I wanted them to.

I couldn't fall back to sleep. I kept thinking about Auntie Rose as my birth mother; I was going to have to get used to that. Would it alter how I felt about Mother or Dad? Or Auntie Rose and Uncle Jake? Would there be awkwardness with any of them when I brought this up in the morning? Could Steven and I be both brothers and cousins at the same time? Was it possible that I'd been put up for adoption, nobody wanted me, and as a last resort I'd been brought right back into the family? Was I actually rejected, resented? Would I ever tell anyone else?

I couldn't really envision Auntie Rose being a mother, what with her hibernations and odd behaviors, something I could deal with as a nephew but honestly, if she'd been my mother, I'm not so sure it would've worked out the way it did with Mother. And Uncle Jake, well, he wasn't the fatherly type, no, Dad sure had him beat on that score.

All this spinning about finally took its toll, physically and mentally, but just before I fell asleep as the sun was coming up, I realized that the third important thing that occurred after Papa returned from his trip down south was neither a piece of news nor a disclosure, but rather it was the understanding that I could put things together on my own. Up until that point in time, my instinct had been to run to adults for explanations and answers; this was the innate reaction, a manifestation of the dependency of children. While there are certain things children need from adults, the exclusive nature of the adult *give* and child *take* is unalterably changed at a certain point in life, and it was pretty clear that this was that point for me.

32.

Uncle Jake had a premonition

In the morning, I wasn't quite sure how to start the conversation with Mother and Dad, whether to get them into a discussion on another topic and then slide over or to begin, point blank, without any warming up. I settled on the latter, otherwise I'd just be postponing the discussion even more. Steven got up early and went out to ride his bike over to Zippo's; I made the decision not to say anything to him until I'd talked with Auntie Rose. I found the perfect time, as Auntie Rose was making her way over from her house and Papa had gone to the fish market in Brookline. Mother and Dad were in the kitchen, Mother fussing about with pots and pans and Dad pounding away at an adding machine on the breakfast table so Mother would have an audience.

I plopped down in the chair across from Dad and started right up.

"I know that Auntie Rose and Uncle Jake are my birth parents," I said, not alarmingly, not in an accusatory fashion, just matter-of-factly.

Mother turned around and gave her husband the *I knew this was going to happen someday but despite ample warning I never prepared for it* look while holding the frying pan in midair.

"We were going to tell you, of course," Dad said, a bit startled, "but to be honest with you, we weren't sure when."

I nodded that I believed him.

He acknowledged my nod and continued, "Can you tell me how you found out? Did Auntie Rose tell you? Papa?"

I felt a bit squeamish. I mean, no one had told me and if I went through my revelation from the night before, they probably wouldn't believe me, thinking it was an elaborate cover-up, that I was protecting someone who shouldn't have said anything.

"I just kind of guessed, really," was how I answered, "no one said anything to me. You know, as I get older I look so much like Uncle Jake, that's all," and left it at that.

I'm not sure that they bought it, but it didn't matter that much; they'd have to assume it was unlikely that someone inside the family would've been responsible for a betrayal of confidence. So I supposed that if they had any doubts about my response, they'd chalk it up to someone on the outside having made an inadvertent comment that resonated with me and assume that the combination of such a remark with my observation about looking like Uncle Jake was what triggered my declaration that I knew who my birth parents were. Being Mother and Dad, in front of me at least, they seemed satisfied and, while still a little nervous, gingerly continued the conversation.

"Are you upset?" Mother asked.

"That you didn't tell me?"

"No," she responded, "that's not what I meant," glancing at Dad to crack the code that faces emit silently, an ability that's acquired only after living many years together. She went on, presumably after getting the unspoken "okay". "That your aunt and uncle decided"—here she paused, choosing the precise phrasing—"not to raise a child, to give you up, although," she quickly added with a bright smile, "it wasn't as if you were given *away* because you stayed right here with us."

At that point I knew what I should say and came out with, "You're my parents, and I love Auntie Rose and I loved Uncle Jake, but they'll always be my aunt and uncle, and Steven's my brother."

They both came over to me and gave me a hug, Mother kissing my cheek. I'd been in one of my growth spurts and noticed it was difficult for her to do now, unless I was sitting down. Dad was rubbing his hands against my arms from behind. After a minute or so, they both pulled back a bit and looked at me with warm smiles framed by tears rolling down their cheeks, a sweet and salty moment all at once.

"Does Steven know?" I asked.

They shook their heads no.

"We'll tell him when he gets back," Dad said. "You'll have to tell Rose, she's on her way over for breakfast," he said to Mother. She nodded her head yes but I could see her eyes flickering, darting, trying to find a place to alight, to fix on, to steady herself, to steel herself in anticipation of how she was going to do it.

"I'll tell her, Mother, let her hear it from me, I found out on my own anyway and this'll give her the opportunity to tell me how it was best for me."

"You're such a good boy," Mother said, "come here, let me kiss you all over," which she did. It made me feel good.

In a few minutes Auntie Rose arrived. I waited until she'd gotten settled in the kitchen. BlueDog was at her heel. I started up by asking her about the name-your-baby book that she kept by her bedside and took the seat next to her at the kitchen table. She seemed startled for a split second, and in that infinitesimally small moment, I could sense her uncertainty as to whether this was about *the issue* she'd been waiting to confront all these years or if she were misinterpreting an innocuous gesture.

I jumped in to avoid any ambiguity. "I know; I know all about what happened when I was born, about giving me to Mother and Dad."

A mysterious force pulled me into her arms, and we both cried softly, a happy cry, for a few minutes. She pushed me back a foot or so, smiled, wiped my tears with her thumbs, and hugged me again. We began to laugh uncontrollably.

I wanted to know all about it, the circumstances, how she came to the conclusion that she didn't want to be a mother, that she could give the baby, me, to her sister, that they'd make up a story and then decide when to tell me, if not the whole thing, at least the major parts. As eager as I was to know the answers to these questions, I could sense that *I* needed to tread gingerly as well, so I started out by asking how she named me, why she picked Joel.

"It had to be a *J*, it couldn't be Jacob, of course, Joel was just fine." At that moment I realized that Steven was named for Sylvia, but I was in the dark as to whom I was named after. I persisted, not wanting to upset her, yet quite curious as to whether I was going to find out about some relative who'd died before 1939 and what story that might trigger.

"Why a *J*, Auntie Rose?"

"It was Uncle Jake's idea. Come, let's move to the living room, it'll be more comfy." BlueDog traipsed behind her, then put his head in her lap and closed his eyes the moment she plopped down on the sofa, whereupon Auntie Rose absently stroked his ears. I sat on her other side. I thought that was all she was going to say, and despite my wanting more, I wasn't going to agitate, for I knew this whole episode was very hard for her. Suddenly, Mother and Dad appeared in the room; they'd followed me in case they were needed and now was the time that Mother stepped in to help both Auntie Rose and me.

"Uncle Jake had a premonition," she began. "He saw it the night he and Auntie Rose witnessed Kristallnacht in the hospital in Hamburg. He'd lived through the degradation of our people since 1933. Each year, the situation had gotten worse. He'd waited in vain for ordinary Germans to come to their senses. Jews had gone from being mocked to being disenfranchised to being attacked, and this downward trajectory could only result in them being expelled, or worse. For a while, he thought they'd all end up in another country, the US perhaps, or Palestine. But as the restrictive laws were passed and Jews were subjected to the whims of street mobs, he came to the terrible conclusion that as a group, they were doomed. That's when he made the fateful decision."

"To leave," I added.

"Surreptitiously, yes," Auntie Rose said. "Uncle Jake waited for the right moment; he needed a death certificate. During Kristallnacht, with the bodies in the streets, he implemented his plan. Then he made the deal with the customs official; paid him a lot of money and gave him a car as well."

"But what's this got to do with my name beginning with a *J*?" I persisted.

Auntie Rose turned her head to look directly into my eyes, and with her hands still stroking BlueDog, said simply, "You were named for the Jews."

It never occurred to me until many years later that I might have been burdened with the memory of the six million who had died at the hands of the Germans. For the time being, however, I was enthralled to have corroboration as to the truth of how Uncle Jake had met Auntie Rose and how they had left Germany together after Kristallnacht.

I had successfully leapt over the hurdle of my origins and my name but still didn't know why I'd been raised by Mother and Dad. Was this too delicate a question? I mulled over how I could inquire, cognizant of Auntie Rose's potential defensiveness and sensitive to the possibility that discussing this so soon after losing Uncle Jake might be too much for her to bear. A real schicksalsfrage, I thought, and the dredging up of this term from Old Uncle A's recollection of Uncle Jake's tale made me smile brighter than the hundred-watt bulb in the reading lamp on the end table.

"Can you tell me, Auntie Rose, what happened at the hospital, not the one in Hamburg and not here, a few months ago when Uncle Jake died, but when I was born?"

She started out pretty matter-of-factly, but within a few moments, her eyes filled up and I waited for them to spill over, just as I would anticipate her cupcakes rising to the lip of the baking tins and would bet on whether they'd cling or spill down onto the pans.

Auntie Rose said, softly, "My pregnancy had not been, um, *planned*." She hesitated, waiting to hear if I would interrupt with a question as to its meaning. My silence prompted her to continue. "Long before Uncle Jake and I got to the hospital, we'd struggled with our feelings about being parents. Uncle Jake intimated that he would go along with whatever I decided; I attributed this deference to his European upbringing and his acknowledgment of my primacy in this regard. While he was offering support for the position of keeping the baby, I could detect it was given without genuine enthusiasm, inasmuch as his demeanor was respectful and conciliatory but without passion. As the weeks went by, I suspected his ennui was related to a resignation that he would have to assume a paternal responsibility for which he felt ill-suited. Do you understand?" she asked, and I interpreted this as meaning could I follow since she had used the word *ennui,* and although I couldn't give her a definition, in the context of the story I didn't need her to stop and explain. I nodded affirmatively.

"When I was about four months pregnant, Uncle Jake confided to me that he could no longer pretend that he wanted to be a father. It was enough, he declared, for him to minister to the horses at the track where he could immerse himself for eight hours a day and temporarily not worry about the possibility of a horrendous fate for European Jewry. He spent all week dealing with eye and gum infections, torn muscles, abrasions and scrapes, pus and blood and bile, never investing his emotional capital in the horses' futures, either as individuals or as part of a group. That's what got him through each day."

I was about to ask Auntie Rose how distressed she was at the time Uncle Jake told her of his decision, when she sighed, as if reliving the moment, and said, "In fact, I'd been looking for an opportunity to tell Jake that I wasn't sure *I* wanted to raise a child." She hesitated and I could tell that this was related to her not wanting to offend me, because she put her hand tenderly on the side of my cheek. It was a gesture that was meant to convey her eternal bond with me, and I reciprocated it by giving her a clinging hug, burrowing my face into her shoulder. She gently rocked me back and forth, her tears dripping onto my neck, one by one. She was silent.

After a bit, Mother took up the slack, beginning slowly as if she were attempting to drive a car from a dead stop in third gear. "Auntie Rose was overwhelmed," she started, "with all *my* responsibilities, all the attention your brother required, nonstop. She followed me around, making notes, *dozens* of them—to do with caring, feeding, playing, teaching. Why, it got so that each time your brother cried, she scrambled through her notes frantically, looking to find a similar situation in the past so that she could then hopefully recognize what to do when she had her own baby."

With her eyes closed, Auntie Rose gave a gentle laugh, resurrecting a long-ago memory. "I had a collection of scribblings a mile long that your father"—here she meant Dad, not Uncle Jake—"helped me organize in his usual efficient, accounting way, by alphabetizing the categories of my observations. Each night, I'd flip through my three-ring notebook and have your father"—now she meant Uncle Jake—"quiz me on the topics before we turned the lights out. I was more exhausted than your mother, for Pete's sake, and she was the one with the baby!"

It all made sense and I decided not to interrupt, but I wasn't convinced that this was the whole reason. I suspected that it had as much to do with her eccentricities, with her hibernation, with her not having been brought up by her own mother, a deprivation that manifested itself in her not being able to relate to motherhood.

"It was Uncle Jake who came up with the idea of a stillborn, and we discussed it with Papa first; he was flabbergasted but eventually saw the wisdom in making the adoption an intrafamily affair. It was, clearly, a superior alternative to losing the baby, you, altogether. With his blessing secured, we approached your Mother and Dad"—here she looked up at both of them and then continued—"the night I had them feel the baby's kick, your kick! for the first time."

Auntie Rose declined my appeal to provide specifics as to those discussions; only later, when I became an adult, did I recognize the distinction that Auntie Rose was making by refusing to let me peek into some of her most private moments after having revealed so much previously. I would have to learn about boundaries later, especially when it was safe to cross and which other times it was prudent not to try.

"We fabricated the stillborn story that would be used until such time as you and Steven were old enough to be told, but we never set a date."

What amazed me was that everyone must've known the truth yet no one ever slipped up. What eggshells they must have been walking on when I first began to speak and interact and comprehend.

At this point, Mother and Dad melted away, an acknowledgment that their presence was no longer necessary, now that they'd witnessed Auntie Rose deal with the situation, with me, in a way that maybe they hadn't anticipated. Even I, right before I talked with Mother and Dad that morning, hadn't known quite what to expect from her. I couldn't have predicted: Would she withdraw? Curl up in tears? Not be able to speak?

Auntie Rose got up slowly so as not to disturb BlueDog, opened her purse, and pulled out a few old pictures. She searched for one specific photo. When she found it, she checked the back to make sure the inscription described what she was looking for and then, with an electric smile that I didn't remember ever seeing before, handed it to me. It was a picture of a boy mugging for the camera, holding a leash. The dog was a black Labrador and it looked much like BlueDog. The boy in the photo looked like me, but I never had those ridiculous clothes, knee pants they were called, britches by some, and socks like the girls wear up to their knees.

"Is this Steven?" I wanted to know, not really believing my question but wondering who it could be, it wasn't me, that was for sure.

"It was your father, Uncle Jake," Auntie Rose said.

I peered closer and could see that it was, it really was.

"You should have this picture for your scrapbook," Auntie Rose said. "Each time you look at it, you should know how proud he was of you, how proud he was that you were his son."

Only when I was older did I stop to think about how Auntie Rose and Uncle Jake pushed me away and simultaneously pulled me close. How awkward it must've been to make the decision to give me up and then to make me an integral part of their lives. When, I wondered, did they make the transformation from mother and father to aunt and uncle? Did they have regrets? Or was it a relief?

My initial reaction was a mixture of acceptance, excitement, and confusion.

I accepted what Auntie Rose, Mother, and Dad had just told me; for once, it seemed to be the truth, the whole truth, and nothing but the truth, the kind of thing that they say when they swear you in on a stack of Bibles. And the fact was there was nothing that could be done. Auntie Rose was still Auntie Rose and Uncle Jake would forever be Uncle Jake. I didn't think of myself as having two sets of parents and vowed that I'd never let Mother and Dad have any reason to doubt my filial loyalty.

Part of me was feeling on top of the world, as if I'd hit a home run in the bottom of the ninth to give the Braves a come-from-behind victory. I'd figured this out on my own and had handled myself in front of Auntie Rose in a manner that could've provoked Mother into one of her ace of spades comments such as, "HE'S A FINE YOUNG MAN OF WHOM SYLVIA WOULD'VE BEEN PROUD."

And, let's face it, I hadn't actually suffered a loss.

But I wouldn't be able to avoid some confusion. I lived with a woman who was my mother but not my birth mother and spent a lot of time with another woman who was my birth mother but also my aunt. I was concerned about mixing up salutations, calling Auntie Rose "Mother," for example, by mistake, and Mother overhearing and feeling hurt, thinking perhaps that she was diminished somewhat in my eyes despite all the mothering that she'd done.

Auntie Rose's reaction was a mixture of acceptance, excitement, and relief.

I was gratified that she accepted this as if she knew not only that it was coming but that it was coming that day. She was like the understudies who've practiced their lines over and over to be in the right place if the call comes so that they can fit in seamlessly to the role. Had she and Uncle Jake practiced? How could they've anticipated all the alternative ways in which this could've played out?

What I hadn't anticipated was the pure joy that exploded from her. She'd kept this secret hidden for so long that no one could imagine the fireworks display that'd ensue once the fuse had been lit.

Yes, and relief: now she could unravel her stories and pictures, unencumbered by thoughts of pretending, not worrying about holding things in, not concerned that she'd say the wrong thing.

I stayed with Auntie Rose for most of the day, alternating between enthusiastic periods of hugging and kissing and more even-keeled talking about everything imaginable except, of course, *the troubles*. I asked her about being a little sister; I wanted to know if it was the same as being a younger brother. I clamored to find out more about Papa as a father, not just a grandfather; did he regale her with stories too? I probed to find out if Mother's ace of spades comments were something she invented as an adult or if she'd used these expressions when she was a kid. Had she fallen in love with Uncle Jake at first sight? Could she really hear animals talk? On and on I inquired, in jeopardy of being a nudge, but I didn't care, I wouldn't be able to stop my engine from overheating until all my questions had been answered.

For the most part, I was sitting next to her and she had her arm around me, which enabled her to gently guide me closer to a picture on the coffee table or to pull me in to her, the mama bird sitting on her egg.

We sat for a while in silence with her just rubbing my arms, with me leaning into her side. Then I turned so we were face-to-face and asked directly if she missed me.

"What do you mean, sweetie?" she asked.

"Well, you know, not *missed* missed, you see me practically every day, that's not what I mean." I stopped, searching for the right words, and then began, not knowing if what I was going to say would indeed be the right words. "Do you miss me as your son?"

"You are my son," she replied evenly.

"No, Auntie Rose, I don't mean it that way, what I mean is that I'm Mother's son and you're my aunt, and I wonder if that's still okay with you or do you ever, you know, wish . . ." I trailed off.

"Wish that I never gave you up?" she interjected.

"Yes."

She sat perfectly still for a while and also looked straight across the room when she answered. She seemed to be in a trance for a bit, and I knew not to break it. Finally, she said, "Just know that I love you with all my heart, I always did and I always will, that I'm your Auntie Rose and your birth mother and I don't see a conflict in any of that."

She gave me a kiss that went on for a little too long, normally something I would've squirmed out of, but because it was this day, I let it go without resistance or comment.

I probably received more kisses that day than any other, and I can tell you that when I went back to my room, BlueDog started to sneeze nonstop, a reaction to the perfume and lipstick that covered me from head to toe.

It was years before I could fathom what Auntie Rose had said, her real schicksalsfrage: if she had said yes, she regretted the adoption, it would have caused a Pompeii-like eruption in our household, and if she had said no, it could've come across as cold or selfish.

As soon as Steven came home, I showed him the picture of Uncle Jake with a black Lab and asked him who he thought it was. He said it looked just like me and BlueDog, but where did I get those crazy clothes? I told him it was Uncle Jake and then took him through how I'd connected the dots, about Auntie Rose and Uncle Jake being my real parents. I gave him the play-by-play of what happened when I spoke earlier that day to Auntie Rose, along with Mother and Dad, who joined to explain things that were too difficult for Auntie Rose to say herself.

"So you're still my brother, aren't you?" he wanted to know.

"Of course."

"Okay, that's weird," he said, then smiled and went on, "cuz you went to sleep one thing and woke up another."

It took me a few seconds to register that by saying "cuz," he was making a double entendre, and I gave him an admiring laugh, something I truly meant.

And then, for the first time, he hugged me, really hugged me.

I spoke with Papa about all of this in the evening when we were working on our stamp collections, and I appreciated the fact that he didn't pretend that this was the first he knew that I'd found out about the adoption, Mother having called him at work. He told me that any time I wanted to speak to him about what he called "the situation," I shouldn't hesitate to do so, but that it was imperative to keep this within the family.

So on the surface, everything was normal. But there were times, especially at night, all quiet with the exception of BlueDog's slow, rhythmic breathing, that I fantasized about what it would've been like to've had Auntie Rose and Uncle Jake as parents and Steven as a cousin. It was all dreamy, of course, which is what we do as kids, discounting the possibilities of strife, eliminating any considerations of negative outcomes, and hardly ever giving heed to the daytime facts, preferring instead to create a patchwork alternative, which we tuck in tightly around us, giving ourselves over to the illusion that warmth equals truth. And then we wake up, from either a noise or a voice, and ask ourselves was what I just went through real or did it come from the imagination? And not really knowing is disorienting; it jumpstarts our fears into high gear in a flash, our serenity transforming into anxiety and doubt.

On the night I confirmed my authenticity, I found myself sitting up, then pacing the bedroom, mumbling a bit, going to the bathroom, getting a snack from the icebox, walking around the kitchen table, slapping the backs of the chairs with an ever-increasing severity, asking the questions I wouldn't pose to Auntie Rose: Couldn't you've at least tried? Why did I have to find out on my own? Did you love me any less? What would Uncle Jake have said if he were still alive? Did you ever have any regrets? *Did you ever think of how I would feel?*

It was all for the good, I eventually reasoned, referring to the intra-family adoption, and came to the conclusion that this wasn't the last time I was going to wake up in a fit to pace the house, to talk to myself. I was right, of course, as I followed this middle-of-the-night pattern for many days, once bumping into Dad, who told me he couldn't sleep, he'd gotten up to work on a particularly tough accounting problem, and another time into Mother, who seemed fidgety, not making any sense about why she was up. For many years, even when I was in the army, I had the recurring dream where I asked the same questions, over and over, always consoled in the end by the refrain from that night: it was all for the good.

Steven once asked me if I had I been upset or even angry about any of this. I wasn't, probably because I remained in the family. But I did wonder if I would've been hostile had I been shipped out to a stranger and never known my birth parents.

I was dying to tell someone, and I was pretty sure that Susie would keep it a secret, but you never knew. Kids who are fast friends one day can turn on each other in a split second and say the cruelest things; they have little regard for the consequences once they perceive the friendship to be over. But in the end, I heeded Papa's advice and told no one. Ever. Until now.

December 29, 1952

Someday was today. I have lost a husband and gained a son.

Auntie Rose

33.

We were meant to focus on Kristallnacht, the Nuremberg laws, and mischlinge

The last time we saw Old Uncle A, Steven and I met him at North Station; he was almost unrecognizable from afar, all stooped over, slow of gait, and drastically thinner than he'd been just a few months earlier. It was only when we were about twenty feet away that I was sure I knew who it was. He did perk up when he saw us. That's when we rushed to relieve him of his bags; it was a competition between us in a way. He wouldn't surrender his scarf, which he wore practically as a vest.

In the taxi on the way home, he talked softly and haltingly about Morone, referring to him exclusively as Mordecai, which wasn't really all that surprising since Morone had started referring to himself that way in the phone calls we got from him at Sal the barber's.

I wondered how Morone referred to himself when he talked with his father and uncle on the phone. In a close-knit Italian family, a Mordecai would've been as out of step as a real Moses in the O'Neil clan or a real Murph among the Feldman *mishpachah*. It occurred to me that Big Alfredo and Rocky probably lit a candle for him as if he were gone, the same way Jews sat shiva when someone married out.

Old Uncle A's voice had been reduced to a whisper. He simply didn't have the lung capacity to speak or move the way he used to. However, his mind hadn't withered, not one whit. Back at our place, he was still able to teach us about liberty and justice for all, not by the rote of the Pledge, rather by means of his vast knowledge of stamps, including the three-cent George Washington Carver 1948, the Justice Harlan Fiske Stone 1948, and the Samuel Gompers 1950. When he finished, he then presented us with plate blocks for these three stamps, treasures of unrivaled value I have today that I could sell for a couple of dollars each.

On that last visit, Old Uncle A and I went for a short walk around the block. He was all bundled up, more than what I thought was necessary for the weather. We walked slowly; he was holding on to me for balance. After a few minutes of silence, he looked up to me and said, "Promise that you won't let Palus Island die." He squeezed my arm as he said it, so of course I said I wouldn't. I didn't have a clue as to what he meant. The next day, he took the train to return to Maine.

As frail as he was, it wasn't much of a shock to me when Papa announced somberly a few days later that Old Uncle A had died in his sleep; from old age, he quickly added, which made Steven and me feel better. But I couldn't stop thinking about the pledge that I'd made to him about keeping his island alive. I must've thought about this nonstop for days after he died. I had this recurring dream in which I'd watch a giant earthquake swallow the small island off the coast of Maine, whole, knowing that because I hadn't prevented this from happening, I was responsible: I'd let Palus Island die, I'd disappointed Old Uncle A. I was driving myself nuts tossing and turning every night. I moved around the bed so much BlueDog finally sat up one night and gave me that dog look that meant to cut it out or sleep on the floor.

I woke Steven up and anxiously told him about my promise to Old Uncle A and my inability to make sure an island didn't die.

"I know, I'm being silly, islands can't die, they can't just go poof and disappear—but why'd he say it?"

"Hey, you know the funny thing is, islands *can* die. I read in the *Weekly Reader* that when they dropped the first hydrogen bomb over the island of Elugelab in the Eniwetok Atoll in the South Pacific, eighty thousand tons of soil were lifted into the air. The island was vaporized. Now it doesn't exist. It said so, on the very first page."

"Come on, that's not what I mean."

Knowingly, Steven got up and sat cross-legged on the bed and continued on a different tack. "Jeez Joel, it's not that Old Uncle A wanted you to actually make sure the reds don't destroy Palus Island. He was using what's called a metaphor; that's when they say stuff to illustrate something, they give an example, and what he meant was that you, you're the one who's going to carry on the tradition, you know, the storytelling about the family, about the folks on Palus Island, about politics, and about things that go on. He was handing it over to you; he knew he was dying, Papa's really old, and Uncle Jake has died. Think of your obituaries, the scrapbooks, how you're able to finish other people's stories, that's what Old Uncle A was talking about."

It hit me. I looked over at BlueDog and imagined that he was a little Greek boy from Papa's stories and that I could continue to talk to him, to practice my stories so that one day I could talk about Steven, Noodge and Susie Mauer, Myandrew, Frankie, Zippo, and all the grown-ups we interacted with in 1952, the year the Braves decided to leave Boston, the year I found out about my uncle Jake coming to America, the year I found out about Little Alfredo's death, the year I helped the congressman win the Senate race with the aid of a theft and a bribe, the year I found out about my origins, as well as the year I found out that my grandmother had been murdered.

"You're right," I said, "it didn't matter that Uncle Jake told us how he arrived in Boston from a ship directly from Germany and met Auntie Rose for the first time on the dock, where she took him to HIAS, yet Uncle A told us a completely different story."

"Who knows if Peek even existed?" Steven said.

We'd seen him at the zoo, but the truth was we'd seen an ostrich, and yes, Auntie Rose spent an inordinate amount of time with it, and yes, it seemed to like her, but then again, what zoo animal known to be friendly doesn't like some human contact, and why should we have believed all this about the woman who went into hibernation for the month of November?

We were silent for a while and then my brother said, "I don't care about the truth of how Uncle Jake became a vet or how he met Auntie Rose. We were meant to focus on Kristallnacht, the Nuremberg laws, and mischlinge."

That was the point.

"And who knows if half the stuff Old Uncle A told us was true, about Nana, about Uncle Jake, and even about stamps?" he added.

One thing we found out was true was how the congressman came from behind in the last few weeks of the campaign, roaring ahead, fueled by the endorsement from the *Boston Chronicle*, the newspaper owned by Mr. Wolf, who suddenly swung his paper to the congressman's side. Some of this was eventually reported in the *Herald Traveler*, although no names were ever mentioned; it was all hush-hush, off the record, no official would talk about it.

Papa told us all about the polls that were posted on the front page of the paper that compared the congressman to his opponent that day as well as the previous day and week.

"Well, the polls were phony, made up, numbers pulled out of thin air," he told us. "I'm going to let you boys in on a secret," he continued, a tribute to us that was more rewarding than Murph Feldman's quarters; he was now taking us into his confidence, something he did with Moses O'Neil, Murph Feldman, and Chief Stinkowski. "Murph Feldman paid off the guy who conducted them and Derby Canurbi bet the poll numbers each day, making a killing, of course, because he knew in advance what they'd be. The *Chronicle*'s endorsement, the momentum of the polls, and the extra cash we could share with the campaign pushed the congressman over the top," he said without a trace of guilt. Then he winked and walked out.

"That must've been the fix that they referred to that night at Faneuil Hall when you and I went to the rally for the congressman," I said, once Papa was beyond earshot.

"Yeah, but that's probably not the whole thing," Steven said. "Look, there was that rumor we overheard in Papa's office that Mr. Wolf was in desperate need of cash on account of a mistress he had to keep quiet. So it must've been what they call a shakedown: Mr. Wolf would endorse the congressman, publish the results of the phony poll every day, and get a slice of Derby Canurbi's winnings, or else the story about the affair would appear on the front page of the *Herald Traveler*."

Papa reopened the door to our room a crack, poked his head around the opening, and said, "One last thing boys. Another secret. Don't ever breathe a word of this, but you should know that the whole thing with the *Chronicle* was set up by the congressman's old man."

34.

You mean Little Alfredo wasn't a hero?

Steven and I were eager to meet Dr. Burgas when he returned from duty in Korea. Tall and thin, quick-witted and a real take-charge guy, Daniel Burgas, MD, was the pride and joy of Isaac, the kosher butcher, the boy who justified Isaac's own father's decision in 1890 to come to America from a small city on the Black Sea in Bulgaria. Steven wanted to copy everything Daniel did, from the moment we met him at a party that Papa held at the furniture store.

Our job was to move most of the furniture to the sides so there'd be room for all the partygoers, leaving a freestanding bar and some cocktail tables in its place. We arranged things according to a plan that Murph Feldman gave us. When he handed it to me, I told him I wasn't a nincompoop, prompting him to respond that he knew that, kiddo, then look back and smile at me, an acknowledgment of the first time I scored a gotcha with him. We knew just about everybody and we were the only kids, celebrities kind of, which was okay with us.

Daniel came to the party at Papa's store directly from making rounds, wearing his loose-fitting, hospital-issue blue smock and pantaloons. To Steven, he was glamorous.

Daniel told us about what it was like to be a physician, particularly in the emergency room, and Steven begged him to let him come one night and visit. He told Daniel that he wanted to see the stabbings and the gunshots and then watch as he sewed them up and saved their lives.

"It's not like what they show you on Saturday mornings at the movies," he said. He explained what a typical day was like and didn't mince words when it came to vivid descriptions of blood and guts, accompanied by pain, howls, confusion, and a barrage of physicians, nurses, and attendants who instantly swarmed over the patients, trying to do doctoring and detective work at the same time, making decisions on the spot that could always be criticized in the cool light of the following days, when it would all look so obvious.

This drew Steven in like a magnetic force.

My only thought was that the pantaloons were ridiculous.

At the end of that evening, Daniel came to say good-bye to us at the same time as Rocky and Big Alfredo made their way in our direction. They hugged and thanked Daniel, addressing him as Dr. Burgas, for the lovely letter he'd sent and for letting them know how Little Alfredo had died. After Rocky and Big Alfredo left, Daniel lingered. He didn't take his leave as he'd planned. He stood there for about a full minute, then turned and asked us if we wanted to know how Little Alfredo died.

We told him we knew, that we'd heard it from his dad, first when he came to our house to tell Papa and then when he read the letter at the wake for Little Alfredo.

Daniel told us that what we'd heard was what he'd wanted us to hear. What he'd wanted the story to be.

"When I observed my initial death as an intern, the chief attending told me that the first thing that you say is the matter of record, so you should make sure that you say and do what you want history to acknowledge. I wanted Big Alfredo and Rocky to be proud of Little Alfredo, to think of him as an American hero, the son of immigrants who gave his life for his country. So I spent hours determining what it was I was going to say and how I would write it in a way that Little Alfredo's family could take some small measure of solace from his death."

"You mean Little Alfredo wasn't a hero?" Steven asked.

"Oh, he might very well have been," Daniel replied, "but he didn't die the way I described in the letter."

Daniel told us what had happened.

"I did indeed go up to the main line of resistance, although as a doctor, I wasn't allowed to go out on patrol. It was just too risky; there were so few of us that they couldn't take an unnecessary risk of losing even one of us. A patrol came back one night, a group of men I'd never seen before, carrying a dead marine.

"A few days later, I was back in Seoul and was approached by a marine who recognized me from that night. The marine told me that he needed to talk about what'd *really* happened up there. I suggested he seek out a clergyman, but the marine declined and simply started to talk.

"The marine told me that he'd been out on that patrol and been involved in the firefight. When it was all over, they stepped around the bodies of the dead guys, and that's when they all realized that they weren't *North* Korean, who we call PROK, or Chinese, who we call CCF; no, to their horror, they realized the soldiers were *South* Korean, ROK troops, our allies, dead on the ground along with one of our guys, too.

"Friendly fire. He said they held a powwow. Some guys wanted to tell the truth when they got back, others said let it be. 'Who'll know?' The marine who told me this said he went from body to body, trying to discover if there was life left in any of them. There wasn't. Apparently, the South Korean troops had shot at the marines first. Our guys voted, majority rules, and it turned out in favor of saying they'd been attacked by enemy troops, returned fire, and made their way back, end of story.

"It was simply a group of ROK troops who did the reverse of ready, aim, shoot and paid the ultimate price. And the one of ours who got it? A poor kid, Alfredo Morone, who was clipped in the head from behind, probably when he was running for cover at the sound of the first salvo."

He paused; it was obvious he was still affected by all of this.

"I couldn't," he started and stopped. "I couldn't. I tried and tried to tell the truth in the letter to my father. I threw several drafts away, it just didn't seem right. Don't ask me how I came up with the idea to concoct the story, for which I have some guilt, I must admit. I tell myself it was the right thing to do. Seeing Little Alfredo's father and uncle here, I guess it was.

"You know," he said to us in a way we later thought was him practicing how he'd say it to others, "it's pretty clear to me now that Little Alfredo died in vain."

The three of us stood awkwardly without talking for a while, then Daniel made a few minor head and hand motions, indicating that he was really leaving, his way of saying good night, which I'm not sure he could've done if he'd actually had to utter the words.

I wonder now, somewhere out there today, do a little Steven and Joel exist, dropping pretend smart bombs filled with water off of buildings, working joysticks in front of consoles, zapping figures over the horizon, snapping to and saying "Sal-u-tay" to men in camouflage uniforms, wondering if they'll ever see them again?

Somewhere out there do a Papa and Murph Feldman and Moses O'Neil exist, prepared to pierce through the political protective vests worn by the elected officials, without firing any ordnance, simply by taking actions to counter the vanity of the men who dream up these conflicts but never have to fight or die in them? And somewhere out there does a young Dr. Daniel Burgas live, undertaking his responsibilities to those who come back from the battlefield to stitch them up with the threads of dignity?

I grieve today, still, for Little Alfredo, for the other Little Alfredos Dr. Burgas couldn't help, and for the Little Alfredos I'll never know about.

I remember crying at Little Alfredo's funeral and again back at Big Alfredo's house after the service. I remember the waterworks when I first showed Little Alfredo's obituary to Big Alfredo and Rocky.

As a kid, I thought that grief might be quantified on a device that measured tears in the same way that a thermometer records temperature, it was that simple. But now it's all more complicated, as today they tell us it's hotter than it actually is because of the temperature-humidity index and the wind-chill factor makes you feel colder than it actually is. Nowadays, expressions of grief are not always apparent on a face or in body language; more often than not, they manifest themselves as searing abdominal pain, what Old Uncle A would call a twisting of the *kishkes*, a part of the body Steven looked for but never found inside his first cadaver at medical school.

Now that I'm an adult, I hoard my tears, as if there were a finite supply and letting them go without appropriate provocation would cheapen the impact of their release when I face real loss. Although they're reserved, I never know in advance when they'll want to come out. As I've gotten older, they gather right below the eyelid, peeping out, waiting for the command to charge, sometimes giving me a look of vulnerability, something that's perceived as weakness in a child but as sweet and sentimental in an older person.

35.

And that's how I met your grandmother

Often when Steven wasn't around, I'd be in our room, pretending to be on the air, practicing with BlueDog as the audience, and sometimes Papa would walk in, always begging off when he saw what I was doing, me always insisting he stay, him protesting, nevertheless heading for the leather chair that'd once been at HIAS, so I guessed it was as old as he was. He'd close his eyes and I'd wonder if he was imagining that he was telling other people *his* stories from the time that he was back on the boat that took him to Nova Scotia and Palus Island at the turn of the century, when he met Nana. That was, of course, the boat on which he'd entertain the passengers with his wild tales of places he'd never been, experiences he'd never encountered, people he'd never met.

One time, I thought Papa had dozed off, but the second I finished my monologue, he opened his eyes and asked, "Do you want to know how I met Nana?" I assumed that this was purely a rhetorical question. I knew that not paying attention was taboo, clearly disrespectful, and despite the fact that I could practically recite parts of the story myself, I said of course and moved over to the bed where BlueDog rearranged himself to fit snugly into my curvature.

So he started in with, "There was an old immigrant at HIAS who'd be awakened by demons each night. His screaming was bad enough, but his sleepwalking was frightening all the other occupants and he needed to be restrained. I'd sit on him, pinning his arms down, while another kid held his legs against the bed. It was my job to shut him up, but this wasn't easy. He'd throw his head around and spit, making it hard for me to get my fingers near his cheeks; he'd start to snap like a turtle, snap, snap, snap." He made the sounds with his thumb clicking off his middle finger.

"So I got to wearing gloves, the thick ones that coal deliverers like Rocky use. Anyway, one night when he was in a particularly bad state, the men who ran HIAS called Sylvia's mother when they looked up in the records that she was someone who might've known the old man from his village in the Pale," he continued. "Nana was just sixteen years old and had to learn English on the street as her parents only spoke Yiddish, telling each other that English was too hard to fathom. By the time Sylvia and her mother got to HIAS, I was sitting on the old immigrant's chest and the other boy had secured his legs. Sylvia's mother screamed at us and we were so startled that we leapt off the bed and practically stood at attention. She brushed by us like a medic ignoring his officers and attended to the old immigrant. Her soothing voice calmed him down, and she asked her daughter, in Yiddish, to get a towel soaked in cold water. I told her, in broken Yiddish—I'd forgotten so much as I was speaking English almost exclusively—to follow me, and we went down the hall together. We came back and handed the compress to Sylvia's mother, who'd by then gotten the old immigrant to sit up. He looked dazed. She told everyone to get out, and the three of us kids scrambled through the door awkwardly, causing Sylvia to tell the boy who'd been holding the old man's legs, Murph Feldman, to stop pushing her. Murph Feldman's Yiddish was as good as his Irish, which is to say he could order a knish from a street vendor or ask a girl in a tartan skirt to kiss his Blarney Stone; in other words, he didn't know what Sylvia was saying. I held him by the shirt collar and Sylvia slipped through the door first, walking fast ahead of us into the reception area. I thought she was beautiful and said so to Murph Feldman. When she turned around, blushing, telling us in English to go away, I was smitten. She wanted nothing to do with us, calling me a hooligan. Murph Feldman told me later that this was an Irish term for handsome man. I was doubly smitten. We sat on chairs at the reception for half an hour, waiting for Sylvia's mother. When she appeared, exhausted, she took her daughter and exited. I followed them, out of sight, to find out where they lived. The next day, Sylvia and her mother reappeared to find out that the old immigrant had slept through the night, peacefully. Sylvia's mother then explained to us that the old immigrant had seen unspeakable horrors in the village in the years since she herself had left, including the torture and death of his wife and daughter, which he rewitnessed every night.

"I saw Sylvia almost every day after that. She'd show up at HIAS to assist her mother, but she managed to spend her time with me and Murph Feldman, who taught her how to play dice, crank a car, and run her fingers through the sofas to search for the coins that the immigrants would leave.

"And that's how I met your grandmother," Papa said.

No boat to Halifax, Nova Scotia, no stopover on Palus Island, no meeting Mr. Auerbach—Old Uncle A—not a word. The story that we could recite, word for word, was gone, replaced by a memory dredged up of what, another event that he was confused about? Or was it a story with hidden meanings, something that I was supposed to unpack as I grew up? I told him that this was a beautiful story. He got up to leave my room, patting me on the head.

I couldn't tell if his eyelids were fluttering or if he gave me a wink, perhaps the same wink he gave me at the end of his stories about the little Greek boy. Of course, it could've been nothing more than an involuntary tremble.

After he closed the door, I said out loud, "When you're a kid, they don't always tell you the truth."

I let that linger for a while, then opened my scrapbook to the very first page. I took out one of Dad's sharpened number-two pencils and wrote at the top the words I'd just uttered.

It wasn't beyond Papa to've made up the HIAS tale to compete with the Palus Island story just to create some mystery and thereby keep himself alive. Papa is still very much there for me to touch, to feel, to talk to, to talk about, to debate, to discuss, to reminisce about, alive in anecdotes and remembrances I pass down to *my* grandchildren about a man they never met but could describe to a T: Solomon Mischal, a.k.a. Solly to the Irish pols, a.k.a. Frenchie to the passengers on the boat to Halifax, Papa to his grandchildren, furniture dealer, benefactor to immigrants, the man who helped rig an election for the grandson of immigrants, who arranged to sneak his son-in-law into the country as a refugee from Nazi Germany, who took advantage of inside information about a horse so he could make some bucks to provide for his family, and who organized the kidnapping of a marine so he wouldn't be in a position to die in vain.

36.

No record of citizen Jacob Goldblum

When I told Mother I was going to volunteer for the army in 1961 right after graduation from college, she gave me a tight hug then stepped back, looked me in the eye, and channeled her enthusiasm by repeating the second part of the president's "ask not" line from his recent inaugural address: "What You Can Do For Your Country," as if it'd been one of her ace of spades pronouncements that had been co-opted by a White House speechwriter. She took Polaroids of me in uniform and sent them to all her friends.

I was going to get drafted anyway. I figured it was worth the extra year if I volunteered in order to get to do Armed Forces Radio. Naturally, after basic training, I was assigned to the motor pool.

I took a ten-week course on how to fix every piece of transportation equipment in the army. They had manuals that even a cretin could follow, mostly pictures with names underneath, that kind of looked like a puzzle. On each page, a specific piece of the puzzle was shown in close-up, indicating where it was supposed to fit. Underneath, there was a list of what could go wrong on the left and suggestions for how to fix it on the right. They had a book for each vehicle, and we had to be able to pass an exam at the end of the course before we could be assigned to a particular motor pool squad. The incentive to pass was the realization that if you failed, you'd be assigned to the kitchen, and trust me, it was difficult enough to *eat* the chow, you didn't want to be part of the team that had to make it and clean up afterward. Remember, it's called *mess hall* for a reason.

At night, I'd doodle in the manuals they gave us, making notes with arrows that pointed to the places where I'd found things they hadn't illustrated or mentioned, along with some pithy comments that had something to do with the illustrations in the manual and a lot to do with tangents that allowed me to pass the time with interest. My buddies were always asking me what I was writing.

I told them I was taking notes on what I'd learned during the day, not wanting to be ridiculed as "college boy," doing my best just to be "plain folks." Inevitably, given the competitive instinct, one of the guys found my manual and began to read it in the barracks after dinner one night. Perhaps he expected me to be defensive or to demand he give it back. I figured if anyone wanted to read it, so be it. That defused him and he started to read it out loud. They gathered around him and within a few seconds, they laughed, amused by my critiques, observations, and suggestions.

Word spread quickly and a group of guys from other barracks came over each night and ask me to go through additional parts of my manual. Flattered, yes, but pressured, too, as I had to anticipate that a group would want to hear a little bit of what I'd written the previous day, so it had to be fresh. Least intimidating was the actual reading; it wasn't much different from going through my scrapbook, which I'd done countless times in front of BlueDog.

After I'd read my manual to the guys in the barracks every night for a week, our NCO called me out at lineup in the morning. He'd heard about the increasing traffic to my barracks at night and was suspicious. I showed him the manual and gave him some samples of what'd been going on. The next day, a captain we called Hook, on account of his culling volunteers to do his personal chores, came to see me and asked if I'd like to bring my manual to a wider audience. I imagined a stadium. He brought me to a little room with a desk and a microphone. He told me that I could have fifteen minutes that night at eight. He told me the chair squeaked so I'd better not move and sit straight and that with fifteen seconds to go I'd hear some music in my headphones, which meant that I'd have to wrap up. He pointed to the clock on the wall and said, "Watch Big Ben, it drives everything that we do," and then he walked out. This was my introduction to radio.

The guys in my squad spread the word, and I'm told that there was a transistor radio turned on in all the barracks, so I had an audience of hundreds, at least. I got the same slot each night. No one ever said anything to me about time after the first session so I took an hour, getting back to my quarters a little after nine. I never had to worry about having enough material. In addition to the motor pool, I had my own experiences with the infirmary (they insisted I needed a rectal examination when I went in for a tetanus shot after I cut my finger on a rusty drip pan, perhaps because I answered "my ass" to something that they asked me when I was giving my medical history), the mess hall (I stumbled in on a "silent but deadly" tournament following a lunch of franks and beans), and with frog giggin' (the good ol' boys from South Carolina taught the Yankees about that special post-midnight after-the-rain flashlight-and-rifle-butt exercise that wasn't found in any of the instruction manuals for how to be a good GI). Frankly, none of this was much different from the day-to-day experiences that Steven and I'd had with Noodge Mauer, Myandrew, and Frankie, except that we were nine years older and supposedly adults training for the defense of our country.

At this point, Noodge Mauer was engaged and working for the girl's father in a clothing store in Providence, which was okay, he wrote, except that the old man didn't speak any English, and he had to learn Portuguese and go to Mass every day. Myandrew was living in Greenwich Village, going to coffee houses, playing guitar, smoking marijuana, and being very vague about what he did to pay his rent. And Frankie? He was in jail.

At the beginning of 1962, I got my orders to ship out. I was sent to West Germany, to USAREUR in Heidelberg, to serve in a large motor pool where I'd be in charge of a group that worked on tanks, keeping them battle-ready at all times. The wall had been put up on August 13. We were on high alert. I couldn't write much in letters home, they were being monitored, so I kept a diary of sorts, scribbling on matchbooks, napkins, folded paper cups, really anything that didn't look like a letter or a traditional piece of paper. When I called home, Mother and Dad would share one phone and Auntie Rose and Papa the other, listening to tidbits from what I wrote, which made my experiences sound more adventurous than dangerous, fooling none of them as I'd be reminded by you-know-whom at the end of every call to "Be A Good Boy And Do What They Tell You," Mother's way of urging me to be on the lookout and stay out of harm's way, though God knows, it hadn't made a difference to Little Alfredo.

One day in March of '62, I was summoned to the commanding officers' quarters and greeted by Captain Hook, who'd also been transferred to Germany. He asked me if I would do a program on Armed Forces Radio, although *ask* isn't the right word for the kind of question that the higher-ups know the answer to in advance, as evidenced by the papers he handed me when I said yes, orders that indicated I'd been switched out of the motor pool the night before. He told me in the most serious way to be funny.

They allowed me to travel to other bases, where I could do interviews on the air or simply gather material for a broadcast at night. From the base at Heidelberg, I could get transport via my buddies in the motor pool to any other base and to every major city in West Germany. I went southeast to Stuttgart and Munich, north to Frankfurt, Bonn, Cologne, and Düsseldorf, and over the hump to Berlin. I picked up stories on the way, camped out with the motor pools in the bases to get new material, and made my way through the city streets, never getting a second glance from the children of the volk who passed me by without their eyes measuring the shape of my head, the slope of my nose, or the space on my sleeve where Juden like Uncle Jake had to wear the yellow star.

I went everywhere. Everywhere, it seemed, but to Hamburg. After a year of making excuses, I arranged for a trip in May of 1963. I'd picked up enough German to be able to get around, except that the farther south and east I went, the stronger the dialects became so that I had to rely on menus and other printed materials. But in Hamburg, I was reasonably self-sufficient. I went to the parks around the lakes and to the docks on the Elbe, looking for where there might've been a tent that once housed a circus. I had a few clues. I started with the Planten un Blomen, but this turned out to be unlikely, insomuch as the signs everywhere practically kept you from touching or smelling so much as a flower. I couldn't imagine what someone would've had to go through to get a permit for a circus, what with the construction of the tent and the effluvia from the animals. Old Uncle A had told us that when the circus hands left the harbor with the bird princess of Africa and Peek, following the accident, they sped around the ornate city hall and found a hospital across from a museum. I spread a map of the city on a bench at the side of the landlocked Binnenalster and tried to work backward to the spot where the kid threw the marble that knocked Peek off his feet, sending Auntie Rose crashing into the pole, resulting in her chance meeting with the veterinarian who'd spirited her away after Kristallnacht only to be felled at fifty-two by the sound of a baseball crashing into a glass window during a game being played by his nephew, who didn't find out he was his son until after he died.

I sketched possible routes, asking older people along the way about circuses and hospitals, careful not to mention anything about before the War, not wanting to have them clam up if they suspected I was seeking to extract recompense or guilt. I got nowhere. Finally, I decided to check at city hall itself; surely there would be a record for Uncle Jake, somewhere, of a permit, a tax, a license, a form of some kind.

I remembered how Steven and I were awed by the John Hancock Building, built in 1947, rising twenty-six stories, almost five hundred feet if you include the weather beacon, which everybody does. One of the first things we learned after we saw the beacon was:

Steady blue, clear view
Flashing blue, clouds due
Steady red, rain ahead
Flashing red, snow instead.

This was what I was thinking as I approached the city hall in Hamburg, although had I been more of a world traveler, I would've had images of Versailles or the Hermitage or Buckingham Palace in mind, or just about every European king's castle. Instead of admiring the granite and limestone coat under a copper hat with a neo-Gothic spire at attention, inspiring some to pause and instinctively salute its strength, its Germanness, I approached it as the potential repository of a part of my history, nothing more.

Having been frustrated in my attempt to find the site of the circus or the hospital where Uncle Jake and Auntie Rose had met and witnessed Kristallnacht, I was in search of traces of Jacob Goldblum. He was a doctor, there had to be a medical license. He was an employee of a hospital, there had to be a tax document. He drove a car, so he needed a driver's license. Or maybe he got a speeding ticket one day so there was a court record. Something. Or perhaps, it wasn't impossible, there was even a certificate of a marriage to someone before Auntie Rose.

After hours of asking where to find records, getting directions to one of the more than three hundred rooms, sorting through names, sifting through variants of Goldblum and of Jacob, finding pieces of official paper approving or denying the most mundane of events, I'd come up with nothing. I retreated to a bench by a window and started to think the unthinkable: that the story of his meeting Auntie Rose, of living through the Night of Broken Glass, of coming to America, was just that, a story, a tale that I now might have to realize was simply a fabrication. Perhaps this was the reason I'd delayed coming to Hamburg for over a year. I didn't want to discover that there was no truth to the narrative that'd become a central part of my life.

I didn't realize that I'd been sitting for almost an hour. I was exhausted. I walked down the stairs to the reception area and was nearly out the door when I passed a woman holding an application for a visa.

Lightning struck. I bolted back up the stairs and retraced my steps to a microfilm station that contained customs documents and frantically moved the levers to get at the documents from 1938, which I could see through the magnifying glass. I went through page after page for November 10, 1938. My eyes were blurred, my heart raced,

I sweated feverishly. I was nervous that I wouldn't find what I was looking for and nervous that I would. There was a huge amount of material to sift through as most international travel and movement of goods took place by ship at that time. When I saw it, I must've screamed and a couple of people came running toward me, picking up speed when they saw the blood on my brow, caused by smacking my head against the viewfinder when I'd pulled up instead of out. I applied pressure with a handkerchief for a minute, concerned that when I reinserted my eye, after coagulation, I'd find I'd misread or misinterpreted what I thought I'd seen. With my pulse racing to catch up with my need for oxygen, I looked again and saw the name I was searching for on a ship's manifest for the day after Kristallnacht. There it was, the name Uncle Jake had assumed, Dieter Harald Eberhart, as well as the signature of Gunter Schuttmann, the customs official who gave him an exit card and stamped his ticket for a boat trip to Montreal in exchange for some cash and his car.

I paid a small fee to have a copy of that document made and walked out of city hall emotionally exhausted and physically pained. I went to an outdoor café by the Binnenalster and ordered a beer. I sat there pressing a napkin filled with ice on my head, the swelling generating a riveting ache, the dried blood liquefying as the ice melted. I downed the anesthetic and wrote the following notes on the back of the copy of the ship manifest with Uncle Jake's pseudonym on the front:

> No record of citizen Jacob Goldblum. No residue of Dr. Jacob Goldblum. No trail of a Jewish doctor who lived and worked in Hamburg. However, evidence of Dieter Harald Eberhart, who made the North Atlantic crossing to Montreal on November 10, 1938 as an imposter, a Jew, traveling from Hamburg with an injured American circus performer and a wounded ostrich.

I stuffed the piece of paper in my pocket. Eventually, it too wended its way into my scrapbook.

A month later, in June 1963, I was assigned to go to West Berlin to do the army's "man on the street" interviews when the bigwigs were in town. They announced that the president was coming on the morning of June 26. I was stationed in the crowd interviewing American soldiers and the Germans who'd come to see him give his speech and then was to hustle into the building to cover the reception afterward, but under no circumstances was I to have the microphone on when the president was in the room.

There were more than four hundred thousand people out in front of the Schöneberg Rathaus, West Berlin's city hall, at the Rudolph Wilde Platz across from Checkpoint Charlie. It was a beautiful day. The crowd was in a festive mood. You have to remember that Berliners were cut off from West Germany, from the world, when the Russians put up the wall. There were times they suspected they'd be traded in some cold war card game and would end up behind the Iron Curtain. Having the president of the United States come to West Berlin was an affirmation of their worth to the West. I looked at the president's trip as a reflection of the American ethos to forgive and forget. You know, as an abstraction, I'll sign up for that, but in the real world, forgiving isn't so much an act of charity as it is naïveté, and forgetting is an insult to the victims.

Anyway, he gave a great speech. The most important one of his presidency. Really. Better than the inauguration speech when he said, "Ask not what your country can do for you . . ." and, "Let the word go forth from this time and place . . ." Here it was, only eleven years after I'd heard a young skinny congressman give a speech at the Badgers Club, a guy with a great sense of humor, who was there at that time as much because he was Honey Fitz's grandson as anything else, standing in front of us as a symbol of everything the other side was not. We all remember the punch line—"*Ich bin ein Berliner*"—but not how he set it up. "Two thousand years ago," he told the crowd, "the proudest boast was *civis Romanus sum*. Today, in the world of freedom, the proudest boast is *Ich bin ein Berliner*." The second he said it, there were more *Gänsehaut* in that crowd than if you'd had a million geese assembled to listen to the head gander.

All of us in the military converged into the conference room following the speech. In a few minutes, the president came around and made it his business to speak to every soldier in the room. We'd been told beforehand what we should do. We were to salute, remember he was our commanding officer, and not say a word; he had to address us first. That was part of the protocol. Which he did, one by one. He asked you where you were from, your name, what you did, that kind of thing. He could tell your rank; you weren't supposed to say, because as the commander in chief, he was supposed to know.

It all went pretty routinely. The president approached me, smiled, and asked me where I was from.

"Boston, sir." I saluted.

His eyes lit up, as I was someone from his hometown.

"What's your name, private?" he asked.

I'd given no thought as to what I might say if he addressed me. So when I opened my mouth to reply, I blurted out, "I'm Papa's grandson and I deliver envelopes on my bike, with my brother, we go all over the city and we get a quarter a day from Mr. Feldman."

No one breathed. The room was still. After a brief hesitation, he asked, "What's in those envelopes, son?" and I kind of raised my shoulders up a couple of inches, turned my palms up, and had the look of a kid who'd been caught red-handed and couldn't think of anything, nothing, that he could say that wouldn't get him in more trouble.

He was laughing although you couldn't hear it, you know the kind of laugh that gets transmitted without sound. He nodded and proceeded down the line. After he exchanged salutes with the next GI, he turned around, smiled, paused, stared at me, and said, "I knew we could count on you fellars," in his best imitation of The Boxer, who'd said precisely that to Steven and me at the Badgers Club meeting before the Senate election of 1952. His wink and broad smile were caught by his official photographer. Then he went on to the next soldier.

Five months later, he was dead.

37.

Everyone is going to want to know who's who

A year later, in Boston, I met The Guy on the Radio. I was just out of the army, back from West Germany. There was a blurb in the *Herald Traveler* that he was going to be a guest on a radio show in the city; he was promoting a book. I figured that if I could meet him, I could ask him some questions, the usual stuff, how to break in, could he point me in the right direction, that kind of thing. I waited for the show to be over at 10:00 p.m. and approached him as he was leaving the lobby. I remember I didn't rush up to him, tell him my name, say I was a fan. I knew that wouldn't get so much as a glance and that he'd never break stride.

Instead, as soon as I saw him, I took a kazoo out of my pocket and went into a rendition of his theme song, "The Bear Missed the Train." So many times I heard him play that, it's the phonetic English for "Bci Mir Bist Du Schön," what Uncle Jake used to sing on our car rides.

"The bear missed the train, the bear missed the train, the bear missed the train, and now he's walking."

"I'm going to the Copley Square Hotel," he said, not addressing me directly, "so you can be my guide to make sure I don't get lost." In a few minutes, we were at the bar. Here I was, at the literal elbow of someone who'd been successful, famous, for what I was thinking I wanted to do. I wouldn't have this opportunity again, so I launched into a monologue of what happened to me in 1952, telling him about my brushes with betrayal, disease, gambling, death, bribery, persecution, kidnapping, war, politics, escape, loyalty, forgery, unconditional love, depression, marines, theft, girls, and a dog.

I could tell that he'd been engrossed, but not wanting to push it, I stood up and said good night.

He shook my hand and said, "Hey, kid, someday you, Steven, Noodge Mauer, Myandrew, and Frankie are gonna be as well-known as the gang in my stories." He then added, "As important as it is that you remember your Mother, Dad, Papa, Uncle Jake, Auntie Rose, Old Uncle A, and all the other people who were central to you when you were growing up, you should embrace them more as an adult, especially as you get older and the distance between you and them becomes less significant."

I hesitated, then asked, "Are all of your characters *real*? Are your stories based on stuff that happened to you when you grew up?"

"Does it matter? Would you decide, one way or the other, to listen or to tune in somewhere else if you found out I made it all up? Or most of it?"

"No," I answered quickly, "it actually wouldn't make a difference."

"If it's just reporting on the events of the day it can be entertaining for a while, especially if there's a lively way of retelling, but it'd get tiresome, and truth be told, I'd never have enough good material for a show that goes on most nights if I had to give a verbatim account of interactions I'd had with friends, family members, and others I've met.

"Fictional characters have lives as well," he went on, "they inhabit our spaces and we interact with them; it's still a give-and-take, just not in the same sense as what's going on here, in our conversation tonight. But never forget that a made-up person can speak to us just as well as someone who's here in the flesh. There's no difference whether you hear something from the point of view of first person actual or third person fictional if it interests you, moves you, or gets you to think about things from another perspective.

"Look, kid, I don't have a clue whether the things you told me are true or not. What's important to me is that you've painted pieces of art that need to be displayed, and you know what? I don't care if they're fakes.

"For me, life's usually better as fiction. Yeah, you heard me right, because that way, no one can disagree with, challenge, or sue you. Now there's no harm starting with a *kernel* of truth, but make sure when you cook it up it turns into something that can't be traced back to its original form, you know, so think in terms of omelets, they begin as chicken eggs, but tell me, would anyone looking at an omelet who'd never seen a chicken's egg be able to tell you its origin?

"Let your characters speak to you, think of yourself as a translator, there's a million ways to say the same thing, that's why we have synonyms, after all.

"So don't be afraid of going off on tangents or making distortions, and blind alleys are okay too, because no one but you knows what the outcome will be and you can always make an elision to something else to get you back to where you want to be.

"And by the way, kid," he added as he was winding down, heading toward the elevator, "everyone is going to want to know who's who, especially relatives and those with whom you've interacted; they'll spend hours trying to determine if a character is all or partly based on them in disguise. Don't give in to the temptation to discuss this with them. That's all about their ego, pride, and neediness, and all that's gonna do is drain you dry."

He shook my hand, said good night, and disappeared. I made my way across the street and sat on a bench in the square between the library and Trinity Church. I was trying to process what The Guy on the Radio had said to me. I endlessly replayed what I'd heard, the reel looping round and round my brain until I felt something poke against my ribs; I attempted to swat it away, which caused the cop who was rousting me with his billy club to get agitated. I'd fallen asleep on the bench, and while I protested that I wasn't a bum, I was more concerned that he'd haul me in for vagrancy and that Mother would have to come down to the police station and say to me in front of the desk clerk, "For This I Had To Send You To College?"

He never knew my name, and I never asked him anything about how to get into radio. But this I'll say for sure: what he told me is the advice I followed for all these years.

The week after I met The Guy on the Radio was when I found BlueDog pretty unresponsive and took him up to Suffolk Downs to see the vet who'd taken over from Uncle Jake. I could tell from the minute the vet was looking at his eyes and feeling his abdomen that something was wrong. He told me BlueDog had cancer and gave me some medicine for the pain. When I got home, I gave BlueDog a pill and hoisted him onto my bed while I listened to a Milwaukee Braves game. One of my hands was stroking him softly about the ears and neck; the other was riffling through my scrapbook, into which I'd taped the kazoo I'd played a week earlier, the night I met The Guy on the Radio.

May 6, 1970
Dear Diary,

He's gone, I told my sister this morning on our first thing in the morning call. We drove together and went up the elevator to his floor. They said he was asleep. We waited in the lounge. When the attendant walked down the hall slowly with her head down, we knew.

The nurse told us that when he went to bed last night he said Nixon is killing me, pointed to two articles in the paper on the Cambodian Incursion and the Kent State shootings, and promptly fell asleep. I told my sister that we should put these last words on his headstone. We laughed and imagined how Joel might use this on his show. From Dad through us to his grandson. He will live forever now.

I will miss my father so,
Rose

38.

You're going to tell Auntie Rose, aren't you?

As the fiftieth anniversary of our grandmother's death approached, I felt the weight of the burden of keeping what I knew to myself and decided it was time to reveal the truth. Walking through the Fens on a beautiful summer day in 1972, I turned to Steven and said, "I have to tell you one more thing about 1952, something I withheld from you and everyone else, something that I originally thought you might've overheard, but since you've never brought it up, I'm pretty convinced this'll be news to you.

"It's about Nana," I began and proceeded to give him the round-by-round, blow-by-blow description of the conversation I'd overheard at Sal the barber's that day twenty years earlier when Steven was sitting behind me reading girlie magazines. When I finished, he was silent, and I didn't know if this was due to shock at finding out about his grandmother's murder or if he was stewing over the fact that I'd never told him previously.

Then he reached out, touched my arm, held it for a few seconds, and said, "You're going to tell Auntie Rose, aren't you?"

"Well, actually, I think she's going to tell me," I replied.

Auntie Rose looked through the glass beside the front door and excitedly let us in, giving us warm hugs. She then sat in the overstuffed chair in the living room where we used to see her with BlueDog snuggled on her lap, taking in the morning sun, a sleep aphrodisiac for both of them.

I made tea and waited until she'd had a few sips before starting the conversation about her mother, not wanting to risk her spilling the hot contents if she were to somehow become upset.

"Auntie Rose," I began gingerly, "Steven and I want to take you back in time, almost fifty years in fact, and talk to you about the night your mother died."

I waited for a reaction. Candidly, if it'd been negative, a hostility in voice or eye movement or a dismissive wave of the hand or perhaps even a tear, I would've stopped, given her state and my cognizance of not wanting to upset her. I was also concerned that she'd decline to engage with me, preferring instead to drift into a dreamy fog, leaving me to wonder if this wasn't the right time, or worse yet, that she'd never make time to discuss this with me.

As it was, she surprised me by looking directly at me and replying calmly, "Election night."

"Yes, the night Papa came home and found your mother slumped inside your door," Steven said.

"Do you know what happened?" I asked.

"You mean how she died?" she replied.

"Yes," I said.

"Do *you* know?" she asked me forthrightly.

"I heard in 1952, but I'm not sure if it's right," I replied. I gave her an encapsulated rendition of what I knew and how I found out.

She stared at us for what seemed like an interminable amount of time, probably no more than twenty seconds, but time has a way of standing still when you're anticipating an event, the opposite of how it moves afterward, as when you notice that the ride back always seems shorter than the ride out to the destination. I didn't know if this meant she was pulling back.

I was surprised at her answer.

"I've been waiting a long time for you to ask."

Inherent in that was a mild scolding, a small rebuke that I instantly recognized as punishment for my being selfish; she'd been prepared previously to unburden herself of this great weight, and although my motive had been to try to protect her, my postponement had simply prolonged her anguish.

"I'm sorry, we should've had this talk before."

She nodded and gave me a genuine smile, an act of forgiveness.

She started slowly. "I always got up during the night to go to the bathroom, sometimes more than once." Then she began to pick up some steam. "I'd been a bed wetter as a small child and would do anything to avoid the embarrassment, so I'd go even if I didn't feel the urge, you know, an ounce of prevention as they say."

Her voice was soft but firm. Occasionally, she'd pause and take a sip of tea, delicately grasping the lemon that I'd cut into larger-than-normal sizes so she'd have something substantial to squeeze.

"I wanted neither to wake anyone nor to let it be known what I was doing. You have to understand that I hadn't actually outgrown this problem. My constant treks to the bathroom were a means to disguise it. I had the routine down: I'd slink out of bed, put one foot down on the floor, let my eyes adjust so I could see if there was a toy or a book on the floor—tripping and falling would've wakened your mother—then I'd tiptoe down the hall, touching the wall, feeling my way without the light, then shut the door gently in the bathroom, take care of what I had to do, then reverse course, taking the same precautions. I was embarrassed."

She shifted her weight to be able to see more of the window, perhaps a way to avoid direct eye contact with us, but this is only speculation.

"On election night," she continued, "I was coming back from the bathroom and was in the hall when I heard the knock on the front door. Mother had been in the parlor and I heard her get up, walk to the front door, and I recognized the familiar sound that the metal peephole cover made as it scraped to the right, enabling her to see out into the third-floor landing. I heard a man say, 'Western Union,' and another voice said something about the election. When I realized that Mother was going to open the door, I stood still, not wanting the men to see me in my pajamas. Mother always made sure we had proper clothes on if there was someone else in the house who wasn't family."

She readjusted herself in the chair and resumed speaking, but Steven and I had the distinct feeling that she was talking to herself, or to an invisible third party. Her gaze occasionally intersected with ours but there wasn't always recognition; it was as if we were looking at her through a one-way window yet all she could see was a mirror.

"I can see myself now, standing a foot or so behind the hall wall, leaning my head forward just enough to get my left eye past the edge of the wall, supporting myself against the hall wall with both hands, lest I fall and humiliate my mother, who'd narrow her eyes; that was all it would've taken for me to then have scrambled myself up and run back to the bathroom. But I didn't stumble and stayed motionless, expecting that I'd jump out of the shadows once Mother closed the door so I could have her read me the telegram."

At this point, she seemed to acknowledge our presence.

"You boys have to understand that to get a telegram in 1922 was a real treat." She gave us a small smile.

"You saw it all," I interjected quickly, not wanting her to have to relive vocally what she was then reviewing visually in her head.

"Yes, yes I did. All of it, the opening of the door, the man grabbing her by the shoulder, the other man twisting her head like she was a rubber doll, her collapsing against the small table where we put our gloves and keys, her then falling to the ground, the men closing the door silently."

She said this all as if by rote; perhaps she'd practiced this for years, waiting until the right moment to let it all out. It was clear that she didn't want or need me to protect her. I was surprised at how matter-of-factly she described what happened next.

"I stayed put for a while, I don't know how long, it could've been seconds or minutes. But after some period of time, when she didn't get up, I went to where she was on the floor and whispered in her ear, 'Get up, get up, Mother, you can get up, the men have gone, it's okay.' When she didn't move, I started to shake her, lightly at first, her arm, her shoulder, then I started to push her. I became angry and my exhortations to get off the floor, while still in a whisper, carried such an urgency it frightened me, as if I weren't speaking these words, they were coming from somewhere else. I think I remember pounding my fist into her back, but this I'm not sure of. I must've stayed with her for quite a while, crying softly but steadily, the cries becoming moans, maybe you'd call it wails but not too loud, I didn't want to wake my sister, I didn't want her to know what I knew. I started to shake and rock back and forth, crying, wrapping my arms around my sides, calling out in that exaggerated whisper for Daddy: 'Come home, Daddy, come home!'

"I was a little girl, after all," she said as if it were an asidc.

"And then, well, I can't explain it but as excited as I was to hear my father coming up the steps, I ran like the dickens to my room," she said, imitating what we imagined was her voice as a little girl, standing on her tiptoes like a ballerina poised to take flight, then fluttering toward a nonexistent bed, "and I slid under the covers and pretended to be asleep. And wouldn't you know it, I held it for the rest of the night," she exclaimed with a bright smile as if she wanted to be praised, "not getting up again to go to the bathroom, not moving a muscle when I heard Daddy speaking on the phone and then a bit later, when the commotion started and I recognized Murph Feldman's voice.

"In the morning, Daddy came into our room a little earlier than usual, told us to get dressed and brush our teeth, we wouldn't be going to school that day. Your mother got excited, thinking there was going to be a treat of some sort and kept asking me, as we were in the bathroom and then back in the bedroom, to guess what it might be. I was secretly hoping that the news was going to be that Mother was in the hospital and that the doctors were saying that she'd be home in a few days, once the bruise on her neck had healed."

"We do that, you know," Steven added helpfully, "we suppress things that are unpleasant, but then, well, it only lasts for a period of time; the memories come back and weigh on you as if someone were holding you down even though you can't see who it is."

She looked at him with pride, her nephew the doctor.

"Just like Uncle Jake," I said, looking at my brother, but my words were aimed at my aunt.

"Yes, like Uncle Jake. It was fourteen years of pressure for him, boys, 1938 to 1952, but you know that, and then he couldn't take it anymore," she said, trailing off so much that the "anymore" was barely audible.

"And for you, Auntie Rose?" Steven inquired.

She'd moved back into the chair. "The weight never lifted, sweetie," she said, tapping her fingers consecutively against the fabric of the chair. "Your mother was distracted by all her new responsibilities and I didn't want to compound her agonies by telling her that our mother had been murdered, that it wasn't an accidental fall caused by dizziness following a bad case of influenza, which is what everyone was saying."

"So you assumed her burden as well," I said.

"That's what we do," she said, pivoting her gaze back to us.

I wasn't sure whom she meant when she said "we," it could've referred to sisters, daughters, women, Jews, Jewish women, I couldn't tell.

"Each time I thought it might disappear or lessen, like when I was in the circus or when I met Jacob, it came back just as fast as it'd come on, first with Kristallnacht and then with the War. It got so that I only felt comfortable with animals; you saw that in the Fens and with BlueDog, and I felt this intensity with the animals in the circus, especially Peek, the ostrich.

"And as the anniversary of your Nana's death would come around, the image of her being killed would consume me, and then of course, it was unfortunate that Kristallnacht occurred in the same month, which was also the month in which you were born, the month I gave you to your mother."

"This was the start of what Mother called *the troubles*," I said with conviction.

She fell silent and stared out the window. We strained to see what was in her line of sight until we realized that what she was looking at couldn't be seen by anyone else. After a while, she turned her head and said, "Yes, Joel, your Nana's death was the *start*."

"And then Kristallnacht," Steven added, almost as a confirmation.

"Uncle A told you about that," she said.

"Yes, Auntie Rose," I responded, "everything, about the circus accident, the hospital, meeting Uncle Jake, and getting on the boat."

"*All* of it?" she inquired in such a way that both my brother and I inferred that she wasn't sure we really knew the whole story.

"I think so," I said, looking at Steven, who nodded his head in agreement.

"Mischlinge?" she asked.

We nodded.

"Hineini?"

"Throwing up over the rail," Steven said.

She fell back into silence but this time stared at me for a few seconds, then at Steven, as if she were trying to ascertain that we really did know it all.

"There's something else?" I asked hesitatingly, and when she didn't offer a prompt rebuttal, I stiffened, knowing that something was coming that Old Uncle A hadn't revealed to us. I pretended I was listening to him tell us the story of Uncle Jake and Auntie Rose in Germany, searching for any detail that I'd forgotten.

Like Uncle Jake on that long-ago day approaching the port in Hamburg, I wondered if I continued to speak, would *my* voice be affected, would there be a croak? I felt saliva filling my mouth. I got up, went to the sink, and spit. Immediately, my mouth refilled. Gastric juices gurgled throughout my alimentary canal, so loud I was sure Auntie Rose and my brother could hear. I looked at my reflection in the window above the sink to check my pupils. They were slightly constricted. I wasn't surprised; I was anxious and becoming dehydrated but perhaps it wouldn't be noticeable. As I wended my way back to my chair, I made a mental note not to look either of them directly in the eye.

"Yes," she replied, so quietly that if she hadn't given a nod, I wouldn't've been convinced it wasn't just a sigh. We knew not to prod, that a scab was being reopened and that the pain needed to ooze out slowly; a torrent would overwhelm her.

"The body," she finally said.

"The dead body, the one the German doctor was going to say was Jacob Goldblum?" I asked.

"Did you see it?" Steven probed.

It was clear that she was reliving an event. Eventually, she started, haltingly, as if each word mirrored the agony of her experience.

"We went down . . . the hospital stairs, unhurriedly, the doctor leading . . . Uncle Jake supporting me gingerly . . ."

Her eyes were closed, her head bobbed with each descending step.

The pace picked up the closer she came in memory to where she'd been. Her reverie took on an urgency, the anxiety in her voice channeling the thirty-four-year-old incident. Her voice was lowered, as if to ensure that no one would overhear her.

"It's so cooold," she whispered, the o's elongated in line with her quiver.

Steven and I watched as she entered the morgue.

"There's no one here, there's no body," she said, swirling her arms like a maestro in front of an invisible orchestra.

There was silence for a few seconds as she was listening to the doctor.

"Yes," she said, the answer to the unheard question of whether she was ready.

"Let me turn the handle, you pull out the gurney," she insisted.

"Oh my God," she exclaimed, then cupped her mouth to stuff those words back in lest they be discovered.

"He's just a *boy*," she said, turning her head sideways and lowering it into Uncle Jake's neck. Her silent crying elided into a stifled moan.

"Ohhhhh, no, Jacob, oh my God. He's but twelve or thirteen," she continued, stretching her right arm to touch his cheek. "Maybe he just had his bar mitzvah, called up for his first aliyah . . ." She trailed off.

She shivered and started to cry, her tears cascading like rivulets; she made no attempt to suppress them as they fell, first on Uncle Jake's shoulder, then, many years later, onto her shawl.

"Get me a cloth, let me wipe the blood from his head, clean the gurney," she commanded with urgency.

She gasped. "My God, Jacob, look at the gash in the *back* of his head!"

She grimaced, desperately trying to keep her voice low to mimic what had taken place in the morgue.

"It's inconceivable," she hissed.

Her anguish jumped like the arc of an electrical charge to the two of us, who reached out to kiss her cheeks on opposite sides and to rub our hands soothingly on her arms and back.

Then she straightened herself and started up with the Kaddish, "*Yitgadal v'yitkadash sh'mei raba* . . ." which we now joined, standing, paying our respects to the nameless boy, something we now do each year on the anniversary of his death.

We finished the prayer but didn't make a move to sit down. We waited for her to come back from that November night in Germany. We each took one of her hands, and the warmth of those touches seemed to hasten her return.

Finally, she opened her eyes, looked at me, and said, "So, you see?" practically inaudibly, the slightest hint of a smile, of hopefulness.

I moved closer to her, bent down with my arms engulfing her, and said, "Yes, yes I do." And I did.

"I had to," she said, now with some conviction. "I couldn't, you know."

And despite there being no objects to her declarations, I knew precisely what she meant.

She said this without a trace of regret or remorse, an acknowledgment that giving me up to her sister was the right thing to do for her, for Uncle Jake, for me, and for Mother and Dad.

She continued, "The fog would dissipate somewhat in about a month's time and I could function better for the next eleven, then the cycle would repeat, but the images of my mother slumped on the floor and this poor young boy on the gurney were always with me."

We stayed with her the rest of the afternoon, concentrating on good memories of Uncle Jake, Nana, and Papa, not in some way to have these enjoyable recollections balance the events that she'd just recounted; they could never do that. Rather, it was an attempt to give her some solace that despite *the troubles* and all she'd been through, our love was unconditional.

June 30, 1972
Dear Diary,

The boys were here today to tell me what they knew about my mother's death. Out of the blue. I didn't ask them why today. Perhaps because in the fall it will be fifty years. Fifty years!

What Joel overheard at the barbershop was the other half of the story that I've lived with for all these years. It's a blessing that Dad didn't know the truth. It's hard enough to accept premature death. I can attest to that twice over. But murder? And what's worse, a murder by mistake? And not just murder. Robbery. What they took, stole, from my family had no value to them but was irreplaceable to us.

They say time heals everything. I wonder who the "they" were and what they had that was broken.

39.

Timmy was a time, the way historians name epochs

In the spring of 1981, Rocky suffered a heart attack, prompting Morone to return to Boston, almost unrecognizable with his bushy beard that crept high on his cheekbones separated by only a few inches from a black knit hat pulled low over his forehead. He was still AWOL, fearful of being captured and put into the brig. We met him outside of the hospital, where Zippo had let us in to see Uncle Jake twenty-nine years earlier.

He greeted us with hugs that lasted for twenty seconds or so, the kind that can get uncomfortable so you lean back a bit without breaking the bond and stare into the other person's eyes, a prelude to an easy disengagement. He informed us that Rocky had been through the worst, that he was a real fighter but wasn't up to visitors outside the family.

He told us to call him Mordecai and introduced us to a comely woman who held his hand.

"We run the *chavurah* in Bar Harbor, and it's Mordecai who's called every time someone needs an extra person to make up the *minyan*," she said.

Even though his metamorphosis from Morone to Mordecai had taken place many years earlier, it was still hard for Steven and me to comprehend that the marine from the North End, Rocky's son, Little Alfredo's cousin, was enmeshed in a Jewish community in Maine.

"I was grateful to your grandfather, Murph Feldman, and Moses O'Neil for springing me from the marines, but I must confess that in the beginning I chafed at the rules I was required to follow," he said to us as we walked to a nearby restaurant. "Gradually, however, I fell into a routine on the island."

"Where he became the object of everyone's attention and conversation," his wife interrupted. "As the only young man, he had no competition for the affection of the men and women who'd invite him in to their cottages at the end of the day to drink their tea, to listen to their plights, and to encourage him to read their books."

Lacking a daily paper, getting only intermittent reception from the radio console in the main building, and having only occasional contact with people on the mainland, he explained, he had been isolated from much of the current stimuli, except for the weekly call with his father and uncle that he could make from Seal Harbor.

He'd been deprived of his prior haunts and old habits, so he gradually became susceptible to the influences of his surroundings, first the dress, then the food, and shortly thereafter the cadence of life, despite unfathomable horrors many of the island inhabitants had experienced in the past.

"Then, too," he reminded us with that old Morone aplomb, "there was a girl, the granddaughter of one of the men on the island," and he made the never forgotten gesture of running a comb through his still full head of hair and taking a smoke out of an imaginary pack in his sleeve. His wife rolled her eyes, something we do instead of blushing when we become adults, which was her signal to us that she was *that* girl.

My strong suspicion was that she had indicated to Morone that if he wanted to get past second base, he was going to have to become Mordecai.

We relived the days of 1952 with Mordecai and his wife, who was engrossed with the stories and urged us to continue well into the night. When we at last mentioned Timmy, she said, "You mean the kid with polio, who they named the fund after, when they used to collect coins at the seventh inning of the Braves games?" Steven and I looked at each other and realized that she might've been there the day Morone and I caught the foul ball.

Mordecai said, "You say 'Timmy' to me and I conjure up that whole summer of 1952. I can't recall what he looked like, so in my mind, Timmy was a time, the way historians name epochs long after the period has passed."

I wondered what Mr. Pleistocene looked like.

"Timmy was bicycles and baseball and eating all the stuff from Noodge Mauer's parents' store and sneaking upstairs to visit his sister, playing battleship, pick-up sticks, and sticking my tongue down her throat," I recalled.

"Timmy was me wanting to get out of the marines and back to Boston and not ship out to Korea, that was for sure."

"Timmy was Myandrew, who came out at the induction center on Whitehall Street in Lower Manhattan in 1960, flamboyantly heralding the new decade, demanding to be accepted, it was his right and obligation and who were they to deny admission into the army to the guy who was wearing a winking "Uncle Sam Wants Me" T-shirt coordinated with a flag bandana?" I noted.

I thought of Mother and the derivation of Myandrew's name.

"Timmy was also Frankie," I went on. "I think I was the last to hear from him. After a year of community college, he told me he was going to move out of his house but was afraid to tell his father on account of what he might do. He got a place in Somerville, and that's where his father went after beating up his mother, who'd withheld the location from her husband until she thought she was going to die. Frankie's old man announced his arrival on the front steps, raving like a lunatic. Frankie hugged the wall and unlocked the door, and as it burst open, he swung his bat, the autographed bat he bought when we went to the game in 1952 at Braves Field and kept in our garage out back for fear his father would've found out about his spending money on a souvenir. He swung high and hit him square on his temple. Dropped him instantly. Dead by the time he hit the floor."

I remembered him buying the bat, giving it to me, and my using it on July 4, 1952, when I hit the ball that shattered the glass window above the garage, the sound of which had repercussions for my uncle Jake that day and for me until this very day.

I proceeded to give Mordecai and his wife the abbreviated version of my ancestry and adoption. "Your Mother isn't your mother but she's your Mother," he said, and we all knew which *mothers* were capitalized from the way he inflected the words.

I left out the part about being named for the Jews. It's something that I've internalized and has guided me on a regular basis; there isn't a day I don't think about it and wonder if my life would've been different if I'd been a Tom, Dick, or Harry. Is a name just a name, or can it also be a label that stands for something? I've always assumed it can, in the same way my father the accountant attributed value to trademarks for his clients.

After sitting quietly for a moment, I noted that I was sad for Frankie who'd been convicted and sent to prison and embarrassed that I hadn't ever visited him while he was doing time.

"You knew that Timmy died," Steven said in a way that was a declaration that others could interpret as a question.

"My God, no!" Mordecai exclaimed loudly, causing other diners to glance our way. "Alav ha-shalom," Mordecai added quietly, and Steven filled him in on the details, how he'd had his good days and bad, times when he thought he was going to make it and other times when he suffered relapses, the final one happening just a few years before.

After a silence, Mordecai changed the subject. "It's pretty amazing, you guys actually met a man who ended up being president," he said.

"We met him at my grandfather's place, when he came around with his entourage looking for money in the early part of the summer of 1952," I recalled proudly. "And then again at the Badgers Club; you were there too. Remember when The Boxer got me to steal the postcards from the newspaper, the ones that were supposed to be for the Braves to stay in Boston, but which we gave to my grandfather and his pals to be used in the campaign?" This was a question without a raised voice at the end, more of a pronouncement.

We drank toasts to Timmy, to Little Alfredo, to Uncle Jake, and to the congressman who became president. We stood up when we honored the memory of each of them. We sat for a minute, not saying much. Then I got on my feet and proposed one more. With glass raised, I said, "To BlueDog." I couldn't have said any more because I would've choked. BlueDog died during the election campaign of 1964, when it should've been the president running for a second term. Steven traded places with one of the other residents that day so we could be together.

February 19, 1987
Dear Diary,

I have not written to you in 15 years. The time has not gone by swiftly. I hear each second tick. Last Thursday was the yahrzeit for Ida. Two years. I think about her every day. And her Jeffrey, who sends me a card on my birthday.

People remark how young I look. Seventy is the new fifty, they say. What was so good about 50 I don't reply.

Today we buried my sister. When they said my brother-in-law wouldn't come out of his coma, it was just a question of time for her. I grieve for both of them. What do we pray to, my rock and my redeemer? They were that for me.

I am flanked by Joel and Steven and the grandchildren. There are seven, 4 boys and 3 girls. They are quiet and respectful and cry when the rabbi speaks of the lovingkindness within the family.

They shed tears for the woman who doted on them while my eyes water for the girl who did double duty and the woman who gave me a lifeline when my boat was sinking.

She never asked me how it turned out that November became just another month. That the troubles disappeared in 1972. I never told her about the other half of our mother's story. The secret was safe with Joel and Steven.

When I threw dirt on her coffin, I told her that it was her spirit that enabled me to stand up to the customs official during Jacob's and my escape. Her courage to accept an extraordinary challenge that allowed me to not suffer a loss of the most precious kind. Her strength of character that set an example for the boys to follow.

She was an exemplary mother, sister and mother.

Now I truly am an orphan. I take some solace that I can say this for the first time at 74.

Rose

40.

I Miss You Already And You'll Always Be My Baby Boy

The next time the three of us got together was in 1996 at a memorial for The Guy on the Radio in Boston. Mordecai had ridden the Downeaster from Brunswick, and we picked him up at North Station. We were without our wives. After the service, we went to a small Italian restaurant in the North End, Mordecai's idea; he was feeling his oats, Hooch-like, taking refuge for a night in his old haunt, delighting in the fact that he was incognito. At fifty-seven, I was the youngest, Steven almost fifty-nine and Mordecai sixty-three; approximately the same ages as Papa's pals in 1952. We agreed that if offered the opportunity now to spring a marine from Parris Island or steal some postcards from a newspaper or beat up a hood at a fancy restaurant or bribe someone to get inside information so we could make a bet or spread some money around to get people to vote for a candidate, well, we weren't the guys to do the jobs. Was it that we weren't capable? we asked ourselves. Or was it that these were things that couldn't be done today? Or, more than likely, that even if they could be pulled off, we weren't of the right mien?

Pictures of Papa, Nana, Mother, Dad, and Old Uncle A flashed in front of me as we drained our glasses. I saw Dad at the kitchen table working the arm off of the adding machine, throwing crumpled-up yellow pages across the room, rarely getting them in the wastepaper basket. I saw Mother giving me a look, it could've been any number of looks, but they all meant the same thing. I saw Papa at the store telling me stories as I dug my hands into the sofas and searched for coins the way Murph Feldman did at HIAS, the ones the immigrants left for the next generation. I saw Nana through Old Uncle A's eyes, so full of mist you would've thought you were making the crossing from Seal Harbor to Palus Island at night as a nor'easter was coming in.

I imagined Moses O'Neil hanging around Papa's wagon and later, as a young tough, beating up on Leo Tubbs. There was Chief Stinkowski, standing silently, like Babe Ruth or the Shawmut Indian, waiting for one of the pals to finish what he was doing so he could go shake somebody down, like the mayor's men from Milwaukee. I saw Derby Canurbi placing the bets on Hooch and the Senate election and taking the action on the Braves' move, all of which enabled my brother and me to go to college and Mordecai to keep Palus Island going. I saw Murph Feldman asking us if we was deaf and dumb and handing out phony papers to Uncle Jake, Morone, and Derby Canurbi, as well as my birth certificate to Mother and Dad.

And, too, I saw Rocky and Big Alfredo, ever together, lamenting the loss of their sons. They were near Isaac Burgas the butcher and Sal the barber, all gone. As were Sergeant Wilson, The Boxer, Dr. Richards our pediatrician, Mr. Perini and Earl Torgeson of the Braves, Mr. Carlson the sportswriter, Smitty the photographer, Dr. Goodman from the hospital, the bartender from the pub across the channel on Thomson Place, Gray Fedora and Fourth Man from Milwaukee, Canoehatman from the Badgers Club, and the dozens of guys my brother and I met in the summer of '52 when we delivered envelopes on Tuesdays that contained the bets and collected others on Thursdays that held the money that would keep Papa's merry-go-round revolving.

Papa spent his last few years entertaining his companions at the Hebrew Home for the Aged in Roslindale, vibrant and spellbinding until the end. My last conversation with him took place just a few days before he died in 1970. He was eighty-six, slowed but erect, with enough thinned white hair to hold a part that angled toward his left eye, adding an exclamation point to his winks.

"I *have* to ask you something, Papa," I began, and he instinctively motioned for me to accompany him to the far side of the common room.

"Let's get away from the altekakers," he said without irony, many of whom were younger than he.

"Did you . . ." I hesitated, seeking to gauge his understanding that this was not going to be a question about some mundane issue, a message I'd tried to convey by accenting the word *have*, a clear giveaway that something important was on my mind. He nodded slightly, which I interpreted to mean that he was receptive, so I started up again. "Did you have second thoughts about the *events*"—a euphemism that didn't need explanation—"during the summer of 1952? And before, going way back, to the days of Mr. Maguire?"

He didn't respond immediately, so a part of me wanted to rev up my engine, but I stayed in neutral, a pause that I'd learned as I'd gotten older, a verbal ellipsis that's served me well in navigating through uncharted conversations. An observer from the other side of the room would've seen two tall men standing no more than eighteen inches apart, one extending his hand to the arm of the other, which could've easily been misinterpreted as a steadying physical outreach but in this case was simply a way of conveying affection.

"*Tikkun olam*," he finally said, rather matter-of-factly.

"How were you *repairing the world*?" I asked incredulously, though in a tender tone so as not to appear insulting, my mind racing through images of bribes, vote stealing, fixed races, betting on outcomes when the results were known in advance, theft, forged documents, illegal immigration, kidnapping, shakedowns, and beatings.

"Those were different times," he pronounced as if he were an instructor in a classroom, "so context is everything, Joel. It wasn't like it is today, where you, your brother, your children, friends, any of you has access to whatever you want: jobs, schools, you can be a lawyer, work on Wall Street, join a big company, buy a house in any neighborhood, go places, serve in government, appear in a motion picture, and not think for even a minute about how being a Jew would affect you, not having to change your name. For God's sake, you can even wear a *kippa* outside," he added with relish, proud to have used the Hebrew instead of the Yiddish word *yarmulke* for skullcap, which was no longer preferred by us younger Jews, who'd co-opted the Hebrew word from the sabras of Israel.

"But *repair*?" I asked.

"It was *broken*, Joel, the world was cracked, the seam right down the middle. The WASPs ate the cake for three centuries; they threw us the crumbs, patted us on our heads, told us we should be grateful. It had to be fixed; not by anarchy, you've seen how that plays out. We took a page from their book; we started bit-by-bit. The Irish built the railroads, the Italians the streets, the Poles the tunnels, the Jews traded." If I'd been talking with one of Papa's pals, he would've said the micks, the dagos, the Polacks, and the Yids. "We all saved our nickels, had lots of children, bided our time, got the vote, and then we turned on them, yes indeed, we gave as good as we got."

I'd never thought of a revenge motive associated with tikkun olam, most often tied to social justice efforts. I had to process this, and while I was a bit stunned, I wasn't put off, knowing what he and his generation had lived through. And succeeded in doing. They'd elected a descendant of Irish immigrants as senator and president and opened doors for the children of the riffraff, something that was unimaginable for a person born when Chester Arthur was in the White House.

Now *I* was the beneficiary of a reciprocal touch that stayed on my arm as he added, "There's unfinished business, you know, and while your generation's methods may be different from mine, we do have the same goals." He locked eyes with me and gestured to the other side of the room; it was as if my body were a gear he jerked in motion that rotated then stopped automatically at the sight of a young African American employee wheeling the housekeeping cart into the room.

He died in his sleep two days later. We've mourned his passing by celebrating his life in stories shared with our families and in expressions of tikkun olam in our community.

Murph Feldman died of cancer of the mouth, a consequence of too many cigars, his unintentional bathroom deodorizer. Moses O'Neil was found in the trunk of a car with the index finger on his right hand missing. I remember Murph Feldman telling me how Moses O'Neil got his nickname—pointing at guys he was threatening with an Old Testament look—so I guess this was some kind of retribution. Chief Stinkowski took a job as head of security for a Polish retirement home in Milwaukee, which put an immediate end to a string of thefts. The last I heard about Derby Canurbi was that he was living in Macao, but Steven suspected that this was a rumor he initiated himself, to keep the mob at bay. I told him you could bet on it.

I miss them all, those whom I loved and others I knew only briefly, fleetingly, including the congressman who became the president. Some days, I still see him at Papa's office, then at the Badgers Club, or at Faneuil Hall or up on the podium across from Checkpoint Charlie. Each time, he says the same thing: "I knew we could count on you fellars." I try to catch up to him, to acknowledge that he can always count on me, but he's forever running away from me. I've never been able to lock onto his eyes; he keeps an equal distance between us, no matter how fast I try to make up the difference.

I've learned that I can never catch him, although that hasn't stopped me from trying.

I've learned that other dogs are not little Greek boys.

I've learned why when you're a kid they don't always tell you the truth.

Myandrew was an early casualty of the AIDS plague. He'd become an outspoken advocate for research and devictimization, and his death was accompanied by an article in the *Herald Traveler*. After he got out of jail, Frankie languished in a series of dead-end jobs, his uncontrollable anger preventing him from accepting any level of authority. Noodge Mauer became a "revenuer," he liked to say, admired by his peers for his ability to ask a million questions, a tactic that wore down taxpayers and resulted in unexpected payments. Zippo married and divorced at least three times, a pattern I attributed to a restlessness stemming from her failure to find anyone who'd lived up to her ideal: her high school boyfriend who became a physician. Susie regained the full use of her legs and became a well-known runway model, her backstory of overcoming polio contributing to her appeal. Once a year we get together around the holidays for a lunch spent devouring our reminiscences, like former lovers thinking about the what-might-have-beens.

In 1987, Dad was struck by a hit-and-run driver as he was walking from the trolley to his office, where he still spent half days puttering about. He lingered for a week but never regained consciousness. Steven and I visited him every day, sitting by his side, reading to him, pretending he could hear us. So we made sure to tell him how much we loved him before we left. Mother hardly ever spoke a word after that, occasionally mumbling one of her aces of spades, "I Have Nothing To Live For," her response to any attempt by us to comfort her. She died within three months. Auntie Rose was inconsolable, and it was agreed that she would come to live with my family. Steven visited at least once a week, usually finding her holding court on the front porch, entertaining neighborhood dogs and cats, waving to the kids on bicycles, sometimes getting up and pirouetting, dancing they assumed, but we knew better; she was listening to the tuba making the oompah-pah sound, the glockenspiel signaling the parade of the animals, and the calliope announcing the ringmaster's entrance.

On October 31, 2002, Auntie Rose went to rest on the sofa in the family room after the last of the trick-or-treaters had departed. I brought her some tea. She sipped a bit and then, with her eyes closed, asked me to tell her a story. I told her about a woman they used to call the bird princess of Africa who worked in a circus in England in the 1930s with a Canadian who looked like a Mountie with his jodhpurs and brass-buttoned shirt, a Cuban whose tongue was black from chewing tobacco leaves, a Hungarian who'd become apoplectic the moment someone mispronounced *Budapest* without the *esht* sound, a tinker from the west coast of Ireland who'd offer to trade you stuff that you would've sworn had once been yours, and a peg leg from the Faroe Islands who claimed he was descended from Leif Erikson. He insisted that he owned Greenland and had the deed to prove it. I told her about an ostrich named Peek and how the woman would stand up on his back and parade around the ring. I told her about the applause and the huzzahs and the smiles the woman put on the faces of little children who'd clamor for her autograph and put her picture from the newspaper on their walls and bulletin boards.

She seemed to be asleep. I went into the kitchen to reheat the kettle. I put a small Halloween cupcake on the glass table in front of the sofa. She neither moved to get up nor opened her eyes.

She whispered, "Thank you," paused, and then said softly, "I Miss You Already And You'll Always Be My Baby Boy."

In that split second after I savored what she'd said and before I bent down to give her a kiss on the cheek, she died.

October 25, 2002
Dear Diary,

I was determined not to write to you ever again. What more did I have to say? I decided it's time to burn them. They are too personal. I retrieved them from the hidden flap within the inside pocket of the valise. I reread them and am surprised to find only two dozen. I thought there were more. I worried about setting off the alarm in Joel's house. The fire department will come and I will have to explain what I was doing. I cannot simply throw them in the garbage. That would be disrespectful.

I decided to leave them for my son. Let him make the decision. He will know what's best to do.

Perhaps in due course I'll make one more entry. I'll see.

Rose Mischal Goldblum

41.

The man my grandchildren call Old Uncle M

The last guest to leave the shiva was the man my grandchildren call Old Uncle M. He gave me a hug accompanied by a squeeze around the neck, affection that I reciprocated with a kiss on his bushy cheek. Each time he left to go back home to Maine, I wondered if it'd be the last I'd see of him.

He'd been Mordecai for fifty years, a greaser from the North End turned observant Jew, a tough who'd sought *t'shuvah* for his willing participation in a scheme to cancel the contract he had with the US Marine Corps. He'd dedicated his life to redeeming himself by caring for the wounded who'd never been injured in battle, those whose bruises and scars hadn't healed from unimaginable state-sponsored suffering. In divine double-entry bookkeeping, his liabilities had been more than offset by his service assets to the downtrodden. When the rabbi noted Auntie Rose's mitzvah, her giving me a new life with Mother and Dad, it was hard for me not to think of the gift that Rocky's son gave to the refugees off the coast of Maine.

I took my jacket off when the last of the guests had departed and carefully laid it across the back of a chair, making sure the black ribbon wouldn't get crushed, then poured glasses of wine for the rabbi, my brother, and me and moved to the living room in front of the fireplace. The rest of the family left us alone.

"My great-grandfather gave a short speech at the funeral service for your grandmother in 1922," the rabbi said, "so in a way, it's only fitting that I was here for you boys." Steven mouthed the word *kiddos* to me with a grin, which was how the rabbi's great-grandfather, Murph Feldman, used to address us in 1952. Yes, we were still boys, although in our sixties, as grandfathers, there'd be no bike riding all over town, no shaking down compromised businessmen, no stealing postcards.

"I was told of the great mosaic, the many people of different faiths who were there for your Sylvia, so it was especially pleasing to me to see more of the same at Kol Israel today," the rabbi said.

It was true. When word got out that Auntie Rose had died (things move at the speed of light as a result of the Internet), the synagogue overflowed with the descendants of those who knew my family and Papa's pals oh so many years ago. And, too, the pews were filled with legions of my listeners who appreciated my aunt in the way that people call up lyrics from a favorite song, passages from a remembered novel, poem, or speech. As I walked to my seat in the front row, I canvassed the house and saw what Papa noted at the Badgers Club when he introduced the congressman: people of diverse ages, backgrounds, stations of life. They sat where my brother's and my families sit each Friday night and then greeted me at the conclusion of the funeral service in the anteroom where we'd gather on those nights to recite the Shabbat blessings, the *kiddush* and the *hamotzi*, celebrations over the wine and the bread.

The three of us sipped, nodded, smirked, and yawned, movements that substituted for language. Perhaps we were inhabiting reveries, special sanctuaries where we could retreat, knowing that others couldn't enter unless they received our permission, which was rarely given. On the way out, Rabbi Feldman touched my forearm and told me that I'd made the right decision for him to refer to Rose as my aunt. We hugged.

It was then that I mentioned to Steven that I'd discovered a note in Auntie Rose's dresser drawer, in Uncle Jake's handwriting, reminding himself to make sure to set the alarm every day to go off at 6:00 a.m. so he could leave the bedroom and tiptoe into the living room to listen to his shortwave radio at 6:10 a.m., 1:10 p.m. in Israel, when *Kol Zion La Golah* (*The Voice of Zion to the Diaspora*) would broadcast the names of survivors searching for relatives.

"Those ten minutes we were motionless, barely daring to breathe, tucked into our fort in their living room," Steven acknowledged, dredging up memories from long ago. "It was Hebrew, of course," he stated. "We should've known."

"Conversational was something they never taught us," I replied, and it was true, our learning of Torah and haftorah readings bore the same kind of resemblance that Creole does to Parisian French.

Steven and I lingered downstairs. After a half hour or so, I noticed that all of the lights in the rest of the house were out; the silence wasn't just coming from the living room. There was nothing more to say.

Or so I thought.

I was all set to head upstairs to bed when Steven asked, "Do you still have the scrapbook, the one that contains the memorabilia from 1952, including the pictures in the *Herald Traveler* of you and Morone catching the foul ball, of the two of us standing behind Mr. Carlson in front of the paper's building, and of us with Papa, Dad, and the congressman at the Badgers Club, and one of the flyers that we put up on telephone poles near Faneuil Hall indicating we'd found a large black dog?" And another question: "Do you still have the 'I'm a Brave Bostonian' button?"

I told him yes, I had all this stuff, and picked up my jacket, a gesture that meant, "I'm exhausted, I'm going to bed," and went upstairs.

My brother never asked if I had the exit visa for Dieter Harald Eberhart; Uncle Jake's passport, Boston birth certificate, and veterinary school diploma; Morone's orders to ship out and his letter to his father requesting he be baptized; Mordecai's Mount Desert Regional High School records, birth certificate, and Maine driver's license; Derby Canurbi's passport; or Dr. Burgas's letter to his father concerning the death of Little Alfredo.

All this and more is tucked away in drawers and closets, some of it ripped or yellowed or dog-eared with notes in ink attached or inscribed. As nice as it is to occasionally touch and rearrange these materials, for the most part their contents are embedded inside of me, where I recalled them at will when the engineer turned down the light and the green dot appeared next to the microphone. That's when I shared elements from the stories about me and my friends as well as those that Papa told us about the people he met on the boat trips to Halifax at the start of the century, mixed them up with those that Old Uncle A revealed about the people who lived on Palus Island, coupled them with never-ending tales that were spawned from our comings and goings when I was a kid, along with so many others I came across in the intervening years.

42.

The prism that refracted our societal attitudes, values, and policies

On the air, I'd start a riff, either outlined beforehand or spontaneously created from these mementos, fueled by the energy of the moment, designed to knit together the strands of a narrative that'd illustrate the points I wanted to leave as impressions that members of the audience should remember, even if only as fragments, for years afterward.

I can recall the closing of my last show in 2011 without resorting to any notes:

"I've come to the conclusion that it doesn't matter what's the truth, and besides, there could be more than one definition of the truth, depending on the viewing angle that's presented. Moreover, if the person you heard it from believed it to be true, you'd have no compunction about repeating it to a third party and backing up its veracity.

"Was there any truth to my character called The Mechanic, who'll replace a part, 'I meant to say . . .' but who doesn't care to understand why it broke down in the first place? Was this based on a particular person or maybe a composite of several?

"Was I lying when I described an evening in which Auntie Rose sat at the captain's table on her trip to England in 1938 and found herself next to The Mason, who set a mortar of trivial words so thick that neither a witticism nor a clever observation from anyone else could penetrate the conversation? Would the story have more value if it were literally true?

"I can't tell you how many letters I got after I introduced The Historian, who goes through his preset list of anecdotal relics from the past that he brought with him, then retreats into a social coma and rests, motionless, like those replicas we've all seen at the Museum of Natural History. Somehow this species never evolved to develop spontaneity. So many people told me that they knew who this was about, for sure.

"And the same with The Thief, who interrupts the flow of an exchange, picks up on a word or phrase and hijacks it off on a tangent. However, that one isn't as bad as The Plumber, that special breed of social bore who chokes off all conversation with one wrenching 'I know that,' or The Roman, my name for those people whose conversations inevitably lead back to themselves.

"One of my favorite characters is The Patronizer, who would've written off Old Uncle A with a dismissive flick of the wrist by saying something condescending wrapped in a compliment of sorts, 'Oh, we need more people who've chosen sacrifice above all.' Yet to me, Old Uncle A died a rich man, despite there being no visible manifestation of affluence, having accumulated invaluable assets such as admiration, love, respect, and pride. And unlike many of our contemporaries, he left a legacy without having offspring or material wealth.

"Yes, my characters were composites, drawn from multiple sources, whom I then cast in alternate versions of the same story, and while the particulars of each anecdote or narrative were different, most of them originated in forms that were both plausible and acceptable. And interestingly, when I heard an unusual version from another source, it didn't diminish my view of the earlier story or of the teller. It didn't matter if the events reflected accurate recall or were created out of whole cloth; which was precisely the message I got the night in 1964 when I met The Guy on the Radio.

"My favorite characters to whom I returned over and over again in my stories and radio soliloquies were my brother Steven, Noodge Mauer, his twin sister Susie, Myandrew, Frankie, and Zippo. I'd also make occasional references to characters called The Fixer, The Intimidator, The Gambler, and The Enforcer, pseudonyms for Murph Feldman, Moses O'Neil, Derby Canurbi, and Chief Stinkowski, respectively.

"Papa's pals were four of the many characters so colorful you couldn't make them up. They're all gone now, but their legacies are alive, we see them all around us, perhaps not as vibrant or quaint and in many ways more dangerous and insidious to be sure. Or is that merely the observation from one who knew them at the time from a child's perspective?

"They operated in a world with fuzzy boundaries of legality and morality in a time so close to ours by the calendar yet so far removed from how we live our lives today. Nineteen fifty two, when most of the shenanigans took place, wasn't that much different from the era of thirty years before that, when Moses O'Neil and Chief Stinkowski took down Leo 'Tubby' Tubbs, or even thirty years before that, around the time that Honey Fitz and Mr. Maguire were just getting started. But thirty years later, in 1982, we'd undergone a revolution in telecommunications and transportation, in civil rights, in how we conducted wars. And now, almost thirty years beyond that, we've experienced such shocks as terrorism on our shores, a financial meltdown second only to the Great Depression, and a breakdown in societal values.

"We were fighting a different kind of war in Korea in 1952, a conflict initiated only five years after World War II but one that didn't hit us in our solar plexus, didn't cause us to unite; it presaged the wars in Vietnam, Iraq, and Afghanistan where we've fought with a proxy army that's disconnected from our day-to-day lives.

"We were living in 1952 with the delusion that baseball was a game, albeit one played by young adults, but something that was supposed to entertain us with the fantasy that any one of us could've been one of those guys, and whether or not our team won or lost, there was a good time for all, players and spectators both. Professional sports were always a business for the owners, but we fans knew it as a *pastime*. The Braves' move to Milwaukee shattered this illusion and began the inexorable shift that's taken us to the point where as much actual and electronic ink, voice, and video are devoted to illicit performance-enhancing drugs, contract disputes, and abhorrent behavior as are dedicated to the players' feats on the fields.

"The fierce loyalties across ethnic and cultural communities based on immigration through the first two decades of the twentieth century were supposed to have dissipated into the great melting pot of America, but the election of the great-grandson of Irish immigrants to the US Senate in 1952 not only didn't contribute to our congealing, it seemed to be a harbinger of an enhanced effort to fractionalize the public into squabbling ethnic groups fighting over the public trough in the three generations since.

"And our optimism that science would conquer all, that polio would be the last epidemic, was rooted in the can-do spirit of post–World War II exceptionalism, yet this turned out to be wishful thinking of the most naïve kind, for while we were anticipating the end of an era, a new one was just beginning with the ubiquitous transmission of diseases and the availability of intercontinental transportation.

"Our American culture has been profoundly changed, and one can arguably trace the center of this shift to the time immediately preceding and following 1952, allowing us to view this year as the prism that refracted our societal attitudes, values, and policies toward war, disease, politics, sports, business, and immigration.

"I tried to keep this era alive, to use it as a foil to talk about our times today, the way The Guy on the Radio kept the Great Depression and the War front and center, and it just so happens that I did it by reaching back into my childhood, when I too suffered through momentous events of these times."

43

I'll ask him what he meant

I'll finish writing the memoir this morning, but I'll linger a bit in the studio, the way I'd savor Susie after dropping her off at her house following a movie, her dash of perfume and scent of citrus rinse hovering around me for at least the time it took to walk back home. I'm a bit anxious, knowing I won't be returning, but the uncertainty can't be compared to what Isaac Burgas, the kosher butcher, must've felt when he was marking off the days on his calendar until his son Daniel, the doctor, was scheduled to come back from Korea. Good-byes that are commonplace, casual, ritualized exchanges with a literal meaning sometimes can't be distinguished from those that sound the same but are infused with sorrow, loss, and apprehension. So while I'll wave and smile when bid farewell by the young engineers and interns who're arriving at the studio at the dawn of their careers, my rejoinder good-bye will be tainted by a sadness that they won't be able to detect.

I've captured images of the photos that line the walls and will download them to my scrapbook, which I still hole up with in my den late at night, lip-reading notes I've scribbled next to clippings, pictures, knickknacks, stamps, ticket stubs, and the like, occasionally glancing at my black Lab nestled near my feet, imagining her with blue splotches of paint licking my calf below my dungarees, rolled up so I won't get the grease from my bicycle chain on them.

I'm going to take the Braves cap off its hook and put it on; it's only fitting that I wear it as I shake hands with the other personalities, the engineers, and the administrative staff, making my way to the door, a walk that usually takes only a few seconds, though today I'm prepared to stop at each desk and cubicle and express my thanks for their support and companionship. I won't be carrying any papers or memorabilia except for the baseball bat I'll take off the hook, the one that I used on July Fourth, 1952, that broke the glass and that Frankie used years later as a murder weapon. It stayed in the evidence locker at the main police station for years. Now I'm the last holder in the chain of custody. How I got it is another story.

My brother and I have planned to go to the cemetery in West Roxbury, where we'll place small stones on the grave markers for Nana, Papa, Uncle Jake, Auntie Rose, Mother, Dad, and Murph Feldman, remembering to look for his name as Meyer. After all, it was Murph Feldman who assisted me greatly in getting my initial start in radio, as he created the news piece that supposedly appeared in the *Berliner Morgenpost* about my private meeting with the president after he gave his famous "*Ich bin ein Berliner*" speech, the faux article that came from my college newspaper my senior year, 1961, which featured a picture of me with a famous radio humorist sharing a beer at a local hangout, and the phony story from my high school paper that reported on a discussion I had in 1957 with my dog, a black Lab, who was lamenting the fact that the Russians sent dogs into space but we hadn't done so.

We'll say Kaddish for them as well as for Old Uncle A, buried on Palus Island as he requested. On the way home, we'll drive by the row house near the Brookline border, go around out back to the driveway that circles the garages, glance up at the plate glass window, then head off in the direction of the Mauers' store, now a coffee bar. We'll phone Mordecai from the car.

Undoubtedly, I'll think about what happened at the shiva for Auntie Rose when a new neighbor introduced herself and offered condolences to me on the loss of my mother.

I didn't correct her.

Then we'll share a corner spot near where my brother got to second base with Zippo. I'll ask him what he meant when he told me a year ago that I was my mother's son. It could've related to Mother, from whom I learned discipline, responsibility, steadfastness, evenhandedness, and unconditional love. It could've related to Auntie Rose, from whom I learned loyalty, tenacity, risk-taking, self-effacement, and unconditional love. Perhaps he'll say it was an offhand remark, and I'll have no way of knowing if this is indeed true. In any case, for sure, I am my mothers' son.

GLOSSARY

GERMAN

ach	oh
Auf Wiedersehen	good-bye
Außenalster	Outer Alster Lake in Hamburg
Binnenalster	Inner Alster Lake in Hamburg
das Unglück	bad luck
Endlösung	the Final Solution
führer	leader
Gänsehaut	goose bumps
Gymnasium	high school
Ich bin ein Berliner	I am a Berliner
Juden	Jews
Kinder	children
Krameramtsstuben	historic buildings in Hamburg
Kristallnacht	Night of Broken Glass
Kunsthalle	art museum
Lederhosen	knee-length leather breeches
Mein Gott im Himmel	my God in heaven
Mischlinge	half breed
Planten un Blomen	botanical garden park in Hamburg
Prinzessin	princess
Rathaus	city hall
Schicksalsfrage	conundrum
schwarz	black
und	and

Vaterland	fatherland
Viel Glück	good luck
Volk	people
Wandervogel	German youth group
Was ist das?	What is this?
wunderbar	wonderful

HEBREW

Alav ha-shalom	blessing: may peace be upon him or her
aliyah	immigration to Israel; also, called to read from the Torah
bima	elevated platform in a synagogue
boker tov	good morning
chavurah	informal group of Jews who pray or study together
chuppah	wedding canopy
haftorah	part of the Hebrew Bible
hamotzi	blessing over bread
Havdalah	the service at the end of Shabbat
hineini	here I am
Kaddish	prayer for the dead
kiddush	blessing over wine
kippa	skullcap
kol tuv	all good things
Ma nishtana?	What has changed?
minyan	ten Jews at a prayer ceremony
mitzvah	an act of human kindness
sabra	native-born Israeli
Shabbat	Sabbath
shehecheyanu	prayer for celebration
Shema	foundation prayer of Judaism—the declaration of faith
shiva	mourning period
tikkun olam	repairing the world
Torah	the five books of Moses
t'shuvah	repentance

yahrzeit	anniversary of the death of a family member
Yitgadal v'yitkadash . . .	the start of the Kaddish prayer

IRISH

banjaxed	ruined
beor	good-looking woman
bowsie	lawbreaker
boyo	lad
coola boola?	do you understand?
craic	good time
delph	artificial teeth
eejits	idiots
gomey	fool
gurriers	punks
Janey Mac	holy cow
jaykers	Jesus
Jaysus	Jesus
langered	drunk
oul fellaman	father
práta	potato
shebeen	place where unlicensed liquor is sold
sláinte	salute, toast
sleeveen	untrustworthy person

ITALIAN

assassino	killer
capisce?	understand?
criminale	gangster
finito	finished
goombah	hood
salute	health
sicario	hit man
sotto voce	lowered voice
il vecchio	old man

LATIN

Civis Romanus sum	I am a Roman citizen
in loco parentis	in place of the parents

YIDDISH

altekaker	old person
bei mir bist du schön	by me you are beautiful
boychik	young boy
dreidel	four-sided spinning top
gelt	money
kishkes	guts
knish	potato dumpling, sometimes with other ingredients
kugel	noodle pudding
mishpachah	relative
onkl	uncle
oy gevalt	good grief
oy vey	woe is me
rugelach	small crescent-shaped pastry
schul	synagogue
schmuck	fool, from the Yiddish meaning penis
shtetl	Jewish village in the Pale of Settlement
treif	not kosher
tzitzis	ritual fringes attached to a prayer shawl
yarmulke	skullcap
yekke	German-speaking Jew
yid	derogative term for a Jew

ACKNOWLEDGMENTS

I'm immensely grateful to Ann Streger Price, who read every word of each draft, pushed me relentlessly to raise my standards, and offered words of encouragement when I needed them most. It's true what Peachy Levin told us: "You deserve each other."

I can't say enough about the influence that the late Jean Shepherd had on me. One of the great radio raconteurs, he enabled his listeners to imagine that his characters were intimate friends who became part of their lives. We believed in them, knowing full well that although they didn't exist, we could recognize ourselves in them, and by so doing, could gain insight into the world in which we lived.

And heartfelt thanks to the following individuals:

Amy Oringel of Fig Tree Books LLC, for savvy editorial and sophisticated business advice;

Betsy Dunne of Fig Tree Books LLC, for matchless operational expertise;

Rachel Tarlow Gul of Over the River Public Relations, for excellence in publicity;

Christine Van Bree of Christine Van Bree Design, for the elegant book cover and jacket design;

Pauline Neuwirth, Beth Metrick, and Elyse Strongin of Neuwirth & Associates, Inc., for the classy interior book design;

Anne Horowitz, for extraordinary copywriting and editing skills;

DJ Schuette, for outstanding proofreading proficiency;

Matthew Price of Design by Price, for first-class website designs and IT wisdom;

Heather Cameron of Publishers Group West, for unstinting distribution efforts;

Ellis Levine of Cowan, DeBaets, Abrahams & Sheppard LLP, for ever-present wise counsel;

Peter DeGiglio of St. Lawrence Publishing Consultants, for superb assistance in navigating the book world;

Alison Sheehy of Alison Sheehy Photography, for distinctive photographic gifts.

It's been a pleasure working with them, not only because of their exceptional skills, but, most of all, they have an entrepreneurial spirit, understand the value of and see the benefits in collaboration, show enthusiasm that is contagious, and demonstrate keen insight into how best to foster an encouraging and respectful workplace. Kudos to all of them.

ABOUT THE AUTHOR

David Hirshberg is the pseudonym for an entrepreneur who prefers to keep his business activities separate from his writing endeavors. He adopted the first name of his father-in-law and the last name of his maternal grandfather as a tribute to their impact on his life.

Using his given name, he is an accomplished 'C-level suite' executive, having served in the life sciences industry as Chief Executive Officer (CEO) of four firms, Chairman of the Board of six companies, and a member of the board of three other organizations. In addition, he is the founder and CEO of a publishing company.

Hirshberg is a New Yorker who holds an undergraduate degree from Dartmouth College and a master's degree from the University of Pennsylvania.

Much like the narrator in *My Mother's Son*, he is a raconteur in real life as well as through fiction. His interests include American history, Jewish literature and practices, the nexus of science and religion, the current cultural wars in our society, and English, Irish, and Gordon setters.

A Note to Parents

DK READERS is a compelling progr
readers, designed in conjunction wit
experts, including Dr. Linda Gambre
at Clemson University. Dr. Gambrel
of the National Reading Conferenc
Association, and the International Reading Association.

Beautiful illustrations and superb full-color photographs combine with engaging, easy-to-read stories to offer a fresh approach to each subject in the series. Each DK READER is guaranteed to capture a child's interest while developing his or her reading skills, general knowledge, and love of reading.

The five levels of DK READERS are aimed at different reading abilities, enabling you to choose the books that are exactly right for your child:

Pre-level 1: Learning to read
Level 1: Beginning to read
Level 2: Beginning to read alone
Level 3: Reading alone
Level 4: Proficient readers

The "normal" age at which a child begins to read can be anywhere from three to eight years old. Adult participation through the lower levels is very helpful for providing encouragement, discussing storylines, and sounding out unfamiliar words.

No matter which level you select, you can be sure that you are helping your child learn to read, then read to learn!

LONDON, NEW YORK, MUNICH,
MELBOURNE, AND DELHI

For DK/Brady Games
Publisher David Waybright
Editor-in-chief H. Leigh Davis
Licensing Director Mike Degler
International Translations Brian Saliba
Director of Business Development
Michael Vaccaro
Title Manager Tim Fitzpatrick

Reading Consultant
Linda B. Gambrell, Ph.D.

Produced by
Shoreline Publishing Group LLC
President James Buckley Jr.
Designer Tom Carling, carlingdesign.com

For WWE
Director, Home Entertainment & Books
Dean Miller
Photo Department
Frank Vitucci, Joshua Tottenham, Jamie Nelsen
Copy Editor Kevin Caldwell
Legal Lauren Dienes-Middlen

First American Edition, 2009
09 10 11 10 9 8 7 6 5 4 3 2 1
Published in the United States by DK Publishing
375 Hudson Street, New York, New York 10014

Published in Great Britain by Dorling Kindersley Limited

A catalog record for this book is available from the Library of Congress.

ISBN: 978-0-7566-5390-3 (Paperback)
ISBN: 978-0-7566-5389-7 (Hardcover)

Printed and bound by Lake Book

The publisher would like to thank the following for their kind permission to reproduce their photographs:
All photos courtesy WWE Entertainment, Inc.
All other images © Dorling Kindersley
For further information see: www.dkimages.com

READERS

CM Punk™

Written by Brian Shields

DK Publishing

For CM Punk, it was his last chance. His opponent was Extreme Championship Wrestling (ECW) champion John Morrison. It was September, 2007. One month earlier, at *SummerSlam 2007*, CM Punk had battled Morrison for the ECW Championship. That night, he lost. He hoped that this event would end differently.

Morrison stepped onto the ropes and jumped off. But Punk was fast. He stepped away and let Morrison

crash to the mat. Then he lifted the champ, slammed him back down, and pinned him.

CM Punk had won his first championship in WWE.
But it would not be his last.

CM Punk's long road to becoming a top WWE Superstar began in Chicago, Illinois. He was one of four children. At the age of five, his parents nicknamed him "Punk." The name stuck with him all the way to WWE.

"Rowdy" Roddy Piper

As a child, Punk was a huge WWE fan. His favorites were

Jimmy "Superfly" Snuka

"Rowdy" Roddy Piper and Jimmy "Superfly" Snuka. Watching these two all-time greats battle on television, young Punk knew he wanted to be a WWE Superstar one day. He set his mind to that goal and stuck with it.

As a teenager, he became a fan of punk music. Along with the music, he was drawn to punk's "straightedge" fans. Like them, Punk avoided alcohol, tobacco, and drugs. He had seen too many kids get into trouble because of these things. He promised himself that he would steer clear.

Instead, as a straightedge, he worked hard to make himself and his body better. He stayed focused and clean and never lost sight of his goal: to be a WWE Champion.

CM PUNK

After high school, Punk left home to work on his skills. He joined Ohio Valley Wrestling, a training program run by WWE. There, he gained a lot of fans.

He also caught the eye of WWE officials. Would his hard work pay off with a spot in the big time?

In the summer of 2006, he got the call he had been waiting for. WWE wanted him to join! His hard work and great athletic ability had paid off. CM Punk was born!

CM Punk's Stats and Stuff

- Height: 6'1"
- Weight: 222 lbs.
- Birthplace: Chicago, IL
- Finishing Moves: G.T.S. (Go to Sleep), Anaconda Vise

CM Punk's first match with WWE was part of an ECW event in 2006. He defeated Stevie Richards. He used one of his best finishing moves, the "Anaconda Vise." Punk went on a run of ECW wins. He beat top ECW Superstars like Justin Credible, C.W. Anderson, and Shannon Moore.

Like all rising WWE Superstars, Punk faced many challenges. He challenged Mike Knox and defeated him in their first battle. Then Punk teamed up with

WWE Superstars Triple H, Shawn Michaels, and the Hardy Boys in a match against Knox, Edge, Randy Orton, and Johnny Nitro. Punk's team came out on top!

CM Punk wrapped up his first year as a pro with a victory over *Raw* Superstar Shelton Benjamin. But the best was yet to come.

Punk began 2007 with a setback. His unbeaten streak in singles matches was broken by Hardcore Holly. That same year, Punk picked up his nickname—the "Straightedge Superstar." He also joined his first WWE group, the New Breed, teaming with Elijah Burke, Marcus Cor Von, Matt Striker, and Kevin Thorn.

However, just a few weeks after joining, he quit the group in dramatic fashion. He nailed the leader, Elijah Burke, with his signature "G.T.S." (Go to Sleep) finishing move. Punk was a solo act once again.

In June 2007, a tournament was held to crown a new ECW Champion. Punk defeated his old New Breed teammate, Marcus Cor Von, to advance to the finals.

There, he ran into a red-hot Johnny Nitro, who captured the title. This marked the first of many battles between CM Punk and Johnny Nitro. Later that year, Nitro changed his name to John Morrison. Each time the two men met, the ECW Championship was on the line.

Punk and Morrison clashed at *SummerSlam* in August. Morrison defended his title, beating Punk. Then came their September "last chance" battle, won by Punk. CM Punk's dream came true. He was ECW Champion at last.

Like all champions, CM Punk had to defend his title against the best WWE Superstars. He took on and defeated Big Daddy V, The Miz, and Mark Henry. Then, in January 2008, Punk lost the ECW Championship to Chavo Guerrero. The loss was tough, but good things were just ahead.

At *WrestleMania XXIV*, in March, CM Punk took part in a

CM Punk's WWE Championship History

- World Heavyweight Championship
- ECW Championship
- World Tag Team Championship (with Kofi Kingston)
- WWE Intercontinental Championship

Money in the Bank Ladder Match. A ladder is placed in the middle of the ring. A briefcase is hung above it. Inside is a contract giving the Superstar who captures it a shot at a WWE World Championship match. The first man to claim it wins!

Joining CM Punk in this big match were WWE Superstars Chris Jericho, Shelton Benjamin, Mr. Kennedy, Carlito, John Morrison, and Montel Vontavious Porter. Many Superstars made it onto the ladder, only to get thrown off!

Finally, after a long struggle, CM Punk climbed to the top of the ladder. He grabbed the briefcase. This golden chance to fight for a WWE Championship was his. But when would he use it? He wisely chose to wait for the right moment.

CM Punk waited for the right time to cash in his championship contract. Meanwhile, he beat many WWE Superstars. The list included Matt Hardy, Chris Jericho, and Tommy Dreamer. Then, in June 2008, CM Punk decided to make his move. He was going to use his golden contract.

Punk watched from the locker room area as Edge, the World Heavyweight Champion, battled Batista. When Batista knocked down Edge, it was time to move.

CM Punk sprinted into the ring. It took only a few seconds for Punk to pin Edge. CM Punk was the World Heavyweight Champion.

Throughout the rest of 2008, Punk defended his new title against many opponents. He beat the much larger John Bradshaw Layfield, also known as JBL. This made Punk clearly WWE's top Superstar.

At *SummerSlam* that year, JBL challenged Punk again. Once again, Punk beat him to keep his title. At *Unforgiven 2008*, Randy Orton, Cody Rhodes, Ted DiBiase, and Manu ganged up on Punk—before his match even started! As a result, Punk lost his title.

But there were more titles to come. In October 2008 on *Raw*, the "Straightedge Superstar" teamed up with Kofi Kingston. They took on Ted DiBiase & Cody Rhodes in a World Tag Team Championship Match.

CM Punk's Nicknames

- "The Straightedge Superstar"
- "Mr. Money in the Bank"

DiBiase & Rhodes were two of the thugs who had beaten Punk and cost him his title. He wanted to get some revenge.

That's just what he did. Working together as an unstoppable team, Punk & Kingston beat DiBiase & Rhodes. They captured the World Tag Team titles. CM Punk had now earned three WWE Championship titles.

Early in 2009, Punk added the WWE Intercontinental Championship. He beat William Regal to claim his fourth title. Still, he wanted to be top dog again. That meant regaining the World Heavyweight Championship.

CM Punk's road back to the top began once again in a Money in the Bank Ladder Match at *The 25th Anniversary of WrestleMania.* In the match, he fought against Superstars that included Kane, MVP, Finlay, Christian, Kofi Kingston, Shelton Benjamin, and Mark Henry.

Once again, Punk snatched the briefcase! He was the first WWE Superstar ever to win two Money in the Bank Ladder Matches!

Punk then chalked up wins against Edge, Chris Jericho, and Umaga. Then in June 2009, he cashed in his chance—again! Punk noticed that World Heavyweight Champion Jeff Hardy was exhausted after a match. Punk struck! He pinned Hardy to win back the World Heavyweight Championship. Punk was again on top of WWE.

Not Just in the Ring!

This Superstar has also earned fame outside the ring. CM Punk appeared on the TV shows *Monster Garage* and *Ghost Hunters Live*. No surprise there. He's one guy that could probably scare even a monster or a ghost!

The kid from Chicago has come a long way. Whether talking to kids about staying away from alcohol, drugs, and tobacco, or pummeling opponents in the ring, this WWE Champion is a true Superstar!

CM Punk Facts

- CM Punk's arm is tattooed with good luck charms, but he believes you can make your own luck with hard work.

- One of Punk's oldest tattoos spells out "Straightedge" on his stomach.

- Punk created his in-ring style by mixing fighting skills that he learned from his travels around the world.

- No one knows for sure what the "CM" part of Punk's name means. Punk himself has offered different meanings. Sometimes he even says that it has no meaning.

Index

DK READERS

My name is

I have read this book 

Date